'Introduces a ⌐ ⌐ ⌐ hile at the same time explor⌐ ⌐ forces that shaped a nation…th⌐ have hit on a real winner.'

Crime Review

'There's a crime at the centre of the story, but it is the detail of early Australian life, the atmosphere and great writing that make the book special.'

Choice

'The evocation of place and time is splendid.'

Mail on Sunday

'The Keneallys have produced a strong murder mystery of admirable depth.'

Sunday Times

'The Keneallys have done a great deal of able and unobtrusive research. With *The Soldier's Curse* Monsarrat is fairly launched into what promises to be both a troubling future for him and a sure entertainment for readers.'

The Australian

'A series that promises to add a new dimension to the Australian crime scene at the same time as it explores the forces that have shaped a nation Things can only get more interesting.'

…ng Herald

About the Authors

Tom Keneally won the 1982 Booker Prize with *Schindler's Ark*, later made into the Academy Award-winning film *Schindler's List*. His novels *The Chant of Jimmie Blacksmith*, *Gossip from the Forest* and *Confederates* were shortlisted for the Booker Prize.

His daughter Meg Keneally has been a journalist and radio producer, and has spent more than ten years working in corporate affairs for listed financial services companies. Both live in Australia.

THE UNMOURNED

THE MONSARRAT SERIES

MEG AND TOM KENEALLY

POINT
BLANK

A Point Blank Book

First published in Great Britain by Point Blank,
an imprint of Oneworld Publications, 2019

ISBN 978-1-78607-460-7 (paperback)
ISBN 978-1-78607-461-4 (eBook)

Printed and bound in Great Britain by Clays Ltd, Elcograf S.p.A.

This is a work of fiction. While, as in all fiction, the literary
perceptions and insights are based on experience, all names,
characters, places, and incidents either are products of the author's
imagination or are used fictitiously.

Oneworld Publications
10 Bloomsbury Street
London WC1B 3SR
United Kingdom

For Craig
and
for Judy

And in memory of Mary Shields,
Parramatta Female Factory convict and
Meg's great-great grandmother

Prologue

Parramatta, November 1825

He really must do something about that door, he thought as he crossed the yard back to his quarters. Its top hinge was a little loose and the resulting scrape woke the women. What transpired after he entered generally woke them anyway, but there was a moment he relished, the blank wall of their combined unconsciousness, none of them with any awareness yet of what was about to happen to whichever sleeping body was the focus of his current interest.

When that O'Leary woman was still a First Class convict, before her rebellious tendencies had seen her moved to the penitentiary, as the scrape announced his presence she and the others would rise as one, surrounding the bed of whomever he'd decided to take that night, standing there like a silent forest of reproachful ghost gums. There was something welcome to him about their gaze but also something that delayed him in his stroke.

But now he had sent her to the Third Class tower they tended to stay in their beds. They woke up, of course. He could always tell. No arms flopped over the side of the cots, no one rolled with the heaviness of a sack of grain. Their stillness betrayed their consciousness, their breathing was too even for sleep.

If he didn't fix the door soon, though, he might have to start visiting the Second Class women. And really he'd rather not. The First Class ones – they were his preference. So terrified of having to swap their Sunday red jackets for the leather aprons and the harder work and reduced rations of their Third Class sisters. Usually a better class of woman, too – while their circumstances may not have been kind, they were not extreme enough to drive the women to the type of felony convicts of other classes perpetrated. Of course, depending on the boat, the squeamishness of its surgeon, some of them had already been got at on the way over by the sailors. Couldn't be helped. But most of them still had their teeth and some even wore unpocked skin. Yes, a better class of livestock altogether.

Tonight he had been in the First Class quarters to give a personal welcome to a new inmate. She'd come off the *Phoenix*, and its surgeon was a stickler for proprieties so it was a good bet that none of the sailors had got a look in. She was a thief, or so he assumed. Had stolen ribbons at a country fair, perhaps, or taken a florin her master had left on a dressing table. Didn't matter. Her young body – seventeen or eighteen years since its birth, he guessed, hard to tell sometimes – didn't bear the ravages of one used as a commodity in a lane behind a London inn.

So while the watchfulness of the others in the room pricked the back of his neck, all in all he was rather pleased with the evening so far. Now his destination was a long drink of rum. He'd have to remember to tap the barrel he hadn't watered yet. He must start marking them – he suspected he might have watered down some barrels more than once. And that would make it too obvious – more customers might complain, and they tended to do so using fists rather than finely turned verbal abuse.

Crotty had worried him when he'd mentioned that his customers seemed to be unable to get drunk and he might have to find another supplier, one who paid duties and operated within the law. And he looked after his suppliers, Crotty did – he'd hate to see an honest one undercut by someone who was watering his wares. The authorities may need to be alerted to the fact.

We'll see who holds most sway with the authorities, Church consoled himself. A publican on the margins like Crotty, or a highly placed functionary such as himself. In the meantime the promise of undiluted rum in his quarters, his wife asleep, pulled him from the heat and frenzy of the First Class dormitory.

But before he could reach the outer wall of the yard and the gate which separated his quarters from those of the bonded women, a sound snagged his ear. A footstep. Not loud, but firm enough to indicate that the owner of the foot was not taking any significant pains to conceal the approach.

He turned, smiling when he saw who it was.

'You've given some thought to my proposal?' he said.

A nod. No smile to go with it. Good.

'May as well get started on our business now, then,' he said.

'Yes, I suppose so.'

A slight tremble. Even better. Confidence in one such as this would have worried him.

His companion glanced around. It was a clear night with a full moon. Anyone looking out of one of the windows surrounding the yard would have recognised them. He didn't care about that, but he was the one in this particular transaction who didn't stand to lose.

He looked up for a moment, his eyes drawing in the light from the stars. Not a man given to appreciating beauty. Not a poetic soul. But still, when one came from east London, with its smudged, low sky, a glimpse of purity was worth looking up for.

Had his body continued to function for longer than the next half-minute, Church might have been grateful he'd bothered taking a final scan of the night. Certainly it was the last beautiful thing he saw. Because by the time he lowered his gaze, his companion had closed the distance between them. He spread his lips into a half-formed menacing smile that said he was ready for anything, but wasn't sure quite what he was being asked to be ready for. He opened his mouth – maybe to ask a question, maybe simply to assert his authority. But he didn't have a chance to choose the words before the tip of an awl flashed upwards, pushing through the woefully insubstantial membrane of his right eye, and continuing until it found his brain.

Chapter 1

'Now you're mocking me, I swear it. It simply cannot be possible. You're having a laugh at a poor woman's expense.'

Hugh Llewelyn Monsarrat braced himself. The effort wasn't wasted. A second later, the corner of a rolled-up cleaning towel, Mrs Mulrooney's answer to a whip, connected with his temple.

'I assure you, dear lady, it's simply the way the English language works. The King himself has to follow these rules, whether they be logical or not.'

'Well I assure *you* that this is not a language I can take seriously. And I'll hear no more sniffing from your good self about Irish spelling and pronunciation, thank you. Any language that lets the C get away with so much mischief has a lot to answer for. You'd have me believe it makes two different sounds in the same word! It needs to make up its mind, so it does. *Circle* should start with an S, and that's the end of it.'

This was by no means the first pitched battle Monsarrat had engaged in with his housekeeper over the irrational nature of the English language. The tiny kitchen had seen many of them, heard her small, calloused fist bounce in frustration off the over-scrubbed table. Mrs Mulrooney insisted, for example, on spelling

1

war with two o's, like *door.* 'Otherwise you'd say it as *warr,* like *far,* wouldn't you?' she asked, although Monsarrat had no reason to believe she was actually interested in his opinion on the matter.

She would threaten, on occasion, to abandon the whole exercise, but Monsarrat knew she wouldn't. Her admission into the world of readers had been at the request of her previous mistress, the late Honora Shelborne, for whose murder he suspected Mrs Mulrooney still wept and said nightly rosaries.

But for all her complaining, Mrs Mulrooney's progress was exceptional. She had been Monsarrat's student for little more than a month and she was already writing the letters to her son that he used to write for her. If the boy noticed that the letters came with a few less flourishes and a few more ink blotches than they used to, Monsarrat felt sure he wouldn't mind.

This morning, though, he perceived they'd probably come as far as they could. She needed, perhaps, a day or so to adjust to a world in which the letter C could shimmer and change in such a maddening fashion. He stood and gathered the pens, the paper, the small slate on which she had started forming her first letters with a stylus, made redundant by her quick grasp of the language (except those parts she felt had no right to stand as they made no sense).

'May I trouble you, Mrs Mulrooney, for some tea before I go?'

She snorted, exasperated that he felt the need to make such an obvious request.

'I'll bring it to the parlour, so. Out with you now. Out, out, out!'

Strictly speaking, of course, Mrs Mulrooney had no right to order Monsarrat out of the kitchen. It was his, after all, a fact he still found miraculous when barely a few months previously his possessions had added up to two threadbare waistcoats (one eternally ruined by a smear of red dust), a thinning black coat and an ink pot.

In those days, his presence in Mrs Mulrooney's large, distempered Port Macquarie kitchen had been an indulgence, only possible when the commandant of the settlement had turned a blind eye.

But no one save Mrs Mulrooney herself could challenge his right to stand in this small, whitewashed box here in Parramatta.

His purchase of the cottage that housed it had been made possible by a leather sack handed to him aboard the sloop *Sally*, which six weeks ago had ferried him and Mrs Mulrooney from Port Macquarie to Sydney, and then committed them by cutter to the journey up the river to Parramatta.

'The major knew you wouldn't accept this, so he asked me to give it to you when we were too far to turn back,' the *Sally*'s first mate had said as the last of the cruel black rocks which marked the beaches around Port Macquarie slid out of view.

Major Shelborne, Monsarrat's master in Port Macquarie, was born into wealth, while his tragic and beautiful young wife, Honora, was impoverished but of blue blood. The money, said the accompanying note from the major, was by way of thanks. 'This is but a fraction of what I feel I owe you for bringing my wife's killer to justice,' he had written. 'Please do me the honour of accepting it, together with my wishes for your success in Parramatta.'

But while Monsarrat's reward had paid for the kitchen, Mrs Mulrooney had a moral right to the space, or so she felt, and with a passion which had all the authority of an edict. She required Monsarrat to knock before entering, which he happily did.

The Port Macquarie kitchen where he had first met her had been a freestanding outbuilding of the Government House to which it belonged, and this was no different, an outbuilding to the main edifice. Kitchens couldn't be trusted, apparently – had a habit of burning down – so they needed to be kept away from the house to avoid the contagion of flame.

This kitchen had a small room to the side, tiny and tidy, whitewashed walls, a small bed, a table with washing necessities and a rudimentary wall sconce. Monsarrat had offered Mrs Mulrooney the finest bedroom in the small main house, but this was where she preferred to sleep. And while the four rooms of the main house – the sitting room, a parlour and two bedrooms, darkly painted according to respectable practice – were Monsarrat's domain, he did not impose a reciprocal requirement that she knock before entering.

This was just as well as it would have been difficult for her to do so while carrying a tea tray. She put one down in front of Monsarrat after he had obeyed her command and made his way to the main house to sit in the small parlour and try to stretch out his legs (not easy for a gangly specimen when the legs in question had to fit under a small table), fiddling with his cravat as he weighed his new good fortune.

'Anyone would think you'd never seen a cravat before. You've had one of those things around your neck for decades – you'd think you'd have learned the art of them.'

'And so I have, as a matter of fact,' said Monsarrat, feeling the mild irritation that her scolding sometimes brought forth, a blemish on their friendship which was nevertheless easily washed away by her excellent tea. 'But you realise I need to be above reproach. There are those who wouldn't hesitate to characterise a poorly tied cravat as a symptom of an irredeemably criminal nature.'

Some of those people, Monsarrat knew, inhabited this town, and saw from a distance the black streak of a man stalking daily up the hill to Government House. It was one of the reasons he needed the fortification of Mrs Mulrooney's tea before departing for work. As he went, he seemed unable to break the habit of glancing to the side occasionally, expecting to see his old associate Bangar silently keeping pace with him. But the Birpai tribesman was in Port Macquarie and therefore not in a position to soothe Monsarrat with his quiet companionship. In Monsarrat's six weeks here he had not met one member of the Burramattagal, whose name the colonisers had mangled in christening Parramatta. There were very few of them now in the vicinity. They had been shifted towards the area recently christened Blacktown and were discouraged from staying near the river which had been named after them.

As well as taking pains over his cravat, Monsarrat liked to be early to pass below the crudely cut sandstone lintel of the outbuilding in which he worked, across a courtyard from the main structure of Parramatta's Government House, with its white-rendered edifice painted with lines to make people believe it was constructed from the finest marble rather than crude convict-made brick.

He supposed, really, that he should walk up the meticulously paved, curving driveway, before skirting the columns of the main entrance – not for the likes of him – and walking to the side of the building where pristine render gave way to the honest, whitewashed brick. But while Monsarrat claimed to be one for proprieties, he was less fastidious when a convenience could be gained by disregarding them, and when no one was looking. So he climbed the side of the hill leading from his house into the governor's domain, past Governor Brisbane's twin follies of bathhouse and observatory, and arrived at his workplace without passing the glaring façade of the governor's empty residence.

As early as he was, he was not the earliest. The governor's private secretary in Parramatta, Ralph Eveleigh, was always at his desk by the time Monsarrat arrived. Fresh paper, fresh blotter, fresh ink, usually a partly composed document in front of him. In the short time Monsarrat had been working for Eveleigh, he had never walked into the man's office without seeing him push back quickly from his desk, as though caught in some illicit act rather than the drafting of a letter to the colonial secretary or orders for the commandant of a remote penal station.

Nor was his conscientiousness reserved for when the eyes of authority were on him. Eveleigh was between governors. Thomas Brisbane, who had caused no small amount of consternation by making his home in Parramatta rather than Sydney, had recently made his final journey down the winding drive, the first yards in a journey which would take him back to England. And his replacement, Ralph Darling, was taking his time to arrive.

He was in Van Diemen's Land, apparently, and would next spend some time constraining Sydney's bureaucrats, grown wild under the absentee Brisbane. There was no word on when he might come up the river.

Even with a man of Eveleigh's habits in charge, this was the first time Monsarrat had been called at this hour into the office, a spacious room by colonial standards, white-limed with a fireplace and a northern window through which Monsarrat could see a scatter of huts in the shade of grey gums and shaggy barks.

Eveleigh, for once, was not sent reeling back from some document or other when Monsarrat entered. Nor was there any work in progress in front of him.

'Monsarrat. Good morning. On time, I see, and that's all to the good, as it happens. Thank you for your punctuality.'

It was still strange to Monsarrat, being thanked, being spoken to as if his presence was a matter of pure choice. But while he was now an emancipist, and not of a mind to leave Eveleigh's employ, he was not quite free. His ticket of leave had come with the precondition that he serve this man, and with more than his immaculate copperplate writing.

Ralph Eveleigh was one of the few in the colony whose pale skin had, for the most part, escaped discoloration by the sun. A formidable intellect in a frail, sandy-complexioned body, Eveleigh never stepped outside without a hat, and never rolled up his sleeves, even in the worst of the heat. To do so would have creased the fabric, something Eveleigh couldn't countenance. He had enough to deal with as it was, with a crop of hair so unruly that he'd told Monsarrat he had considered having it shaved.

But for all his fastidiousness, Eveleigh didn't share the prevailing view that a convict was rotten to the core by nature. Informed by his master that his request for an additional clerk had been approved, that he would have charge of one with special investigative skills which could be brought to bear from time to time on what the colonial secretary had described, on a visit to Parramatta, as 'more delicate matters where a galumphing police investigation may not produce the desired result', Eveleigh intended to utilise these skills, both investigative and clerical. Monsarrat was a refined tool, and as long as he performed he would be treated well within the walls of the offices where Eveleigh reigned. Yet Monsarrat knew that his deductions, which had brought a killer to justice in Port Macquarie, owed much to the perceptiveness of the woman who now ruled his kitchen. Thus access to first-rate tea was the least of his reasons for employing her.

'I had your morning planned, you know,' said Eveleigh now. 'Preparing the Parramatta tickets of leave for our friend the colonial secretary.'

'Ah,' said Monsarrat. Tickets of leave. The laborious process of trawling through the records to find the ship, crime and transportation date which matched a name he'd been given, the owner of which was about to be released from penal servitude.

'Tedious work, I know. But at least you already have one. It would be something of a cruelty to make a Special write the words which will give freedom to another.'

When Monsarrat had been a Special – a convict with skills beyond muscle, which could be put to use by the government – the chief clerk of the day had not displayed a similar sensitivity, and he had spent years writing freedom for others while the prospect of his own had remained impossibly remote.

'As you wish, of course,' Monsarrat said. Not quite an ally, Eveleigh was nonetheless civil. That fact, and his position, made him someone Monsarrat was anxious to please.

'Well, I have a different wish now. I have been informed of a particular incident,' said Eveleigh.

'Incident?'

'Yes, although that's a rather inadequate term. More accurately, I suppose the word would be murder. And a fierce one, not that any of them are tame. So it seems, Mr Monsarrat, that I'll have to find someone else to scribble out those tickets of leave through half-closed eyes, while I finally have a chance to use your ... more unique skills.'

Chapter 2

The top half of Robert Church's right eye was pristine, white, and seemingly unrelated to its lower extremity, which was punctured beyond repair.

'Precision, then,' Monsarrat said. 'Almost as though he stood still for it.'

'Actually,' said his new friend, 'I'll wager that's precisely what he did.'

Dr Homer Preston had been transported for stealing the purses of his patients while they were under sedation in his surgery. There was also a certain amount of talk of grave robbing, with Dr Preston thought to be the nexus between the disinterrers and the more conscientious students at the school of anatomy, though nothing had ever been proven.

Unlike Monsarrat, Preston had served his first sentence and had not reoffended (or at least been caught doing so), so had not needed to endure years at a place of secondary punishment. Just as well – he would have made a very bad medical orderly, being more intelligent than most colonial surgeons and lacking the tact which would have prevented him from sharing that opinion.

Monsarrat had met Preston a month ago, shortly after his

own return to Parramatta, when a clerk was needed to transcribe a statement on the death of a woman at the Female Factory. She might well have been a victim of the man lying here. Monsarrat hadn't seen Emily Gray's body, but Preston's description had been more than enough detail for him. 'Of course one frequently sees people who can stand a bit more food. Describes the vast majority of people here. But this woman – someone had taken a hide and stretched it over a bundle of sticks, or so it seemed. Starvation while under the care of His Majesty.' The inquest had returned a verdict of death due to hunger and 'hard treatment', a mundane phrase which could be used to stand in for a variety of lurid abuses.

'It's an incision, there's no other word for it,' Preston said now. 'Can you imagine trying to do that to someone who was crashing about, running, turning their head, trying to deflect you in some way? Had he offered any resistance, his eyeball would look like Napoleon's regurgitated lunch.'

Napoleon was probably asleep under Preston's desk at the hospital back in the town, and Monsarrat doubted the cat would lower himself to something as indelicate as an eyeball. Monsarrat was one of the few who knew the creature's name – it might have been considered a little incendiary, a decade after Waterloo, so Preston didn't make a habit of telling people, or indeed of sharing the fact that there was a cat in the hospital at all. In any case, Napoleon did not seem to think that knowledge of his name should entitle Monsarrat to any more consideration than he gave anyone else.

At least the hospital had a clear function: to keep people alive or to ease their dying. No one Monsarrat asked had yet been able to define concisely the Female Factory's purpose. Not that it had no purpose. Quite the reverse – it had several, and they frequently collided in a manner which made the place an administrative headache.

It was a place of incarceration, but with only a fraction of the beds – or mattresses, or area of floor – it needed to sleep all of its inmates. It was a marriage bureau and employment agency, where convict women accepted masters, or husbands they had known for just an hour, purely to get away from the place. It was a business, intended to be self-sufficient and perhaps even to contribute to the colony's coffers by selling the women's sewing and skills as laundresses, yet where inmates went unshod and unfed, their food sold in the free community to fatten the superintendent's purse. And it was a place of asylum, intended to protect vulnerable women from the men in the colony, who outnumbered them at least five to one, exposing them instead to one of the worst examples of the male population – the man who now lay on a table in a stone outbuilding of the Factory.

On the plans, the building in which Monsarrat and Preston were examining Church was called the Room for Useful Purposes. But it was more commonly known as the Dead House as it was the room in which corpses were stored. Its sandstone walls tempered the summer heat, yet before long other smells would mix with the odour of baking dust.

The Dead House was tucked into a corner of the Female Factory's drying grounds, where the cloth woven by the inmates was stretched out and subjected to the sun's full force, watched by the First Class prisoners from their sleeping quarters on the second floor of a long, thin sandstone structure. The superintendent's residence lay on the other side of the drying yard, at the front of the building, near a gleaming clock, a gift from a king who seemed to believe that allowing the women a means of counting out the hours of their incarceration was more important than clothing them properly. The thing had been sent from England by ship, and there were few such pieces in this, until recently, apparently timeless country.

'And was the weapon . . . Well . . . all the way in?' Monsarrat asked.

'Oh yes. It seems so.'

'Would have taken a fair amount of strength, I imagine.'

'I expect so. Whoever it was started low – clearly they were trying to use an upward thrust, put their body weight behind it. But then ... Look here, Monsarrat. Notice how the upper edge of the puncture has pulled away a little? They hit the skull, you see. Needed to stand up straight so they could get it through the optic foramen – that's the hole in the skull that leads to the brain. And that's most certainly where the tip ended up, as the man's dead.'

Monsarrat wasn't squeamish – the squeamish didn't survive here. But he was astonished that Preston could speak with such detachment. 'Did you know him at all?' he asked the doctor.

'Only to nod to. His wife, now, I did know. The matron. They allow us to use this place, you see, from time to time, when the hospital can't cope.'

'So Church's wife has assisted you?'

'She's let me in – we'll leave it at that. I did treat her once, though. For a sprain. Brought about by liberal quantities of rum, judging by the smell of her.'

Over the years, Monsarrat had developed his own shorthand, together with a certain amount of skill in writing without his eyes on the page, so those whose words he was capturing were only peripherally aware he was doing it. He lacked, here, his customary weapons of pen and ink, reduced to a stub of graphite pencil which he carried, wrapped in an old handkerchief, for the purpose. He scratched on a piece of paper as Preston spoke, his eyes dividing their time between Preston's face and the corpse.

'Now,' said Preston, taking Monsarrat's elbow and urging him towards the door, causing him to smudge his shorthand in the process. 'You're going back to the office?'

'Yes. I'm to transcribe the details of our interview.'

'Very well. You may wish to add this. Perhaps the reason Church didn't struggle was that he didn't expect an attack from the person who killed him.'

'Why wouldn't he? I know him by reputation. I imagine it would be relatively easy to find people who believe that the world without Church would be significantly improved.'

'I have no reason to disagree with that. But the angle – I mentioned before, as you recall – it's possible that someone crouched and drove the weapon up into his eye, before standing to their full height and completing the job. There's another possibility, as well.'

'Which is?'

'Which is that whoever did this didn't need to crouch to drive upwards. Perhaps they were already standing at their full height. There are short men, of course. Or the murderer could have crouched. Or a tall man could have dragged Church down to meet the point that ended his life. But it's also possible, barely possible, that the killer was a woman.'

It was time, Monsarrat thought, to go. A mundane decision, but he still relished his unaccustomed liberty – to go where he pleased, and engage in any activity as long as it was lawful, of course. He had no intention of engaging in anything unlawful, having only just acquired his second ticket of leave.

It was crucial, he thought, to start transcribing his scratchings immediately – however effective his method of shorthand (and he fancied it far exceeded that used by other clerks), there was still the issue of language and the connective tissue which needed to be laid over the bare facts, which resided only in his memory, and which smudged as easily as the graphite did.

They would need, however, to remain smudged for a short while longer. He had just settled at the small, unpolished desk in his whitewashed workroom, completed the ritual of laying out blotting paper, pens, and ink, when Ralph Eveleigh appeared.

'Daly's here,' Eveleigh said, turning. He knew that Monsarrat would follow.

Daly was a man of little imagination and even less humanity, in Monsarrat's view. He had an almost perfectly square face that was overlaid with a net of small red lines, his blood vessels having given up the fight against the dual onslaught of alcohol and sun. The sun was one of the inevitable inconveniences of life on the rim of His Majesty's influence – you couldn't avoid it, just as you couldn't avoid convicts, especially in a town where barely one in ten of the inhabitants had arrived free. And Ezekiel Daly hated convicts.

Nor did he make any distinction between Specials and those who were ticketed versus those who were still serving their sentence. Daly considered that the felonious stain could not be removed by a bit of paper, and Monsarrat knew that he was an example of the kind of convict Daly most detested. An educated man who should have known better. Who thought his letters gave him liberty to live a kinder life than those who worked on the road gangs or cut lumber. Who had the hide to act as though his ticket of leave gave him the right to stand equal with free men.

Daly's was a reasonably common perception and Monsarrat had quickly become inured to it – failing to do so would have sent him mad. But as much as he would have liked to discount the man's opinion, he couldn't. Because Ezekiel Daly was the Superintendent of Police.

There was an extra seat facing Eveleigh's desk, a surface which seemed to exist on a different plane to Monsarrat's own, reflecting shapes in its gleaming, polished wood while squatting on ornate, carved legs. But Monsarrat wasn't invited to use it – Eveleigh saw no advantage in needlessly provoking Daly and felt that Monsarrat's continued upright posture was a small price to pay.

'I understand you've spoken to the doctor,' Daly said, ignoring Monsarrat and addressing his question to Eveleigh.

'Yes. Mr Monsarrat, as you know, has considerable experience in taking down depositions and the like. I was given to understand that Dr Preston was at the Female Factory, so I felt it best to have somebody there with him.'

'I know about Mr Monsarrat's experience,' Daly said. 'What I don't know is how much of it – if any – is legitimate.'

'I assure you, superintendent,' Monsarrat said, 'that I am more than capable of accurately reflecting Dr Preston's opinion of the deceased.'

'Be kind enough to share that opinion with us, then,' said Daly, still staring at Eveleigh.

Monsarrat did as he was asked, dwelling on the detail of the injury to Church's eye in the vain hope of unsettling Daly, though he suspected the man saw worse every day before breakfast. 'Judging by the angle, Dr Preston seems to believe the assailant could have been a woman,' he said. 'Or at the least someone of short stature.'

'It'll be that O'Leary bitch, then,' said Daly. 'As I thought. I've had her moved to solitary confinement as a precaution.'

Eveleigh drew back his shoulders. Monsarrat knew he didn't approve of such language, even in relation to a convict.

'I assume you mean Grace O'Leary, superintendent,' he said. 'The riotous Irish woman.'

'It's no coincidence, Eveleigh, that things have been quieter since Church put her into the Third Class penitentiary. Moral decay spreads like a disease, you know. You must know – you must've seen it.'

It was perhaps unwise to question Daly's unthinking condemnation of this woman, but flawed logic offended Monsarrat every bit as much as a false lawyer walking free offended Daly, and Monsarrat couldn't help himself. 'You mention she's in the penitentiary, superintendent,' he said. 'How, then, could she have gained the freedom to commit this act?'

Daly thrust out his lower jaw slightly, an unconscious act which heightened the resemblance between his head and a wooden block. He addressed himself to Eveleigh again.

14

'You know security in the penitentiary is next to non-existent. Church's own wife is frequently reported to be the worse for drinking sessions with the convicts. We all know about the riot, too. God alone knows how O'Leary got out, but I'll warrant she did. Perhaps she offered the only asset she has to one of the turnkeys.'

'You are indeed an astute judge of human character, having been exposed to it in its least edifying forms,' Eveleigh said. He had a narrow mouth that rarely smiled, but those who saw it every day, as Monsarrat did, became adept at noticing a slight twitch in the right-hand corner, which was as close as Eveleigh came to indicating amusement.

'Nevertheless, I imagine a man of your rectitude will wish to make sure that the evidence is beyond reproach before proceeding to trial. Efficiency is dear to you, I know, and the most efficient way to proceed would surely be to close off other possibilities. I believe it's fair to say that Church was not endeared to a great many people.'

'That would be wonderful, Eveleigh, if we all had an army of clerks at our disposal. I, however, am in the unfortunate position of commanding eight mounted troopers and a handful of convict constables of varying quality, from the corrupt to the assiduous. They all have quite enough to do maintaining order on a daily basis – including amongst each other – without being required to exonerate all manner of refractory creatures before the one who is patently guilty is brought to trial.'

'My dear superintendent. You do a remarkable amount of work, given the woeful privations you suffer. And, as you say, you do not have the luxury of an army of clerks. Nor do I, but I daresay I could spare the one I have. Perhaps you would do me the honour of allowing me to dedicate Mr Monsarrat to the task of taking statements. It's the least I can do, especially as your department bore part of the cost of building the Factory in the first place.'

'He is a convict, Eveleigh.'

No, he's not, thought Monsarrat. And he happens to be standing a few feet from you.

Eveleigh echoed his thoughts. 'Mr Monsarrat is no longer a convict, as you know, having been granted a ticket of leave for his role in solving a vile crime in Port Macquarie, which took the life of a woman gentle by birth and, I understand, by nature. If I may say, he has a forensic approach to an interview. I believe I could spare him, barely, from the daily onslaught of paper generated by this office, and certainly his temporary loss to our functioning will not weigh nearly as heavily on the order of the colony as would the diversion of a trooper or two.'

'Very well,' said Daly. 'See that he behaves, though. And I assure you I will be verifying all the statements he transcribes, particularly those which relate to the guilt of the Irishwoman.'

Daly turned to look at Monsarrat directly for the first time, but continued to aim his words at Eveleigh.

'He should not think he may alter these facts to exculpate a fellow convict. Because if he does, well . . . Tickets of leave can always be cancelled.'

Monsarrat stood there for some time after Daly's departure. He was still unused to leaving a room without being dismissed. Eveleigh seemed to have forgotten his presence and scratched away at the document he had been working on when Daly arrived. But after a short while he looked up at Monsarrat and gestured to the seat Daly had vacated.

'I've known the man for a while, and he has adopted the practice of occasionally returning to a room a short time after he has left it in case he catches anyone in an indiscretion. Quite likes flattery, of course, but is intelligent enough to recognise it might be false. I half-expected that block of a head to appear back around the door, to check whether I was maligning him.'

16

Monsarrat did not comment, as he might have done had such a statement been made by Major Shelborne. Two years of being locked in bloodless intimacy with the major, as his clerk, had given him an instinctive understanding of when to speak and when to stay silent. He had yet to develop similar insight when it came to Eveleigh so it seemed wise to keep quiet.

Eveleigh certainly did not seem to expect a response. 'In any case, Monsarrat,' he said, 'I was certainly genuine in my remarks about Robert Church. He was not a well-loved man. It may be that the rebellious O'Leary is the one we have to thank for ridding the world of him, but I'd be more comfortable if we established it beyond doubt before shipping her to the gallows. I'd like you to spend a few days at the Factory, if you would. Talk to O'Leary, of course. Take a statement. But talk to anyone else who seems of interest, as well. Because I'd really rather not hang a woman for a crime she didn't commit, and the truth of the matter may turn out to be rather more complex than Daly would like.'

Chapter 3

I am well plaiced here now. I have a small room by the kichen and only Mr Monsurat (was that how his name was spelled? How dreadful she hadn't asked!) *to look after. It is his hand wich rote all of the letters you have had from me for the past two years. I'm happy and proud to ashore you that these words were put on the page by me without need of anyone else.*

Hannah Mulrooney wrote quickly. Certainly too quickly to avoid the blotched pages for which Mr Monsarrat sometimes gently berated her. She was desperate to catch the letters and employ them to create meaning before they floated out of reach, before they became again what they had been for all but the past month of her life – meaningless symbols whose secrets were reserved for others. And she always felt impatient in getting letters off to Padraig, imagining him reading them in astonishment at the phenomenon of a literate mother.

She was reasonably pleased so far, though. Only a few minor smudges. Until the knock on the door startled her into a more egregious blotch at the end of the sentence. She glared at the pen until she was confident it felt the full weight of her irritation, then put it down and went to the door.

When she opened it, her peevishness transferred itself to the person who had knocked.

'May I come in?'

'And there'd be little use in that, now, Miss Stark. Mr Monsarrat's at his labours. As all people are at this hour. Decent people, in any case.'

Sophia Stark's eyebrows drew together at the slight. You'll have wrinkles if you keep at it, Hannah thought.

Hannah had enjoyed Monsarrat's friendship for two years. And until recently that friendship had lived entirely within the confines of the Port Macquarie penal settlement, where as a free woman and housekeeper to the commandant Hannah was considered a higher class of human than the twice-criminalised clerk.

Monsarrat was one of three people she deeply cared about in that claustrophobic place, with its glowering mountains and voluble seas. Those other two were gone now, one at the hands of the other. And for a time after, her friendship with Monsarrat and thoughts of her son had been the only things keeping her tethered to the earth. Sometimes she had feared they would not be enough.

Odd, then, to be here in Parramatta, Monsarrat's servant instead of his superior. She didn't mind, of course. Not a bit. She was happy to continue to produce large quantities of tea, happy to continue conversing with the man who had made the penal settlement bearable. Not quite so happy to be his student in the matter of letters, but willing to put up with it.

But, still, it required a certain amount of adjustment.

It was even more difficult to adjust to the fact that Monsarrat had not sprung fully formed into the world two years before. That he had in fact existed for significantly longer, and had a past of which Hannah knew only the barest outlines. They had not spoken to each other much about their backgrounds. People didn't here. If you travelled too far down this river you would invariably be snagged by a submerged log. Better to leave threats beneath the surface.

But sometimes the river ejected pieces of detritus on to the bank where they had no business being. And in Hannah Mulrooney's view, the sharpest of these was Sophia Stark.

Hannah knew that Sophia and Monsarrat had had a liaison of sorts. She also knew that Monsarrat had lost his first ticket of leave after being found out of his district, on the way from Sophia's bed; that if Sophia hadn't insisted he increase the frequency of his visits to her, ensuring he was abroad on a Sunday, at a time when the particularly vehement, convict-hating Reverend Horace Bulmer was likely to be plying the roads around Parramatta, he might have escaped detection.

This did not make Hannah look kindly on the younger woman at the door.

'I'm aware of Mr Monsarrat's location, Mrs Mulrooney,' Sophia said. 'And had I wanted to visit him, I'd have come at a time when I knew he'd be home. It is not him I've come to see, but you.'

Hannah simply stared at Sophia's sun bonnet, which bore a fussy cloth flower. Surely the time has passed for such girlish decorations, at least in your case, she thought. She was mildly alarmed at her attitude. She usually enjoyed the company of women, had in fact yearned for it after the death of Honora Shelborne. She would, she liked to think, welcome anyone who could make Mr Monsarrat happy.

But if Sophia was making Mr Monsarrat happy, Hannah had yet to see evidence of it. She was not, it had to be admitted, looking particularly hard. It was difficult to see past the brittle pretensions of the former chambermaid, who had been brought here for the theft of items of far greater value than those stolen by most convicts.

It usually took a far longer acquaintance for Hannah to decide to devote some of her time to truly disliking someone, to doing it properly. Sophia had first walked through the door of the small house on Monsarrat's arm a few weeks before, and Hannah had been fully prepared to warm to her. She was still negotiating her way around the altered geography of her friendship with Monsarrat, and wasn't immediately sure how she should greet Sophia as she stepped into the small parlour, lifting her skirts to avoid snagging them on some crates which had not yet been removed. A tentative smile, Hannah thought, might do it. A few steps in her direction, perhaps to be followed by a word or two of welcome, an offer of tea.

She never got as far as the offer. Sophia took off her shawl, handed it to Hannah, and turned without acknowledging her to comment to Monsarrat on the dust on top of the mantle.

Hannah was generally difficult to offend. Particularly if she believed the offence was unintentional, she was able to shrug it off, a useful ability in this place. But there were people who pretended to be what they weren't. Who aspired to a status they were not born to. There was nothing wrong with this in Hannah's mind, except that those thus inclined tended to be dismissive of their fellow former convicts as a means of distancing themselves from their own squalid histories. They vaulted a chasm that would never again allow them to stand in the Irishwoman's good graces. In treating Hannah like a coat rack, Sophia had crossed that line.

Perhaps Monsarrat had spoken to Sophia after that tense first encounter. In any case, the next time she arrived at the house, she gave Hannah a nod and a clipped good evening. Hannah responded in kind, but no greeting, however effusive, could have pulled Sophia back into the warmth of her regard.

And now Sophia stood here again, interrupting her letters, her new communion, still fragile and tenuous and, Hannah feared, prone to destruction if she was not given the peace to concentrate on it.

'Might I come in,' Sophia said. Not a question. A demand.

'You might, I suppose. Whether you're welcome to . . .'

Sophia sighed, forcing the air out through her nose rather than her mouth. 'This is getting tiresome, you know. Please let me in and I can assure you I won't detain you longer than absolutely necessary.'

Hannah stood aside, watching as Sophia made her way into the parlour and seated herself. She looked at the housekeeper, perhaps expecting tea to be offered. If so, the woman was in the grips of a futile hope.

Hannah sat down opposite her. 'Kindly remove your hat,' she said. 'You are inside.'

Surprisingly, Sophia did so. She put the hat in front of her, its ribbons neatly folded underneath it, and adjusted it so that it sat square. She looked like a goddess looming over a small straw mountain.

'You wish to speak with me.'

'Indeed. I seek your cooperation.'

Hannah said nothing. It cost her – while she had been able to call upon the written word for only a short time, she used the spoken word with skill, and enjoyed doing so. But she also enjoyed the discomfiting effect her silence seemed to be having.

'Your cooperation in the matter of Mr Monsarrat.'

'I didn't know he had become "a matter", as you put it.'

'I am aware that he relied heavily on you in Port Macquarie. That he holds you in high esteem.'

'He does, as a matter of fact. I have given him reason to.'

'Are you aware, Mrs Mulrooney – no, of course not, how could you be? – that a woman in my position, letting rooms and so forth, requires a certain amount of protection if her reputation is not to be irrevocably besmirched?'

'I'll need to take you at your word for that, now.'

'Please do. And the most effective form of protection comes in the shape of a man. I wish it were not so, but my . . . friendships, shall we say, with certain discreet and highly placed gentlemen have ensured I can operate my business without having soldiers knocking on the door in the early hours of the morning, full of rum and shillings.'

'I see. You trade in a different currency, I suppose.'

'If you insist on characterising it thus. I had for some time a particular friendship with a clerk in the colonial secretary's office, a man who frequently travelled from Sydney to Parramatta, and was unable to stay at Government House.'

'Not highly placed enough, I suppose.'

'Perhaps not. Even if he were, he would probably have needed lodgings – Governor Brisbane refused to have guests at Government House. I shall not name this gentleman, but he was very generous. I owe him my business.'

'Only him?'

'Mrs Mulrooney, you and I both came here on ships on which men outnumbered women, exiled to a colony which suffers a similar imbalance between the sexes. We have both seen the sailors and the soldiers and the civil officers and the merchants come and go, offering favours in return for favours. I do not surmise you fell for those blandishments. Pay me the same compliment.'

'Yet those blandishments worked on some,' said Hannah. 'On many, perhaps even on most. I may be the only one honest enough to openly question the source of your money, but I'd be surprised if no one else were thinking it.'

'Then you, and they, are wrong. This friendship with the colonial secretary's man was not ... onerous, I suppose, but it served to provide a measure of protection from those among my customers who might otherwise have expected me to take my hospitality too far.'

'This clerk, he ran away?'

'No. I imagine he is at this very moment sitting in the colonial secretary's office just as Mr Monsarrat is sitting in the governor's. Still there, and still rather happy to be reputed to be my friend. Or he would be, if I had not ended the matter with him.'

'And why did you do that?'

'Mr Monsarrat came back. Need you ask?'

'And I suppose, given his employer, you feel Mr Monsarrat can provide a higher level of, as you call it, protection.'

'Not a bit of it. I'd say he could, of course, but that's not why I ended things with the colonial secretary's clerk. Quite simply, I am rather attached to your employer. And his high regard is very important to me, as you might imagine.'

Hannah grunted.

'So I've come to ask you something of a favour. Given that you have his confidence, and his esteem.'

'That is true.'

'I'm aware, Mrs Mulrooney, that you may not feel I am an appropriate consort for Mr Monsarrat.'

Hannah wasn't certain what a consort was, but she was not going to admit that to this woman, who would have taken it as further evidence that tea and dirt were the only elements she could cope with.

'None of my business,' she said, ignoring the internal voice that chided her when she lied. 'Mr Monsarrat is as free as he was before you convinced him to break the conditions of his ticket of leave – don't think I don't know about that. Two years in Port Macquarie and he never once mentioned you, you know. And then the story came out shortly after we got here.'

'I wasn't responsible for his losing his freedom.'

'Oh? What was he doing out of his district then?'

'You will believe as you wish, Mrs Mulrooney,' said Sophia. 'However, I would like you to think about Mr Monsarrat's future. A man of his years – soon he will be closer to forty than thirty – surely his happiness rests on being accepted by his social betters, and his acceptance rests, at least in part, on marriage. And Mr Monsarrat is not the type to marry for convenience.'

'No. Convenience has never been his chief reason for doing anything. And his acceptance will surely rest as much on whom he marries as on the existence of a marriage itself.'

'Yes, and I'm aware that you are free with your opinions – far more so than most domestics would be with their employer.'

'I am not a domestic. I am his friend.'

'That being the case, may I ask you to cease whispering against me? I know what you say, I can guess. I can read it in between his words to me, in his caution. There is a reserve there now that didn't exist before Port Macquarie.'

'Put there, no doubt, by your lack of correspondence when you thought he was lost to respectable society, in the wilds of the north.'

'It's true I didn't write to him, nor he to me. We both knew that would be the way of it. Now he has returned, though ... I am not asking you to praise me to him, just to refrain from high-lighting what you may view as my inadequacies.'

'Miss Stark, I will make you only one promise. I will speak as I see. I always have and I do not intend to change that.'

Sophia stood, lifting her hat, calmly placing it back on her head, tucking in any strands of hair that didn't frame her face to its best advantage, and tying the ribbon beneath her chin so that it was perfectly symmetrical.

'Very well then, Mrs Mulrooney. Thank you for your candour. I also must speak as I see fit, and while your honesty today is commendable, perhaps you have been less than forthright with Mr Monsarrat when it comes to certain aspects of your past.'

Hannah narrowed her eyes. Of course, in this place you could make veiled references to dark pasts and be right eight, nine times out of ten. She was polishing a retort so it would fly smoothly when she ejected it, when the front door opened.

Monsarrat was flushed, she noticed. Accounted for, no doubt, by his insistence on wearing that black coat in the November heat.

'Mrs Mulroony, I need to ... Oh, hello, Sophia. Unexpected delight, as always. You'll have to excuse me for the moment, though. I am on business, and a rather indelicate variety, not one I'd wish to burden you with.'

'Of course,' said Sophia smoothly. 'I was simply passing the time with your housekeeper. I shall leave you to your affairs.' She glanced at Hannah, and would almost certainly have seen the smirk the Irishwoman was unable to keep from her face.

After Sophia left, closing the door very firmly, Monsarrat turned to Hannah.

'We're to go to the Female Factory first thing in the morning,' he said.

'We? You wish me to accompany you?'

'Of course. It seems there may have been some feminine involvement in a crime which has been committed. As I am teaching you to write, I must beg you to return the favour and teach me to read.'

Chapter 4

For an institution of women, the Female Factory drew an inordinate number of men to the gates in its austere sandstone walls, whose verticals gave the place a solidity and a pretension to authority which other structures in Parramatta lacked.

The men, of course, were there because of the women. The superintendent paraded the First Class inmates before any man who came seeking a wife. Emancipated convicts who had got themselves a piece of land to farm, which could only be reached by day upon day of dusty travel. Labourers and dock workers, perhaps. Rough men who had no romantic notions of marriage, most of them viewing it as a cheap way to get a servant. The man would select a woman and if she was willing the marriage would be arranged.

And the woman generally was, although not always. There were whispers of a fight that had broken out in the room where the women were brought, one by one, to be assessed. One man – a romantic, a rare species here – had brought a bonnet to give to the woman he selected. The object of his attention liked the bonnet. Unfortunately, she didn't like the man who was offering it, and he left, wifeless, with only a black eye and a handful of shredded straw and ribbon.

Monsarrat was grateful that Hannah had agreed to come with him today, grateful to have at his side a woman whose mind naturally ran in the channels of logic and observation, channels into which he had had to train his own thoughts to flow. To tell the truth, he occasionally envied Mrs Mulrooney her analytical brilliance, bestowed as it was on a former convict who in the normal run of things would have had little call for it.

But it had not been the normal run of things for quite some time, and certainly was not now. Hannah Mulrooney had been his friend when he himself was still a felon. Now he had been able to offer her employment, he intended to press her into service not only in making tea but in making deductions as well. While the governor's man might attract attention at the Factory, his housekeeper would become all but invisible among her bonded sisters, and Monsarrat had no doubt she would use that advantage to its fullest extent.

'Sophia was assigned fairly soon after she arrived, I think,' said Monsarrat. 'But she may have been at the Female Factory for a short while. I shall ask her.'

'If you think she'll be open with you,' said Mrs Mulrooney. She was weaving her way along the road, trying to avoid the worst of the ruts and holes and to stay in the shade available from the river gums. 'Madam won't welcome it, the reminder that she used to be a convict. But if you're going to annoy her, it might as well serve a purpose.'

'I'm afraid I don't follow.'

'Well, you're in a deal of trouble already – taking leave of herself so abruptly, and making it clear that you view me as more of a colleague than a servant.'

'Why on earth would that upset the woman? She didn't come to see me, she said as much. And she knows of the esteem in which I hold you.'

Mrs Mulrooney stared at him for a moment, with what looked oddly like pity. He wasn't sure he wanted to know why. And by this time they had reached the Factory, and the scene there made conversation impossible.

On an upturned crate outside the gates stood a small man in breeches, with his shirtsleeves rolled up to the elbow so that those interested in such things could see that his wiry frame may lack fat but not muscle. He moved from foot to foot but, to keep his balance, never looked down. Indeed, he couldn't have seen his feet if he'd tried, as they would have been obscured by a metal hot box he held, which leaked the smell of meat pies.

'You need not listen to me,' he was calling to the small crowd of men in front of him. His voice was deep and resonant. In those few words, Monsarrat recognised the refined accent which had been a feature of his daily life when he was a clerk at Lincoln's Inn.

'We won't, so,' said someone among the audience.

'Very possibly a wise choice, sir,' the man on the box said amiably. 'You have in fact no reason to give what I say the slightest attention. But Aristotle. Now, there, my friends, is a man deserving of your attention. And I ask you to grant him a moment of it. Aristotle said that if liberty and equality are chiefly to be found in democracy, they are best attained when all persons alike share in government.'

'Unfortunately, the government doesn't like to share,' said the heckler, earning himself a chuckle or two from those around him.

'This is true, my friend, for power is all it has, and those with power tend not to give the concept of equality consideration. The key, then, is to make that power dependent on the goodwill of fine fellows such as yourself. And of the wretches behind these walls, whom some of you may be taking home. What I am talking about, my friends, is nothing less than universal suffrage.'

'Don't know what universal suffrage is, but I'm familiar with universal suffering.'

'Precisely so. Universal suffrage, my friend, can put a stop to that. It means that we let everyone vote. No one can hold power – from the most junior functionary to the governor himself – unless the majority says they wish him to. This must be our goal, my fellow colonists, if we are to avoid in this place the inequities which characterise our former home. If we are to escape the enclosure of lands which has made starved shadows out of so many of our friends back across the seas. If we are to escape the rotten boroughs which allow the powerful to exercise yet more power.'

'My suffering would be eased by one of your pies, if you'd be good enough to come down off that thing and sell me one.'

The man on the box smiled and did as he was asked. No sooner had one of his bouncing feet hit the ground than he was surrounded. Shillings were shoved at him, and he opened the lid of his hot box to allow a wonderful smell to escape, and sight of the items responsible for generating it – pies of a remarkably uniform shape and size covered with golden pastry.

Monsarrat glanced to the side and noticed Mrs Mulrooney gazing at the man. Perhaps it was out of interest in the pies, in how the pastry had been made so beautifully, but Monsarrat suspected she was more entranced by the man's ideas.

Behind the thicket of people jostling for pies was the barred gate of the Female Factory. A letter of introduction from Eveleigh convinced the watchman – a different man from the one who had admitted Monsarrat for his conversation with Preston – to open it.

'One of the management committee is here,' said the watchman. 'In the committee room.' The man pointed with his chin, clearly not thinking Monsarrat, whoever he was, worth raising a hand for.

The committee room flanked the Factory's outer yard, kept company by the superintendent's quarters, some of the Factory's several stores and the lying-in hospital, which would certainly have seen the birth of several of Church's spawn. To its left, out of sight now, lay the drying grounds, and Monsarrat tried to avoid glancing in the direction of the Room for Useful Purposes – it was almost inconceivable that in such an inefficiently run institution Church's body had already been removed. Ahead of him was the sandstone slab of a building which housed the First Class women, and a passage through to the yard in which they washed and walked and paraded for muster. To the right were the Third Class yard and its penitentiary, which held, with debatable effectiveness, Grace O'Leary.

He didn't know how much use Robert Church had made of the desk in the committee room, but the person sitting there now had most certainly claimed it, if covering it with papers could be said to equate to ownership. He looked up as Monsarrat entered, exposing a raw piece of flesh on his neck which had been rubbed by sweat and the wool of his high collar.

And that wool . . . Monsarrat was accustomed to the sight of black or brown coats, punctuated by the occasional regimental red. This man, though, seemed heedless of sartorial convention. His cravat was a little too scarlet and his jacket was a more muted shade of the same. His waistcoat was nearly enough the same shade as Monsarrat's, but the former convict's bone buttons could not hope to compete with the gold studs glistening from this man's torso.

His wavy hair was so artfully pomaded that it put Monsarrat in mind of a tossing sea, and his full mouth looked as though it should belong to a poet. But there was nothing poetic in the man's bearing, and Monsarrat realised that anyone willing to dress as he had must have power – an unassailability conferred either by indifference to the opinions of others, or the ability to dictate those opinions.

As Monsarrat knocked to alert the man to his presence, he became aware that Mrs Mulrooney had positioned herself outside the direct line of sight of whomever was inside. She needn't have bothered. Without looking up, the man said, 'Go away.'

Monsarrat glanced behind him at Mrs Mulrooney, who

shrugged. He cleared his throat.

'Sir, I do beg your pardon. I am here on behalf of His Excellency the Governor, sent to assist in gathering evidence in the matter of the superintendent's death.'

'The governor?' said the man, still bent over the papers. 'Would that be the one who has sailed for England, or the one who is dithering about in Van Diemen's Land?'

An interesting question, thought Monsarrat. 'More correctly, sir, I am clerk to the governor's secretary.'

'Ah. Eveleigh's man.'

He did look up then, and Monsarrat wished he hadn't.

His eyes were very light blue, almost a feminine colour. They looked at Monsarrat as though he were guilty of a crime and it was their task to determine the punishment. The man was not old – perhaps Monsarrat's age – but was clearly used to power.

'Is this an inmate?' he asked, nodding to Mrs Mulrooney as she attempted to become one with the door frame.

Monsarrat bowed slightly and entered. 'This is my housekeeper, sir. I thought her services might be useful to the Factory when I'm about my business here. She is ticketed and free.'

'Very well,' said the man. 'Ladies' Committee is here today – one of them, anyway. Have her go to Superintendent Church's quarters.'

Monsarrat turned and nodded to Mrs Mulrooney, affecting a hauteur necessary to disguise their amity, but for which he knew he would pay later.

'Now . . . all here is in disarray. It will be a chore for the new superintendent when we appoint him. Until then, I suppose we must do all we can to find out what happened to the old one.'

'Sir, will you have a hand in appointing the new superintendent?'

The man glared at him for a moment. 'I will excuse your ignorance on this occasion,' he said. 'Please ensure it's not repeated when you're next before me.'

Monsarrat didn't intend to come before this man any more than necessary.

He hated not knowing who the man was, too, but Monsarrat suspected he would find an inquiry as to his identity presumptuous. In any case, he was obviously a member of the Factory's management committee, so could likely make Monsarrat's work here difficult if he chose to do so.

'Sir, you knew the deceased?'

'Yes. And I must say I believe humanity can get along perfectly well without him. Whoever is responsible not only shared that view but seems to have been holding it for some little time. This was no opportunistic attack, I gather, given the manner in which Church was dispatched.'

'So it seems, sir. Mr Eveleigh has given me to understand that certain assumptions are being made as to the identity of Church's killer.'

'More than assumptions, I'd say. We simply need to find the proof that fits the facts we already know. I would say it's close to certain that the killer is a particular convict woman. One of those who resides here involuntarily.'

'May I ask, sir, what gives rise to this certainty?'

'The woman's own behaviour. She has fragments of education, you know. She decided to put it to use by petitioning the governor for Church's removal as superintendent. But she could have left, you see. Didn't want to. I hear whenever she was brought before a man seeking a wife, she would spit or pick her nose or rave or do whatever she could to put him off.'

'Nevertheless, from what I understand, sir, her petition may well have had the support of several others, both within the Factory walls and outside them.'

'I've no reason to doubt it, and would not even think to remark on it had it stopped there. Especially as she was, for a time, of good behaviour. First Class, in fact. She could have been out of the Factory any number of times – a handsome woman, or she was until a few weeks ago. Surprised no one selected her for a wife. Probably regrets she didn't succeed in despatching Church the first time around.'

'She made a previous attempt on his life?'

'Not directly – at least not as far as I'm aware. No, it was the riot. You heard of it, no doubt. Police even came across some of the women in the streets, before they were all rounded up.'

'No. I'm afraid I was . . . elsewhere, at the time.'

'Well,' said the man. 'It all started with an objection the women had over some punishment or other. And they had a grievance with the rations.'

When he was at Lincoln's Inn, Monsarrat had abhorred the more obsequious clerks. Surely someone of sufficient talent and industry did not need to debase themselves. After ten years as a convict, though, he had learned the value of the protective coloration of the toady, while detesting himself for taking advantage of it. 'Surely the management committee would not permit any tampering with the rations,' he said.

The man looked up sharply, eying Monsarrat for an uncomfortable half-minute, searching his expression for any sign of sarcasm.

'No, indeed,' he said finally. 'Nevertheless – one morning during muster the women broke ranks, charged the guards, who didn't defend themselves for fear of killing them. Breaking furniture, breaking windows. Eventually breaking the gate. They surged out and then didn't seem to know what to do with themselves. I never thought women were as susceptible to heedless action as men, but it would seem these ones were just as capable of starting down the path without the faintest idea where it would lead them. So they were all rounded up. I interviewed them, and every woman, without exception, told me the riot had been O'Leary's idea.'

'So she's been held in the penitentiary since, I take it.'

'Yes. Before Church's death she worked with the others during the day and was locked up at night. Since the murder, she has not been allowed to leave her cell.'

'I see. May I have your permission to interview her? In

accordance with my instructions from Mr Eveleigh, of course.'

The man looked skyward, an affected expression of frustration designed to be decoded by its target. 'Don't expect to find a handsome woman now,' he said. 'Apparently Church decided to tie her to a chair in the middle of the yard and crop her hair as punishment. From what I understand, he didn't take particular care with the shears.'

Chapter 5

Hannah Mulrooney thanked Christ and His saints that the Factory had not yet been built when she had pressed her foot to the earth of this place for the first time.

The nine huts along Church Street into which she had been rammed on her arrival were still there. Not a lot of care had been lavished on their construction – particularly as the labourers were not builders by trade but pickpockets, rebels, poachers – and the administration seemed to have believed the huts would be capable of altering their meagre dimensions to accommodate the ever-increasing numbers of convict women.

Perhaps none of this would have mattered, thought Hannah, had it not been winter when she had disembarked. Certainly the cold was not as bad as it would have been at home, nor the damp. But cold was cold, particularly wearing the woefully inadequate cotton and calico the navy had given her. A lot of the other women wore the clothes they had been tried and convicted in under their navy slops – in most cases it was essential just to preserve one's modesty. Hannah had to contend with the chill without the benefit of her own clothes, as her infant son was wrapped in them.

So, while conditions at the Female Factory might have been somewhat more physically comfortable than those in the huts, she would not have traded. Because with the Female Factory came the Orphan School. The Orphan School was where the children of the Factory women went when they reached the age of four. They were supposed to be reunited with their mothers at the expiry of their sentence, but women could be assigned as servants anywhere in the colony, without the means to get back here at the end of the standard seven or fourteen years. Sometimes mother and child never saw each other again.

As a veteran of this place, Hannah had not had to face that particular cruelty among the multitudes she was exposed to. She had been able to keep her son, Padraig; dragged him with her even as she was assigned to service as a hut keeper in the shearers' quarters of a property a day's ride from Parramatta, the river mudflats giving way on the journey to jagged hills, bald in places, and twisted trees with crows in their branches that spoke with the same accent as the children.

Padraig was raised with the property's other children, he played with them, and she engaged in her first transaction with the Protestant faith when she sent him to the local rector, who had an educated convict teach children to read. It was not a gulf she wanted to jump, the one between her faith and the god of the Methodists. But she was willing to do it, to procure for her son the education which could ultimately mean the difference between a labourer who had spent his health by thirty, and a comfortable man of trade. So Padraig sat and learned his letters with the sons of felons, ticket-of-leave men and the occasional native stockman.

As he grew she could see that his features were expanding until they filled a framework laid down for them at birth. With his red-gold hair he looked, increasingly, like his father, and this was why she refused to allow him a pudding bowl cut which would make his hair look like a cap. And his hair was never, ever to be cropped.

At any rate, judging by what Monsarrat had told her of his conversation with Dr Preston about Mrs Church, neither Hannah nor her son would have benefited from the matron's drunken care at the Female Factory.

But this can't be Mrs Church, she thought, as the door of the superintendent's residence opened at her knock. She and the woman who faced her must have been almost the same height, both of them struggling to graze five feet. That, however, was the end of the resemblance. The woman had certainly been in the world a good decade and a half less than Hannah. She was wearing a plain but well-made cotton dress which was utterly spotless, a rarity in this place, where Hannah often believed (and said as much to Monsarrat) that she was the only inhabitant this side of the Indies with half a care for cleanliness. Clearly someone of means, then.

Hannah had already admonished one woman for failing to remove her bonnet inside, and now here was another, vastly elevated in comparison, keeping it in place. Perhaps, she thought, she'd missed a change in the rules while she was in Port Macquarie, where the proper etiquette for bonnet wearers was not a subject of regular discussion.

'Well, I'm not sure how I can put you to use,' said the woman, after Hannah had told her why she was there, 'but I imagine a cup of tea will provide the necessary inspiration. Please do come in.'

There was a kettle already on the hob, with steam vines inching out of its snout towards the corners of the room. Beyond that, on a low couch in the corner near a staircase which might have led to a bedroom, lay another woman, snores leaking out of her. This woman had no bonnet, and the hair plastered to her cheek by sweat was light enough to conceal a small number of grey hairs, which were multiplying and threatening to crowd out the others until no claim to blondness could be made.

'I shouldn't worry about waking her,' said the woman. 'I doubt anything will for some hours.' There was a cheerful clatter of cups as she got them down from the sideboard, and the swishing of the water in the teapot as she warmed it, poured it out and replenished it over a mound of fragrant leaves.

Her name, she said, was Mrs Rebecca Nelson.

'I'm on the Ladies' Committee, you see. Well, at the moment I *am* the Ladies' Committee. Charlotte Bulmer had been running it, but her husband doesn't want her mixing with convicts – he fears moral contagion. My husband fears moral contagion too, of course, but he takes the opposite view – he believes corruption sets in when one makes no attempt to help others. Mind you, he prefers to help from a distance. And I do believe he likes to think of me as the leading lady of philanthropy here, especially since they moved the native school into the bush. Dear Bessie Evans, she does such a remarkable job with those savage children. And now that she's doing it well away from here, there are so few other ladies with the inclination to help.'

She was, she said, the wife of a Quaker merchant. 'Have you seen the store a street back from the river, the large one? Nelson's. His name is David Nelson, you see. Tea. Cloth – the kind you can't get here, not that rough, coloured calico they make these poor girls wander around in. China and glass and cutlery. A bit of silver plate, but he tries to keep stocks low – thieves, you see. To be expected, here, I suppose.'

'I'm sure it keeps him very busy, missus,' said Hannah. Odd statement, she thought. Even by her own standards. But she had to admit to a level of discomfort, sharing tea with this bright creature while the shade breathed in the corner. 'I am to be at your disposal, I understand, while my employer is engaged in the business of helping discern the identity of Mr Church's killer.'

'Wonderful,' said Mrs Nelson. 'I haven't liked to leave poor Mrs Church, you see. Not that she would notice, I don't think. And I do still have a few tasks to complete here, which I'd as soon attend to before the end of the day. May I ask, would you be kind enough to sit with the poor thing? Just have some water at the ready in case she wakes. I'll be back as quickly as I can.' And off she went with elegant, seemingly unhurried steps.

Hannah did not like sitting still. Particularly not now and with a woman she didn't know, who might awake at any moment in an uncertain state.

Mrs Nelson had not even left her the solace of tidying. The windows set into the brown, rendered walls had been flung open, presumably to allow the sour vapours wafting off the sleeping woman a means of exit. The table had been scrubbed, recently and thoroughly if she was any judge. The hob was clean, as was the china. And the floor had been swept. A small pile of dust and detritus lurking in the corner was the only oversight Hannah could see, and she dealt with it immediately.

She picked up a cloth from a hook near the sideboard. It was unwashed – presumably Rebecca Nelson's powers of domestic reorganisation extended only so far. Hannah dipped the cloth in some water and walked over to the form on the couch, recoiling slightly as the smell of rum hit her. Bending down, she used the coarse fabric to smooth the grey, crinkled hair away from the woman's cheek. She got no response.

She washed and put away the cups she and Mrs Nelson had been using, and poured some more tea into a tin cup she found relegated to the shadows in the corner of the sideboard – she preferred the use of her own china and didn't like to impose on anyone else's. Such things mattered.

The elegance with which she'd departed had deserted Rebecca Nelson when she returned, ramming herself back into the kitchen, racing to a seat at the table as though there were others competing for it.

'Mrs Mulrooney, I have the most marvellous idea!'

Hannah glanced over at Mrs Church. She had not moved, and it was highly likely that slamming doors were common enough in her waking life to provoke little response even when she was conscious.

'I mentioned, of course, that I'm the sole representative of the Ladies' Committee here at the moment,' Mrs Nelson went on. 'We do what we can for the girls. Of course, some are more deserving of help than others, but we try not to discriminate. Certainly one of my objectives is to equip them for life once they eventually leave this place. A smattering of letters – sewing and needlework, that sort of thing. But there are more than two hundred women here, and with only one of me, well . . . I'm sure you can see the impossibility of the situation.'

'Certainly. It must be very difficult.'

'It is! It is. That may change, however. Your employer is here, yes?'

'Yes. Mr Monsarrat.'

'Just so. I met him, you see, crossing the yard, and asked him if I could make use of your services during his future visits to the Factory. Wonderful man that he is – five minutes' acquaintance is plenty of time to take someone's measure – he agreed. So you *shall* be helping me here, on occasion, with these unfortunates. Assuming you have no objection to working with convicts?'

'None at all, Mrs Nelson. I was one myself, for a time. So I'm hoping you've no objection to working with former convicts. I've been ticketed for . . . Well, nearly twenty years now.'

'Even better! You will have so much deeper an understanding of them than my own. I feel for the poor wretches, but of course I couldn't begin to understand them. Perhaps you can school me. In the manner of thinking which comes with bondage. It might enable me to help further. It changes one, I suppose. Do you not agree?'

'If one is weak-willed enough to let it do so, perhaps.'

Mrs Nelson laughed, slapping the table in a most unladylike fashion.

'And you are one with the strength to prevent it, yes? Like myself, or so I fancy, anyway. Do you not think, my dear woman, that we might benefit from shoring up the characters of those here?'

She fidgeted with her hat as she spoke, to the extent that Hannah wanted to swat her hands away from it. Her fingers continually sought escaping strands of hair, pushing them back inside the bonnet, which was drawn tight down over her forehead. She seemed insensible to the fact that her probing would draw out more hair in the process. An impossible task, anyway – the strands of Mrs Nelson's hair were so startlingly red that they made the light straw of her bonnet, to which they adhered, look like the veined cheek of a drunk.

'It will be wonderful to have someone ... effective. Poor Mrs Bulmer. She is unavailable due to a nervous complaint, apparently. The kind of complaint I imagine would afflict anyone with a husband like hers, although she doesn't, at least, take solace in rum.'

Hannah had heard the name Bulmer before, and not only from Mrs Nelson. Presumably there were not many of them here, and the only one she was aware of was the vindictive preacher who had ended Monsarrat's first stretch of freedom. If he was the woman's husband, Hannah thought a nervous complaint was the least of her problems.

'Now,' Mrs Nelson said, patting her bonnet as a reward for its efforts in constraining her hair, 'you are a competent needle woman, I judge.'

'Well, yes, as it happens. Having not seen my work, though, how are you able to judge it?'

'Your skirts, dear lady. Patched several times, I see. Please don't worry – done in such a skilful way that few people would notice. Only those with an eye for such things, like me, would have any inkling. I hope you're not offended by the observation.'

Hannah couldn't help drawing her shoulders back just a little, drinking in praise which was rarely a feature of her conversations with those higher up in society. Odd, though, that a woman of Mrs Nelson's station would notice patching on skirts – most of those with money wouldn't think of it.

'So I'm sure you'll agree with me that it's not good for the character of the ladies here to be wandering around in the clothes they were supplied with, little more than rags held together with rough stitching,' Mrs Nelson said. 'No finesse to it. Perhaps I might be able to impose on you to pass on some of your skill to these women.'

Hannah was not sure that she liked Rebecca Nelson's assumption of her agreement, but it had been a long time since she had been able to impart any skills of any sort to anyone, much less been given the opportunity to show off. She decided to let Mrs Nelson assume her consent until she could see where the woman's plans were leading. 'I will of course be delighted to be of service in any way,' she said, with the automatic but shallow deference the Irish had a lot of training in.

'Of course you will! Stout person such as yourself. I shall expect you, then, shall I? At nine o'clock on Monday morning, or as close as you can manage. You and I, I feel, are going to give these ladies something which the recently departed superintendent tried to remove. We are going to give them hope.'

Chapter 6

Monsarrat had been directed to a small passage which led to the First Class yard. The women were at their work now, weaving and sewing for the greater glory of the colony, so there was no one to watch from the windows of the First Class sleeping quarters as he delicately skirted a dark patch of dried blood on the ground.

The women of the Third Class might have preferred to work at the looms of their better-behaved sisters. Certainly today it would have been preferable to the drudgery they were engaged in when Monsarrat passed through the small doorway into their yard.

The women could have gained the river within twenty or so steps, if not for the high sandstone wall separating them from it. If there was any river breeze, the wall was as effective at keeping it out as it was at keeping the convicts in. An awning stretched from the wall, propped up on two sticks, and the women huddling underneath it wore sheepskin aprons over clothes that were in varying states of repair. Some wore blue and white cotton dresses and white caps, although certain items could no longer lay claim to anything approaching white. A few wore their slop clothing, or dresses which had been very obviously stitched together from other, smaller items.

While His Majesty's resources didn't stretch to uniform clothing, the administration made sure everyone who saw the creatures would know them for what they were. Each woman, at her breast or on her sleeve, bore a large yellow 'C'. The imperial coffers had also stretched far enough to provide the women with hammers, which they were wielding with varying degrees of enthusiasm, chipping away at dollops of rock that littered the yard. Their overseer sat on a stone block throwing pebbles at any crow or magpie which came into range and the women looked at him from time to time as though they would quite like to try the hammers out on him.

Monsarrat approached the man now – he was a former convict, or perhaps was still serving his sentence. He wore the same sort of neck handkerchief Monsarrat had been issued on the *Morley* a decade ago, its original colour now impossible to guess at.

'Grace O'Leary,' said Monsarrat. 'Where am I to find her?'

Monsarrat's entry to the yard had not attracted much attention – men from the outside did occasionally come here. Monsarrat knew Reverend Horace Bulmer walked into this yard each Sunday to see to the women's spiritual reform, or at least to remind them how comprehensively damned they were. There were reports of several convicts converting to Catholicism to avoid his Sunday lectures. But the mention of O'Leary's name caused a stillness to settle over them. They didn't look at Monsarrat – the convict who survived, man or woman, was most often the one whose eyes were continually raking the ground – but some hammers paused before they struck the stone, murmured conversations were arrested mid-sentence, and Monsarrat felt the weight of their attention just as keenly as if they had been staring.

Their guard didn't seem to notice, or didn't think the pause relevant. He stood. 'Who are you?'

'You don't need to know my name, only whom I represent – the governor and the superintendent of police. So, Grace O'Leary. Direct me to her, if you please.'

The overseer seemed unimpressed with Monsarrat's credentials. He sat back down on the sandstone block, armed himself against avian invasion with another pebble, and pointed to the building to his left. 'In the cells. Upstairs. Turnkey's there, or should be. If she hasn't killed him as well.'

The turnkey had so far escaped assassination and seemed no more impressed with Monsarrat than the overseer had been, barely willing to rouse himself from guarding the empty ground floor to admit Monsarrat to the cell above it.

Monsarrat was long used to the less savoury smells that accompanied life in a penal colony, which arose from an increase in population for whom hygiene was not a priority. And the odour of Grace O'Leary's cell, when the turnkey admitted him, was just as rank as any male convict barracks, but somehow different. The air was heavy with grease and underneath lay a note of stale sweat, presumably female but no less malodorous for that. The bedding was no doubt the source of it – untreated wool just as it had come from the sheep's back, oily and studded with burrs and what may have been dags, had been laid in the corner, compacted by the weight of the woman who slept on it.

She wasn't sleeping now. She was sitting with her legs to the side in an oddly delicate posture. She looked at Monsarrat as he entered, but said nothing.

Without taking his eyes from her, he reached backwards and pounded once on the door with his fist.

'Already?' said the turnkey as he opened it.

'I am to take this woman's statement. How do you suppose I am to accomplish that without a table to write at?'

Monsarrat was unused, after so long as a convict, to speaking with authority, and was training himself to do so – he found the results were far more effective than any amount of obsequiousness as long as one was addressing the right type of person.

46

'You would like me to fetch a table?'

'Of course, man.'

'I'm not to leave my post. Particularly not when she's here.'

'I assure you I am capable of defending myself against any attack from this creature. However, I am not capable of defending you against the wrath of the governor, should he hear his representative has not been afforded the ability to carry out his tasks.'

Monsarrat had no idea what the governor looked like, and Ralph Darling, yet to arrive in New South Wales, was unaware he was served by a Welsh–French hybrid of a former convict. But the turnkey knew none of this.

After the man moved away from the door, Monsarrat said, 'Had to send the turnkey off. He would have listened, you know.'

'Of course he would have,' the woman said. 'May be the most exciting thing that's ever happened to him.'

Her voice was surprisingly low, sonorous, the voice of a preacher or a revolutionary.

Her face was symmetrical, angular in a way that was both alluring and somewhat fearsome. Her skin was pale enough to host a field of freckles – but they looked as though they had faded since her confinement to the penitentiary. What he could see of her hair appeared to be dark, but there wasn't much of it – it sprang up in black and lustrous tufts here and there on her scalp, in the places where the skin hadn't been abraded to the point where it would not support any growth.

'You are Grace O'Leary.'

She didn't bother to respond, continued to stare at him.

'I am Hugh Monsarrat, from the governor's office.'

'You're here to ask why I killed that man.'

'Did you?'

'No, I did not. And I owe a debt to whoever did.'

'You're known to have worked to destabilise him, undermine him. You have written to the governor about him?'

'Indeed, and would have done so a hundred times more had I thought it would make any difference.'

'So your letters were ignored?'

'I would think so, yes. He remained in place.'

'Until someone sought to dislodge him in a rather emphatic way. The letters, though – they were not the end of it, were they? The small matter of the riot. There are many who believe that alone should be enough to hang you.'

She absorbed this with her strange, direct gaze, unblinking at the prospect of capital punishment.

'Then let them hang me, sir. I'll not argue; I'll consider it a fair price. I'm the only one with a shaved head. A far more effective means of communication than letters, I would say.'

'Were you expecting more heads to be shaved?'

'You haven't heard? I suppose you wouldn't have – not a glorious moment for His Majesty's reign.'

'What wasn't?'

'Church was going to take everyone's hair, you see. Said it was to address a general lapse in discipline, but he probably just had a wigmaker willing to pay well. And he spent a lot of time organising it – the girls were to shave each other's heads, and he paired them up into groups of friends so each of us would be shaving the head of someone we cared for.'

How, thought Monsarrat, can those who control this place be so dense when it comes to feeding the hungry, but so creative in their punishments?

'I can see from the little that's grown back,' he said, 'that shaving your hair would be a sin against all things handsome.' And then he scolded himself, wondering who had instructed his lips and tongue to form those words, as it certainly wasn't him.

'You are kind, Mr Monsarrat, but you should compliment only those women who have freedom over their own beauty.'

Monsarrat gathered himself and asked quickly so as to banish the Monsarrat who allowed unguarded statements to escape him, 'So that's what sparked the riots?'

'That was what convinced a lot of the girls to join, yes, along with being hungry.'

'Ultimately for nothing, though. You were all rounded up.'

'For nothing? No – the others did not have to endure having their hair taken. And we ate better for a little while. Shopkeepers in the town threw their wares out onto the street at us to prevent us breaking in.'

'The rations – did they stay sufficient?'

Grace O'Leary snorted, a noise which might have been disgust, or the symptom of some sort of congestive complaint.

'The bread got smaller. A little bit got shaved off each time. And the meat – they would assure us it was there, in the stew – that it had just been boiled down. But I certainly didn't taste any. So, no – as soon as Church's masters stopped looking in this direction, the rations began to shrink. Although he had the wit not to substitute salt for sugar again.'

'So,' said Monsarrat. 'You have engaged in a campaign of correspondence against Mr Church. And you have instigated a riot against his administration. Yet you ask the world to believe that you are not the one who attacked him.'

'You have a Frenchy name,' she said, as though she had not heard him. She started to chuckle, but the laugh betrayed her and transformed into a cough. She stood, walked to the corner and spat some phlegm into a rag which Monsarrat noticed she clutched in her hand. She turned back to him, wiping her mouth. 'Are you French?'

'No. It's a relic, my name. A remnant from a time of persecution, long gone now.'

'Well, Mr Monsarrat . . . Monsarrat . . .' She rolled the name around her mouth as though tasting it. 'You can be thankful your persecution was long ago,' she said. 'Mine continues.'

'I understand.'

'You do not.'

'Miss O'Leary, I did not myself come to this place as a free man.'

'I don't doubt it, Mr Monsarrat. That would only make you like most here. But to claim you know of persecution, when you came here in a male form rather than a female one – forgive me if I don't believe you. Tell me – have you heard the name Emily Gray?'

The convict Homer Preston had mentioned. The one who had starved to death.

'Emily died in this room,' said Grace. 'She was so hungry she ate the bones from her ration, then started on the weeds on the drying ground. And to punish her for that, for chewing on His Majesty's weeds, Church had her held here. She had a metal collar, ropes tied to it, and the other end tied to spikes in the floor. When she started thrashing about in here, they put her in a straitjacket. That's how she stayed until she starved to death. Look.'

She pointed, slowly, deliberately, to four deep indentations in the floorboards. She had positioned herself in the middle of them. Where Emily would have sat. Where Emily would have died.

'Church wanted to rob me of hope, to sap my spirit. He failed. I lost hope a long time ago. I have nothing tethering me to this earth. So I have no reason to let fear or anything else temper my actions when it comes to stopping the worst of the abuses.'

'Please don't say that to anyone else,' said Monsarrat. 'In some lights, it could be seen as a confession.'

'It's not.'

'What was done to you recently – your head – that is wrong, I can certainly see that. And by someone whose objective was to demonstrate power rather than punish an offence.'

'Well, I think he was happy to do both.'

'Yet for all the short rations, the overenthusiastic discipline, you have not taken one of the chief options available to you, which would enable you to leave here.'

'To marry, you mean? Or be assigned? I've never had the opportunity.'

'Miss O'Leary, I have not come here with any preconceptions, nor with the intent to find you guilty if you are not. But I must ask you, please, for your honesty.'

'You have it. You've had it since the moment I opened my mouth.'

'I've been told you made yourself disagreeable to potential suitors. Deliberately did everything you could to ensure you weren't chosen.'

'Who told you that? The magistrate?'

Monsarrat said nothing.

'I imagine it would have been him,' she said. 'He wasn't one of Church's admirers, that is certain. But he's a lazy man, and it takes far less effort to believe any lie the superintendent tries to feed you than to try to ascertain the truth.'

'And what is the truth?'

'That I was never brought out and marched in front of the men. That Church wanted me right where I was.'

She leaned forward, covering her mouth and expelling another cough, a moist rumbling in her lungs demanding release.

He waited for her to finish, looked up at the splintery timber ceiling so she would not feel embarrassed. The public humiliation she had already endured was more than enough.

'Why?' he asked when she had finished and wiped her mouth on her sleeve. 'I've been given to understand you were a significant problem for the man. Why would he not be happy to get rid of you?'

'Do you know, Mr Monsarrat, how Church and that sottish wife of his, and the rest of them, are paid?'

'One presumes in money.'

'Then one would be presuming incorrectly. They get some money, certainly. But it wouldn't do for them to be too much of a drain on Governor Brisbane's purse. So they also get centage.

A proportion of everything we produce here. Cloth, twine, everything. And that's where the real money is. If they were paid as they were in the old country, they'd make half as much. And if they were paid what they're worth, they'd make nothing.'

'Yes, I can see how such a system might be open to abuses. But why would that prevent you from marrying?'

'I was a seamstress, you know. In Galway. Quite good. And of course my talents came with me over the seas, and I applied them with great industry when I first arrived. Thinking it might be a way into the good graces of the rulers, you see. Better rations, wheat flour instead of that India stuff. Indeed, work by my hand tended to fetch a higher price than that done by a housekeeper or a dairy maid. Church wanted me at my work table, making a valuable product for him. So even though I was in the First Class at the time, I was never paraded before such men as came here to select wives.'

'But surely that's against regulations.'

'Whether it is or not, I can't say. Those on whom the laws rest most heavily are not often told what those laws actually are.'

A scraping sound now slid underneath the crooked door, followed by one of the milder and less imaginative of the curses regularly employed by the colony's men. Monsarrat opened the door and the guard, key in hand, gave a startled jerk, then lowered his head and looked at Monsarrat as though he had just grown horns and was about to charge.

'You'll not be mentioning to anyone that the door was unlocked, I trust. After I went to the trouble to procure this for you.'

'This' was a low wooden bench, perhaps long enough for one and a half well-fed people to occupy.

'Thank you for the seat. As for the table . . .'

'The bench will serve as a table,' the guard said.

'And I should sit . . .'

'The floor is sturdy enough.'

'Thank you. I shall test its sturdiness while I decide how much detail I shall put in my report.'

The turnkey jutted his chin out. 'Do as you please. There are no tables to be had.'

He dragged the door back into its frame, and this time did lock it, using a few more expletives and leaving Monsarrat with the impression he may not be disposed to unlocking it.

Monsarrat laid out his writing implements on the bench like a priest preparing a ritual, aligning his pen precisely with the edge of the paper, uncapping the ink and placing its stopper to the side. He bent and brushed the floor near the bench, but a glance at the muck which adhered to his hand told him it was futile. At least his trousers were dark, but he would have to brace himself for an assault with Mrs Mulrooney's cloth for putting her to the trouble of washing them.

Then he carefully knelt in front of the bench and got from his pocket the paper and pencil which he used for shorthand.

We will choose our words carefully, now our friend is back at his post, he wrote.

He had no idea whether she could read, but she must have been able to as she nodded. Using words carefully was a skill Monsarrat had developed, consciously working at it, gnawing it into a shape, a tool appropriate for any purpose he needed to put it to. It was a matter of survival. Grace, he imagined, would have a keen understanding of its importance.

He held the pencil suspended over the page.

'I charge you to tell me, Grace O'Leary, whether you did take the life of Robert Church on Thursday last.' It was theatrical, overly so for him, and he had an uncomfortable suspicion that some colour had begun to rise on his cheek. Certainly, Grace had noticed his discomfort, if her small smile was any indication.

'No, sir, I did not.'

She took an obvious inventory of his face before deciding to fix her gaze on his nose. She seemed to him altogether too perfect in her denial.

'And why should you be believed?'

'Sir, you have seen the security under which I'm held.'

She was smiling openly now. Monsarrat raised his eyebrows, motioned his head towards the door. A warning. Getting lost in wordplay could carry a cost, such as the secondary sentence that had followed a particularly elegant comment he had made about natural justice to Reverend Bulmer two years ago.

'Now, yes. But at the time of the murder?'

'Why, the very highest level. It was night-time, of course. They do not wish to allow us the opportunity to wander, in case we decide to sample the delights of the town. I was in a room with five other women, just down the corridor at the end of the building. I am not the only person who sleeps in this building.'

'Were any of your cellmates missing at the time of the murder?'

'I couldn't tell you, Mr Monsarrat, having been asleep myself at the time.'

Her eyes left his nose to its own devices for a moment, flicking towards the window. She was very possibly unaware of their momentary rebellion.

'So your contention – to which you will be required to swear – is that you were under guard, sleeping, but in the company of others, at the time the superintendent was killed?'

'Yes.'

Monsarrat nodded. He dashed off a statement to that effect, cursing the conditions for interfering with his penmanship while taking a perverse pride that it was still better than any other clerk in the colony.

'I will read your statement now.'

'No need. I am perfectly capable of reading it to myself.'

'Had you an education, then, in Galway?'

'None that didn't involve needle, thread and cloth. No, I received my letters here, courtesy of Mrs Nelson. As did many of the other girls. Now, if you would give me the paper?'

He blotted it and did so. As she read it he had a strange sense she was checking for errors in spelling or grammar. Evidently finding none, she looked up at him, nodded and reached out for the pen, using a florid signature which Monsarrat observed was common to the newly literate, who enjoyed stretching their wings in this manner. Hannah Mulrooney liked to curl the edges of the first letters of her name, and tended to give the 'y' an elaborate tail.

Grace handed the statement back. She may believe this is an end to it, thought Monsarrat. She may not be aware that this place's most senior law officer has already mentally convicted her. And Monsarrat was not entirely convinced Ezekiel Daly was wrong.

He stood, rapping on the door with the back of his knuckle. He heard weight shift on the other side but the guard seemed in no hurry.

'Mr Monsarrat,' Grace O'Leary said, taking the opportunity the delay afforded. 'I did not do this. You have my statement. I know it is what you're expecting me to say, whether I'm guilty or not. And I am happy it was done, but it was not done by me. There are others you may care to look to. The rations which didn't come to us must've gone somewhere. And there is Mrs Church – rum disagrees with her. Gives her something of a temper.'

'I see. Well, thank you for that information. Coming as it does from someone who I believe has something of a temper herself. Was it that, I wonder, which prompted the superintendent to visit such violence on your scalp?'

'No. A few new ones came in. One reasonably young – I'm surprised they weren't assigned straight off the boat. And during muster the superintendent decided to give one of them a more detailed inspection. He took off her neck handkerchief, made to put his hand down the front of her dress.'

'And?'

'I hit the bastard. And I will happily sign a sworn statement to that effect when next you visit, as I'm sure you will. Good day, Mr Monsarrat.'

The guard had obviously decided enough time had passed for him to make his point, and the key was driven home into the lock and twisted, with a few attempts before it decided it would move the latch.

Monsarrat saw that as he left Grace was already lying down, her back to him, her head on the dirty wool which, despite its filth, would hopefully provide at least a fraction of the protection her hair no longer could.

'What's your name?' Monsarrat asked the guard.

'Felton. Tom Felton.'

'Well, Felton. I have a lot of work to do, and I may not get around to noting that the door to O'Leary's cell was unlocked for quite some time if you are able to show me the room she was in on the night of the murder.'

Felton nodded, set off down the corridor. The room he led Monsarrat to was small but amply served by windows. They had once had panes, judging by the few jagged teeth jutting from the frames. The women here had the relative luxury of bedrolls, which had been pushed into the corners of the room, probably to avoid the worst of the summer rain when it lashed in through the pointless windows. At the end of the room a small, barred round opening let in a little light. Monsarrat wondered why anyone would bother barring a hole barely large enough for a child to fit through while leaving the windows unrepaired.

The window yielded only a view of the Third Class women at their work and the overseer, who seemed to have given up on the birds for now. But the round opening looked out on the widest part of the Third Class yard, and the storeroom opposite. And from this perspective Monsarrat noticed something he had overlooked before: a sturdy wooden gate set into the corner of the yard.

'Felton – where does that gate lead?'

'To the wood yard and then down to the river. It's always locked, before you ask.'

'Who has the key?'

'The superintendent – or he did, anyway. Maybe the management committee. The storekeeper and a few others. Not me, so it's not my doing if it's unlocked. Not that it's used much. The woman from the Ladies' Committee – she's got her fingers in everything, can't stand mess – was in here cleaning the muck out of the keyhole the other day. I told her not to bother but she said the sight of the dirt clogging it up irritated her.'

'Hmm,' said Monsarrat. His eyes traced the path he had taken an hour ago, when he walked from the First Class yard, which still bore a smear of Robert Church, through a gap in the wall to the Third Class yard, until he was standing just a few feet from the gate, without noticing its existence.

Had Robert Church's killer known of it, perhaps had a key? It would be a very convenient route down to the river and away.

The murderer might not have needed to get away, of course. He or she might have only had to climb the stairs to one of the bedrolls in this room. He was disconcerted by an image which suddenly placed itself before him, a picture of Grace standing by this small aperture, her eyes absorbing what light they could from the moon while someone who was happy for her to bear the consequences slid through the gate to the river.

Chapter 7

'She denies it, of course.'

'Naturally,' said Eveleigh. 'And I'd assume she was telling the truth if the security of the Third Class penitentiary was as it should be, but I've gathered it's not.'

Monsarrat decided not to tell Eveleigh about the unlocked door. Even though he wasn't sure whether he believed Grace, he did feel there was scope for further investigation.

'She told me she had written to the governor about Church, sir,' he said. 'If you can spare me, perhaps some time in the cellar might prove illuminating?'

'Hmph. Not just trying to escape the heat?'

The cellar had thick stone walls surrounded by earth, and in Eveleigh and Monsarrat's estimation was the coolest place in Parramatta aside from the river itself. But it was the administrative version of the Augean stables. Monsarrat had only been down there for a short time, so had only briefly been able to assess the state of the shelves, with ledgers and scrolls jumbled together, many of them wearing a fine coating of dust. The place also housed all the correspondence, files and documents that nobody had got around to organising yet, some of which dated back to the previous decade.

'Certainly not,' Monsarrat announced. 'I thought I might be able to locate her letters to the governor, if we still have them. I also think it would be wise to acquaint myself with the details of her original offence. It might provide me with some idea of how to approach her when I'm at the Factory next.'

'She's hardly likely to have confessed to a murder she hadn't yet committed,' said Eveleigh. 'And your work is complete, Monsarrat. You have her statement. Send it to Daly and we'll be done.'

'Yes, but it simply occurs to me, sir, that her correspondence might touch on other abuses going on at the Factory, which might in turn lead to other lines of enquiry. We want to make sure the right person pays for the crime, as you said.'

Eveleigh sighed. 'You know, I always complain about time-serving clerks. Those who simply do what I ask of them and not one iota more. Those who never show any initiative. Oh, how I wished for somebody with a bit of spark, a bit of willingness to look further, do more.'

'Thank you, sir.'

'It is not a compliment, Monsarrat. Now that I have you, I'll take the time servers back any day. Very well then, might as well see what you can find. But please don't act on the information without telling me first. We don't want to embarrass the management committee. At least not without a plan.'

'Ah. Speaking of the management committee – there was a man at the Factory, sir. The guard on the gate told me he was on the committee, but he didn't introduce himself and I got the strong impression he would have been offended if I'd asked who he was.'

'Describe him, if you please.'

So Monsarrat did – the flamboyant clothes, the crenellated hair. He left out the poetic mouth and cruel eyes.

Eveleigh said something under his breath. It sounded like a more extreme version of the curse used earlier by the penitentiary guard.

'You, Monsarrat, have had the honour of making the acquaintance of Socrates McAllister. Not a man whose attention you want to attract.'

Something in Monsarrat's stomach decided, then, to slither and turn. McAllister he had heard of. McAllister was dangerous. McAllister was a magistrate. But he wielded more than judicial influence. His uncle, Philip, was the most powerful landowner in the district, a grazier whose profitability dwarfed that of surrounding farms.

Philip McAllister, not one given to sparing the feelings of others, made no secret of his disappointment in his nephew's business skills, and Socrates, who had once had a place reserved for him at the centre of the growing McAllister empire, was now relegated to managing one of his uncle's smaller farms. The McAllister name was sufficiently respected to procure him not only a seat on the bench but also on the boards of various civic institutions, including the gaol across the street and the Factory. So while Socrates was the least of satellites to his uncle, he still wielded considerable power. And in the absence of the governor, all of those with at least some power were stretching and flexing, testing to see how much influence they could appropriate before the new man arrived.

Respectable though McAllister looked, there were rumours, if one cared to listen – and Monsarrat always did, prided himself on being a silent receiver of information – of under-the-table deals involving rum, fabric, wool. Suggestions of usury. Rumours too of threats, and beatings administered at arm's length – in this place where the majority of the free folk used to be otherwise, it was not hard to convince a man to accept a monetary inducement for bringing street justice to another.

There was even talk that a particular man known to be late in his payments to his creditors – and whether those creditors included McAllister could only be guessed at – had returned home one evening and found the structure which had housed him until that morning had been pulled to the ground.

'Well, I shall make sure I stay out of his way then, sir,' said Monsarrat.

'You might not be able to. If he takes an interest in you, you will suddenly find him around every corner. Let us hope he's decided you're not important enough to be bothered with. Especially since he's become an ally to the good reverend now.'

Monsarrat had heard that the Reverend Horace Bulmer had achieved his long-held ambition of a seat on the Parramatta bench. An alliance between him and McAllister, especially one directed at Monsarrat, was not one he wanted to contemplate.

'Nevertheless,' said Eveleigh, 'if you can stay out of his way, it will be all to the good. There have been ... consequences ... in the past for those who haven't.'

Monsarrat wanted to ask what those consequences were, and on whom they had fallen. But Eveleigh held up his hand. 'Enough of that for now. You have my permission to spend one hour in the cellar – God rot you and your cursed luck, getting out of this heat – however, if you're unable to find anything in that time, that will be an end to the matter.'

Riffling through the papers down there, Monsarrat tried to find Grace's transportation records and any letters she might have written to the governor. He didn't know when Grace would have written the letters, which was just as well as the documents weren't organised chronologically. Nor by surname, he discovered when he went to look for Os and found them scattered between Ws, Qs and Bs.

After a while a rudimentary system of organisation began to emerge. The documents relating to the Female Factory appeared to have been jumbled together on one section of the shelves. He got them down, one by one. The ledger which listed women transferred to the Factory had Grace's crime as 'stealing cloth'. Hardly surprising when the overwhelming majority of the Factory's residents were transported for crimes committed in the name of survival: a great many women had stolen at the behest

61

of an unforgiving hunger, particularly in the summer grain-for-cash season, only to find that hunger had followed them here.

The records shed no light on the details of Grace's crime, but they did note that she was 5 feet 6 inches – tall, very tall – with brown hair and blue eyes. That her occupation was seamstress. That she was tried at the Galway assizes and was sentenced to transportation for seven years. And that when she was transported, she was 27 years of age, unmarried and childless.

Monsarrat ignored the rest of the ledgers and concentrated on the loose documents, looking for her name. When he saw it, he stopped. Flipped through the pages, seeing how much was there.

There was letter upon letter. Ten, twelve, fifteen pages' worth. All addressed to his Excellency the Governor. And no note had been made on them as to whether His Excellency had replied. Monsarrat thought it unlikely.

'I was transported for a crime I did not own,' Grace wrote.

Of course you were, thought Monsarrat. Weren't we all.

And since arriving here, many other women and I have been punished twice – once in being transported, and a second time by being assigned to the Female Factory, where our rations are kept so short that one of our sisters has recently expired.

The superintendent, meanwhile, visits the most degrading and depraved abuses on the women, particularly the younger ones. I have attempted to prevent this on numerous occasions and have paid by being beaten, deprived of food, and with other punishments.

If women are to help build this colony then I despair, for they will be in no fit state to do so with the current hard treatment they receive.

I beg Your Excellency to intervene, to turn out the corrupt and brutal administration of the Factory so that those of us who wish to make honest lives here once our sentence expires can do so unimpeded.

Grace had been protecting the younger women, then. Or trying to. Had been punished for it, and kept doing it. Monsarrat couldn't help but admire her. He asked himself whether he would have the courage to do the same in her position but decided he did not wish to know the answer.

She was more, though, than an instigator, a stirrer of pots. She had used the language of her rulers in that letter. To be able to do so, after a relatively short time in the ranks of writers, showed a nimble mind. It was possibly a symptom of her Irishness, as he knew from Mrs Mulrooney that the Irish could show an eloquence more marked than their education might warrant. It was also, he thought, evidence of a finely honed protective instinct. She, like he, was prey adopting the coloration of the predator.

Judging by the date on the letter, it was sent before Eveleigh took up his post. And in any case the documents dated after Eveleigh had arrived were in meticulous order. He wondered if his employer would know whether the letter had been replied to. There were more, too, detailing beatings and head shavings and rapes and starvation punishments – a parade of horrors. Whether or not Grace had received a reply from the government, through her letters she posed a question for Monsarrat. Had she, in her attempts to protect the women, taken subsequent steps to ensure they would never be molested again?

Chapter 8

Sophia Stark had remained lodged as a hazy though promising presence in Monsarrat's mind during his time in Port Macquarie. It was the sort of remembrance that took grace and beauty for granted, in a way which might not be credible in a relationship with a real woman daily encountered. Sophia radiated even more lustre when compared with Port Macquarie's prostitute Daisy Mactier, whose ageless and flat face had defined Monsarrat's dull existence while Sophia decorated his dreams.

He had called on Sophia a week after his return to Parramatta. The shrubs which guarded the small pathway leading to the front door of her guesthouse were as neat as he remembered them. He had chosen a mild evening. The unnatural daylight which persisted beyond the dinner hour was beginning to fade, and flights of white cockatoos were trailing the tips of their wings across the sky and rousing the bats. It would probably have been more convenient for Sophia had he knocked at the door of the Prancing Stag during the day, when the majority of her guests could be relied on to be out. He couldn't countenance it though. Midday's enveloping heat would have called forth a slick of sweat he did not want her to see. He feared it would remind her he was a beast of burden, even if his tool was a pen rather than a hammer.

He had been imagining her reaction when she set eyes on him. A gasp, colour rising at her throat. Perhaps a tear. Most certainly an embrace.

'Oh,' she said when she opened her door to him. 'I thought you had another year.'

'Yes,' he said, trying to keep any peevishness out of his voice. 'I thought it might be longer, in point of fact. I had made myself rather indispensable. But I did a service to the commandant, who procured me a ticket of leave. I am now as free as you.'

She was looking at him oddly, her head slightly to the side as though she was trying to see whether he was in fact there and not a shimmering falsehood. She seemed, after a few moments, to have satisfied herself of his solidity, and she opened the door wider and gestured him inside.

They went into the parlour, passing a small sitting room swamped in opulent swagged curtains, with fussy, flocked wallpaper and inexpertly stuffed with cheap furniture modelled on what Sophia believed one would find in a country house. A neatly dressed man sat there with a copy of the *Sydney Chronicle* on the table in front of him.

Sophia's private parlour was small and tidy like everything else associated with her, though slightly cramped. They sat on opposite sides of the table at which they had once drawn the chairs close together, shoulders and elbows touching.

'Have you employment? Now that His Majesty has ceased feeding you?'

'Well, His Majesty has contented himself with paying me rather than feeding me. I am clerk to the governor's private secretary.'

Both of Sophia's eyebrows shot up, but her mouth did not share their surprise, her lips pinching into a sceptical moue. There was a sharpness to her that he didn't recall, a jagged quality which she had tried and almost – almost – succeeded in sanding away.

'The governor's secretary,' she said. 'But we've no governor, do we?'

'We do, in point of fact. He just happens not to have arrived here yet. He will, however.'

'And when he does, you'll be working for him?'

'Well, for his man, yes.'

'And do you intend to make yourself as indispensable to him as you did to the commandant of that place they sent you to?'

'Certainly. It is the only path to safety.'

Her mouth relaxed, and she attempted a ladylike smile which hid her teeth. She rose, then, as did Monsarrat, unfolding his long legs from the small ornate chair he had been sitting on, unwilling to stay seated while she was on her feet.

She walked over to him and slowly, as though performing a ritual which depended on absolute precision for a successful outcome, reached up her arms and put them around his neck, drawing his head down towards her.

'Welcome back, governor's man,' she said.

⌒◦⌒

The luminous Sophia who had lived in Monsarrat's thoughts in Port Macquarie could not, however, coexist with the hard-edged, pinched woman whose eyes constantly slid to the side. He tried, with increasing desperation, to call the angel back. She must surely have existed. He would not have risked his freedom for her otherwise. And if she was there once, she might be again. A few nights a week he tried – arriving after dark and leaving before dawn to avoid Bulmer's maniacal surveillance – to excavate her, visiting the bedroom which had once sent him into a fever but now had little more allure than Eveleigh's office.

While the night-time visits were only just beginning to feel like a dry duty, Monsarrat would have done almost anything to avoid Sunday mornings.

The stroll with Sophia down Church Street was pleasant

enough, as one was never frustrated by unmet expectations of transcendence on a stroll to the Sunday service. The church was a serviceable building, the genteel sandstone of the main building flanked by two towers made of bricks shaped by convict hands. There had been no attempt to make the spires on these towers conical, and certainly they lacked the flourish of the stone spires of his boyhood, rising in unapologetically flat, triangular planes to meet at the crosses that topped each one. Even the church had its guards, its overseers.

Monsarrat's freedom brought with it the right to occupy one of the pews to the rear of the church, looking over devout heads towards the box pews reserved for Parramatta's first families. He would have been happy, actually, not to occupy any part of the church but he was still a man on the margins, and chipping away at the walls that separated him from the Eveleighs and McAllisters required visible attendance. He told himself it was necessary to give him access to the people and places he needed to reach to carry out his duties, on which his continued freedom depended. He did not like to stand directly in front of another possibility – that he hungered for the approval of those who would never give it, who viewed him as irredeemably corrupted.

The walk to church with Sophia had, however, become less agreeable over the past few weeks, it had to be said. Sophia's conversation had previously ranged over a wide landscape, from politics to art to the doings of the local worthies. But now her focus was becoming increasingly restricted. She wished to know when they would marry.

Monsarrat had no objection to the idea of marriage. The respectability he had hungered for since his days posing as a lawyer in Exeter was very possibly closer than it had been since his arrival in the colony, and a wife would do no end of good in enhancing it. But, he told himself, he wanted to be more settled, more assured, before he married. He ignored, when it insisted on presenting itself, the image of him and Sophia in her cramped parlour, silent, joined by God but separated by a slab of polished mahogany and a wall of mutual disappointment.

In Port Macquarie, he had mapped the invisible traps, the people who could be engaged and those best avoided; he had constructed a barricade of words and become adept at changing his form to meet each circumstance. That place, hemmed by mountains and sea and river and containing 1500 souls – and only a few dozen who had any power over him – had been easy to negotiate once the pitfalls had been identified.

Parramatta was a different proposition. An outpost, certainly, but one with far more people, and closer to the seat of power. And the greater the proximity to power, he had learned, the greater the danger. Six weeks had been barely enough time to identify the most obvious of pitfalls, let alone to intuit the hidden traps and construct a way to bypass them. Then, of course, there were the traps laid by those who saw no benefit in approaching things obliquely, the people whose antipathy was easily won, and worn like a cloak. And chief among them, alongside Socrates McAllister, was the Reverend Horace Bulmer.

Bulmer had very firm views about the nature of convicts, their character and whether it could be improved. He was of the belief that a criminal gene existed, and those unlucky enough to receive it from their parents were irredeemable, doomed to bring to life the criminal acts which were already engraved on their souls.

Monsarrat would very much like to ask the reverend one day how this belief sat beside the assertion that God gave man free will. That would have to wait, though, until his position was unassailable. Bulmer, like the superintendent of police, felt that those who had had the benefit of education should know better, and that someone who could take their advantages and turn them to evil ends was dangerous enough to deserve the noose.

Monsarrat was exceptionally grateful that Bulmer was not in charge of convict punishment. But he was in charge of St John's Church, and he used that position to ensure Monsarrat got at least a little of what the clergyman felt he deserved: the clerk had been the framework upon which the reverend had laid the fabric of a great many of his homilies. There had been two alone since Monsarrat's return, since his presence in the church, seated and free, had caught Bulmer's attention and inflamed his indignation, never far from the surface at the best of times.

Monsarrat saw no sign that the reverend was tiring of his subject.

'Much will be expected from those to whom much is given,' Bulmer had screeched last Sunday. 'But what can be said for those who take those gifts and instead of dedicating them to the Redeemer and to the service of man, dedicate them to sin and Satan? Are they not more culpable than those who were given no gifts to begin with?'

The reverend said this while looking directly at Monsarrat. It was the chief reason the clerk didn't sit beside Sophia – there was no need to present Bulmer with another target, as well as a reminder of the sin of fornication. Sophia was probably grateful for the distance, too. She emerged after Bulmer's first homily with a thunderous face, refusing to glance in Monsarrat's direction until Ralph Eveleigh greeted him warmly. 'I've come to rely on him, you know,' Eveleigh had said to his wife. 'It will be quite an adjustment if they take him away from me.' Suddenly Sophia was at his elbow, with the tentative smile worn by those seeking an introduction.

This Sunday, however, was one of the first during which he had not given the reverend a moment's thought as he and Sophia walked to church. He was thinking of Grace O'Leary. Grace's punishment would have been far more distressing for someone like Sophia, he thought. Sophia had always equated cleanliness with wealth, and hoped her attendance to the former would hasten the appearance of the latter. Grace didn't seem to care all that much about such things, unless her seeming indifference was a self-protective ruse. He was adept at constructing those, and liked to think he was equally skilled at spotting them in others.

If Monsarrat was astonished to realise when they arrived at the church that he had forgotten all about the reverend's impending homily, he was equally astonished, half an hour later, to find that he was not its subject.

'There are those among us,' the reverend said as he poked an invisible sinner with his finger, 'who feel education entitles them to subvert the will of God and the King.'

The words could easily have applied to Monsarrat, but the reverend's gaze was directed somewhere over Monsarrat's left shoulder. He was tempted to turn, but he kept his own eyes down as the venom skimmed the back of his neck on the way to its target, and he was grateful for the reprieve.

'There are those who feel justified in filling the hearts and minds of men with poisonous fantasies of universal suffrage, of spreading the notion that voting, a say in the workings of government, is a natural right.

'Like the most effective works of Satan, their argument seems reasonable – reasonable enough to lead many a sensible man down a dangerous path.

'But these clever men, the ones who preach evil disguised as good, know the truth of it. They know the ridiculous, obscene and un-Christian concept of universal suffrage will lead to chaos. They know there are those whom the Lord has equipped to govern, and placing that burden on others will lead to ruin.'

Monsarrat discovered the identity of Bulmer's victim after the service. He came upon Dr Homer Preston outside the church, clapping the shoulder of another man. 'I hope you don't feel too neglected, Monsarrat,' Preston called when he saw him. 'I'm sure the reverend will return to you next week.'

His companion was replacing his black cloth cap, having removed it in church – probably more out of respect for God and convention than Reverend Bulmer. Small, wiry and constantly in motion, waiting for Monsarrat to join them he shifted from foot to foot.

'Now, even someone as recently returned as you cannot have failed to hear of the Flying Pieman. You know this fellow runs into the mountains and back in a single week, with that ridiculous hot box of his,' Preston said, indicating his companion.

Monsarrat shook the man's hand. 'Yes, I believe we met outside the Female Factory. I'm not clear, though, whether it was pies or ideology you were selling.'

'More of the former than the latter I'm afraid, though I wish the quantities were reversed,' the man said in a clipped accent. 'And while there are some excitable souls who refer to me as the Flying Pieman, I much prefer the name that God and my parents gave me, which happens to be Stephen Lethbridge. At your service, naturally.'

'Well, Mr Lethbridge, I am in your debt for drawing the hellfire of the reverend away from me. It won't last, I fear, but a Sunday's respite has been delightful.'

'I am sure. When that man warms to a topic, he rarely lets go. Quite a feat to become the focus of such attention, especially for one so newly arrived.'

'Newly returned would be more accurate. I have enjoyed his attention before, when last I lived in Parramatta. A convict with an education, you see. He could not resist.'

It was Bulmer who'd had a geographic restriction placed on Monsarrat's first ticket of leave, preventing him from seeing Sophia in her Parramatta bedroom. It was a restriction he had ignored, at her urging, and Bulmer had taken great delight in reporting Monsarrat to the magistrates when he was caught on the road from Sophia's bed. Sophia must then be more than she currently seemed, he thought. It would be an unbearable cruelty if he sacrificed his freedom for one whom he did not have a hope of loving.

'I may be able to provide you with more relief next Sunday,' Lethbridge said. 'I will be staying in Parramatta for two weeks,

71

and I have no doubt that in that time I'll manage to do something to offend the man's sensibilities. I'll consider myself a failure if I don't, actually. Especially as there are so many who are eager to escape condemnation from the pulpit by placing someone else in front of the man.'

'I see. And who do you believe placed you in front of him?'

'Well – when I triangulate my location on Saturday, and recall the man within the Female Factory that morning, I come to a particular conclusion.'

Monsarrat looked confused.

'I understand it has been some time since you have lived here, Mr Monsarrat. So you may not have had the pleasure of hearing the reverend on the subject of immorality at the Female Factory – he's on the management committee too, so I'm not entirely sure he should be drawing attention to his own failures, but still. Half the windows on the second floor are broken, which forces the women to huddle in one corner of their rooms, which, to hear the reverend tell it, urges them to acts of depravity that defy description. And of course there is Church's well-known liking for female convicts, and his wife's well-known liking for rum. All of which, to Bulmer, could have been prevented by the oversight of more effective management.'

'Well, it seems Socrates McAllister is managing the place at present. I thought Bulmer and he were on friendly terms. They are on the bench together, are they not?'

'They're friendly for as long as it benefits both of them. But what if the new governor decides to look at the Factory records and finds certain irregularities during the late superintendent's tenure? What if he decides to call the management committee to account? Well, then the reverend can point to his continued warnings from the pulpit, say his push for reformation in the committee room was ignored.'

'Why does he not simply leave the committee?' said Monsarrat. 'Why risk soiling his cassock with the muck of the women?'

'He's an evangelist,' said Lethbridge. 'He feels divinely

directed to bring the word of his vengeful God to the wretches. Do not make the mistake of thinking Horace Bulmer is motivated entirely by the pursuit of earthly power. He is a zealot, and that makes him dangerous.'

'Well, whatever drives the man, hopefully he and McAllister will make a better selection this time around. The committee does not seem to be mourning Church.'

'Possibly not. And nor are the innkeepers who have been receiving watered rum of late, so they tell me: I stop at a lot of places between here and Blackheath, and people seem to trust me – I'm familiar, but not around all the time to cause embarrassment.'

'I see. And are any of your confidants significantly more aggrieved than the rest?'

'Not as far as I can tell. But some are closer than others. Michael Crotty, now – he owns a shebeen nearby, and he's losing customers over the rum. He's not philosophical about it in the least.'

Sophia, having finished a discussion with the wife of a less prosperous farmer in the district, was employing one of her more disconcerting strategies, standing at some distance and staring, silent but eloquent on the fact that she felt it was time to leave.

'Mr Lethbridge, I should be glad of the opportunity to sample one of your pies before you leave. Are you selling them this coming week?'

'Indeed. On Thursday I plan to be at the crossroads. A wonderful place for the curious, Monsarrat – all kinds of people and information wash up there. And people do seem to enjoy discussing scandals there while they eat. The superintendent's departure from the world is being feverishly dissected at the moment. Whatever crimes the man committed in life, there's no denying that in death he's been awfully good for business.'

'I hope to see you on Thursday, then.'

'And I you, Mr Monsarrat. In the meantime, mind yourself. The ruts in the road are the least of the dangers for those who don't watch their footing here.'

Chapter 9

Monsarrat seemed to be getting into the habit of defending Grace O'Leary.

'I honestly don't believe it was her. Quite apart from the fact that her door is guarded – inexpertly, it has to be said – I simply don't believe she has it in her.'

'Making quite a number of assumptions there, Mr Monsarrat,' said Mrs Mulrooney. 'For a logical man, you are being quite illogical. How on earth would you know what she has or hasn't in her?'

Monsarrat sighed. It was fast becoming his favourite time of the week, Sunday evening supper at the kitchen table, enabling Mrs Mulrooney and him to drop any external pretence of a master–servant relationship and converse as the friends they were. But sometimes he wished she was just a little less intelligent, a little less perceptive. Might make things more restful, but it would also make them less interesting.

'I don't know, I really don't,' he said. 'It's instinct – and before you say it, yes, I know that mine has been proved wrong in the past – but she seems to believe she has a role, still, in protecting the others. And how can she do that from the end of a rope?'

For all Monsarrat and Mrs Mulrooney had been through together in the past two years, they still addressed each other formally, for the most part. In Port Macquarie their conversations took place in the Government House kitchen, with intrusion likely at any time. It was true that overfamiliarity would not have any damaging constructions placed on it – given the age difference, very few people would be believed should they start to spread rumours of a non-existent romantic liaison. Nevertheless, any deviation from accepted practice would likely have brought them unwanted attention.

Here, though, at a table which belonged to Monsarrat rather than the government – and which received regular scrubbings from Mrs Mulrooney in penance for its very existence – there was no one to clatter through the door, heedless of anything they might be interrupting, and lock themselves down in one of the chairs demanding tea. The young man who had once done that was gone now, and not mentioned between them for all that an empty chair was still always kept at the table.

Given the change, Monsarrat had invited his housekeeper to address him by his given name.

'I don't choose to be employed by a Hugh,' she had said. 'A Hugh might be anyone and might do anything, you know. Whereas, Mr Monsarrat . . . I trust a name like that.'

'I suppose I had better continue to address you as Mrs Mulrooney, then,' he said.

'You will do as you please, of course,' she had answered, with a stern look which left him in no doubt that any liberties would be taken at his peril.

'Well, Mr Monsarrat,' said Mrs Mulrooney now. 'I prefer not to believe it of her either – you say she is an Irishwoman, so I may be a little swayed in that regard, but nevertheless . . . I learned a good deal of the character of that Church.'

'And how did you manage that, while assisting the woman from the Ladies' Committee?'

'The woman's name is Mrs Nelson, I'll thank you to remember,' Mrs Mulrooney said sharply. 'A good woman, too. Practical, unlike some of my acquaintances. And I didn't do much to assist. She bade me sit with Mrs Church while she went on an errand.'

'Yes, so you said. Unconscious, I understand. Yet she still managed to tell you something of her husband?'

'Indeed, and the only reason I haven't raised it until now is because you've been rather taken up with a certain individual today.'

Monsarrat smiled weakly. The tension between his friend and his lover was beginning to pierce even his male consciousness. He could not guess what the cause of it was, but was sure they would come to some form of accommodation with each other. He did find it mildly amusing that these two women seemed to be competing for different parts of him – Sophia for his heart, Mrs Mulrooney for his head. That amusement was clouded by the fact that any serious breach between them would make life very difficult. He hoped it wouldn't come to that, but was aware of a certain core of stubbornness in which the two of them were more alike than different.

'So,' he said, 'what did the unconscious woman manage to tell you?'

'Well, very nearly nothing. I had to work my way up to it, you see, to get close – stank so much, she did. Sweat and rum – it's a combination I particularly dislike, and one which rarely manifests itself in a woman. But this one . . . You could almost see the haze around her.'

'But get close you did, eventually? The noxious substances which you had to clean up when dear Mrs Shelborne was ill . . . The sweat and fumes from a drunk woman must be nothing in comparison.'

Mrs Mulrooney sat down opposite him, now, bracing her elbows on the table and resting her forehead on the palm of one hand. 'Don't speak of her. Not yet. The affection I had for that woman – I would have cleaned a thousand times worse. I would have waded through a river of it.'

'Of course, my friend. I am sorry.'

Mrs Mulrooney lifted her head, stood and placed her hands on the table, leaning on them for a moment to regain strength. Then she pulled her shoulders back and set about sharpening a knife, which had already undergone similar treatment the day before.

'I felt no affection for Mrs Church, of course,' she said as she moved the blade across the whetstone. 'I know women might be driven to all sorts of actions to maintain their survival in a place such as this, but I find it hard to understand anyone putting up with a husband like that, if he is guilty of even half the crimes that are laid at his door.'

'Yes . . . Well, not everyone is as strong as you. I'm certainly not.'

She turned from her work then, quickly pivoting at the hip and flicking out her cleaning towel, catching him as always with remarkable precision on the temple.

'Of course you're not, Mr Monsarrat. That's why you need me – it's why you pay me the pittance that you do to keep me around.'

Monsarrat, who was paying Mrs Mulrooney more than he could afford, smiled and nodded. 'Indeed, I am fortunate that you consent to such mean treatment rather than taking yourself elsewhere.'

She had returned to her sharpening, but spared one eye to glare sideways at him.

'Now,' he said, 'you were telling me what you learned from Mrs Church.'

'Yes, I was, before you interrupted me with your prattle. I eventually accustomed myself to the smell of her. And I noticed that a mass of her tangled hair was stuck to her cheek. I suppose she'd been sleeping on it and had rolled over because when I smoothed it back from the face – using a cloth, mind you,

I wouldn't touch it with my bare hands – I noticed small marks in her skin. And then I noticed scars on her cheeks. A misshapen nose, which looked as though it had been broken. And her hands – the knuckles were raw, the nails were broken, and all up her arms there were scars, short straight ones, as though somebody had been cutting her with a knife. Regularly.'

'And you believe each of these injuries was inflicted by her husband.'

'Now, I don't go making assumptions with the regularity that you do. But that's a fairly safe one, I would say.'

'So would I. Especially given what I learned of him from Grace O'Leary.'

'But there's something else, Mr Monsarrat. Something which makes me believe she may not have acquiesced, at least in the end.'

'And that is?'

'Underneath the couch she was lying on – I noticed it as I knelt down to examine her hands – there were scratches, deep gouges in the wood.'

'And why would that be significant?'

'Because the instrument which I believe made those scratches was lying there as well. Long, and pointed like the weapon the doctor believes dispatched Church. It was an awl.'

Hannah hoped she wouldn't start the week in the position of nursemaid to an unconscious drunk. Now Monsarrat had convinced Eveleigh to let him go to the Factory again, she was accompanying him to be of what assistance she could to Mrs Nelson. They took a track downhill and then a wider trail, which had been churned by wagons after rain and had set into hard corrugations and ridges of clay.

'It's quite a fortunate turn of events, actually, that you've been asked to help her,' Monsarrat said. 'Your keen eye may yet light upon something which has further bearing on the investigation.

Certainly I can't think of anyone else who would have noticed the awl under the bed.'

Hannah was delighted by the praise, while also accepting it as simple truth. And when she sought out Rebecca Nelson in the superintendent's quarters, she was further delighted by her reception.

'How marvellous! To have you here on a Monday is an unexpected blessing. Today, you see, is when I tend to visit those unfortunates who are somewhat unsound of mind.'

Mrs Nelson grabbed Hannah's arm, dragging her by the arm across the outer yard and into the Factory. Weaving in and out through dining halls and workshops, past looms attended by women dressed in odd patchworks of clothes. A few looked up and smiled at Rebecca as she went past. One even said good morning.

'Good morning, Ann! Looking forward to tomorrow?' Mrs Nelson didn't wait for an answer, especially as the question implied Ann had some choice in tomorrow's activities, whatever they were.

'I'm teaching Ann to read, you see. A few of the other First Class women too. I'd love to expand into the whole Factory, but I'm not allowed to, and in any case there's only one of me. Well, two of me now,' she said, smiling at Hannah.

'Ah. A difficult process, with which I have first-hand experience.'

'You have taught someone to read?'

'Not a bit of it. I have been taught – am being taught. Only for the past six weeks.'

'And how do you fare?' Mrs Nelson stopped her headlong progress through the halls, drawing Hannah aside, looking at her intently.

'Tolerably, so I'm led to believe. I am now writing letters to my son. I can't speak for the grammar or the spelling, but I'm told I'm doing well.'

'I don't doubt it. I knew you were intelligent the moment I met you. It's in the eyes, you see. Now, tell me – I've had no one to ask this question of, no one who has the wits to answer it, anyway. What is the most difficult part of it?'

'Surely you remember learning to read yourself?'

'No. My father was a schoolteacher, my mother a governess: I was schooled in my letters very young. I certainly remember hating it though. Some of it must've sunk in, however, for I can read as well as anyone, and there are those who say my hand is among the finest in the colony.'

'I know someone who'd like to challenge you for that honour. As to the hardest . . . I would have to say that the letters won't behave themselves. They keep insisting on doing different things in different words. There is no logic to it, no organisation. If I ran a kitchen the way the English language runs itself, it would be in ruins.'

Rebecca chuckled. 'I'm sure you're right, my dear Mrs Mulrooney. So if you were to teach someone else to read, how would you go about it?'

'Get the exceptions out of the way before teaching the rules. Otherwise you have people driving themselves demented to learn the logic of it, only for them to find there is no logic. I'm not surprised many throw their hands up and walk away from it. Especially when they don't need it to make money – they can get that selling dresses, or sailcloth, or . . . other things.'

'Sound advice. Something to think on, at any rate. Do you object to discussing this further with me in due course?'

'No reason why not, I suppose.'

'Excellent. This morning, though, I fear we are spending our time with those beyond reading, beyond understanding of most things. Halfwits, some call them. But then they're not lacking a certain intelligence. They're just not very keen on engaging the world, you see. It would hurt them were they to come into any contact with it. So here they stay. They have long served their sentences but have nowhere else to go. I hope you have the stomach for this?'

'I've the stomach for whatever is required of me,' said Hannah, drawing herself up to her full five feet in height.

'Forgive me, I can see I have offended you. I didn't mean to imply that you are squeamish, or weak. I simply wish you to be prepared. They're not violent – not generally. But they are ... disconcerting, I suppose you could say. At any rate, there's only two of them. One each, eh?'

'And what will we be doing with them?'

'Just sitting with them, really. Soothing them, giving them greater peace of mind. I like to think that somewhere, under the madness, as long as I am there they realise they have not been fully abandoned.'

They were outside a wooden door. It didn't look particularly strong – none of the doors here did. Mrs Nelson drew a ring of keys out of her pocket. 'Remind me to return this to its place in the superintendent's lodging, would you, please?' she said as she selected one and inserted it into the hole.

The room was small, sparse, but remarkably clean – Hannah had heard stories of Bedlam and other asylums, places where the insane drifted to the floor like dust. And most of those lurid tales included at least some mention of an overwhelming smell, the stench of humans who were beyond caring whether they offended anyone else's nostrils.

This really didn't smell, though, at least no worse than anywhere else in the Factory, in the colony for that matter. And the floor was clean, as clean as could be expected. There weren't too many surfaces for dust to gather on anyway. The room contained two beds, and one woman.

'Good morning, Lizzie!' Rebecca Nelson said, with the same delighted tone she'd used to greet Hannah. 'Where on earth is Pamela?'

'She's pretending to be asleep,' said Lizzie. 'She's been pretending since last week – they came with our breakfast, I tried to wake her. She just stared at me. I gave her a slap, then, told her not to be so rude. You always tell us how important manners are. She kept it up, though. Kept staring, kept refusing to eat, even when I put some of her breakfast in her mouth. Then they came and took her away. Maybe they're punishing her for being naughty, for pretending too much.'

'I see. No one told me . . . Well, I keep forgetting I'm not part of the staff here. So you're by yourself now, Lizzie.'

'Yes, until they bring Pamela back.'

'Lizzie, dear, I don't believe they will be bringing Pamela back. Have you been lonely?'

'Hard to tell, isn't it?'

'I suppose so, Lizzie.'

For all of the childishness, Lizzie was perhaps the same age as Hannah, or a touch younger.

'And they've be treating you well?'

'They aren't treating me at all, missus. No treats. Not like the fair at Tyburn.'

Hannah had only been to England once – when she was held on a prison hulk pending transportation to the colony. But she'd heard of Tyburn – a notorious place, where hangings attracted huge crowds, and the crowds in turn attracted merchants who sold all sorts of treats. That was a world away, and years ago.

'Well, Lizzie, I have a treat for you,' said Rebecca. 'I brought a friend for you to meet. This is Mrs Mulrooney. She's housekeeper to one of the governor's clerks.'

From the arch of Rebecca Nelson's eyebrow, Hannah assumed that what she did next surprised the woman – she went and sat on the bed next to Lizzie and said, 'Good morning, Lizzie. I'm very pleased to meet you.'

Lizzie gaped at her, seemingly astonished. Then she opened her mouth wider and began to wail.

'You're like them,' she screeched. 'The ones who took him, and they've come for me now, haven't they? All this time I was wondering, I thought I'd escaped, but I haven't, have I? They've sent you to get me!'

With that, she hauled back one shoulder and slapped Hannah across the face with all of her admittedly diminished might.

Rebecca Nelson darted to the bed, dragged Hannah away by the shoulders.

'Lizzie, there is no call for that! I've brought you a friend, and you're not being very friendly, are you?'

'Why, Eddie, why did you do it? I trusted you, Eddie. Why did you?'

The name – the odd, unclaimed name – brought on a frightening change to Rebecca Nelson. Her even features, which seemed to have been designed to convey polite neutrality, twisted and contracted until her face was all flashing eyes and snarl. Then she, too, drew back her hand and struck Lizzie.

'You will address me as Mrs Nelson,' she shouted.

Lizzie lay back on the bed, holding her cheek where Mrs Nelson's hand had connected, breathing out small whimpers.

Mrs Nelson inhaled deeply, smoothed her skirts. Her features dissolved back into neutrality before her mouth arranged itself into a sympathetic smile. She knelt beside the bed and began stroking Lizzie's hair.

'You're distressed, Lizzie. No one is taking you anywhere, you're just confused. We'll leave you now. Leave you to calm down. And perhaps the next time I bring my friend you'll have a few more manners about you, will you? Rest now. I'll send someone in with some water shortly.'

She shuffled Hannah towards the door and closed it, taking care to lock it securely.

'My dear, I am so sorry! Are you all right? There's something of a bruise there, coming up.'

'I'm perfectly fine, thank you, Mrs Nelson. I am somewhat hardier than I look. Simply surprised.'

Hannah did not mention that her surprise arose mostly from Mrs Nelson's attack on Lizzie. She had seen this kind of thing, mind you, plenty of times. The mercurial nature of the rich when they felt a liberty had been taken. She had not expected to find such changeability in Mrs Nelson. But there you are, she thought, making assumptions like Mr Monsarrat. You hardly know the woman.

'You know you mustn't take the slightest notice of anything she says, no one does, all she comes out with is a demented stream of unconnected sentences,' said Mrs Nelson. 'I know it's hard to ignore them when they're accompanied by a slap, but if you're the extraordinary woman I believe you to be, you may be able to forgive poor Lizzie.'

Hannah had no hesitation in forgiving Lizzie. What was giving her pause was the surprisingly lucid nature of Lizzie's speech, for all that Rebecca thought she was rambling. It was true her words bore no resemblance to her current situation, but they retained a kind of sense.

'Do you know what she was talking about?' she asked. 'Why did I disturb her so?'

'Perhaps it was the Irish accent. She lost family in a rebellion there, I believe. Seems to have made her destitute, you see. Forced her onto the streets, into prostitution.'

Then Mrs Nelson seemed to catch herself. 'Forgive me again. You are such a steady person it slipped my mind that you were transported. I hope ...'

Hannah was astonished to have a gentlewoman apologising for offending her sensibilities, especially one who had just dealt so brutally with a lapse in decorum. In the eyes of many, Hannah knew she was thrice damned – a former felon, Irish and a woman.

'Nothing like that. I stole to feed my baby,' she said. While true, the statement sounded far more hollow even to Hannah's ears than it once had. Its power had been eroded by its use as a justification by every female convict with a baby. But it must have had some resonance with Mrs Nelson, who nodded. 'Everyone does what she must,' she said. 'As did Lizzie. Not condonable, but understandable.'

Hannah had rarely heard anyone freely express such views, and it was particularly odd coming from one who had just struck a woman for familiarity and using the wrong name. But that was the quality for you, a high-handed goodwill which evaporated in the face of a slight. It was the opinion of the majority that a great many people suffered hardship and loss but not all of them turned to crime.

'You seem to have an uncommon understanding of them . . . of us,' said Hannah.

It was intended as a compliment – Hannah liked to think that those she intended to insult could not mistake her intent – but Mrs Nelson's lips parted slightly, then pursed, while she looked at Hannah, confused at first, then lowering her eyebrows, which gave her face a look of pinched offence.

'I am nothing like these women. I share no history with them; I have no basis for any special understanding. It's common among the convict class to confuse charity with something deeper. A simplistic view, of course. Please do not dishonour me by conflating my kindness with some sort of bond.'

'Of course. I'm sorry, I meant no offence,' Hannah said. Although to tell the truth she had taken a small amount of offence that Mrs Nelson would feel somehow diminished by anything more than a superficial association with a convict. Or a former one.

She knew she had succeeded in masking her irritation when Rebecca's face softened, and her mouth relaxed into a smile. The change was rapid, jarring. Hannah had not viewed Rebecca as changeable, but it seemed there was a hazardous unpredictability within her. Hannah would need to be careful.

'I'm so glad you understand,' Rebecca said. 'You've seen what I have to deal with, all the work that needs doing, and I would hate to lose your help.'

'You show great patience,' said Hannah, hoping she sounded sincere. 'Perhaps Lizzie reacted as she did because she has no distraction, no choice but to dwell on what she's lost. Perhaps if she can rage at me – from a safe distance – it will bring her some measure of consolation. I would be willing to visit her again, if you thought it would help.'

'Maybe.' Mrs Nelson sounded unsure. 'For now, though, we will return to the superintendent's lodging. You and I have much to do.'

'We do?'

'Yes, of course. You are going to help me find a way to teach letters more effectively.'

Hannah spent the first half of their transit across the yard wondering if she dared ask the most pressing question the morning's events had thrown up. She did not want to risk offending Rebecca again. But if she decided to ask no questions, she would get no answers, and Rebecca's reaction might prove more telling than any verbal response.

'Mrs Nelson, I wondered – why did Lizzie refer to you as Eddie?'

Rebecca frowned again, but this time seemed more perplexed than angry. 'I've never heard her do that before. Maybe it was her husband's name. I wouldn't set too much store by it, my dear. You never know what she'll come out with.'

'Can it be, though? If it was her husband's name, would she not have said it before now?'

'Perhaps she has,' said Mrs Nelson. 'Perhaps she has screamed it into the night when there's no one to hear. Really, Mrs Mulrooney, I find it best not to follow people like Lizzie down their tangled paths. There's no telling what horrors they lead to.'

Chapter 10

Mrs Mulrooney's tea was by far the finest Monsarrat had ever tasted, and was largely responsible for maintaining his sanity in its current – although sometimes he felt questionable – condition during his confinement at Port Macquarie.

'Very odd, to be honest,' Mrs Mulrooney was saying. Her hands were working independently, using a knife to remove the skin of a potato while she leaned forward in her seat to allow the peel to fall into a small bucket. 'Exceptionally familiar, for one thing. I've never had a gentlewoman speak to me that way, with the exception of dear Mrs Shelborne, and that was only after a period of acquaintance. The woman's met me twice and she's treating me as a friend.'

'Possibly she's a good judge of character, then.'

'Don't you be thinking you can flatter me into failing to notice that you haven't finished your tea, Mr Monsarrat. But while she seems delighted I'm there, she takes huge offence at the implication that we might have something in common. And she hit a woman – a madwoman too. It's off, that's all. It's not right.'

'Despite the oddness, do you think you can continue to put up with her?' said Monsarrat.

'Indeed, for she has my interest. She was the soul of patience until the madwoman called her Eddie, then she cracked her across the face. She claims not to know anything about the name, and possibly she doesn't, but it certainly seemed to disconcert her. I intend to find out why.'

'I am glad to hear you say that.'

Mrs Mulrooney was very good at taking someone's measure, better than just about anyone Monsarrat had met – and he considered he was no slouch in that department himself. Perhaps that was why he was disturbed by her attitude towards Sophia – her reservations made it harder to ignore his own. And perhaps that was why her tea was not sliding down his throat as easily as it usually did.

He had said the other night, slightly ruefully and half-seriously, that he would miss their evening discussions after he and Sophia married.

'Well, I would be very surprised if I miss them, Mr Monsarrat,' she had said.

'Oh. I see. Well, I hope my company hasn't been too much of a burden on you.'

'Don't be an eejit, you ridiculous man. Of course I would miss our talks were they to end. However, I very much doubt that they will.'

'They might have to for a time. I imagine Sophia will want my undivided attention. Of course you will always have a situation here, with us – I could not do without you and you know that very well, but when Sophia and I marry there might need to be some adjustments.'

'And I'm well aware of that myself. What I was getting at is that I think the chances of you marrying her are small. And I consider that to be all to the good.'

Monsarrat was shocked. A small amount of tension was to be expected between them, he supposed – they had both played such crucial roles in different parts of his life that they no doubt felt they had a claim on a piece of his soul. And God save him from strong-tempered women, despite the fact he seemed to surround himself with them. But they also tended to be people of character, and Hannah and Sophia were no different. He'd had full confidence that what he saw as a minor crinkle, their antipathy, would be ironed out with the passage of time. This declaration from Hannah Mulrooney spoke of an acrimony which went beyond that.

'Why do you think that Sophia and I will not marry?'

'Don't misunderstand me, Mr Monsarrat. She'd be a lucky girl, so she would. But I don't believe you're enough for her, you see.'

Monsarrat nearly choked on his tea.

'For the love of God. It wasn't a slight against your manhood, Mr Monsarrat. I'd never do that to you, knowing how delicate your pride is.'

He opened his eyes as wide as he could, aping surprise. 'I thank you for your consideration. It is uncommonly kind of you.'

And that, of course, earned him another swipe with the cleaning cloth.

'What I meant,' the housekeeper said, 'is that madam craves respectability. Marriage to a steady clerk – one who has a colonial offence against his name, as well as his original one – may not bring her to sufficient heights on the social ladder. You seem to be the best she has right now, but I would not doubt for a moment that she is searching for a better prospect, one perhaps with a greater income and less of a criminal taint.'

'I really must ask you to stop speaking like this, Mrs Mulrooney!' he said, sharply enough for her to take a startled step backwards.

He felt immediately guilty at alarming her, annoyance at himself for feeling guilt, and further irritation with her for introducing him to such a noxious stew of emotions. Still, he made sure to speak somewhat more gently. 'I don't know what Sophia has done to offend you, but you are accusing her of the most appalling, calculated marital strategy.'

'Very well. I'll stay silent on the matter,' she said, 'and hope to be proved wrong.'

The problem was, he thought, Hannah Mulrooney was rarely wrong.

~~~~

Second

Rebecca's husband, David Nelson, was known as hard-nosed but honest.

From what Monsarrat knew of Quakers, he assumed Nelson approved of his wife's philanthropic activities at the Female Factory. Possibly had even suggested them. And it could do no harm for Monsarrat to be seen to be supporting these activities.

So he wrote to Mr Nelson, introducing himself and offering the services of his housekeeper for a full month to assist Mrs Nelson in her endeavours. He knew the offer would be accepted with alacrity and didn't wait for a response. The next morning he walked Mrs Mulrooney to the Female Factory and delivered her to Rebecca Nelson.

Back, then, through the Factory gates, past the bell on its filigreed stand, around the same height as Monsarrat himself, which told the women when it was time to wash, to work, to eat, to sleep. Which had failed to tell the superintendent it was time to die.

He asked the guard whether McAllister was here. Thankfully he wasn't. Clearly the leader of the management committee felt he had done enough managing for the present.

Just in case McAllister or some other worthy did present himself, Monsarrat checked the cuffs of his coat, flicking away a leaf which had drifted down and got caught in one of them. As no greater authority was currently present, he would assume the role himself, he had clearly decided, and pretend to be comfortable while doing so.

In this bell-regulated place, the women had not yet heard the peal which would tell them to pick up their hammers. They were gathered, instead, in tight knots around the Third Class yard. When Monsarrat had first seen them, they had seemed simply appendages of the one, rock-breaking organism. Now, at what passed for leisure here, their individual characters asserted themselves.

There were a number of quarrels taking place, the louder ones seasoned with words the women had definitely not picked up from one of Bulmer's Sunday lectures. A few were singing, either to themselves or to the others, sea shanties or folk songs which had flown over the water behind them, trailing in the wake of the ships that brought them here. The woman with the largest audience had a high, sweet voice which would have been admired after dinner at a fine house in the home counties. A few sat on rocks or the ground smoking small clay pipes; others appeared to be sleeping, with one snoring in a manner which made Monsarrat suspect intoxication – liquor was forbidden, of course, but he knew such prohibitions counted for little.

Here and there, the women embraced one another. Monsarrat had overheard scandalous stories related behind hands outside the church about the kind of comfort the women were said to provide each other. But there was nothing lascivious about these embraces. Two girls, probably not yet in their twentieth year, had their arms slung companionably around each other's shoulders, while nearby a woman cradled an even younger girl, stroking her hair while she silently sobbed.

A different overseer was here today, a man with the shoulders of a bull, a snub nose and a bald head reddening in the sun while his grimy neckerchief tried to spare his throat from a similar fate. Monsarrat informed him (taking care not to make it sound like a request) that he would be interviewing prisoner O'Leary.

'Do as you wish,' said the man, without taking his eyes off the women. 'They've sent me over from the convict barracks to keep an eye on these tarts. Hopefully I'll be back there by tomorrow – men are a lot more straightforward.'

One of the women heard him and made a rude gesture in his direction. He pretended not to notice.

Tom Felton, the turnkey, was inside the Third Class penitentiary.

'I hope you have by now been able to procure a suitable table,' Monsarrat said.

'I have not. The bench is still there, though, if the bitch hasn't destroyed it.'

Grace O'Leary was still there, too. Still on the same patch of floor, hemmed in by the marks left by Emily Gray's spikes near the matted, greasy wool of her mattress.

'Ah, it's my Frenchman,' she said as Monsarrat entered. She reclined, propped her head up on one hand and tilted over on her hip like a gentlewoman at a picnic. 'And you've come to try again to get me to confess, I shouldn't wonder.'

'I'll not hide it from you, Miss O'Leary, that there are men who'd be delighted if you would. As to whether I've come to secure your confession – that very much depends on whether you're guilty or not.'

'Well, as I've already assured you, I am not. I fail to see what else you could possibly achieve here.'

'I've been asking myself the same question. I must warn you, I am among the few willing to entertain the possibility that you might be innocent. But that will do you no good at all unless I am able to uncover something less tenuous than an instinct.'

'I shall try to find the time for you, so,' she said, the last word transforming into a wet cough.

'Have they sent a doctor to you?' asked Monsarrat. 'How long have you been coughing?'

'Oh, since I've been up here. No doctors for the likes of me, or for Emily Gray. At least while she lived – in their wisdom they brought one in after she'd died. I will die or survive without help or hindrance from a surgeon.'

She coughed again, but this time seemed to be trying to constrain it, covering her mouth.

'And you might as well call me Grace. It's been years since somebody referred to me as anything other than my first name or a curse, so when you address me by my surname, for a moment I don't know who you're talking about.'

She spoke quickly, trying to get her statement in before the next cough rose. When it did, she kept her mouth closed, so the rumbling violence was trapped in her lungs and throat. I'll ask Homer to examine her, Monsarrat thought.

'Very well then, Grace,' he said. 'I have read some of the letters you sent to the governor. I've also read your transportation records. You claim you're innocent of the crime which sent you here. Now you claim innocence of another. You can see how it looks.'

'I don't care how it looks. I am innocent of both.'

'An interesting position. I believe my own crime had certain . . . mitigating factors. But I would never disavow it. Many people are here for crimes which shouldn't have required commission, but under the strictures of the law they are crimes nonetheless. Is that your situation?'

'No. When I say I am innocent, I am.'

'You didn't take any cloth, then?'

'Oh, I did. But with my mistress's permission. I was maid to the wife of a cloth merchant – employed for my skills with a needle and thread. This lady's husband would give her his finest wares, which I made into gowns for her, and she would sell the designs if other ladies admired them. Any leftover material was mine to keep, she said. Sometimes I had enough for a handkerchief, sometimes enough for a skirt. Her husband noticed one skirt made of a fine cotton, and he asked his wife what I was doing wearing it.'

Monsarrat wanted to believe Grace, with her dangerous kindness. 'She denied giving it to you?' he asked.

Grace stood and moved to her small window, which afforded her the sight of a small patch of the yard she was no longer allowed in.

'Yes. She was meek, you see. Feared her husband would be angry if he knew she'd given me the cloth. So she accused me of theft without a second thought, and my protestations counted for nothing. At the time, I thought I was lucky not to hang.'

Grace's expression at rest was generally a half-smile, half-sneer. Ready to encourage or mock, laugh or scowl, but ready to react. Not the dead look of many convicts he'd seen, their expressions permanently washed away by the brutality of their penal experience. Now, though, this was what settled itself on Grace's face.

'I wouldn't mind hanging, I sometimes think,' she said, turning from the window. 'Whoever dispatched that man did the world a service, and I was thinking, actually, last night, that I would be happy to do them a similar service by taking their place.'

A bubble of half-formed alarm rose in Monsarrat's throat. The colony, he thought, would kill someone like Grace, and people such as Daly would be too stupid to realise they were poorer for it.

'But then where is the justice?' he asked.

'A very good question, Mr Monsarrat. One which I have been asking myself since I arrived here, as I've seen precious little evidence of it. And you, a convict yourself. Why should you put such a high value on justice? You must've seen through it, seen that it's just a word those in power use to justify their actions.'

'It can be, yes. I've certainly seen that happen. But there's a finer, clearer version of it as well. Doesn't always manifest itself, of course. Isn't always given the chance to. But where I can help it do so, I will.'

To do less, he thought, would be to sink into the pool of human refuse until he was indistinguishable from the rest of them. 'And you seem to be making a decent fist of it yourself, or trying to. It is you, is it not, who protects the weaker ones here?'

Grace scowled and turned away.

'I try,' she said after a while. 'You see them arrive with some brightness, a fragment of soul. He could never stand that. Those were the ones he went for, you see. He didn't base his choice on beauty. He based it on spirit. Anyone who had it needed to be brought into line. And they were, for the most part. And I couldn't bear it, Mr Monsarrat. I couldn't bear to see the soul drain out of these girls, one after the other, until they became slack-faced shades. My life is of no use to me, but it might still benefit someone else.'

The malnourished, slack-faced shades here may be beyond your help, Monsarrat thought. But to say it would be a cruelty.

'And was that why you convinced the other women to rise up?' he asked.

'I never said I did, now.'

Monsarrat stood up, walked to the window and stood by Grace. He still wondered why she had glanced at the window the last time he was here while she was claiming to have stayed away from its counterpart in the cell she'd been in at the time of the murder.

She couldn't have seen the murder, though. That much he knew. Even from the room's position at the narrow end of the Third Class penitentiary, the First Class yard where Church had died wasn't visible. The best she'd have had was a view of one of the stores.

'Grace,' he said, 'as I've said before, if we are to have any hope of saving you – whether you wish to be saved or no – you must be honest with me.'

She sighed. 'Very well. The abuse and short rations were one thing,' she said. 'But it was the head shaving – the way it was done.'

'The way yours was done certainly seems more than a little brutal.'

'Ah, well, you see I had the personal attention of the super-intendent himself. But he couldn't have shaved two hundred heads at once, much as he may have liked to.'

'This event – I should have asked last time – when did it occur?'

'It did not, it couldn't be allowed,' Grace said, pounding her fist against the wall as Mrs Mulrooney did on the kitchen table when he became too irritating. 'We didn't let it get that far. That was where the riot happened, in the drying yard where we were mustered to do the terrible thing.'

'I see. And you organised it.'

'Organised – that's an interesting word, now, and not one I'd necessarily use. I suggested. I passed messages, I put forward possible signals, possible ways in which the thing might be done. I even had an objective – once we had escaped, we were going to march up the river to Government House and demand justice. But when we got outside everyone scattered, seemed to run out of will, didn't quite know what to do with themselves.'

'At any rate, they pointed the finger at you, as the one who organised it?'

Grace went back to her matted wool, lay down as though the memory of the betrayal was too much to remain standing. Another cough escaped, propelling itself out of her before she had time to block it with her hand.

'Some of them did, yes. There was chatter, you see, not all that discreet. Grace said this, Grace said that. So I was demoted from First Class to Third, had my head shaved – the hair had only just grown back before Church had another go at it last week – and I've been worried about the First Class women ever since.'

'Worried?'

'The superintendent had a special interest in them. I did what I could to protect them. Not always successfully. Now they have no one.'

Monsarrat wasn't sure about that. It must – *must* – have taken more than one woman to organise the riot. Grace could not have spoken to everyone. There might be others, probably were. Grace could well, he realised, be the leader of a sort of resistance.

But resistance leaders didn't have a habit of admitting it.

'They'll have even less if you hang,' he said.

'Which is the one thing that makes me want to avoid it. Who's to say the next superintendent won't be worse?'

'No one, at the moment. But before you can assess him and mount a campaign against him, we need to clear you.'

'You are making assumptions now, Mr Monsarrat.'

'I am doing no such thing. Simply starting with a premise, which I'm going to test to see if it holds up. Now – you were asleep, you say, when Church was killed?'

Grace was silent.

'Were you really?' asked Monsarrat.

'Continue with your premise, Mr Monsarrat.'

'Very well. No one from this part of the Factory can see the First Class yard. But those on the upper floors of the other buildings can. So who lives there?'

'The First Class women. A few others – the pregnant, the infirm, the mad.'

'So I suppose there is slim hope one of them might have been awake, might have been looking out the window at the exact moment it was done.'

'You are right, next to no hope at all. Unless . . .'

'Unless?'

'Unless Lizzie Ball was awake. Poor thing, it's been a long time since she and her wits knew each other well. And she has a terrible time sleeping, you see. Has nightmares. You can sometimes hear her at night. There are some who like to tell the new arrivals she's a ghost, standing at her window in her nightdress.'

'But she's insane, you say. Wouldn't make a very good witness, then.'

'I didn't think you were interested in identifying suitable witnesses, Mr Monsarrat. I thought you were interested in divining the truth.'

'And so I am. Very well. Let's see if this woman's insomnia is able to illuminate the situation.'

Chapter 11

'I suppose a confession was too much to hope for,' Eveleigh said.

'Seems so. The new governor, by the way, may be interested to hear of some of the punishments being meted out in that place. Church did not appear to operate according to regulations.'

Eveleigh snorted. 'If that's the most incisive deduction you can bring forward, Monsarrat, we may have to review your special status.'

'Sir . . . I know Superintendent Daly is very anxious that the O'Leary woman be tried, convicted and sentenced with all haste.'

'Indeed. He's not one for nuance.'

'Do you share his views? Or would you be interested in . . . perhaps, an alternative theory?'

'Only if it doesn't remain theoretical – what had you in mind?'

'Well, Henrietta Church was found in possession of an awl. And with marks from it, all over her arm.'

'An awl in a place which engaged in leather-working is hardly remarkable, no matter how Mrs Church was using this one. No, Monsarrat, I'm afraid I can't give any serious consideration to her, certainly not in preference to O'Leary.'

'And there are rumours Church was selling misappropriated rum ...'

'They are of somewhat more interest, and significantly more credible. Church has long been suspected of misappropriating some of the Factory's supplies, although the rum supplies aren't significant – for the use of staff only, of course. However, his returns are all present and correct, so no one has put any significant effort into investigating. And if he was selling rum, it wasn't to anywhere with a licence. They wouldn't touch it, or him. Duncan at the Caledonia, he goes and buys his straight from the ship.'

'Indeed. I'm assuming the shebeens that were here when I last resided in Parramatta are still in operation.'

'Very much so. All right, Monsarrat, you have my permission to look into some more of Church's contacts – discreetly. Be careful – he wasn't the only one to deal in sly grog, and if the rumours are true he was by no means the most highly placed individual to do so. Tomorrow you can go back to the Factory to see if you can find any evidence, of anything at all, from anyone. For now, though, to your desk. There are several tickets of leave requiring attention, and they're not going to write themselves.'

The administration would have loved it if all the public houses in the colony were licensed. But many existed on the margins of both the law and the settlement, in the fringes of the bush, in remote gullies where misanthropic ticket-of-leave men lived, and some had nudged their way in as far as North Parramatta. They were places of mad fiddle music and the singing of discontented songs, where gambling outcomes were decided with fists rather than by the numbers on the cards, where the justice administered was not codified in governor's writs or magistrates' decisions. And they could exist anywhere there was a building. It was perfectly legal to put a sign outside your own home advertising your parlour as a place where grog could be had. It was less lawful to fail to pay tariffs on the grog you sold.

Michael Crotty had sold the questionable stuff for some years, finding the rewards more substantial than those associated with labouring. While being unlicensed meant that he attracted a less refined class of person, it also meant no one was looking over his shoulder to examine the drink he served and where he got it. Barrels appeared at his house, but no one recalled seeing him down at the docks negotiating with the masters of newly arrived ships.

When Monsarrat entered Crotty's parlour, he realised he was the only one with a cravat, the only one with a pearl waistcoat, the only one who looked like he'd spent the day indoors. And the place certainly didn't appear the type of establishment an indoor person would frequent. It didn't look like an establishment at all, actually. There was no bar, no shelves of glasses. A few barrels, a few worn seats. Two men dressed in canvas and soiled neckerchiefs sitting cross-legged on the floor playing dice. And Crotty, ferrying drinks in earthenware cups from the other room.

When he saw Monsarrat, he put cups in the hands of two of his customers without taking his eyes off the stranger.

'Invitation only,' he said as he strode up. 'And you don't have one.'

There must be a reasonable amount of money to be made in the semi-legal public house industry, thought Monsarrat, judging by the man's girth – not rotund, but certainly not malnourished. Bald, although by the looks of his skin probably prematurely. This was a man who looked as though he'd spent a significant proportion of his life outside – the dark-brown splotches on his pale cheek testified to that – yet the sun hadn't gouged the deep lines in his face which Monsarrat saw on those who had served their sentence on a road gang.

'I'm sorry,' said Monsarrat. 'I gained a few extra shillings last night, you see. Thought I'd see if I could make them go further here than somewhere like the Caledonia Inn. But I didn't realise it was a private club, so I'll leave you.'

As he turned to the door, Crotty grabbed his arm. The grip was surprisingly strong, almost painful.

'As you're here, I'll get you a drink. You're not to bring anyone else, nor tell anyone. But you may spend your winnings here.'

He gestured Monsarrat to a stool in the corner with slightly uneven legs. For a moment Monsarrat assessed the other patrons, all ticket-of-leave labourers, by the looks of them. The unfriendly stares he received in return convinced him to keep his eyes down.

Crotty came back with a cup, holding out his hand for payment before giving it to Monsarrat. He deposited a few shillings on Crotty's palm but the man showed no sign of moving off. He watched as Monsarrat took a swig. He stood by, bottle in hand, as if he wanted a flattering appraisal of his liquor. Monsarrat detested rum – always had – but was willing to make the sacrifice.

'Odd. It doesn't taste like the Caledonia's stuff,' he said. 'A bit more . . . watery.'

'If you're going to be casting doubt on my grog, you'll have to leave.'

'I'm sorry, I meant no offence. I just wondered, that's all. Perhaps you have a different supplier.'

'My suppliers are no concern of yours. But if there were any problems with the rum – which there are not – recent events would have seen them dealt with. I'll leave it at that, except to say that if you wish to return, you'll pay and drink in silence.'

Monsarrat nodded, downed the rum and ordered another, hoping it was indeed watered – he had no wish to be admonished by Mrs Mulrooney for returning home drunk.

Though he didn't think there was anything more to learn here, he bought a third cup to maintain the fiction of a lucky gambler after cheap grog. As he drank it, unable to stop himself wincing, one of the dice players turned to him. 'You can try your luck with us, if you want to buy more of the muck. It's not so bad. Better than the swill he's been getting in recently.'

'Really? The rum's improved lately?'

'It had to – people weren't coming. If they want muddy water, they can get that in plenty elsewhere. But he said he'd deal with it, and when Crotty says he will deal with something, he tends to do it. There are other attractions, too. Crotty allows . . . well, I will simply say that those with goods they wish to sell without troubling the troopers are welcome here. So . . . are you gaming, or not?'

'I'm sorry but I spent the last of my money on that rum.'

'No matter. Next time, come with a heavier purse. It would be an honour to play with a man of your . . . distinction.' The man laughed, and in his throat it was a mirthless, predatory sound.

Monsarrat stood, nodded (a gesture that made the man laugh again) and walked to the door. Crotty was standing in front of it, his arms folded, but he moved aside as Monsarrat approached, opening the door and giving a mock bow. He followed Monsarrat out, and Monsarrat felt a momentary prickle, a constriction of the lungs, the same tensing of the muscles that had preceded the beatings he'd been given on the road gang.

Crotty made no move though. He stood leaning against the doorframe, watching as Monsarrat unsteadily navigated the ruts and bandicoot holes which lay between him and the safety of his kitchen.

Chapter 12

'He's not at home, I have no knowledge of where he is or when he'll be back.'

Hannah started closing the door, but Sophia did not turn to leave. She stood on the threshold of the cottage, staring at Hannah. A cold, steady gaze. She seemed unaffected by the heavy heat which was making many women wilt in their long, restrictive gowns. The unadorned yard and unrestrained scrub beyond the cool blue of Sophia's dress, her pristine appearance, looked somehow shameful. The effect was almost disconcerting, or would have been had Hannah cared for the opinions of the likes of the Stark woman.

'So I'll be saying goodnight now,' Hannah said.

Sophia put her hand out, palm against the door's rough wooden face. 'I told you, I haven't come for him.'

'Oh. Our last conversation was so engaging, you'd like another?'

'I have recently come by knowledge of a certain matter. It concerns Mr Monsarrat, it concerns me, but mostly it concerns you. Of course, I would be happy to take this knowledge back to the Prancing Stag with me and lay it before Mr Monsarrat tomorrow morning.'

So Hannah found herself inviting Sophia into the kitchen rather than the parlour. She had never thought to admit the creature into the place she thought of as hers, although her name did not appear on the deed of the house. But the kitchen was where she felt strongest, and there was an air of satisfaction about Sophia which made Hannah believe she would need strength.

It was a pity, having to deal with this awkward visitor. And after such a fraught day.

Sophia wasn't the first woman Hannah had sat across from since the sun rose. Although Hannah would hardly have believed it possible, Henrietta Church had eventually regained sufficient control to haul herself upright at the table of the superintendent's residence, and that morning Rebecca Nelson had brought Hannah in to meet Mrs Church, asked if she'd be kind enough to sit with the woman again, perhaps tidy up a little bit.

Henrietta Church's face was almost as slack as it had been the other day. Her muscles did not seem to see any point in arranging her face into an expression of welcome, a scowl, or anything approximating a reaction.

'You're a new woman,' Mrs Church had asserted, her voice rasping from lack of use, after Mrs Nelson had left to check on Lizzie.

'I'm not an inmate. I'm helping Mrs Nelson.'

'What happened to Bossy Bulmer?'

'I don't know, Mrs Church. I just know she's not involved in the Ladies' Committee anymore. I'm assisting Mrs Nelson while my employer looks into the murder of your husband.'

There was cruelty in mentioning the murder so baldly and Hannah chastised herself, making the sign of the cross in hope of forgiveness from both the Almighty and the woman at the table.

'I'm very sorry to hear of your husband's death, Mrs Church. Mrs Nelson has asked me to do anything I can to help you today.'

'Are you any good at making tea?'

'If you have leaves, I'll make the best cup of tea you've ever had.'

The leaves were tolerable. They were in a cheaply made chest which had let in a small amount of moisture, but not enough to fully destroy them.

'Have you anything stronger for it?' Henrietta asked.

'Now, forgive me for being blunt, Mrs Church, but it's my way, you know. I watched over you while you slept the other day. And, to be honest with you, I don't think anything stronger would do you any good. You're going to need a clear head. Difficult days ahead, of course – a new widow – and who's to say whoever killed your husband won't come after you?'

Cruelty again. I must stop this, Hannah thought, before it starts to come easily. But this time there was a purpose. The woman's reaction, particularly to the idea her husband's killer might not have finished his or her work, could be instructive.

'Difficult times ahead, as you say,' Henrietta said, her authoritative tone diminished somewhat by the tremble in her voice. 'All the more reason for some assistance.'

'Not the kind of assistance you have in mind. There could have been a kangaroo bouncing around in here the other day and you'd never have known it. See how you go with the tea, that's my advice. I'll make you some shortbread, if you've the butter, flour and sugar.'

Mrs Church inclined her head to the left. 'Go to the store. Ask them for what you need, tell them it's my request. They won't begrudge a grieving widow.'

So Hannah did as she was asked, the storekeeper raising his eyes when he knew the request was from Mrs Church.

'Butter and sugar and flour, if you like. Don't bother asking me for anything else though – anything that comes in a barrel.'

Henrietta hadn't moved when Hannah got back. Good, she thought. She'd been half-concerned that Henrietta had some rum stashed away and was sending Hannah on the errand as an opportunity to ferret it out.

'I wish I could do more for you at such a difficult time,' Hannah said as she got a mixing bowl and started on the shortbread.

'But tea and shortbread are the extent of my powers, so that will have to do.'

'I need nothing from you in terms of consolation, although tea and shortbread I will take.'

'Gracious of you, missus. Ah, but to think someone with the strength to do the terrible thing that was done to your poor dear husband – to think someone like that is at large, possibly outside the door now. You should not be alone.'

'I am perfectly safe, thank you,' Mrs Church said.

'But how can you be sure?'

'I can be sure.'

Hannah was unable to provoke her into further discussion that morning, on the reason for her certainty or on any other topic. And now the afternoon had put Hannah across the table from another woman who seemed equally confident in her position.

After she and Sophia had sat in silence for a few minutes, Sophia's eyes lighting on one object after another, Hannah rose and said, 'Well this has been quite a lovely visit, but I must be about getting Mr Monsarrat's supper. I do not know when he will be returning, but I imagine he will be hungry when he does.'

She searched for a skillet which could be trusted not to let itself get dented.

'I know what you're doing,' said Sophia.

'I'd be worried about you if you didn't.'

'I don't mean supper. I mean the remarks to him, the asides, the suggestions that I am interested in marrying him only as long as no better prospect is available.'

'What I say, to whom, is of no concern of yours, and nor is it your right to tell me to stop.'

'But stop you will if you wish to keep his friendship and your position. Mr Monsarrat is a man of integrity, yes?'

'Yes.'

'And what would he think of a friend who had been concealing something fundamental about herself – do you not think his regard might be reduced somewhat?'

Hannah left the stove, sat down again. 'Miss Stark, there are a few things that I feel I need to make very clear to you. The first is that I did not set out to be your enemy; however, your rudeness when we met, and your refusal to do anything since to atone for it, has made my enmity inevitable.

'The second is this: Mr Monsarrat and I had to support each other in Port Macquarie, particularly towards the end, when we watched one of our friends hang for the murder of another, of whom we were very fond. Nothing you say will make him change his view about me.'

Sophia smiled. 'Some old secrets lie beneath the earth for a long time, gaining in strength. They grow through concealment, until they become so powerful they simply beg to be revealed.'

Old secrets . . . There was no way Sophia could know.

'You recall I told you of my friendship with the clerk at the colonial secretary's office,' Sophia continued. 'Well, I asked him, recently, if he'd be kind enough to look for any records in which you were mentioned.'

It wasn't possible, Hannah thought, for the malignancy to cross such a vast ocean. It was to stay in Ireland and starve, not slither under the waves to reach her here. It cost her significant effort to keep her face neutral, but her stomach felt full of boiling liquid, and panic buzzed in her ears.

'Did you know, Mrs Mulrooney, that about twenty years ago there was a census of the marital status of convict women? Quite extraordinarily detailed.'

'Well, my understanding is that it was wide of the mark, in many respects,' said Hannah. The statement was delivered in a calm voice, for which she was absurdly grateful.

'That may be true, I suppose,' said Sophia. 'Would you believe, the charming Reverend Bulmer was responsible for compiling it, and where there was no marriage certificate, he put women down as concubines or unmarried.'

'Concubines!' Mrs Mulrooney said. 'Are we in France, now, I ask you.'

Briefly a smile passed between the two women, until their mutual mistrust reasserted itself.

'Nevertheless, a lot of people set a reasonable amount of store by this document,' said Sophia. 'Particularly as the Reverend Bulmer has interesting ways of ensuring people give credence to his views.'

This, of course, was true – Hannah had no trouble believing that the reverend would use the pulpit to condemn anyone who questioned any statement he chose to make.

'And interestingly there is a Hannah Mulrooney listed in this document. Same year of transportation – my friend at the colonial secretary's office cross-checked it against your other records – and a son the same age as yours, who shares a name with your son.'

Of course there was, Hannah thought. There she had been, two decades ago. Another woman in the same body, two years left to serve on her sentence, taking on extra piecework in addition to her housekeeping duties to pay for an education for her son.

'The only real difference between you and that Hannah Mulrooney,' said Sophia, 'is the honorific. You see, that Hannah Mulrooney went by Miss, not Mrs. Because that Hannah Mulrooney had never been married.'

⁓e⤳

The house was dark when Monsarrat came home. He forced down a small spasm of irritation. Not only did he not feel quite himself after his unaccustomed consumption of three cups of rum, watered or otherwise, but he was disappointed – he had been hoping Mrs Mulrooney would be up: he wanted to share his observations before they became hazed by sleep.

He made his way towards his small wooden bed, in a room almost as sparsely furnished as his convict hut at Port Macquarie had been, though he no longer had to sleep on the floor. He was drunk, to be honest, so he nearly missed the light leaking underneath the back door.

He went through into the kitchen and there was Mrs Mulrooney at the kitchen table. Something was not quite right, though. He cast around his mind trying to work out what it was, thickets of rum fumes and tendrils of nausea impeding him, until he realised. She wasn't moving. Not at all. He had rarely seen her completely still, except in moments of great despondency. She had not done so much as turn around when he walked in.

He rounded the table, sat down opposite her.

'By the Blessed Virgin, you smell awful,' she said.

'It will be the rum, no doubt. I'm not used to it. Suspect I'll pay tomorrow, but visiting a shebeen without drinking would have marked me out even more than doing so dressed like a clerk. It is awful stuff, though. I'll need gallons of your tea to wash it out.'

'And I shall make you gallons, before I leave.'

'You're going to the Factory tomorrow again? To Mrs Nelson?'

'No. I don't know where I'm going. I hope I can rely on you for a reference, though.'

'Were you ever to need one, it would be the most glowing possible, and I would use my best hand to do it. But you have a position, Mrs Mulrooney. Here. Why in God's name would you be talking about leaving?'

Mrs Mulrooney inhaled, straightened up, and finally looked directly at him.

'I am offering you my resignation, Mr Monsarrat. And I hope you'll do me the kindness of accepting it.'

Monsarrat braced his hands against the table, pushing his chair back and standing up.

'I most assuredly will not! Nothing on earth would induce me to. You are not a ridiculous person. Stop behaving in this ridiculous fashion.'

'Ah, but I'm not being ridiculous. When you hear the reason, I've no doubt you'll be at the Female Factory tomorrow seeking an assigned convict to make your tea in my place.'

'I will not. Absolutely not.'

'Not even were I to tell you I've been lying to you since we first met?'

'You're the most honest person I know. Painfully so, sometimes. Don't scowl like that, Mrs Mulrooney, you know the truth when you hear it.'

'Yes, I do. And the truth is, Mr Monsarrat, that I have never been married. Mulrooney was the name I was born with.'

Chapter 13

County Wexford, Ireland, 1798

The young Hannah would play with Colm Dempsey sometimes. They would draw pictures in dirt they didn't own, run up hills which belonged to some lord or other, who had one eye on the rents and the other on next week's hunt.

Hannah hit Colm sometimes, when she thought he was being particularly stupid. Making faces, or sprinkling leaves in her hair, which she hated as she considered her hair sovereign to her and was jealous of his red-gold.

Colm's brother Seamus often played with them, and a smattering of other boys and girls from nearby farms – she could not remember most of their names now. But Seamus's name she would never forget, both for what had happened later and for his influence on their play. Seamus was the one to edge forward into a stream at full flood, or to test whether a particular branch would hold their weight. And when it didn't, and they came home with muddy clothes and were chastised (with Hannah already hating the state she had been persuaded into), Seamus's grin tended to draw most of the adult annoyance, even when Colm would say, 'It's not his fault, Da. Not all of it. We went along, didn't we, Hanny?'

She couldn't remember exactly when she had decided to stop playing with the boys, and perhaps the decision was made for her: it was around the time that her clothes, when wet from a Seamus-led dip in the stream, began clinging to her in a way that made the boys look at her strangely.

She still saw Colm, though. Of course she did. Their farms were next to each other, outside the town of Enniscorthy near the Milehouse crossroads, and when their father died, Hannah's da helped them run the place.

'Although all we've inherited is the right to pay His Lordship,' Seamus would say. Colm told him to shut up. He knew, as did the children of many Irish smallholders, that such talk could draw hazardous notice.

She was jealous of the boys, actually. Of the attention they got from her father. She tried to bring it back to herself by working as hard as any man, harder – cutting and felling, planting and harvesting barley like a demon. But it didn't stop her father shaking his head some nights, saying he wondered what would become of the farm when he was gone and there was no one to tend it.

Hannah's mother had produced only girls, and her older sisters were all married now, scattered around Wexford. She was sure her parents had hoped for a boy. She had ended those hopes: her mother died giving birth to her, and with her father taken up with farming there was no one to warn her against running around the countryside with the wild Dempseys. No one warned the Dempseys against her either – one winter their mother was also carried beyond, by the fever.

She never saw Seamus at the Mass stone, the blade of rock which marked the secret place where the illegal priest conducted services. Colm was always there though, devout in his way.

Hannah's father, Padraig, approved of their friendship, and made it no secret. So Colm might have been hoping for a more enthusiastic response when he suggested he and Hannah should marry.

'I don't know, Colm,' said Padraig. 'It depends.'

'Depends on what?'

'It depends on her. I'm not a brave enough man to promise her to you without her permission. What do you think, Hannah? Would you like to marry this long streak of a boy? Might not be the prettiest, I'll grant you, but he will look after you, of that I'm sure.'

Hannah pretended not to be delighted. She had been drawn, secretly, to the young man with the muscled back who wore in mature form the face and red-gold hair of her childhood friend.

'I suppose he'll have to do, Da. Best of a bad lot. But do you think you can get him to promise not to sprinkle leaves in my hair?'

Colm made no effort to hide his joy. 'I'll use flowers this time,' he said. 'And I'll wish they were jewels. For in a world set to rights it'd be jewels you were wearing.'

But it was not a time for weddings. Not when farmhouses were burning and people being shot by the side of the road.

Colm understood the importance of keeping his views to himself; Padraig Mulrooney had views which needed to be kept to himself. He belonged to a group called the United Irishmen, which had drawn inspiration from the French Revolution, and more recently had taken heart from a promise of French troops to back up an Irish rising, should the people stir.

And it looked increasingly as though they would.

Hannah was aware of her father's sympathies but pretended not to be. Still, there were times when they were hard to ignore. Their cottage was one room, and while pretending to be asleep she sometimes heard whispers outside or inexpertly imitated birdcalls, which would make her father abandon the steaming tea that was his chief solace, indeed seemed to the young Hannah the only reliable source of comfort the poor farmer could depend on.

The governor, sitting in Dublin Castle, hit on a strategy to disarm a population he was becoming increasingly afraid of. It was decreed that all men should go to their nearest town to hand in any weapons they possessed. Most complied, hoping to avoid a flame being set to their roofs, and some who didn't have pikes were so eager to show their cooperation they acquired weapons to hand in.

Padraig had walked with his pike into Enniscorthy earlier in the week. He hated having to do it, and planned to acquire another as soon as possible. He might have been more reckless still, but when they burned farmhouses they did so at night, and he did not wish to see his daughter running into the darkness as flames ate her home.

'I know where they're holding the weapons,' said Seamus. And for a moment he put her in mind of the boy saying he knew where there was a good hill to climb.

'We'll be raiding it, so we will. Soon. The captain hasn't set the date, but plans are being made. And once we get all the pikes back, and any muskets we find, we'll need somewhere to hide them.'

'What about your own home?'

'Ah, first place they'd look. Two young men, and one of them known to be something of a croppy.'

So it was true. Hannah had wondered, when she'd first noticed that Seamus's hair was no longer curling down the back of his neck. Many United Irishmen liked to keep their hair closely cropped, a habit borrowed from French revolutionaries who'd wished to distance themselves from wig-wearing aristocrats.

'I'd not know where to put them, Seamus. Our house is no larger than yours, and our farm only half as big.'

'I'll help you dig a hole, so. We can cover it with boards and put dirt and leaves over the top.'

'And what does Colm say?'

'Colm has his mind on his wedding, on keeping the farm going. He keeps his head down, that one. Something I've never been very good at.'

In the end her father agreed.

She did not know when the raid was to be, when to expect men in the night bearing bundles of sharp metal wrapped in cloth. She suspected her father didn't know either, nor Seamus. They were told to await a signal. Simultaneous raids were planned for strongholds all around the district.

But they were raids in which Seamus would never participate. At around the time he and Padraig were whispering, a detachment of militia was making its way towards the village of Milehouse. In the dwindling light, they saw what looked like an impediment ahead on the road. The impediment, as they got closer, resolved itself into ten or so croppies, all holding pikes. As the detachment turned, they found a further twenty had filled in the patch of road they had just vacated.

When the croppies were done, they robbed the bodies. They didn't particularly mind about the one soldier that got away to raise the alarm.

This enraged the militia, men who, because of pressure from their landlords or out of a conviction that Britain must own Ireland, served as semi-regular infantry under the orders of British officers. They rode all over the county, indiscriminately burning houses and shooting on sight anyone they suspected of being a rebel sympathiser. They weren't very careful in their assessment of a man's leanings before they took his life; it was convenient for them that so many rebels had distinctively close-cropped hair.

Hannah and Colm would never know whether Seamus had heard the yeoman riding up behind him. He was found by other tenants. They put his body in their cart and drove it up to the larger of the two farms that sat beside the small stream. Seamus spent that night where he had spent most of the others of his life, in the cottage where he was born, staring up at the thatch. And the following day he was buried without a gravestone on the farm's furthest boundary.

'Should you not erect some sort of marker?' Hannah asked. 'How will you know where he is?'

'I'll know,' said Colm. 'I'll always know.'

Colm spent that night in a farmhouse which was unused to having only one occupant. When Hannah saw him the next day, the first thing she noticed was how closely his hair had been cropped.

She tried to reason with him, but he would not be persuaded.

'What good will it do, Colm, to die like your brother? Your sense was telling you to keep your head down, and your sense was right. Seamus's death hasn't changed that.'

'It has changed everything,' he said. 'I would rather die than live in a world where they can kill my brother for the way he cuts his hair.'

'But I don't want you to die!'

'Hannah, I'm not that happy with the idea myself. But my hope is there will be a rising to remove the parasites who have burrowed into our earth.'

'This is not how you used to speak, Colm. You used to say a full-scale rising wasn't the way, that we would be outnumbered and ultimately slaughtered. You were right then; you are now.'

'I was a fool. Thinking the British would leave if we asked them nicely. We will ask them in a way they cannot help but understand.'

So it was Colm who helped Padraig dig a hole behind the house, cover it with planks, and Hannah fancied she felt some sort of tug from it, some sort of nascent intent every time she walked past it, as it waited to swallow the weapons to be captured during the raids.

But those raids, they had to be coordinated, Colm explained. No point hitting one house, however successfully, if the others would then shore up their defences, making themselves less vulnerable. Everything had to happen on the same night.

The United Irishmen, of course, couldn't meet openly. Their business was conducted in cottages and copses. Each area had a leader who must find a way to make sure their scattered forces acted together when the time was right. Hannah didn't know who the Enniscorthy leader was. Few people did, unless they were actively involved in the movement. Whoever he was, he could hardly ride from house to house himself. He needed messengers. Ones who wouldn't attract attention.

And while women were certainly not above suspicion as far as the yeomanry were concerned, they had a better chance of escaping attention.

Hannah made journeys to and from the town, past the farms and houses of the countryside from time to time. Occasional trips to the Enniscorthy market. She was alarmed each time at the ever-increasing presence of the militia on the streets, the suspicion with which everyone looked at everyone else, the lack of the conversation which had been almost a part of the currency of the place. She was even more alarmed one day to hear her father's raised voice in the cottage when she returned.

'I won't permit it, Colm,' he was saying as she entered. 'The hole out the back, that's one thing. But this is something you shouldn't be asking.'

She had entered silently, so neither her father nor her fiancé noticed her at first.

'I know that,' said Colm. 'But Massey needs messengers. And without them, nothing else can proceed.'

'I'm to be a messenger girl, am I?' she said.

They turned to her, two sets of agitated eyes rolling over her face.

'No, you're not,' said Padraig. 'We're doing enough.'

'Are we, though?' said Colm. 'Padraig, do you think that if you just stay quiet, this will pass you over? Things have gone too far for that. If the United Irishmen disbanded tomorrow, it would not stop the British killing us and burning our farms. Rising is the only way out now.'

'But Hannah can't be part of it.'

Hannah was certainly not sure that she wanted to be. She cursed the necessity for this rising. But it was a necessity that she could see. So she sat down next to her father, put her head on his sloping shoulder.

'Da, you let me decide about marrying Colm. Will you let me decide on this as well?'

She wondered, not for the first time, whether the British were a stupid race. Might and money seemed to be all they understood, but surely they could see that destroying those from whom they made the latter would ultimately rob them of their means to find the former.

The standard methods of extracting information from captured rebels, flayings and beatings, were being joined by other, more imaginative inducements. One magistrate travelled the region accompanied by an executioner who bore a noose and a cat o' nine tails with him. A short frame was invented for the purposes of half-hanging – suspending a man by the neck, keeping him alive until he gave away the information that was wanted.

And, in what seemed to Hannah to be a horrific imitation of the croppy hairstyle, there was pitch capping. Men were forced to kneel as hot tar was poured over their heads. Sometimes it dried and was then torn off, with whatever parts of scalp came with it. Sometimes it was mixed with gunpowder and set alight, and put out only when the British had the information they were looking for.

The only way to stop the bloodshed, it seemed to Hannah, was to stop the English.

'I will do it,' she said to her father, and felt his shoulder slump a little more.

Massey, whoever he was, came and gave her the oath of secrecy. 'Do you walk a lot around this area?' he asked her.

'As much as I need to. Which is a fair amount.'

He reached into his pocket, pulled out a blue ribbon. 'I don't want you to wear this ribbon until you receive a message to do so,' he said. 'But when you're asked to, put it on and walk – slowly – past the houses you would normally pass. That's all. *Erin go bragh.*'

The United Irishmen's rallying cry. 'Ireland forever.'

'*Erin go bragh,*' she repeated, as though it was a response in a Mass.

She kept the ribbon on her, and a few days later a message was brought to Colm of a rebel victory in Oulart.

'Do you know how many we lost?' he asked her. 'Six! Brave men, of course, and their loss is tragic. But only six dead. Miraculous. The yeomen drank an inn dry and burned it, and charged up the hill and we consumed them. They've abandoned Gorey now too, cramming themselves into Arklow instead.'

The British would now be wanting a demonstration battle to show their strength, reassert their dominance over the island. And if they wanted a battle, Colm was among thousands, emboldened by good luck, who were more than willing to oblige. To do that, they needed weapons.

A few days later, Colm came by the house early in the morning to see Hannah. Their embraces had become more heated of late. The danger, the threats they breathed in with the air, made them believe they were counting a finite number of kisses. And they were as good as married anyway. So Colm was fond of saying, and she did not know then that all men said that sort of thing.

That morning, though, there was no embrace, no attempt to kiss her which she would playfully try to rebuff before yielding.

'Wear the blue ribbon today,' he said, and turned, walking away from his farm and hers.

As the night fell and she imagined she heard the occasional distant shout carried on the breeze, she wondered whether her blue ribbon had killed Colm. But he came after midnight. 'Get dressed, you'll not believe it,' he said. She got up and made her bed neatly to show her father she hadn't been dragged from it unwillingly.

She and Colm walked into the valley and up the opposite hill to the residence of the magistrate, who trotted about the countryside with his personal executioner. His house was empty of people – they had fled when they saw the rebels advancing – and of weapons. Hannah's blue ribbon had been the signal for a raid on every loyalist home where weapons were believed to have been stored. She wondered whether some of them, even now, were on their way to the hole behind her house.

'I want you to realise,' said Colm, 'that you're entering this house as a free woman who bows to no one, not as a servant. Tomorrow you will not be able to do the same. The only hope you have of standing equal with the owners of this house is through revolution.'

It was odd, on this night of smoke and noise, to be walking through the dark and silent house, looking into rooms which were larger than the cottage where she and her father lived.

At the top of the stairs, the family's bedrooms. The magistrate's chamber, finely decorated with rich dark fabrics and a high bed with curtains. The bed clothes were disturbed.

'You know, the man who was sleeping here a few hours ago would happily see me half-hung by the side of the road, then killed when I'd given up whatever he was after.'

'I know.'

'And you know he'd do the same to you, given half a chance. And of course your father.'

'Yes, I know.'

'But we've chased him out, you and I and the others. And we'll do the same again, all over the country. It's my hope, my Hannah, that this won't be the last time you lie down on a bed like this.'

After all, thought Hannah, we're practically married, and in calmer times it would have been done already. So what harm was there? And leaving her virginal blood happily on the sheets of such a disgraceful man seemed to her, somehow, fitting.

Chapter 14

Hannah didn't tell Monsarrat of the magistrate's bedroom. Of the kisses, or of Colm's red-gold hair.

'Colm died on the same day as my father. Before we got the chance to marry,' she said. 'Padraig is his son.'

It had been a long time, in such a far-off place, but whenever she gingerly prodded those memories, they rose up and snapped at her. Colm was no longer on this earth, and he had died unmarried. That was all Monsarrat would be told.

She would not, ever, speak of Vinegar Hill, the battle where Colm was taken, or of returning to the house to find her father piked through on the doorstep. Of watching Colm's execution weeks later, and not recognising at first the man they'd shot in the back of the head, his scalp ruined from pitch-capping.

And she would certainly not be telling Monsarrat of giving birth in the cell where she was taken after she had sold stolen butter to the wrong person.

Monsarrat was silent for a long moment after he had heard the story. Too long, probably. Hannah had risen from the table, started towards her sleeping room to pack.

'My God, but you must hate us,' he said.

'Us?'

'The English. You are a remarkable soul, Hannah, to still be speaking to me after what was taken from you.'

'Why shouldn't I speak to you? Did you do the taking? No, you're a victim of the same people. The ones who look at us and see a disease to be cured, rot to be cut out.'

'Still – I don't think I could have done it. The hatred would have destroyed me. How has it not done so to you?'

'For a time, I wanted it to. But why would I let them take my soul, when they had taken everything else? And I had Padraig to consider as well. That whole voyage – we buried a few babes at sea, you know, and when they slid the little bundles into the ocean I always imagined it was Padraig. Everything, everything I did or said was to help him survive. When we got here – well, I thought, this is his chance. His chance to live without the old hatreds glowering over his shoulder, forcing him to take up a pike. And my chance, too. The hole I left in Enniscorthy after I was transported would have closed over quickly, no one left to miss or mourn me. So if I was to vanish, why not reappear in a guise which would help me navigate this place, that of a married woman rather than a fallen one?'

'You are not fallen, Hannah. Far less so than me, at any rate. Please, reconsider your resignation. I'm sure you would get on perfectly well in another household, but this one would fall apart without you.'

She stared at him for a moment, but said nothing and went to her room. Monsarrat did not know whether his words had had any effect. But when the next morning brought tea, and there were no signs of possessions being bundled together, he began to hope. And when she scolded him for spilling his tea on the kitchen table – 'I'll be scrubbing that for the next week, eejit of a man' – he knew he had succeeded.

As relieved as he was that he had managed to talk her out of leaving, Monsarrat couldn't help feeling a little bit offended. He made a scowling progress along the riverbank, having decided the water might restore his equilibrium, as he paced his way towards Government House, past small, low houses with mean windows, modelled on English houses that were designed to keep out the cold of English winters, and unequal to the task of catching a river breeze in a strange summer. They stood on land which had been pristine, untouched by anything other than a native's hand or the pad of a kangaroo, just a few decades past.

Monsarrat had forgotten about the smell of the bats, dripping now in their thousands from the branches of the river trees, wrapped in their own wings like fat black flowers, insensible to the pique of the man who, for once, was making no attempt to avoid the muddier parts of the bank as he chewed at his irritation. The bats' stench climbed down through the air to meet the smell of rotting river plants, set free by the low tide. The stink was not helping the state of either his mind or his stomach, which had not yet finished complaining about last night's rum. And when he tripped in a hole dug by a bandicoot – odd little animals, grey dollops of fur with the nose of a rat, but three times the size – he decided to try out the word he had heard one of the convict women use on the overseer.

Why would she think such a history, in this place of unfortunate histories, would matter to him? And why hadn't she confided in him earlier? He had saved her, after all, from the gallows, even though at the expense of someone she loved. And while it felt awkward, sometimes, to have stepped into the role of her employer, he had thought that they were both becoming accustomed to the arrangement, and that their friendship had survived the transition.

Still, this was a place where pasts became smudged. Usually either over-dramatised or underplayed in the retelling. And who was to call out the teller of the tales, when the stories – factual or not – were generated by events which had happened in a place of different seasons, different livestock, different lives.

He would get over his offence, he knew. Especially as he had secured continuing access to her company, her intellect, and her tea.

Getting over Sophia's role in the revelation – that was far less certain.

Sophia knew, of course, that he was anxious to sand down the jagged edges of his *own* past, eager for a reputation which would insulate him from pulpit salvos. She must've presumed that he would distance himself from the Irishwoman should anything stain her reputation. In this, she was catastrophically wrong.

He intended to call on her later. Ask her what she thought she was doing. Listen to the answer, make a decision.

Now, though, he had a more important task. One given to him this morning by his servant.

'Don't you go thinking that this tea comes without a price,' Mrs Mulrooney had said, her small, scurrying steps propelling the rest of her, and the tray she was holding, into the parlour.

'Good morning, Mrs Mulrooney,' he said. He had known she was up, of course. Had heard the creak of the pump in the yard, the bucket being dragged out from under the drip stone – a large granite bowl on a stand that purified the water poured into it. Monsarrat sometimes thought the fluid which worked its way slowly through the granite was the only thing here to become more pristine with the passage of time. The water that had recently dripped from the stone into the pail below was now in the teapot.

Monsarrat frequently offered help with the heavier tasks like pumping and carrying water, and was always glared at as though he'd offered insult. 'Sure, you couldn't be trusted to do it properly,' she frequently said. 'You'd galumph around and spill it all, big streak of a man as you are, and who cleans it up then?'

This morning, he'd made no such offer. He understood her well, or fancied he did, and guessed she would use the domestic rituals of the morning to calm herself, take an inventory, make sure each part of the contraption which made up Hannah Mulrooney was in working order, if not spotlessly sparkling.

'As for the price,' he'd said, 'one might remind you that one pays considerably more than one can afford for the excellent tea and the pleasure of your company, as well as the occasional swat with the cleaning cloth. I know, I know, it's a bargain, but still – it isn't nothing.'

'A small step up from nothing, I suppose,' Mrs Mulrooney said as she laid out the tea things on the table in front of him. 'But it's not more money I'm after.'

'No? What may I do for you, then?'

'Pens, paper and ink will do for a start.'

'Of course. But I do recall giving you a quantity of paper very recently. You must be writing letters to Padraig several times a day.'

'Not for me. For the women.'

'The women? Which ones?'

'Now you can't expect me to know all their names, not yet. It will be at least next week for that. But this Mrs Nelson, you see, is very keen on teaching them how to read. And I have found that the best way to learn to read is to write.'

'Have you indeed?'

'I have,' she said, with all the authority of a professor.

'So you would like me to procure pens and paper for Mrs Nelson's use in teaching letters to the women of the Factory.'

'Did I not just say that? Are you still drunk?'

'I don't believe so, but my head is nowhere near as clear as it usually is, a situation which I am relying on your tea to alleviate. Can Mrs Nelson not get the items elsewhere? I am not sure Mr Eveleigh will give me leave to make off with his stationery, and David Nelson – I have passed his house a few times – is more than wealthy enough to spare a few writing implements.'

'I'd agree with you there, if I did not think that procuring them myself would provide us with certain advantages.'

'I see.'

'I very much fear you don't, Mr Monsarrat, if you're asking questions like that. You want me to listen, keep an ear out for notes which sound a little off. It's far easier to listen if people are talking. And far easier to get them to talk when you're teaching them something. And far easier for me to convince Mrs Nelson to allow me to assist her if I am making a contribution myself.'

'Ah. You are right, as usual.'

'Of course I am. So you will do as I ask?'

'My dear lady, despite your assertions to the contrary, I am not an eejit. Therefore I may be relied on to accurately assess where my interests lie, and at the moment they lie in fulfilling your requests in the hopes you will continue to help me.'

'I certainly don't think we can rule out Crotty,' Monsarrat said, hoping he did not still smell of grog. 'I found his belief that his problems with watered rum are over rather interesting.'

Eveleigh got up from his desk – an unusual move in itself – and began pacing the perimeter of the office, head down, carefully measuring each step.

'Monsarrat, do you know how I felt when I was told you were coming?'

'No, Mr Eveleigh.'

'I was delighted. I thought to myself, how remarkable, someone with investigative instincts and clerical skill, so rare to find in one individual. It should simplify matters greatly, I thought to myself.'

'And now?'

'Well, I can't say I regret your arrival. But I was certainly mistaken with regard to your ability to simplify things. You seem instead to be making them rather complicated.'

'I assure you, sir. They are complicated without my intervention. I'm simply thinking to untangle them.'

'And there are those, Monsarrat, known to both of us, who would say that no disentanglement is needed. That the guilty party is obvious, and that nibbling around the edges is wasting time.'

'Is that your view, sir?'

Eveleigh sat back down, rather heavily for such a slight man.

'I don't know, Monsarrat. I just don't know. I do know, however, that the superintendent of police – and others who, shall we say, believe they have a role to play in secular society – are very anxious to proceed to the trial of the O'Leary woman, and would be alarmed by your activities of last night.'

'But surely, sir, you would not wish to see an innocent woman hanged?'

'No, no of course not. But I do want to see this business dealt with. Tidied away. It's interfering with the efficient running of things.'

Monsarrat knew that interference with the efficient running of things was in Eveleigh's view the worst crime anyone could commit.

'So, Mr Monsarrat, I feel that we do need to set some boundaries. You are not – absolutely not – to investigate this or any other matter outside of official hours and without my express permission. You will not involve any third party in this investigation. You will inform me of your intended course of action each day.'

'Of course, sir.'

'And, Monsarrat, one more thing. You have until the end of next week. Should you fail to discover anything germane, I will depose the O'Leary woman myself and prepare a brief for trial. And your status in this office will be less secure than it was.'

Monsarrat felt something inside him wake, shiver, stretch. It was a short step from losing his position to losing his ticket of leave. And he firmly believed a third penal stretch would kill him.

'Now, Monsarrat, if there's nothing else, I suggest you go and talk to O'Leary one last time, to see if you can find a hole in her story.'

'Of course, sir,' said Monsarrat, standing. And then swallowed. If he were to have a black mark against him anyway . . .

'Sir, if I may have one more moment of your time. An acquaintance of mine is engaged in some charity work with convicts. Promoting literacy. I wondered, if it's not too much trouble, would this office be able to spare a few sheets of paper?'

Chapter 15

In the early days in the little home, before Mrs Mulrooney and Monsarrat had settled into the rhythm of Sunday suppers, Mrs Mulrooney had insisted on serving Monsarrat his supper in the parlour. But in all honesty he preferred to take his meals in the kitchen with her. She acquiesced – to a point. She would rarely sit down and eat with him, always flitting from one task to the next. He hoped she ate properly at some point. Quite happy to carry on with her frantic activity in his presence, quite happy to put a plate of root vegetables, cauliflower and spinach in front of him while she muttered at the sugar snips for failing to cleanly slice the dome off a piece of sugarloaf, or berated a pannikin for displaying a hairline crack.

Monsarrat had told Mrs Mulrooney about his conversation with Grace, and about Grace's suggestion that Lizzie might have been one of the few people who could have seen the murder.

'Do you think you can face talking to Lizzie again?' Monsarrat asked.

'Well, I don't see why not. I'll ask Mrs Nelson if we can visit her again today. I'll just keep a reasonable distance.'

'Thank you, Mrs Mulrooney. I'm uncomfortable about the

whole business, to be honest, and particularly about asking for your involvement. But there is a very small chance it could be crucial.'

'Don't worry, Mr Monsarrat. Mrs Nelson will be with me. And I rather hope Lizzie calls her Eddie again. Her reaction may teach me something.'

She reached into the bowl of sand where the eggs were kept – they lasted longer that way – wiped the grains off the one she extracted and cracked it into a mixing bowl.

'Thank you for the paper, by the way. It will come in very handy. It's taking them a little while to pick up the skill of forming the letters, I must say, but still it's a joy for them and me.'

Monsarrat knew from watching her in Port Macquarie that Mrs Mulrooney was never happier than when she was coaxing people along, or compelling them, bossing or cajoling. He realised it must've been strange for her to have only him to take care of, after, for a time, having such a sizeable flock. And he had to admit that it was a relief she wasn't objecting to the task. He'd had more than enough objections from women for one day.

He had visited Sophia on his way home that evening, at the small white boarding house. He had opened the gate and walked up the path which bisected the neat little front yard, knocked on the door until its neat little owner answered. Fortunately, there were no guests at home, so they were able to use the parlour. There was, in particular, a small chaise on which Sophia loved to recline before drawing Monsarrat down to her.

'I would like to ask you,' he said, once he'd settled into a seat and refused the offer of tea, 'why you felt it necessary to attempt to blackmail my housekeeper?'

'Ah,' said Sophia, sitting down opposite him. 'Blackmail? You really think so?'

'What else would it be?'

'An attempt to persuade, that's all. You have been very slow to put in place any firm arrangements for our marriage. It occurred to me that your housekeeper's attitude may be part of the reason. And you know, of course, that it is important for both of us that such an event proceed. I was simply attempting to remove one possible obstacle.'

'So you have,' said Monsarrat, standing up. 'For there can be no obstacle to an event which is not possible.'

'Now, please, Hugh. Be sensible. This is a match which will help us both advance, and any qualms you may feel over the discomfort of a domestic servant are really neither here nor there.'

'They are, though, Sophia. Very much so. The authorities can take our freedom away again in an instant, you know. It just takes someone like Reverend Bulmer to catch either one of us in the tiniest transgression, and you or I, or both, would be back in slop canvas and government muslin. All we can control is our ability to be better than the animals they think we are. Yes, even you, my dear – do not think for a moment that Bulmer doesn't see you as soiled goods, as an outcast woman. We cannot change his mind – none of us, none of the fallen. But we can make him wrong. It is the only real decision open to us. That, and the company we keep.'

Monsarrat turned, opened the front door and walked slowly down the path, towards the river and the rank smell of the bats.

The next morning Hannah was up before the sun, with breakfast ready a full half-hour earlier than normal. She had the fresh sheets of paper in her basket, thanks to the largesse of Mr Eveleigh, and was looking forward to Rebecca's delighted reaction.

For the first time, she arrived earlier than Rebecca. She tucked herself away just inside the Factory's arched gate, hearing the bell which seemed to be doing its best not to be melodious as it told the women it was time for work.

Rebecca must've heard it too and realised she was late for she came trotting around the corner at twice her usual sedate pace, slowing and smiling when she saw Mrs Mulrooney. But she did not slow quickly enough and, catching the hem of her dress under the pointed toe of her shoe, she pitched forward.

Hannah was at her side in a moment, trying to set her to rights, but Rebecca seemed oblivious to all but her hair. The fall had knocked off her sun bonnet – an item for which she seemed to feel considerable affection, for she never removed it, even inside, and it now sat at the end of a small stream of copper-red hair, almost indecently bright against the dirt.

When Rebecca realised her bonnet was no longer carrying out the task she had set to it, that of constraining the red waves, she snatched it up with one hand while trying to gather her hair at the back with the other, twisting it in a way which must surely have been painful, jamming the bonnet back on her head and stuffing the hair in, wide-eyed and breathing hard.

It had been a long time since Hannah had seen anyone in the grips of panic. But in the bloodied days of the rising, she had seen it often, and she recognised it now in Rebecca. The tendency to focus on the trivial to the exclusion of everything else, to try to scrub the spot out of an apron while the house burned, to try to make sure the milking was done when the redcoats were muddying the fields with their boots on the way to the house.

Or the tendency to worry about unconstrained hair when your hands were bleeding.

She took Rebecca's wrists, looked her squarely in the face and marshalled the stern voice she usually saved for the worst of Monsarrat's transgressions.

'Now, you've had a shock, but you must stop this scrabbling about in the dirt fixing your hair. We have to get your wounds attended to, so we do. Stand up now, and come with me into the superintendent's residence. We'll get you cleaned and set to rights and you'll feel the better for it.'

Rebecca let Hannah lead her inside, and she seemed to have recovered much of her composure by the time they sat down at the table – which had borne significantly harsher scrubbings since Hannah had taken to tidying the place each day.

Henrietta Church was often at the table, in varying states of consciousness and sobriety. Hannah tried to urge tea on her when she could, but Henrietta rarely acknowledged her, and when she did she seemed to be under the impression that Hannah was a Factory woman, still a convict.

Heavens knew where Henrietta was today – possibly drinking with some of the women. The kettle showed no sign of having been used since yesterday, and the tea leaves in the caddy were dwindling, becoming damp as they did so. Hannah did not know how long the tea would last, or when it would be replenished. Nevertheless she set the teapot and kettle to the business of making something palatable, perhaps even restoring, out of the leaves.

Once the best cup of tea she could produce under the circumstances was in front of Rebecca, Hannah said, 'I was a little worried about you just then. You seemed in fear of your life. Have you hurt yourself more than is apparent?'

By this time, Rebecca had all of that startling red stowed neatly under her bonnet again, and it had been tied so tightly at the chin that flesh was bulging out on either side of the ribbon.

'I am absolutely fine, dear. Thank you for worrying about me – I must admit, it's something of a luxury to have someone else doing the worrying. I do apologise, I don't know why I acted as I did – very silly, and I flatter myself that I am not a silly woman. A momentary lapse. Please do your best to put my unseemly display out of your mind.'

'Of course. You shouldn't scold yourself. I find there are plenty willing to scold us, without us adding to it. Ah, I'd forgotten – I brought this.'

Hannah reached into a basket and extracted the blank pages, which stared accusingly at her as she remembered it had been a few days since she'd written to Padraig.

'Marvellous! We were nearly out, you know. Tell them to take more care, they do tend to gouge with the pen. All part of the learning process, I suppose.'

'Will we be using them today?'

Rebecca frowned. 'Perhaps not ...' she said absently. And then, 'I have a far more joyful duty for us in mind today, as it happens. I thought we might visit the lying-in hospital, you see. Time with new people will do us good. Two last week, and another yesterday. I suspect all three of them will look like Robert Church – unfortunate, particularly for the girls – but that's not their fault.'

Spending time with babies was not something Hannah considered a chore, no matter how loud they were or how distasteful their emissions. By the time she'd arrived in this place, she'd had enough of the kind of noise death made, and the emissions which followed the firing of a musket.

'I'll not object to that,' she said. 'But I had thought to perhaps visit Lizzie again. Convince her I'm not a monster. It might bring her poor mind some comfort.'

'Lizzie ... She's not making a lot of sense at the moment, even for her. Leave her, for now.' Rebecca reached for the stack of papers, riffling through them as if expecting to see a message written on one of them. 'It occurs to me,' she said, without looking up, 'that you and I are doing the same as the late superintendent, except in reverse.'

'Oh?'

'Yes. He spent all his time trying to remove things from the Factory; we are trying to bring them in.'

The lying-in hospital was supposed to be the sole preserve of women about to give birth, but the reality was that Dr Preston's wards were often unable to cope with the dysentery and other ailments that seemed to flood the hospital in waves, so the women sometimes found themselves joined by these patients, whose moans had nothing to do with childbirth but came instead from the pain of gangrenous limbs or poisoned blood or bones.

Unusually for this place, the women in the Factory's hospital were well cared for. In fact, their free sisters often chose to come and give birth here rather than braving the solitude of their homes.

Hannah had no idea, then, what she would face at the end of the short walk across the yard. Three women and their babies, certainly. But possibly the wife of a merchant or a sailor or a labourer, bringing into the world a child she would be allowed to take home and keep after its fourth birthday, assuming the infant could survive until then.

Today, though, the only women in the hospital were the three inmates. Two of them were nursing their babies and a third was asleep with her child so the place was oddly quiet – a situation the babies would no doubt remedy soon.

Rebecca led Hannah over to one of the women feeding her newborn.

'Ann, isn't it?'

'Yes, missus.'

'And who is this? I don't believe I've had the pleasure.'

'This is Tobias, missus. Four days old.'

'And how is Tobias faring?' It was more than a polite enquiry, it was a question of the utmost significance – a great many babies did not reach their first month.

'He's feeding well. Seems to be gaining weight. Not sickly.'

'He's a good lad,' said Rebecca, smiling. 'And, tell me, who is Tobias's father?'

Ann flushed, lowered her head.

'There can be no secrets between us here, you know,' Rebecca reassured the girl. 'He was not born in wedlock, we know that, and I for one make no judgement. However, I may be able to bring some influence to bear on this young man's father, depending on who he is, in terms of upkeep. Tobias's, and possibly yours, when you are freed.'

'Tom Felton, then,' Ann said. 'The Third Class turnkey. He gives me bread when he can. A little extra meat sometimes.'

Rebecca smiled as though Ann had just told her Tobias was the son of the King of England.

'You are to have no worries, Ann,' she said. 'I'll make certain that Mr Felton continues to meet his responsibilities to you and his son.'

Ann smiled back. There were very few who troubled themselves with ensuring anyone kept their promises to the women here.

They moved on to the next new mother. Unlike Ann, this one was not stroking her baby's head or murmuring maternally. She seemed detached, as though the feeding were just another task to be accomplished before the dinner bell went.

'Sarah,' said Rebecca. 'How's your daughter?'

'Well enough,' said Sarah. No elaboration, no boasting.

'And her name?'

'Eve.'

'What a beautiful name.'

'The first that came into my mind.'

The baby came off Sarah's breast, full of milk, sleepy now, insensible to her mother's apparent lack of interest in her.

'She looks . . . a strong young lady,' said Rebecca. 'May I ask who her father is?'

Sarah turned away. There was no embarrassment in her, though. Anger, perhaps.

'Sarah, the child's father?'

'Who would you think the child's father is? Who has fathered half the children in the orphan school? Most of the babies born in this room were put into their mother's womb by him, I shouldn't doubt.'

'I see. So this is Robert Church's baby.'

'No father left to keep any fine promises to me,' said Sarah.

'I do see your point,' said Rebecca. 'Nevertheless, I'm sure we can come up with something to ease the burden on you. May I hold her, do you think?'

Sarah handed the little girl over to Rebecca without question.

'You should rest now, Sarah. Can't you see, over there – Amelia and her child are sleeping. Best way to build strength, to manage whatever might come next. So you roll over now and try to sleep.'

Sarah did as she was told. The rise and fall of her chest soon became even and deep, and she seemed almost to sink into the thin bare mattress which lay on top of the narrow iron bed.

Rebecca jiggled the tiny baby up and down somewhat awkwardly, but the infant seemed happy.

'Why don't you offer to take Tobias for a little while so Ann can rest too?' Rebecca said to Hannah. Hannah needed no urging. She'd crossed the room and was holding the boy within moments, moving gently from foot to foot, humming in a way that had always settled Padraig. She became lost in her own movement, in the low thrumming sound coming from her chest as she breathed out the sounds of an old Irish lullaby. For a short time little Tobias was everything in the world.

But when she glanced up the enchantment shattered. Sarah was still asleep, but her daughter was not, and Rebecca was looking down at the baby, her expression untroubled by any emotion.

The child was certainly feeling something akin to emotion. Probably fear. The little girl's arms and legs were thrashing wildly, as the hand which cupped her small head forced her face into the fabric covering Rebecca's chest.

Ann was not yet asleep and Hannah thrust her baby back at her, running to Rebecca in a few steps.

'She's suffocating! Turn her around!'

Rebecca looked up, seeming as entranced as Hannah had been, and for a moment she kept holding the baby's head against her as the little girl's arms and legs lost power. Then she seemed to remember herself, gave a small gasp as though woken from a dream by a loud noise, looked down at the baby and immediately rolled her over.

'Hannah! I was thinking about something. She must've slipped. Thank goodness you spotted it. Poor heedless thing, my head was full of the miseries ahead of her. The orphan school, though she's not an orphan, and then . . . But no, here she is pink and perfect, and all thanks to you.'

Hannah nodded, smiled, said it was nothing.

It wasn't nothing, though – it was a long way from nothing. It was hard to believe that Rebecca could have been so caught up in her own thoughts that she hadn't noticed the baby thrashing about. Because in all the years of cuddling babies, and watching other women do the same, on convict ships and in traps and on farms and in gaols, Hannah Mulrooney had never seen one accidentally suffocated.

Chapter 16

Monsarrat was forbidden from visiting Crotty's shebeen again. But Eveleigh had said nothing about pies. And the drinkers of the colony were known to enjoy them when they could get them, when the vendor was not racing up into the mountains clutching his hot box, but instead hopping from foot to foot on the banks of the Parramatta River.

Stephen Lethbridge seemed to have a good sense of where to position himself to best advantage. Certainly the hungry men outside the Female Factory where Monsarrat had first met him had taken every pie he had to sell. And the same fate looked to be awaiting the pies Lethbridge had today. He stood at the nexus of George and Church Streets, known to residents simply as 'the Corner', where he had told Monsarrat he'd be, where news from the river flowed to meet word from the hinterland.

Lethbridge was making no attempt to attract attention. He didn't have to. The flotsam which flowed past the Corner often snagged a pie on its way past, leaving payment in its wake. And the gaol wasn't far away, with its hungry guards. But the prison looked like a rough draft of the building that was now rising opposite it. The stippled sandstone of the older structure was unformed next to the smooth stones of the new one, with each block perfectly straight and showing to best advantage the stone's lines and patterns.

Ironic that the building opposite the prison was a church. Even more ironic that it was a Catholic one.

Mrs Mulrooney would never have given a second's consideration to joining Monsarrat for services at St John's, even had its pastor been a less vicious example of the species than Reverend Bulmer. She cheerfully referred to Catholicism as the one true faith, and Monsarrat didn't take any exception – his religious observances sprang from social and political considerations, not theological ones.

In any case, it would have felt a little mean-spirited to take exception to the profession of a faith that had been outlawed for so long, whose adherents risked shadowy, terrible fates simply for sending their prayers skyward. Monsarrat had just enough understanding of the situation to know that he didn't understand anything.

Mrs Mulrooney, he knew, spent her time rather differently while he went to St John's. She, out of a quiet and genuine faith, went to the small room above the gaol where the Mass was said, with the priest using a plank on two chairs and an earthenware cup in place of a marble altar and silver chalice.

Monsarrat felt a vague unease that she celebrated her genuinely held conviction in these conditions, while he professed his nonexistent belief sitting behind the box-pews purchased by Parramatta's wealthy. But soon she would have a church to rival his. Those engaged in the work of building it were hungry. And Stephen Lethbridge had an unerring sense of where the hungry were to be found. But his customers were mostly the overseers. Those doing the truly backbreaking work lacked the funds for pies.

'Mr Monsarrat!' Lethbridge yelled when Monsarrat was still dozens of yards away. He must have been relatively easy to see from a distance, given his height, his habit of walking with his hands clasped behind his back, which gave him an identifiable rolling gait. This, together with his black coat and somewhat prominent nose, had earned him the nickname of Magpie in Port Macquarie.

'Mr Lethbridge,' he said as he arrived on the colonised corner. 'It occurs to me that I have heard much of your pies, yet not had the chance to sample one.'

'I'm afraid it's a pleasure you will have to wait a little longer for, Mr Monsarrat. I am fairly sold out, apart from this misshapen thing, which is promised to a foreman who has gone to fetch the means to pay for it.' He looked down at a torn pie.

'Well, I shall have to content myself with some conversation for now, then.'

'A commodity I am always happy to dispense, sir,' said Lethbridge, swaying slightly from foot to foot. 'Is there a particular topic on which you would like to converse?'

'There is, as it happens. But I must ask, Mr Lethbridge, may I rely on your discretion? You've no reason to give me any assurances, of course. However, there is a matter of justice which hinges on my discovering the truth of certain things, and you seem a just man. So have I your word that this conversation will not be reported to anyone?'

'Of course, Mr Monsarrat. I adore Justice, blindfolded whore that she is. If you're in the business of tidying her up a bit, I shall not impede you.'

'Excellent, and I thank you. The topic on which I would like to converse, then, is sly grog.'

'An interesting matter indeed, Mr Monsarrat. Homer – that's the Greek gentleman of antiquity, of course, not our friend the good doctor – said no poem was ever written by a drinker of water. I shall have to resign myself to my failure to write poetry, as I don't touch the harder stuff. While drinkers of water might not write poems, they have a better chance of running up mountains and back at the pace I can produce. And in any case, poetry is usually the last thing on the minds of those in this place who drink substances other than water.'

A man with a red face and the look of one familiar with sly grog ran up to Lethbridge, handed him a coin, received the pie in return and walked off eating it. The whole transaction was accomplished wordlessly. The man clearly had a better use to put his mouth to.

'Well,' said Monsarrat, when the man was out of earshot. 'When our mutual friend of whom you speak tells me of the dysentery he so regularly sees at the hospital, and of the foulness it produces, I might argue against the health-giving properties of water from our river. But I do see your point. I do touch grog, on occasion, but far less often than I used to. It seems I lack the constitution for it.'

Lethbridge nodded. 'Wise to recognise our limitations, don't you think?'

'Were I to list mine, I would be on this corner too long. And in any case, it is not the drinking I would like to discuss, but the procuring.'

Lethbridge nodded. 'A pleasure to converse with someone with enough wit to realise the two are not necessarily the same,' he said.

'Nor, it seems, does all of the grog in Parramatta flow from the same source. You mentioned Crotty to me when we last spoke.'

'Ah, yes. An example of one of my main contentions when it comes to the properties of drink – that it cannot enhance poeticism when there is none there to enhance.'

'I fear you may be right. However, it's not the man's artistic sensitivities, or lack of them, I'm chiefly interested in. It's where he and others like him are getting their grog.'

Lethbridge raised one eyebrow, a gesture which carried more impact because his face was the only stationary part of him. 'Now that's an interesting topic to be enquiring about, if I may say, Mr Monsarrat.'

'Interesting? I suppose so.'

'And you're not going to enlighten me as to your interest in this matter?'

'I'm afraid I can't at this stage, Mr Lethbridge. However, I do assure you that the possibility of sparing an innocent life hangs upon it.'

'Well, I can tell you – as I already have, of course – that Crotty was one of the unlicensed publicans who got the grog from Church.'

'Yes. But as you pointed out last time we met, that man's death does not seem to have stopped the flow of the stuff into the shebeens of the town.'

'Nor has it. You recall, of course, Socrates McAllister.'

Despite his uncle's low opinion of him, Lethbridge said, Socrates was not without a certain entrepreneurial spirit. While he would never come close to Philip McAllister's acumen, he was nevertheless alert for opportunities to profit. One of these, according to Lethbridge, was sly grog.

'The unlicensed publicans – they can't really ask for fair dealing because they're not fair dealing themselves,' said Lethbridge. 'So they have to pay whatever their suppliers demand. Especially when they are outside the law, and their supplier has the power to sit in judgement on them.'

'Can you be sure Socrates was selling rum to unlicensed publicans? How did you come by the knowledge?' said Monsarrat.

Stephen Lethbridge smiled. It was a genuine, wide smile, but there was a set to it that told Monsarrat there were lines which could not be crossed.

'We agreed I would respect your need for discretion, Mr Monsarrat,' he said. 'Equally, I think it only fair to agree that my sources should remain obscure. I will say that drinkers get hungry, and sometimes so do publicans, and everyone enjoys a chat after a cup of wine or two.'

'Of course. I meant no offence.'

'Oh, none taken. However, now we know where the barriers are, I think it would behoove us both to stay within them.'

'Very well. So Socrates was dealing in sly grog.'

'Yes, and making a reasonable sum at it as well. Of course, he was only able to do so while he had no competition.'

'And the competition came from Robert Church?'

'It seems so. In any case, a number of Socrates' customers began to complain about the amounts they were being charged. Socrates' usual response was to say that if they didn't like the price, they couldn't have the product. But for the first time some of them responded by saying, very well then, we'll have none of yours.'

'And you're certain it was Church who was providing the competition?'

'Oh yes. I wasn't at first. Crotty and his wife were a bit tight-lipped initially. But then they began to suspect that the rum was being watered. And they were vocal about that, I can tell you. To their detriment, of course.'

'So why didn't they just go back to Socrates?'

'Well, Socrates put his rates up, you see. To compensate for the downturn. Most couldn't afford them, so they decided to stay with Church.'

'And since Church's death?'

'Interestingly, my understanding is that most of them – the ones who want to continue trading – went back to Socrates. Tail between legs, paying more than before.'

Monsarrat recalled Crotty's comment – that his supply problems were now taken care of.

'Mr Lethbridge, there is one question I need to ask you, one of the greatest import. As far as you're aware, did Socrates McAllister know the identity of the man who was undercutting him? Did he know it was Robert Church?'

'Oh yes, most definitely. He made sure he found out, you see.'

'And how did he do that?'

'Well . . . I'd talk to Crotty if I were you.'

'Unfortunately I'm not in a position to do so. For various reasons, it's best I don't visit his establishment again.'

'And nor do you need to – he'll be in town today. Comes in every Thursday to run his errands – one of which is paying McAllister, of course. And afterwards he's not above visiting the Caledonia Inn. As my pies are all sold, Mr Monsarrat, I'd be more than happy to accompany you there, if it suits you.'

The Caledonia Inn was a far more congenial establishment than Crotty's pub. Cups that looked clean; chairs and tables, unupholstered but free of dust. And at one of these tables, as Stephen Lethbridge predicted, sat Michael Crotty.

Lethbridge approached him from behind, clapping him on the shoulder as he walked up so that Crotty turned with a start, already halfway out of his seat with a balled fist before he saw who it was.

'I'm not hungry,' he said, sitting back down.

'Just as well, my friend, as I've no pies left. Them at the crossroads site ate them all.'

Interesting, thought Monsarrat, that use of 'them'. He would have bet his ticket of leave that Stephen Lethbridge knew the correct usage, was pitching his speech to his audience. In London or Exeter it might have made him trust the man less, but not here. Verbal disguise was a survival skill he couldn't blame the man for adopting.

'Actually,' said Lethbridge, 'I was just conversing with a customer of yours. We saw you, thought we'd say hello.'

Crotty looked at Monsarrat for the first time. 'Yes, Mr . . .' he said, his eyes widening slightly.

Monsarrat began to cast around for a fabricated name, but Lethbridge said, 'Hugh Monsarrat, Government House, no less. An important man.'

Crotty stared at Monsarrat. 'And what would such an important man be doing in my establishment? I took your word, sir, when you said you were a clerk.'

He would have to be more careful around Lethbridge in future, Monsarrat thought. For all the man's skills, discretion was clearly not amongst them.

'So I am, I assure you,' he said. A lie in spirit, maybe, but certainly not one in fact. He was a clerk, and he had come into some money. Crotty need not know that it was the major's gift rather than a lucky win.

'I'm concerned to think that someone from the governor's cabal is sniffing around my little establishment,' Crotty said.

'Tell me, do you have other more illustrious people sniffing around? Anyone expressing an interest in where you get your grog and what you pay?'

'My business attracts attention from the right people, I'll say that. They can tell a smart man even if he's not dressed like an undertaker. They are persuasive. And they can actually drink. I don't suppose you'd care to get one for yourself, and me while you're at it?'

'No, thank you. I don't . . . That is, I don't feel like . . .'

Crotty snorted. 'I could tell you have no stomach for it,' he said. 'When you left you looked like you were being driven by a gale. After just three cups, albeit three of the new stuff.'

'Ah, yes, the new stuff,' said Lethbridge. 'I'm given to understand that the fare at your place has improved significantly of late.'

'What would you know of that? You never touch it.'

'Ah, drinkers talk, you see, when they're buying pies. Even when the rum they've just had has been watered.'

Crotty stood, banged his fist on the table. 'I don't water my rum! My grog comes from the same batch as what they serve here.'

'I know,' said Lethbridge. 'I told you, people are saying it's improved a lot.'

'And so it has.'

'Suppliers, though. I make my pies myself, the only way I can make sure they haven't been messed around with. Can you trust your new man to do the same?'

'None of your concern, Lethbridge. It's well known you can't keep yourself to yourself,' he said, before turning to Monsarrat. 'If you are of any importance – and even if you manage to stay on your rung when the new man comes – I can assure you, my supplier would eclipse you. And he goes to great lengths to look after his customers.'

Chapter 17

Hannah didn't know what she was going to say to Lizzie when they met. But she didn't anticipate any problems getting into the same room as the poor woman.

In this, she was mistaken.

It had now been two days since she'd first asked Rebecca if she could visit Lizzie again. Each time she repeated her request, though, Rebecca had another task in mind.

There was the reading and writing, of course. Then the sewing, helping with the leather-working so that the poor wretches could have shoes for a change, checking in on the mothers and babies in the lying-in hospital – Rebecca had made no attempt to take young Eve or any of the other babies again, at least not in Hannah's presence.

Then Rebecca said she simply didn't know whether Lizzie was up to another visit from someone who spoke in the cadence of people Lizzie saw as killers.

'I must confess, I've never seen her react like that,' Rebecca said. 'The way you speak – yes, I know it's not your fault – but it seems to call forward something quite dark in her. A little frightening. She was calling me some nonsense name, as you recall, and accusing you of all sorts of terrible deeds for which you couldn't possibly have been responsible. Maybe best to let her regain her equilibrium before we try again.'

If Lizzie had not regained her equilibrium at this point, Hannah thought, she never would, and she was doubtful about the benefits of leaving the girl sitting in a room by herself, staring at the walls and chewing over the unfortunate fate of her husband, whoever he was.

'The rebels were dreadful, you know,' said Rebecca. 'They dragged some of the captured yeomen onto a bridge once, and shot them where they stood – terrible barbarity. She talks about that sort of thing from time to time. One of the yeomen could've been her husband.'

Hannah's grief at her own losses at the hands of those yeomen was dull, crusted over, but it was still there, and had heard an answer in the anguish of the madwoman, in whose mind those events had occurred yesterday. Hannah wanted to spare Lizzie, if she could, some of the worst of the pain. Today, however, was another day she would not get the chance. Rebecca had drawn her aside yesterday, conspiratorially, in the corner of the drying ground. Robert Church no longer occupied the dead house, she told Hannah. He had been buried in St John's, the Protestant cemetery.

'I wonder if anyone went?' Hannah asked.

'Oh, a few,' said Rebecca. 'Those on the Female Factory management committee attended – obliged to do so, of course. Henrietta wasn't there. God knows where she was, but I doubt she shed a single tear for him. Apart from the official mourners, no, there were very few.'

But one of them, thought Hannah, had been Rebecca. At least, she spoke as though she had been there, although Hannah couldn't begin to imagine why.

'I have a very special task for you tomorrow, my dear,' Rebecca said now. 'You are to help Mrs Church pack.'

'She's going away, so?'

'Yes, permanently. A new superintendent has been appointed, you see. A steady man, by all accounts. And a matron, too, but she will take some time to arrive – she's been at the Female Factory in Van Diemen's Land. It's to be hoped their kindness matches their efficiency.'

Hannah had been wondering how long Henrietta Church would confine herself to the half-light of the superintendent's quarters, pretending when she had visitors to be lost in grief, while in reality lost in rum.

'Of course, I'll be delighted to help her.'

'Excellent. Do be careful, though. She has an awful temper when sober. One hears stories . . . Oh, and mind she doesn't take any of the crockery or cutlery, or furniture. That belongs to the government. It's her personal effects only she's allowed to take with her.'

'Where is she to go?'

'Hannah, I worry about a great many things in regard to a great many women, but on that point, I must tell you, I am completely indifferent.'

It wasn't the first time Hannah had noted a lack of sympathy from the usually tender-hearted Rebecca towards the superintendent's wife. 'I don't know why you persist in getting her to give up the drink, trying to get her to eat,' she'd said to Hannah a few days previously. 'If she wants to drink herself to death, why not let her?'

So this morning Hannah knocked gently on the door of the superintendent's quarters, heard a mumbled invocation and entered. Henrietta was sitting at the table, a cup in front of her which Hannah knew did not contain water.

Brusqueness, efficiency, activity – they'd helped her through a great many situations in the past. As long as you kept moving, it meant you weren't dead. 'Right, so,' she said to Henrietta, clapping her hands and pretending not to notice the smell. 'I'll make a pot of tea for us to get us through the packing. You'll let me know, of course, whether you've a trunk or some other means of conveying your possessions, and what you'd like placed in there.'

She didn't wait for a reply, which was just as well as there was none. Henrietta watched closely as Hannah darted around tidying the kitchen, but the woman was mute.

Hannah put a cup of tea in front of Henrietta and deftly removed that other one at the same time. Empty, of course. She washed it, put it away.

'Get that down your throat,' she said, 'and we'll get to work.'

'Not much work to do, really,' said Henrietta. 'I have few possessions.'

'Ah, but a woman still has to wear clothes, missus. How are you to get another position without them? Where are they to be found?'

'If you insist on packing, you may find some clothing underneath the couch,' said Henrietta, with a weariness that indicated she didn't particularly care whether Hannah found anything or not.

In the dusty recesses under the couch Hannah did indeed come upon an apron, balled-up and stiff, and a grey skirt which had been treated likewise. Again, there were those marks, those striations. Gorges cut in the floor's geography. Might as well be hung for a sheep as a lamb, Hannah thought. Last chance, anyway. She extracted the abused garments and threw a question over her shoulder, as casually as she could. 'Mrs Church, what made these marks in the floor? Is there some sort of insect infestation? I know some of them can play havoc with wood.'

'No, it wasn't an insect,' said Henrietta. 'It was me.'

'You? I see.'

'No, actually, you don't. I know it's not common practice to carve lines into the floor of your residence with an awl.'

'Well, that's true enough,' said Hannah. 'So why did you?'

'Better than carving in flesh.'

'Your flesh? I'm sorry, Mrs Church, but I couldn't help

150

notice ... When I was tending to you the other day, when you were sleeping ... The scars on your arms.'

'None of your business, and how dare you examine me when I am not conscious nor in any fit state to object.'

Hannah sat down opposite Mrs Church, reached out and tried to take her hand, but it was snatched back as though Hannah's own fingers were burning.

'Of course,' she said quietly. 'It's your concern and none of mine, so I'll not mention it again. Unless you feel it might do you good to discuss it? With someone who will give you an assurance they won't speak of it outside this room?'

'It would do me no good at all. Nor do I trust you to keep silent. If there was anything to keep silent on. The Irish are dreadful indiscreet, it's well known. Now, make sure you find the key to the tea caddy as you're packing. I'd hate for some of those leaves to be filched.'

❧

Hannah felt oddly sad that afternoon when the trap arrived for Henrietta and her baggage. The woman was rude and a drunk, and Hannah's attempts to pour tea down her had been rebuffed. There was still the slim possibility that she was a murderer – Hannah had not ruled it out. True, it would make more sense for her to have avenged herself in the privacy of the superintendent's residence. But Henrietta could have slain Church in the yard to draw suspicion away from herself – or rum might have carried her there and made her heedless of consequences. Still, Hannah thought it unlikely. And when the trap pulled away, she felt a rush of torpor, as though she herself had been at the rum.

Henrietta's departure left Hannah without a focus – a situation she never enjoyed. Looking after people, whether they wanted you to or not, was an excellent means of fending off memories of ruin, and worries about a boy who was now a man somewhere in the expanse behind the mountains.

Chapter 18

That Sunday was one of the most disturbing Monsarrat had ever experienced. Unexpectedly, the Reverend Bulmer played only a small part in the upheaval. He was still utterly focused on Stephen Lethbridge and his evil doctrine on universal suffrage and the Rights of Man, concepts that threatened to undermine society and lead to rampant immorality, rioting and other ills. Lethbridge sat there and allowed himself to be drenched in a torrent of Bulmer's bile, condemned as a bringer of false hope, a violator of God's order, a silver-tongued disciple of Satan, an unnatural man who wished to overturn the natural order. After the service he looked around, nodded and smiled at anyone who met his eye, seemingly unperturbed by the onslaught. All in a day's work for a silver-tongued servant of the devil, Monsarrat supposed.

Monsarrat, actually, was relieved, and guilty for feeling so. If Lethbridge could accept Bulmer's hatred with such equanimity, even wear it as a badge of honour, did that not say something about Monsarrat's own moral constitution?

But after the service the day took an alarming turn. Monsarrat was attending church by himself, of course. His arrangement with Sophia was at an end, and he'd decided not to offer to accompany her regardless. A clean break was painful but probably necessary, and he congratulated himself on his judgement as he strolled to the church that morning.

Until after the service he saw Sophia with her hand on an arm in a red sleeve, belonging to a red coat, in turn declaring its wearer a soldier.

Perhaps it was the intensity of Monsarrat's stare at this man – astonished that Sophia had found his replacement so quickly – that made Lethbridge walk to his side and place a hand on his shoulder. 'Difficult, I know, dear fellow, but that poor man will soon feel his hair smouldering if you continue staring at him like that.'

'Ah, Mr Lethbridge,' said Monsarrat. 'Yes, rude of me.'

Lethbridge nodded and smiled sympathetically. He knows, thought Monsarrat, about Sophia and me. God rot the man, he collects information as easily as I collect enemies. And this thought made Lethbridge's next remark even more disturbing.

'One must mind who one stares at, Mr Monsarrat. It is disconcerting for some to be the object of your attention.'

'I try not to stare at all, Mr Lethbridge. This was an aberration.'

'Ah, but it seems you've been doing nothing but staring, in one way or another. And some of those in power do not like it.'

'I answer to the supreme earthly power in the colony, Mr Lethbridge.'

'But you know – a man of your intellect – that the governor is not the only power here. Particularly when the colony is being ruled by a name and an outline into which a man is yet to step. Hard for such a figment to govern with any authority, especially when the Holy Trinity is arrayed against him.'

'The Holy Trinity?'

'Yes, Mr Monsarrat. Church, courts and commerce. When those forces are in alignment, empires fall.'

'Although you're not suggesting that this one is about to, surely,' said Monsarrat.

'Not at all, Mr Monsarrat. I am simply observing. And now I must go, before the Holy Trinity notices my continued presence. If you'll excuse me.'

Monsarrat knew to whom Lethbridge was referring. Church, courts and commerce could be found in one man. Reverend Horace Bulmer. And standing with Bulmer, having to raise his chin slightly so that they could continue their whispered conversation, was the man who embodied two out of three aspects of that trio. Socrates McAllister. Gentleman farmer, magistrate and purveyor of sly grog.

While people like Sophia craved the attention of those on McAllister's social stratum, Monsarrat would have been delighted to escape his notice. It seemed, though, that he was not to get his wish, because as Monsarrat watched, Bulmer's and McAllister's eyes turned to him.

He probably should have left at that moment, but fearing drawing further attention to himself by a quick escape he froze, and then it was too late because McAllister had clapped his hand companionably on Bulmer's shoulder in a jovial farewell and started towards Monsarrat. He started talking before he stopped walking. A busy man, clearly, unwilling to waste time, particularly on a man such as Monsarrat.

'And how is Eveleigh's errand boy?'

Monsarrat inclined his head in what he hoped was a bow respectful enough not to cause offence, but not too obsequious. He was confident McAllister was the kind of man who delighted in spotting weakness in others.

'At your service, Mr McAllister.'

'You remember me, then.'

'Of course, Mr McAllister, as I do all men who have influence in this place.'

'You're still sniffing around the Female Factory, I hear.'

'Mr Eveleigh sends me there to attend to certain administrative duties, yes.'

'What's more interesting, Mr Monsarrat, is that I hear you recently acquired a taste for rum?'

'I rarely indulge, sir, but occasionally one succumbs to temptation.'

'But surely a chap such as you would be more comfortable at the Freemason's Arms or the Caledonia? Not at some shebeen. Dangerous people go to places like that, you know.'

'Yes, I'm aware, sir, and thank you for your concern. I assure you that my future indulgences, rare though they will no doubt be, will occur at one of the establishments you mentioned.'

'Ah, that is good to hear, Mr Monsarrat. And I'm told that you have something of an interest in business.'

'In so far as I have an interest in anything which bears on the functioning of the colony, yes.'

'Well, it seems to me that the business taking up your time of late centres on the supply of drink to various establishments. I must warn you that such business can be hazardous. So I've heard, anyway.'

'Thank you, sir, I will bear your warning in mind.'

'Wise fellow. It would turn your hair white, Mr Monsarrat, to hear some of the tales which come before the bench – the most deplorable acts of violence visited on the unwary who stray into some of the less salubrious establishments. I would hate to see a rarefied man such as yourself subjected to such treatment. Best confine your drinking to the established public houses. Or, better yet, don't drink at all. It can be very bad for the health, you know.'

Chapter 19

Hannah was sorely tempted to visit Lizzie without Rebecca's permission but she did not want to lose Rebecca's trust, nor access to the Factory and its inhabitants.

She was standing outside Henrietta's rooms and toying with the idea of leaving, as it seemed nothing more useful could be accomplished, when Rebecca walked through the gate with a man Hannah didn't recognise. His clothes were not as meticulously maintained as Mr Monsarrat's, but they were clean and well made, his cravat passably tied – and Hannah considered herself an authority on such matters.

'Just the one!' said Rebecca, when she saw Hannah. 'I told you, did I not, Mr Rohan? Here she is, at her post. Mrs Mulrooney, may I present Mr Rohan, the Factory's newly appointed superintendent.'

Rohan bowed slightly.

'Mrs Mulrooney has been my right arm, Mr Rohan, she truly has. I swear to you, with her assistance I can help you out of your present predicament, at least until you get the matter of a matron resolved. Shall we go in?'

Without waiting for an answer, Rebecca was already opening

the door of the superintendent's quarters, urging them all inside. Once there, she clapped her hands again and exclaimed over the tidiness, the lack of dust, the fresh smell of soap and the windows thrown open to catch the breeze.

Hannah moved to the hearth and put on a pot of tea, before realising that the leaves were currently being conveyed to Sydney as part of Henrietta Church's possessions.

'Not at all,' said Rebecca, in response to Hannah's apology. 'We've far more important things on our mind than tea, have we not, Mr Rohan?'

'Indeed,' he said.

'Mr Rohan, you see, has his own house in town, Mrs Mulrooney. He has no need of lodging in the matron's quarters, as of course he is not married to the matron, unlike the previous fellow.'

'No, my wife has no interest in being the matron here,' said Rohan. 'Nor has she the qualifications, to be honest. I have a candidate on her way on a ship from Van Diemen's Land, but the wind must be against them for she hasn't arrived yet. In the meantime, I believe this establishment has been without a matron – or a functioning one – for quite some time.'

His eyes darted between the two women, and Hannah was astonished he was including her in the discussion. But with his next statement, it became apparent why.

'Mrs Nelson has been telling me of the work you and she have been doing with the women. I understand your employer is on the governor's staff, so he will appreciate the need to restore order here as soon as possible. I intend to write to him and request he release you to continue to assist Mrs Nelson until such time as the ship from Van Diemen's Land arrives.'

Hannah said nothing. Several questions pushed their way past each other to be first to her lips, but they would have to wait. Because she had no wish to prematurely pierce the thin membrane surrounding this moment with words. Having her work recognised by an offer of employment, however temporary, was beyond gratifying. And, of course, it would put her in the ideal position to continue her investigations. She had no doubt that Monsarrat would instantly accede to Rohan's request, even if it meant making his own tea for a time.

'Is that agreeable to you, Mrs Mulrooney?'

Again, a strange sense of dislocation – being asked whether a course of action was agreeable. Such a thing had rarely happened, at least not during her time in New South Wales.

'Of course, Mr Rohan. I would be delighted to be of service.'

She should, really, have stopped there. Expressed her delight at the opportunity to serve, and then served in silence. But if she remained invisible, she would make no progress. It was a risky moment, and Hannah's response to risks had always been to take more of them.

'If I may make so bold,' she said, feeling a moral necessity, which didn't stop the first few words coming out in a croak, 'as to venture an opinion. I was wondering about the treatment of some of the women whose wits are not fully together. Some more company for them, perhaps, may be beneficial.'

Rebecca Nelson frowned. 'Bear in mind, Mr Rohan, Mrs Mulrooney has no qualifications in the matter,' she said. 'We simply speak from our observations, and I am sure the lady from Van Diemen's Land will make her own arrangements once she arrives. We will endeavour to do our best to keep things functioning as they have been – perhaps a little better – but of course it is not our place to make any irreversible changes to the functioning of this establishment.'

When she finished speaking, she turned to Hannah and pointedly raised her eyebrows.

'Your observations are welcome, of course,' said Mr Rohan, 'as they are my primary source of information until I have the opportunity to make my own. As you say, the new matron will have her own idea on the matters at hand. But I see no harm in a little more company for the afflicted, if you think it may be of use.'

'We'll just be delighted to keep things running along happily,' Rebecca said, as though discussing a garden party rather than a penal establishment. 'Mr Rohan, it would be a terrible thing to make too many changes. There's no telling how things would unravel from there.'

But there was one change Rebecca was going to make. Hannah had no idea how Rebecca had managed it, but managed it she had.

She was going to get some women out of the Factory.

One afternoon, over tea, Rebecca had told Hannah of her plans.

'They are so stupid, some of them, are they not? Those who set the policies as to how these women should be treated. They claim they want to rehabilitate them, make them good colonial citizens when their sentence expires. But all they do is create future whores, beggars, and corpses.'

Hannah was surprised to hear Mrs Nelson speak so bluntly. She usually stayed on the right side of propriety.

'Honestly, Hannah. They show them this place. They show them the town – the squalid parts of it, in any case. They show them men like Robert Church. And then they expect them to aspire, to behave, in the hopes of inheriting something better when their freedom comes. Yet they've been shown there is nothing worth inheriting, that freedom will just be another form of slavery, but without any certainty of rations.'

'I suppose many of them would rather starve in freedom than in confinement, though,' said Hannah.

'Maybe, although in my experience if you're starving or brutalised, or worse, whether you have a ticket of leave in your pocket or not doesn't make much difference.'

'In your experience?'

Rebecca Nelson had told Hannah something of her story. She was a governess when she moved here with her father, who had inconsiderately died a week after their arrival. Rebecca had secured another position as governess to the widowed David Nelson's children, and had made herself so indispensable he had married her. Hannah was sure Rebecca had faced some difficulties, particularly after her father's death. But she didn't believe those difficulties had extended to starvation and brutality.

'My experience listening to the stories of these women,' Rebecca said.

'And what would you show them, if you could? What would you have them aspire to? Would you spin them some kind of fantasy to keep them quiet, well-behaved? Because that is an abuse in itself.'

Rebecca looked at Hannah, eyebrows raised, head slightly down like a beast about to charge. 'I will thank you, Mrs Mulrooney, not to accuse me of perpetrating a cruelty on these women.'

'I meant no offence, Mrs Nelson,' Hannah said. 'But you know me to be a plain speaker, and I did imagine it is something you value, so I am speaking plainly when I say that it is difficult to aspire to something which does not exist. Lying to these girls will not help them, not in the long run.'

'No, it won't. And that's not what I propose to do. I'm sorry for getting cross, Mrs Mulrooney, especially as I'll need your help in bringing my plan to fruition.'

'And your plan is?'

'Well. We've been doing what we can to give them at least something of what they'll need when they walk under that ridiculous clock for the last time. Sewing, housekeeping, cooking. Letters, most importantly. But what we need to do now, I feel, is to show them where the industrious application of these skills might lead.'

'And where might it lead?'

'Why, into a situation such as yours – domestic service, a fine roof over one's head, certainty of food, protection from molestation, all of these wonderful things. They may even find themselves living under a distinguished roof. A roof such as that of my husband.'

'You want to bring them home?'

'Only for a little while, of course. An afternoon here and there. My husband is something of an aesthete – we have a great many paintings about the place. It will do the women good to see that humans can express themselves in ways other than through lust or violence. And in keeping with that, I thought we'd make a sewing circle: proper sewing – embroidery. Imagine sitting in a pleasant room for an afternoon with needle and thread for no other purpose than to make something beautiful. I don't know what you think, Hannah, but I think that could be the making of some of them.'

It was certainly an interesting idea.

Mr Rohan had given Rebecca permission to select ten of the best-behaved First Class women, and today they were to be escorted to the Nelson houschold to perch themselves on the fine furnishings in order to stitch birds, flowers and butterflies into existence.

That afternoon it fell to Hannah to lead the selected women around a few curves of the river to the Nelson home. There were guards with them too, of course. It had been made clear to each of the women that any attempt at escape would fail, and would mean a revocation of their privileges. Each of them was accustomed to the superior rations of thc First Class convict, and the better clothes and treatment. And now this – an afternoon in a fine house. It seemed unlikely anyone would attempt to run, particularly when they had no idea what they would be running to.

There were two women in particular to whom Hannah's eyes were drawn as they walked. Bronagh and Peggy, their names were, and while they weren't sisters, they could have been. Hannah often saw them together crossing the drying ground or at lunch in the dining hall. Their accents told her they were from a long way south of Wexford, and at first she'd wondered if their fathers could have been in the treacherous North Cork militia – Catholics doing the work of the Crown by killing croppies during the rebellion. But they sometimes greeted each other with a phrase Hannah had not heard in decades. Not whispered, but said quickly enough so it was disguised in the general babble, sinking into the pool of noise around them so only a trained ear could sieve it out. And Hannah's ear was trained, at least when it came to this particular phrase. The United Irishmen's battle cry. *Erin go bragh.* Ireland forever.

Perhaps not militiamen's daughters, then.

For the present, though, they seemed anything but revolutionary. Peggy, who had fair hair and unmarked skin, was walking beside one of the guards, giggling when he reached out to squeeze her waist. Bronagh was smiling indulgently, as though she were chaperoning a well-behaved couple on a walk along the river. These two seemed especially unlikely to try to escape their afternoon excursion.

But they were slowing the group's progress and Rebecca would be waiting for them, Hannah knew, having begged off the journey so that she could make the house ready. Her husband would be there, too. David Nelson had decided that it was acceptable to deal with his business matters at home for the afternoon, while ten convict souls, corrupted but not irredeemable, sat nearby.

'He is a devout man, truly, and a believer in redemption. I think, though, that he would prefer the redemption not take place in our parlour,' Rebecca had told Hannah.

So the women, as it turned out, were not to ply their needles under the gaze of some of David Nelson's finer artworks.

'I wanted to bring them into the house,' Rebecca had told Hannah the previous day. 'But my husband forbade it. He said there was no necessity for the women to know what we had, or where we had it. So it will be the verandah for us today.'

It was the grandest house Hannah had seen since she had padded through the empty rooms of the magistrate's home near Enniscorthy. She had never quite understood the British obsession with taming nature, expressed in their gardens through minutely measured flower beds and precisely trimmed hedges. That obsession was in evidence here, with spherical hedges lining the walkway up to the house and plants rising at exactly the same height from the beds next to the verandah.

But some plants had been allowed the freedom to run, to climb through the earth so that their roots broke the soil here and there, loops in which a shoe could easily be caught. And here and there gum trees stood, no pattern to their location, clearly growing where they themselves had decided to, without any influence from the Nelsons.

Passionfruit vines threaded through the lattice at the side of the verandah, not artfully arranged, as they might have been elsewhere, but making their own path through the slats of wood. There had been passionfruit vines at Port Macquarie, and Hannah felt a debilitating but mercifully brief stab of melancholy as she thought of another verandah on which she had sat talking to a young woman, who should still be alive.

The day was warm but the smothering cloak of humidity Hannah remembered when she had been a convict here had not yet made itself apparent – it would probably be another few months before they had to contend with it. Because of the heat, and the anaemic breeze which periodically managed to make its way up the hill from the river, the verandah was actually the best place to be.

Rebecca was wearing a simple muslin gown that fitted her precisely, unlike the dresses of her visitors, which hung on their frames and were mostly a little too short. She was seated in front of a table with twelve sewing frames on it, as well as a tin full of pencil stubs, and skeins of indecently bright thread.

She stood when she saw the party arriving, waved as though the women were her dearest friends on this earth, beckoned and sat them on wicker chairs far more comfortable than any seating available at the Factory.

'Now.' She clapped a hand excitedly. 'You are going to be doing so much more than mending and darning; so much more than just making clothes or keeping them together. You're going to create something entirely new. But, as with all creation, or even recreation, there is a price.'

The women looked at each other uneasily. A price? Wasn't there always? What would this one be?

'I am going to start by teaching you to embroider letters, words. Far easier, when you're starting out, than a bird or a flower or a leaf, where you have to mimic the shadings that the natural world gave those things. Letters are ours, they owe nothing to nature, they have straight edges and regular curves and are far easier to sketch and sew.

'So, each of you is going to embroider a word, one word, on a piece of cloth. But I will not hand you a frame until you tell me what the word is and how to spell it.'

The women looked at each other, and then back at Rebecca. A trick? Some sort of trap, testing their devoutness or their rectitude? Several clearly thought so, for the word they nominated was God – believing, no doubt, that it wouldn't do any harm to be seen as devout. Thanks to Hannah's efforts, they were able to stammer out the letters and were rewarded with a sewing frame.

A few of the others – some of the younger ones – gave their own names.

'M-A-R-I,' said Mary Smith. One of the more recent arrivals, she had been transported for theft of livestock.

Rebecca seemed to know all their stories. She had told Hannah that Mary had seen a cow straying, and had been attempting to lead it back when she was apprehended. She was a good girl, apparently, caused little trouble, and rarely spoke.

At the misspelling, Rebecca winced at Hannah, handing her a sewing frame. Hannah carried it over to Mary and whispered in her ear, 'Put a Y on the end, there's a good girl. But well done.'

Then it was the turn of one of the youngest of the group.

Helen Down had been barely fourteen years when she was sentenced to transportation, for whacking her stepfather over the head with a piece of wood. She had never disclosed how he'd provoked the attack. Nor did she need to – most here could take a reasonable guess.

'Eliza,' she whispered, as though fearing to disturb the heat that lurked in the air, lest it turn on her. Hannah had noticed, on the walk here, that Helen's eyes were continually scanning the guards, the road ahead, the slope leading down to the river bank. She had assumed Helen was taking in as much as she could of the world outside the Factory walls. Now, she wondered if the girl had been looking for threats.

'Say that again, if you please, Helen,' called Rebecca.

'Eliza – E-L-I-Z-A,' said Helen, more loudly.

And then she began to wail.

It took some time to get her to stop – she was gulping in air in gasps so violent that it seemed to Hannah she might tear open her own chest.

'Mrs Mulrooney,' said Rebecca. 'Kindly go to the kitchen and get the vial of laudanum from the second shelf beside the fireplace. And a cup of water, too.'

Hannah welcomed the opportunity to step into the shade. Until she saw the dining room was green. Rooms of that colour made her nervous these days. This was paint, though, not paper like the last ill-omened green room she had entered. In every other aspect the room was a handsome one – elongated as though built around the long dining table it housed, with a large fireplace which stood unused for the moment, and would probably see its hiatus extend to March or April, when the weather started to cool. Beautiful filigree statues on the mantelpiece, below a picture of a man she didn't recognise, who was sitting with three-quarters of his body turned towards the artist, looking directly out from the frame as though trying to probe the viewer for deception.

A door at the other end of this room led through to a sitting room, which gave out to the backyard and the kitchen beyond it. There must be servants, but Hannah couldn't see them – perhaps Rebecca had sent them away for the convicts' visit. And at the side of the room another door opened to a study where an older man – the embodiment of the man in the painting – sat at a desk. He was frowning at a piece of paper, while its companions were weighed down against the breeze with a small bronze statue of a wolfhound. A much larger, living example of the species was attempting to imitate a rug on the floor in front of the desk, raising his head and growling when Hannah passed the room.

The man looked up, saw her and rose, closing the study door behind him as he walked towards her.

'I trust my wife has explained to you that no convicts are to be inside the house,' he said. He sounded firm, authoritative, but not necessarily angry.

'Of course, I'm sorry. But I'm not a convict. I'm assisting Mrs Nelson, and she's asked me to fetch an item for her from the kitchen.'

'Ah, you're the housekeeper she speaks of so highly. How did she persuade you to act as her factotum?'

Hannah bobbed, introduced herself. 'I don't think there was any persuasion,' she said. 'I'm pleased to assist her.'

He smiled slightly. 'Yes, a common experience, I think you'll find, among those associated with my wife. She seems happy out there.'

'Indeed, Mr Nelson.'

'Surprising. She was once suspicious of convicts – I had to prevail on her to do this work. But I'm glad to see her taking to it. It distracts her from her grief, you know.'

'Her grief, sir?'

'Her father died shortly after the two of them arrived here. She is still in mourning for him. Now, kindly fetch what she asked you for, and please do see that none of the rest of them come in.'

Hannah located the glass vial of laudanum in a cupboard next to the cloves, got a cup from the kitchen and scooped some water from a pail beneath the drip stone. The yard between the house and the kitchen was damp, almost muddy – odd in this heat. There was a small puddle surrounding the nearby pump, with water leaching up from the ground, slowly colonising the space.

By the time she returned to the verandah, Helen seemed somewhat recovered. Her young skin was blotchy, and her eyes were still red and leaking, but she was no longer gasping. She was half-reclining, and being fanned by Bronagh as Peggy held her hand.

'She didn't know me on Sunday,' Helen was wailing. 'Or she pretended not to, which is worse. She wouldn't come to me, wouldn't let me hug her. What must they be doing to her?'

Hannah sat down beside her. 'Eliza is a lovely name,' she said quietly.

'It was my mother's, who is dead, thankfully – she didn't live to know that her granddaughter was born in servitude and has never taken a free breath.'

'And how old is your girl?'

'Four.' The word seemed to shatter Helen's voice for a moment, remove her ability to speak.

Hannah finally understood: the age children of Factory women were taken from their mothers to the orphan school.

'I'm sure she's being well taken care of,' she said, sure of no such thing.

'Do they sing to her, though?' said Helen. 'Do they know that she's scared of magpies? That she likes braiding leaves? That she's good at running but gets a pain in her tummy if she goes too fast?'

She began to cry again, and Hannah cast around for any small mercy to cling on to.

'Soon you'll be able to show her how beautiful her name looks in needlepoint,' she said, cursing herself and His Majesty's excuse for a government that this was the best consolation she could offer. 'And not everyone here is without kindness: you may find she is being better looked after than you had hoped.'

'You mustn't worry,' said Peggy. 'A lot of them have trouble at first. I'm sure it won't last, and her rations are probably better now.'

Bronagh took the cup and held it to Helen's lips. 'As for you, you're too thin, you are,' she said. 'We'll have a word to the pirate queen, see what can be done.'

Hannah was most certainly not aware of anyone matching the description of a pirate queen residing in Parramatta. In fact, the only one she'd ever heard of had harried the coast of Ireland long ago.

Though distracted by Bronagh's strange comment, she noticed now a young man standing by the verandah. He removed his broad-brimmed hat. His hair should have belonged to the man in the house, far too white for his years. As the heat danced around him and soaked into the fires of his coat, he couldn't stop himself glancing briefly at the cup.

'Ah, my friend from the markets,' Hannah said.

And so he was. Hannah hated asking for help with anything, but sometimes, if it was offered on a hot afternoon while carrying home some heavy parcels, she forced herself to accept. Not many people offered, though, but this man had, and while his face was unremarkable, the white hair made him memorable.

He bobbed his head. Rebecca had noticed him too. 'Henson! How nice to see you. All well at the warehouse, I trust? Do go inside. He's in his study, trying to stay as far away from all this femininity as he possibly can.'

Henson smiled, nodded and walked into the house.

'He works for your husband?' asked Hannah.

'Yes, he runs David's main warehouse, down by the river. Serves in the store sometimes too. He inspects the goods off the ship, off the carts. He has a small amount of discretion within strict boundaries in regard to what he can buy. He stores it and catalogues it and generally makes sure everything is in order.

He's not a bad clerk, either. Not much of a sense of humour, but you can't have everything. He's a Quaker – David employs them when he possibly can.'

Hannah had rarely heard one of the social rulers of this place go to so much trouble to explain an acquaintance, especially to a housekeeper.

Helen was now recovered enough to begin to sketch the word which had upset her onto her piece of muslin stretched across its frame, and to start plunging a needle trailing a vivid scarlet tail in and out of the cloth.

Rebecca spent the next hour walking among the women, inspecting their work. 'For God's sake, Ann, what has that cloth ever done to you? There's no need to stab it, now. Gently ease the needle in through the fibres – far more effective and leaves a cleaner result.'

'Harriet, please try to keep your stitches a little smaller. If you make them too big you simply pull at the fabric, see? Small and delicate, like a duchess's footsteps.'

'Never been near a duchess to see what her footsteps are like,' said Harriet, one of the older ones, and, judging by her pitted skin, a survivor of smallpox.

'Ah, but you have such a vivid imagination! Like my dear Lizzie. You can surely create a fictional duchess and observe her gait.'

Harriet did not look particularly inclined to create anything, out of thin air or otherwise, but her stitches gradually became smaller and neater.

Hannah realised they must've been there for longer than she had thought when she stopped having to shield her eyes from the sun to examine the convicts' work. Perhaps Rebecca noticed as well. In any case, she withdrew a small, delicate pocket watch from her skirts, checked it, put it away.

'It appears our time is up. I mustn't be tardy in getting you ladies back to the Factory, otherwise they might not let you come again. Mrs Mulrooney, would you kindly collect the frames? I'll let the guards know their rest is at an end. Cook will be back soon anyway, and she wouldn't be happy to find those galumphing louts hanging around, probably with their feet up on her table.'

At that moment her husband came out with Henson, who was blushing slightly and smiling. They were trailed by the wolf-hound, who jumped onto one of the benches next to Helen, giving her a fright.

'Nemesis! You appalling thing, get down,' said Rebecca. Nemesis ignored her, sitting on his haunches and examining the group of women, assessing them for their ability to provide food.

'He's brought me the most marvellous news, this lad,' said David, clapping the young man on the shoulder.

'Oh? Have you made a particularly advantageous purchase, Mr Henson?'

'Better than that, Mrs Nelson.'

'Better indeed!' said David. 'Henson has informed me that the thieving has stopped. I'm sure it was hiring some night guards that did it, but whatever the reason, for the first time in six months everything is there. Nothing is missing, nothing at all! Odd that I should get this news when I was staying home to prevent a potential theft myself – I will look more kindly on your ladies in future, Rebecca. They seem to have brought us some of the good fortune we have been praying for.'

Chapter 20

It had turned into a particularly pleasant evening. As the summer drew towards its peak, the evenings lengthened beyond anything known in the damp islands Monsarrat and Mrs Mulrooney had come from, and tonight a gentle breeze cooled by the river was finding its way through the kitchen window, which had been opened to receive it. The evening was warm but cool enough, for once, for Hannah to put some dough into a small indentation of the wall where, heated by the fire, it would become bread.

'I have seen people in all sorts of states,' she told Monsarrat as she worked. 'Especially when they first arrive. You should have seen the state of me, now, when I stepped off with a baby in my arms. I was more fortunate than Helen, though. I got to keep him, grow him to manhood. If he had been taken . . . Well, I would have lain there at night imagining him crying for me, wondering why I had abandoned him. Later – and this would be worse – I would have imagined him hardening, making a shell for himself, one which wouldn't have room for me. No wonder she was panicking.'

Panic had always shimmered around the edges of Monsarrat's own consciousness when he was a convict, and occasionally it threatened to return even now, invited back by people such as McAllister. Monsarrat occasionally envied women for their ability to exorcise it by screaming it into the air, something his gender prevented him from doing, dearly as he would have loved to on a few occasions.

Hannah never spent more than a few minutes seated, at least not in this kitchen. She stood, checked on the bread to ensure it was behaving itself and unconsciously started boiling water to warm the teapot.

'But then,' she said, hanging the kettle on its hook to allow the fire to do its work, 'I have to wonder whether there was something else to it, too. She was acting as though it had just happened. Do you think, perhaps, that her soul is so used to insult, so injured, that it tears afresh at the slightest touch?'

'It is a mystery to me, my friend. Why people act the way they do. Particularly women.'

Only very occasionally did Monsarrat wish he had been able to afford a larger kitchen, so he had more space to avoid Mrs Mulrooney's flick of the cleaning cloth.

'I get thoroughly fed up with men complaining that women are incomprehensible. And in that you're no better than any other man I've ever known, Mr Monsarrat, although in other regards you're above most of the rest. All that is required is for you to open your eyes as well as your ears.'

Monsarrat was mildly irritated. For years observation had been his chief strength – one of the only things he was at complete liberty to indulge in. 'Forgive my dullness, then, but perhaps you could advise me on interpreting female communication?'

'Yes, well. As a service to the people of Parramatta, and particularly to its women, I'd be delighted to. When a woman – when anyone – is speaking, you listen to the words, yes?'

'Of course. I believe that is standard practice.'

Mrs Mulrooney narrowed her eyes. Had she not just flailed him with the cleaning cloth, he was certain she would have done so now.

'But do you attend to *how* the person is talking?'

'With their mouth, presumably.'

'Eejit of a man! Are they talking slowly, choosing their words carefully? Are they talking quickly, nervous perhaps, anxious to get everything out? Are they looking directly at you? Is their head down, up, to the side? Are they smiling, frowning, emphasising any word in particular? Do you pay the slightest attention to any of this?'

'Well . . . Of course.'

'Of course you don't. Kindly do me the courtesy of telling me the truth. If you did, you'd have seen the trouble with herself coming.'

'Herself? You mean Sophia?'

'Had you noticed, I wonder, how she was beginning to choose longer words, and say them slowly so that whomever she was speaking to would notice; how she was beginning to hold up her chin and angle her eyes downwards?'

'As it happens, I hadn't. Clearly I require your services as a translator.'

'And I will give them to you, freely and loudly. The first thing I'll say is that if I were a betting woman, I'd wager Sophia didn't speak like that when she boarded the ship in London.'

'I wouldn't have the faintest idea.'

'I would. A London chambermaid? Very few of them speak like duchesses. But she does now. Lord knows where she picked it up. Possibly been keeping an ear out whenever someone of quality's around. Holding her head the way she imagines such a woman would do. She wishes, Mr Monsarrat, to join the gentry. And to hasten that day, she is acting as though it has already happened. And a clerk, even a ticket-of-leave man working for the governor, is not going to get her there.'

'Especially one who has managed to earn the enmity of what passes for aristocracy in Parramatta. Have you heard of Socrates McAllister?' Monsarrat said.

'Of course. Unlike you, I keep my eyes and ears open. I'm surprised Sophia did not make her play for him. Exactly what she's looking for, I'd imagine.'

'He's married, of course. Six children. Wife not well, from what I understand. But that's of no concern.'

'Is it not?'

'Well, at least there is a far greater concern. He warned me against looking too closely at the sales of rum in this town. It's my understanding that he was in competition with Robert Church.'

'So now he has no competition, I take it.'

'None I'm aware of. What he does have is a reasonable amount of influence. Rich, and a magistrate. A formidable combination, and one which I gather he is not hesitant to deploy.'

'Do you believe he might have deployed a weapon deadlier than mere influence?'

'Hard to know. I suppose I will just have to be vigilant.'

'Which will get you nowhere. It may have occurred to you that sadly the killer is not going to confess to the crime if we wait patiently, or ask nicely.'

'Yes, I'm aware of that, Mrs Mulrooney. Thank you very much for the reminder.'

'So we keep an eye out for wrinkles, don't we?'

'I see. And have you noticed anything particularly wrinkly?'

'I have, as it happens.'

'Of course you have.'

'Don't be cheeky. The Nelsons, for a start.'

'The Nelsons? I can certainly see why *she* would worry you, after that incident in the lying-in hospital. But surely *he* is above reproach. Nelson even came by his fortune honestly, from what I understand, which makes him something of a rarity.'

'I've no doubt of it. Mr Nelson seems a fine enough man, although not overjoyed with the idea of convicts in his home, for all that he insists his wife help them.'

'No, well, I imagine he is not alone in that.'

'And his wealth is now more assured of continuing than it was. He was being robbed, you see. Items disappearing from his warehouse.'

'Pity. But not uncommon.'

'Interesting, though, that the thefts stopped at roughly the same time as Robert Church's heart.'

'Perhaps. Hard to see a link, though.'

'Of course it's hard! If it were easy we would not be discussing it. And perhaps there is none. But perhaps there is.'

'And how do we determine that?'

'There's a young fellow named James Henson. A Quaker, like Mr Nelson. He runs one of the warehouses, the one where the thefts were occurring. Seems a nice enough boy. I doubt he would welcome questions about thieving from me, though,' Mrs Mulrooney said.

'But you feel I might have more luck.'

'He can be found down at the docks most mornings. He has a measure of authority to make purchases on Mr Nelson's behalf. He's easy to recognise, too. He is a young man, but his hair is almost entirely white.'

'I shall see what I can do, then.'

'See that you do. In the meantime, I have a few wrinkles of my own.'

'Oh?'

'Well, I've told you about the madwoman, Lizzie. Rebecca has a great deal of affection for her, it seems, despite striking her. But she's reluctant to let me anywhere near her now. After introducing me to her in the first place. Quite odd. And one more thing – I've heard two of the convicts refer to someone called the pirate queen. Any idea who that could be?'

'None at all.'

'Nor I. Except . . . we were told stories of a woman called the pirate queen as children. And the woman's name, as I recall, was Grace O'Malley.'

'Hmm. You think there's a connection with Grace O'Leary?'

'Perhaps. I will see what else is to be known about it, and you have your job to do.'

'And all this time I thought Ralph Eveleigh was my only master.'

'That was foolish of you. I don't know what Mr Eveleigh's like but, as you know, I can be rather unforgiving.'

Monsarrat wasn't sure how forgiving Eveleigh would be were he aware of the course of action his clerk intended to take.

Monsarrat had, as instructed, reported the next morning to Eveleigh before setting out for the Female Factory.

'Mr Monsarrat,' Eveleigh said as he walked in. 'I understand you have been in conversation with Mr McAllister.'

'Yes, he approached me outside church on Sunday,' said Monsarrat. There was no point in dissembling. Eveleigh may already be aware of the details of the conversation, in any case. 'He suggested to me that it might be hazardous to make any further visits to unlicensed drinking establishments.'

'Did he indeed? An interesting caution, coming from him. You didn't discuss any other matter?'

'No, sir. It was my impression that beyond steering me away from the likes of Michael Crotty, Mr McAllister had no interest in me.'

'Probably true. But why he was steering you away in the first place, that's a rather more interesting matter. The man is probably right about the dangers of shebeens. But he himself poses the greater danger. A rich man with the legal power and few discernible scruples is not someone I would wish to see you provoke.'

'Nor one I would wish to provoke myself, sir.'

'In any case, Mr Monsarrat, you're well aware that you are forbidden from looking into this matter except at the Female

Factory itself, during daylight hours. So I suggest that you set about on your business this morning.'

'Of course. With your permission, Mr Eveleigh, I'd also like to call on Dr Preston. Not only was he the man who examined Mr Church's body, but he has treated a great many of the women at the Factory. He may have a useful perspective, now that he's had some time to think about his initial findings.'

'Very well. The hospital, the Factory, and then back here. I look forward to a full report of your activities by tomorrow morning.'

Monsarrat bowed and left the room. He did indeed intend to call on Preston. But first he had a task that had been set for him by a far more intimidating force. He decided to try the docks.

Monsarrat didn't like the docks. There was always a sense of unease when he saw a ship being unloaded, a remnant of the times he'd been unloaded from one himself, against his will. But he also knew that Eveleigh would be carefully quantifying the minutes Monsarrat was out, so his trip there must, of necessity, be a short one.

He stood off to the side as Henson negotiated with the master of the *Phaedra* over some bolts of calico. The proprietor of the Caledonia Inn was also there this morning, doing business with the ship's master over several barrels.

As Henson finished, jammed his broad-brimmed hat on his head and turned to leave, Monsarrat stepped forward. 'Mr Henson?'

'Indeed.'

'Forgive me for accosting you like this. I understand you met my housekeeper, Mrs Hannah Mulrooney, yesterday?'

'Ah, yes! The Irishwoman.'

'Quite correct. It will surprise you, I'm sure, to hear a servant spoken of in this way, but she is a woman of exceptional character whom I hold in high esteem. She told me you might be able to assist me. Your employer is a merchant, I understand? I am interested in purchasing a tea service. The best quality. Does that sort of thing happen to be your line?'

'Most certainly, and as it happens we are expecting a shipment of some of the finest Meissen. Quite delightfully decorated, too. Perhaps you would care to call on me at the warehouse?'

Monsarrat agreed to do just that, and walked away cursing himself for committing to exhaust some of the major's dwindling gift on a tea set which he had not, five minutes before, known he needed.

Chapter 21

Rebecca Nelson, Hannah thought, seemed to quite enjoy ringing the bell on its ornate stand. The bell which marked out the stages of the prisoners' march towards freedom or the grave.

While the new superintendent was finding his feet, Rebecca had made herself indispensable. Already with a good understanding of the daily workings of the Factory, she had so completely occupied the role of unofficial matron that Hannah wondered whether it would cause her some sadness to give it up when the lady from Van Diemen's Land finally sailed up the Parramatta River.

Over the past few days Rebecca had spent hours closeted with Superintendent Rohan in the matron's residence, taking him through the Factory's workings in a detail Hannah had not known she possessed. How many women wore clothes that would need to be replaced. How many had proper shoes – this number counted in the tens. Realistic expectations for the Factory's output, and the adequacy of the rations for the First, Second and Third Class women, including those who were expecting babies.

She even suggested that the superintendent repair the windows in the Third Class penitentiary. 'I'm sure a man of your discernment will understand this,' she said to Mr Rohan. 'We must be above reproach in our treatment of the prisoners, including the one who seems to have ended your predecessor's life. An efficient prison is a humane one, don't you agree? Particularly when the prisoners are partly responsible for producing the funds needed to run the Factory.'

Hannah all the while stood by, cleaning and making tea or being sent out on a variety of errands – to the storekeeper to check on the rations of flour and salt beef, for example, and to the guard outside Grace O'Leary's room for information on her condition.

Entering the Third Class penitentiary today, Hannah was unable to see the turnkey, but had no trouble hearing his low voice and Peggy's giggle from the shadows inside. She crept back out and waited quietly a little to the side of the penitentiary door, so she wouldn't immediately be seen by anyone exiting.

Whatever Peggy was doing with the guard, she was not doing it quickly. Perhaps half an hour passed, and Hannah was wondering whether she would need to abandon her vigil – Rebecca would surely be missing her by now – when the door opened and Peggy stepped out.

She wasn't alone. A moment later, Bronagh followed her and the pair started across the penitentiary yard.

'*Erin go bragh*,' Hannah said.

They immediately turned, gaping at the source of the phrase they had thought was theirs.

'You've a full tummy and clean clothes which fit you,' said Bronagh, in her Cork accent. 'You'd not know the meaning of those words.'

'I said them when you weren't yet born,' said Hannah. 'When they did have a meaning. And they might mean something still, if some from the south hadn't rolled over to have their full tummies rubbed by the British.'

Hannah refused, usually, to give the ancient anger its head.

Not in this place and time. Its rightful targets were dead or across the seas or both, and she feared that if she allowed it to run, it would consume her in the place of those who shot croppies.

But hearing these girls – speaking with the accents of the North Cork militia, of those who had carried a Catholic missal in one hand and a pike covered in Catholic blood in the other – use the phrase as though it were a game, as the price for entry to some childish club and then tell her she understood nothing of their meaning, Hannah felt rage unfurl, push its way to her fingertips so she half-expected to see sparks flying from them.

Bronagh stepped backwards, as though expecting to be struck. 'You were there. The revolution. You saw it?'

'Saw it, took my own part in it, lost everything to it,' Hannah said, in a voice which amazed her, as she had expected it to shake. 'Shall I avenge a few drops of Wexford blood by reporting you? I noticed no guard at Grace O'Leary's door, but I heard him well enough – and you, Peggy. You'd get to spend more time with him as a Third Class prisoner.'

'Do you think I want that? He's foul and rough – not as bad as Church but near enough – and if you understood what we were doing, you would praise me for my sacrifice – one such as you would, anyway, if you really lived through it.'

'Make me understand then.'

Bronagh sighed. 'You've seen how thin everyone is. You know how little food we receive – less even than the pitiful amount rationed for us. Even with the new man, we've not seen an increase in our rations. He's not yet tried to take any of the girls, but who's to say he won't turn into as big a monster as Church? And who's to say he won't start skimming our rations, profiting from our hunger? You profess to care about the fate of the women here. Surely you can see how poorly we are fed and how badly we are clothed.'

Hannah had held out some hope that Mr Rohan's arrival would have put an end to the near-starvation of some of the women. The fact that he had not yet addressed this most urgent of problems concerned her. What was Rebecca doing closeted with him all this time if not urging him to protect the women? Were her pleadings falling on deaf ears, or – and Hannah tried to silence the thought as soon as it occurred to her – was she not pleading at all, beyond the platitudes she used in front of Hannah?

Still, she merely nodded. She did not want to give Bronagh and Peggy any encouragement, any comfort which might stop them revealing the true nature of the situation. And, she had to admit, she was still angry.

'So,' said Bronagh, 'Grace is helping us do what we can.'

'And what can Grace do from her cell? Were you with her, Bronagh, while Peggy was entertaining the turnkey?'

Bronagh looked up to the sky, a futile hope if she was expecting help from that direction. 'I don't suppose Grace's situation can get any worse, even if you do report us. Mine can, though. I am trusting you, now, and praying my trust isn't misplaced,' she said. 'Grace is smart, you see. She seems to know exactly how much the women need to eat to avoid dying from hunger, and how much we can take from the stores without being noticed.'

'But what can she do from behind a locked door?'

'She can tell us what to take and when. From behind her door she can hear when the guards are moving about and when they are not. And she can hear them planning card games. On those nights, we know they'll be drinking rum, we know they'll be less vigilant. So that's when we act.'

'Act? How?'

'We raid the stores, of course.'

'Are you not in fear of your lives when you do this?'

'Of course we are. But all our lives will end from hunger if we do nothing. And we do have some protection. Grace can see the store from her window and she's wonderful at imitating bird-calls. What's that owl one, Peggy? A tawny something or other?'

'Frogsnout, is it?'

'Frogmouth! Tawny frogmouth. They make the oddest sound. And Grace's call could fool even another owl.' Bronagh made her best approximation of the sound. 'But Grace's call is far better than that,' she said. 'And when we hear it, we know we have time to leave the store before whoever is approaching finds us. If she does it twice, we hide in there until the danger has passed, until we hear the call again.'

'How do you transport the food?'

'Oh, we don't take much. Only as little as can be carried in our aprons. And then we share it out in tiny amounts, so that the other women think we're giving of our own rations.'

'So *Erin go bragh* is your watchword. And Grace is the pirate queen?' said Hannah.

'You know the story?'

'Of course I do, eejit of a girl. Wasn't I told it before your ma met your da?'

'If you say it so,' Bronagh said through lips so tense the words were barely able to escape. This woman, Hannah thought, would be used to rebukes and worse from the men who kept her confined, but would not take well to an insult offered by another woman. 'But now I must ask you – what do you intend to do?'

'Nothing,' said Hannah. 'Beyond taking a report back to Mrs Nelson on the condition of Grace O'Leary, as I've been asked to. But I must urge you both to leave off with the raids for the moment. There are going to be more watchers with the new man in place. Be careful. Especially with a murderer about.'

'Murderer? I say saviour,' said Peggy.

'Is your saviour Grace O'Leary?' said Hannah.

'We would be even more grateful to her than we already are if she were. But she can't have been, you see. It is not possible,' said Peggy, twitching her arm to dislodge Bronagh's suddenly encircling hand.

'Why?'

After being so profligate with detail, Hannah saw a sudden caution descend on them. They glanced at each other, as if in mutual warning that they might already have told Hannah, countrywoman though she was, too much.

'There's no question that Grace is an innocent woman. But innocence has no value here for any of us. We were raiding the stores the night he died,' said Peggy. 'So Grace was looking out for us from her window. We saw her – we always look to check that she's there. And while we were inside, we heard two calls. Normally whoever it is passes by quickly, but this time we must have waited ten minutes. Then we heard footsteps – running footsteps – and we thought the guards were running to arrest us. But they passed. And then we heard the signal from Grace. We hurried back to the First Class sleeping quarters, and that was that.'

'Did you ask Grace what happened?' asked Hannah. 'What she'd seen from the window?'

'Of course. But she said it was too dark to see anything and urged us not to ask again.'

'Do you believe she saw something related to the murder of the superintendent?'

'Well, after she told us not to ask anymore, just to accept the fact that the monster was gone, she said, I think, that help can come from unlikely places.'

⁓

Hannah returned to the matron's residence to tell Rebecca and Superintendent Rohan that the turnkey had informed her Grace O'Leary said nothing and did nothing. The turnkey, of course, had said no such thing, but she was confident she would not be contradicted. The man would not want to admit he had been absent from his post.

Hannah knew that Mrs Nelson intended to sit again with the superintendent that afternoon, to present to him a list of supplies she felt the women in the lying-in hospital needed. The midday meal, she thought, would be her best chance to talk to the other women. It was possible Grace may not have been the only watcher that night.

So when Rebecca Nelson reached up her expensively gloved hand towards the bell-pull, Hannah said, 'Would you like me to supervise, today?'

Mrs Nelson always stood by as the mass of women surrounded the communal cooking pots eager to make their rations palatable enough to swallow and knowing they had only a short amount of time in which to do it. Anyone who had not managed to cook and eat their food by the time the bell next rang would go hungry. So if Mrs Nelson saw anyone struggling, perhaps saw one of the newer inmates being pushed aside by long-timers, she would step in, take the girl's rations and cook them herself before handing them back (probably, Hannah suspected, with a prayer of gratitude that her own victuals were considerably better).

Now, Rebecca Nelson frowned slightly at Hannah's suggestion.

'It was just a thought,' Hannah said. 'I watch, of course, the way you manage things. You're an absolute paragon of efficiency, and I seek to model myself on you, you see. So I have a fair idea of what to do, and I know you've been busy enough with Mr Rohan.'

As she was speaking, Hannah was chastising herself for allowing the flattery to reach heights she hadn't intended to scale. She feared Mrs Nelson would feel mocked or, worse, would guess at the truth – that Hannah was trying to get her out of the way.

Indeed, Mrs Nelson did not seem convinced by Hannah's suggestion. As she rang the bell, there was a slight frown when normally the action would make her smile.

'Well ... I suppose ... Having been a convict, though, I'm not sure you'd be allowed.'

'Ah, well, that's no trouble then. I just thought it might be a help to you, you know, with everything you've to do this afternoon. And of course as it is not an official task, I thought it might be all right if you were to hand it off to somebody such as myself. No matter, though. How can I assist you while you're supervising, then?'

Mrs Nelson's eyes were unfocused. She moved her mouth to one side, so that the outline of her teeth was visible underneath the stretched skin of her right cheek.

'Well, as you say, it's not an official position. I suppose it could do no harm, and of course I am extremely busy. You are certain you know what to do?'

'Yes, indeed. Although I'm sure I won't accomplish it with the same finesse as you.' Rebecca smiled, didn't contradict Hannah.

'Very well then. I shall be in the residence, do send a guard if you need me. I look forward to hearing about how you got on!'

So now it was just her. Well, her and two guards and an unaccountable mass of women.

She met the guards' sideways looks with a frank, open stare as she waded into the middle of the group which surrounded one of the cooking pots, looking for those too weak to push their way to the front. Looking, if she were honest, for Helen. Distress was abundant here, but the keenness of Helen's pain spoke of a soul which had not yet grown a callus, and therefore might be open to accepting help and, perhaps, letting slip some information.

Hannah found her on the outskirts of one of the groups of women. She walked up the girl. 'Have you eaten yet?'

Helen shook her head, looking at the ground.

'Well, you'll not find your dinner down there in the dirt. Come on.'

She took Helen's arm and they fetched an earthenware bowl of stew, with its sparse meat and the arse end of a stale loaf, and found a seat on the edge of one of the long benches which hemmed in the dining hall tables.

'Now, you know me, child,' Hannah began. 'You know I'm a friend to you, to all the women at this place.'

Helen nodded.

'Good, very good. Now, you must forgive my bluntness, but I'm concerned about you. Anyone would be in a state, anyone in your position. But I can't help thinking you also seem a little – well – frightened.'

Helen looked down. 'You must think me weak, I suppose.'

'Not a bit of it. Haven't you reason enough for sadness and fright, with little Eliza at the orphan school?'

'I've not done anything wrong, you know.'

Hannah felt a small, burning frustration rising. Mustn't give in to it, she thought. Any sharpness now would just send the girl scurrying back behind those downcast eyes. 'And I'm not suggesting you have. But tell me what scares you.'

'I'm scared the new superintendent will be like the old. And I won't have the pirate queen to protect me.'

'The pirate queen – she took some risks on your behalf?'

'He would come to us at night, you know. To the First Class sleeping quarters. He said he liked young ones. The younger the better.'

Helen's breathing had quickened quite suddenly. Hannah put her arm on the girl's shoulder.

'He said he would never let any other man near us. We were for his personal use, he said. He would come and visit us. He would choose someone and simply lie down on top of them, get to work. The youngest, the most innocent. Some of them virgins. He appeared to like the screams.'

'And Grace O'Leary, she tried to put a stop to it?'

Helen pulled away, looked at Hannah. 'I did not say that name.'

'Neither did you, and there is no need. You are not alone in trusting me. If I was intending to inform, I would have done so.'

Helen exhaled, but her eyes were moving now, skimming over the landscape as they had on the way to Mrs Nelson's house.

'She did what she could,' she said. 'Tried to make him uncomfortable, to organise the other women to stand around him. It didn't work very well. But sometimes, if he was drunk enough, she'd haul him off before he could get underway. Roll him right over so he landed on his back on the ground. He'd looked up at her and laugh. Said she would be punished. Then he'd say we were all whores anyway, and a man of his distinction shouldn't be forced so low, and he'd stagger out.'

'And she did that for you.'

'God, I tell you, his breath was almost the worst of it. The man stank, in a way in which no free man has a right to. And he was heavy, lying there, breathing rum.'

'So he didn't get you some nights. But there were other nights?'

'Yes, for years. It's how I got Eliza. He didn't care about her, about any of them. She would be asleep, delicate as glass, holding my hand, and he would come and dump her on the floor to get her out of the way. She watched. Always. She is spared that, now, at least, in the orphan school.'

'Did the pirate queen try to stop that?'

'When she could. But she disappeared. After the riots. And as soon as she wasn't here, he came back.'

'For you.'

'He wasn't drunk the next time. He smiled when I cried. He pressed my arms, held them so hard. And then he left and came back the next night. And every time, afterwards, I would cry and say I wanted to go home. The others, they all pretended to be asleep, but they can't have been. So they would have heard me saying it. Home is lost to me, but I wish I was home.'

Helen had begun to cry. Rocking backwards and forwards, her stew uneaten. Hannah tried to get her to take a mouthful, but she seemed not to see. All she would say was 'home', over and over.

One of the guards rang the bell. Hannah helped Helen to her feet. Whispered in her ear, 'You must calm down now, my love, you must. I am sorry for causing you distress. Dry your eyes now.

I don't think you weak, but others might. And you know yourself what happens to the weak here.'

Helen nodded, wiped her eyes on a calico sleeve that was too short for her arm, and joined the rest of the women going into the workrooms.

How many of them, thought Hannah, had suffered visits from the foul Robert Church? Would she have encountered Church, or one like him, if she'd arrived late enough to be sent to the Factory? She suspected she knew the answer.

Chapter 22

Monsarrat watched Dr Homer Preston dab ineffectually at an ink spot on his shirt. The stain had only been there for a minute or two, the ink droplet sent flying through the air towards him by Napoleon, who had decided that a conference without him could not be allowed to proceed. The cat had very deliberately left his nest near Homer's feet, jumped onto the desk and walked across, trailing his tail under Homer's nose, languidly stretching until his front paws reached the ink pot, and then stretching that little bit further until it moved off the desk and onto the floor.

'So – can I rely on your discretion?' Monsarrat asked.

'As much as you can on anyone's, Hugh.'

'Not exactly the firm commitment I was after, Homer.'

'Listen, Hugh, I'm not the type to spread rumours, you must know that. And there are some I could spread, oh my goodness, yes. You see everything in this place. Dysentery, smallpox and death do more for equality than any revolution.'

For his part, Monsarrat was somewhat relieved to be here on an Eveleigh-sanctioned visit. The secretary's growing frustration with him and his lack of progress was all too evident, and

Monsarrat suspected that once Eveleigh had made a decision that a cause was lost, he was not to be easily swayed.

'So,' Homer continued, 'it's that Church business you're here on, I suppose.'

'Yes, it is.'

'I understood you had a rather convenient perpetrator, a convict who was all but caught in the act?'

'Not as simple as that, I'm afraid. And somewhat too convenient. I don't know about your life, Homer, but convenience has not been a hallmark of mine. Not unless someone stands to gain from it.'

'So, you have someone else in mind?'

'Well, a great many someone elses. Mr Church was unmourned.'

'You're thinking of McAllister?'

Monsarrat fervently hoped that Homer would keep the conversation to himself. An accusation against Socrates McAllister, unless backed by the strongest evidence, was almost too dangerous to contemplate. He employed a crude but effective instrument which had served him well in the past – answering with a question of his own.

'Ah. You saw that conversation, did you?'

'McAllister loves delivering warnings outside church. With his good friend Bulmer looking on for spiritual support. You are not the first to have been warned about this or that – in the most urbane way, of course. If something cannot be accomplished with urbanity, Mr McAllister doesn't attempt it.'

'I see. And have you been the recipient of one of these warnings yourself?'

Homer's office had a door every bit as flimsy as the one inexpertly hung on Monsarrat's convict hut in Port Macquarie. And Monsarrat suspected very few people thought twice about opening it without the courtesy of knocking. Perhaps that was why Homer was standing now.

'Do you know what, Mr Monsarrat? Hospitals are dreadful places. They smell. And they're full of the sick, the dying, and of course the dead. I fancy a walk by the river, myself, and I believe Napoleon needs to be left in Coventry for a while, to lick the ink off his paws and contemplate his transgressions. Would you care to join me?'

The river seemed to be feeling the heat too, once they got to it. The earlier high tide which had enabled the merchant ships to come and do business with the likes of Henson had bled out, leaching the waters all the way back along the river's length and out to the Tasman Sea, promising to replenish them a while later.

But at the moment the grass sloping downwards from the low riverside buildings met exposed mudflats, which gave off the smell of rotting vegetation, while the water that remained was brown and moving so slowly it was hard to discern any movement at all.

'Not much more fragrant here,' remarked Monsarrat.

'Sadly not. Somewhat more private, though. You asked if I'd been warned about anything by McAllister. One of the few things more dangerous than bringing yourself to his attention to the extent that he feels he needs to warn you, is discussing that warning later.'

'You fear him, then.'

'I fear what he can do. Did you enjoy your time as a convict, Hugh? No, nor did I, and I do not wish to revisit it. Sending either of us back into penal servitude would be a minute's work for him, sitting there on the bench.'

'So what did you do to bring yourself to Mr McAllister's attention?'

'I was unwise enough to be in a position to be useful to him. You worked for a time, did you not, for a magistrate called Samuel Cruden?'

'Yes, I did. I was a tutor to his sons.'

'You may have noticed, then, that he is no longer on the bench.'

Monsarrat had, actually. He intended at some point to find out what had become of the man. Perhaps even find him, thank him. Cruden had been as kind to Monsarrat as was possible within the strictures of the man's position, and while it was his ruling that had sent Monsarrat to Port Macquarie as a second offender, he had done so with reluctance, bound by the very specific laws governing breaches of the conditions of tickets of leave.

'Do you know what has become of him? Is he still out in Windsor?'

'As far as I'm aware. He's had some success as a pastoralist, like Bulmer and McAllister – God knows how these judicial types manage to get sheep to fuck each other, but they do.'

'And the circumstances of his leaving the bench?'

'I shall tell you, Monsarrat, but I must warn you to listen to the end before passing judgement. Because, you see, I was instrumental in his removal.'

Monsarrat stared at Preston. He knew the man was no paragon. But he hoped the doctor hadn't been a willing tool for McAllister. He didn't want to stop liking him.

'Very well, I'll listen.'

Preston was silent for a moment.

'My listening, of course, is conditional on your speaking,' said Monsarrat.

'Yes, yes. All right. Just gathering my thoughts. So, a year ago – it must've been, because I remember the heat – I was asked to examine a woman who was an assigned convict in Cruden's household.'

'Asked by who?'

'By Socrates McAllister. It was known, generally, that he and Cruden did not get along. They disagreed on certain matters when it came to severity of punishment – Cruden felt the lash never reformed anyone, while McAllister felt the more of it the better, and often lamented Governor Macquarie's soft-heartedness when it came to restricting the maximum number of lashes to one hundred.'

'I see.'

'Not only that, but Cruden might have discovered something of McAllister's less . . . shall we say . . . magisterial activities. Certainly he remarked – often enough for it to trickle its way through to me, and no doubt others – that McAllister was not a fit character to sit on the bench. And Cruden, well, he was known as a man of conviction. He would not say such things unless he intended to act on them. So it is reasonable to assume that McAllister felt his position was under threat.'

'And why did he ask you to examine the convict woman?'

'He asked me to look for signs of molestation. And he asked me to enquire of the woman as to the identity of her molester.'

'Did you find anything?'

'I found marks which could certainly have indicated molestation. Bruises on her upper arms, as though someone had pinioned her. Certain injuries in relevant areas, which I'd rather not go into. So, as I had been instructed, I asked her who'd injured her. She claimed it was Cruden.'

'I can't believe that for a moment, Homer. The man doesn't have it in him.'

'So I thought. But it wouldn't have been the first time someone with an outwardly moderate bearing turned out to be a monster. And it must be remembered that Mr Cruden had an unorthodox domestic arrangement.'

This was true. When Monsarrat was tutor to the Cruden boys, it was an open secret that the man shared a bed with his housekeeper, an Irish ticket-of-leave woman like Hannah Mulrooney, who indulged his boys as though she were their mother. Their own mother had died in their infancy, and with a distracted father and a woman whose response to infractions was to bake them little cakes, they had no reason to moderate their good-natured but sometimes disruptive exuberance.

Monsarrat had seen no harm in the relationship then, and didn't now. But harm there clearly was, for it had obviously been used against Cruden.

'So you reported your findings to McAllister?'

'Of course. I might add that it was entirely reasonable to do so – to tell the authorities what I had seen and heard. I didn't feel I was in a position to judge Cruden one way or the other, only the physical evidence in front of me.'

'What did McAllister do?'

'Well, he publicly accused Cruden. Using my report as evidence. Cruden denied it, of course, but there were a great many who were not inclined to believe him. Ultimately he resigned from the bench. It's my understanding he intended to set in motion a process to clear his name, but if he continues to hold that objective, I don't know how far he's come with it.'

'Was that the end to it?'

'Not quite. I became aware shortly afterwards that the convict woman in question had suddenly been given a ticket of leave – two years early. She'd also been married off to a former convict – a relatively prosperous one too, a farrier. I gather she is now living out in Camden in a handsome cottage with her husband. Had her sentence been allowed to run its course, she would still be an assigned convict servant, or back in the Female Factory.'

'So you think McAllister bribed her to speak against Cruden.'

'I'm not saying that, Hugh. I am simply noting a series of interesting events. But I'll be honest, if I had known in advance what the outcome would be, I might have moderated my report.'

'You were complicit in calumny, in the destruction of a good man!'

Preston tensed, kicked a river pebble with his shoe. 'A few things you need to understand, Hugh. I am not a saint and have never claimed to be one, so any attempt to hold me to saintly standards will only frustrate you. I was following procedure, and obviously did not predict the events to come.'

'Do you think him capable of it? McAllister?'

'I would like to think not, particularly given the power he holds. But . . . I think most people are capable of doing whatever is required to ensure their survival. Or the survival of their reputation, which is as precious as life to someone like McAllister.'

'A grim assessment.'

'And an accurate one, I am afraid.'

'A shame the man's tall, given what you told me when we looked at Church's body.'

'Don't set too much store by that, Hugh. I only said the murderer could have been a woman. It could also have been a man, either short or crouched down. Anyway, McAllister certainly has the funds to hire people, male or female, tall or short.'

Monsarrat sighed. The more he found out, the less he knew.

'Tell me, Homer. Moral corruption among the great and good is no surprise. But what of moral rectitude among base criminals? Can that be found as easily, do you think?'

Preston thought for a moment.

'I've seen it, from time to time. You must have as well. The man who shares his rations with someone weaker. The man who takes punishment for another on the road gangs. And very little thanks they get for it, unless there is thanks in the afterlife, to which they commit themselves early if they behave in that manner. Now, this is no philosophical question. You have a reason for asking.'

'I do, and I'd be happy to enlighten you. On a confidential basis, of course. But if you'd indulge me another question? You treat the women in the Factory from time to time. Have you noticed any change in their condition recently? For example, since the riot?'

'What sort of change?'

'Well, anything. But particularly, I suppose, something that would point to a change in their rations. Or evidence of violence, perhaps. Anything like that. Perhaps even marks similar to those you saw on Cruden's convict.'

'Well, the poor things are still underfed, and the riot wasn't long ago. I was there the week before Church was killed to see the women in the lying-in hospital and checking over a few of the others while I was at it. They all claimed they were going hungry, but that's not unusual.'

The edge of Preston's boot had been unconsciously turning up pebbles as he walked, and then drawing back and kicking them. He smiled when any of the stones plopped into the river then stared for a moment at the ripples they made.

Now he stopped short. 'I'll tell you what though. Something I have noticed, and since the riot, too. The new girls. They asked me to look them over, make sure they're not carrying any sort of pestilence which could infect the whole Factory – God, can you imagine what a plague could do in those close quarters? And of late many of them have exhibited the same type of injury.'

'Injury? You mean they were wounded?'

'Nothing open, no blood. But a number of them had bruising on their upper arms. Almost encircling them, actually. And worse than the bruising on the woman I examined for McAllister.'

'How many had those marks, would you say? What proportion?'

'Hard to say. But I'll tell you this – I only saw those marks on the young ones.'

'And what do you think made them? Could it have been a hand?'

'Could have been. But maybe not. Maybe the old lags like to assert their superiority over the new ones. Women attacking other women is a fairly common occurrence behind those walls, I understand.'

'Or maybe it was a man's hand,' said Monsarrat.

'Or maybe it was no hand at all. I asked the girls if they were being ill-treated – I always do – and they said no. Not with a great deal of conviction, but I don't think those new to the Factory do anything emphatically. I think, for the most part, they try to escape notice.'

'Homer, will you do me a great favour? Will you let me know whether, on your next visit to examine the women, you notice the same?'

'Only if you tell me what you're driving at. God's blood, Hugh, you're harder than a corpse to get information out of.'

'Very well then. But I must caution you, nothing's confirmed, nothing is double-checked, nothing is confessed. The information is all supposition and speculation on my part.'

'My favourite kind!'

'Well, that convenient convict you mentioned earlier. Her name is Grace O'Leary. From what I understand, she used to protect the younger ones from the nocturnal attentions of our one-eyed friend. Then of course she started the riot, as a result of which she was demoted to the Third Class and is no longer in a position to intervene.'

'That's what happens to rebels. It's why I try to rebel as little as possible.'

'Ah, but Homer, some things are worth a rebellion or two. And saving this woman's life may well be one of them. Because those marks, you see – I believe they were put there by Church. And I don't think it's a coincidence that they appeared more often after O'Leary was moved to the Third Class. Because without her, there was nothing standing between the girls and Church but a stroll across the yard and a flimsy wooden door.'

❧

He had only done what his superior had instructed, after all, he told himself. A trip to see the doctor on the way to the Female Factory. All approved. But Monsarrat knew Eveleigh would not have approved of the content of the conversation. He hoped there was never any need for his master to hear of it.

Next he set his mind to another task for which he could not be reproached. Eveleigh had asked Monsarrat to introduce himself to the new superintendent. Now Monsarrat planned to have another conversation of which he hoped Eveleigh would never hear.

Scores of female voices scurried through the hot air to reach him, the vibration of footfalls burrowing through the dirt underneath his boots. It must be the meal hour.

The gate guard directed him to the superintendent's residence, the place where the wasted Henrietta Church had poured rum down her throat until she could no longer taste it. Monsarrat didn't know quite what to expect, but he knew the place would be clean now, scrubbed and scoured and aired: Hannah had told him she'd given it a going over.

It wasn't the superintendent who answered, but Rebecca Nelson.

'Mr Monsarrat! How marvellous. I do hope you're not finding the continuing absences of your housekeeper too difficult. You certainly look none the worse for wear, but I'm sure it can't be easy and I am so grateful to you for lending her. I was just telling Mr Rohan what a tremendous help she's been to me.'

Monsarrat stepped out of the glaring sun into the small front room, blinking to adjust his eyes, aware it must make him look somewhat myopic.

The man at the table may have been somewhat myopic himself. He had a pince-nez perched on his nose, a glass butterfly with smudged wings, through which he had no doubt been perusing the great number of documents spread out on the table. Not the neat stacks which decorated Eveleigh's desk, and Monsarrat's own. A blanket of paper which may have had some organising principle, but not one Monsarrat could discern.

Monsarrat introduced himself as the clerk to the governor's secretary. 'Mr Eveleigh begs your pardon that he has not had a chance to call on you himself, sir, and intends to do so at the earliest opportunity. In the interim, he has sent me to assure you that the governor's staff will provide you with any assistance you need, and to inquire whether we can do anything for you at present.'

Mr Rohan nodded, mumbled polite acknowledgements, and said (perhaps a little sceptically) that of course he understood the governor's secretary was a man with a great many tasks to attend to, especially in the empty space between one governor and another.

The Factory's management committee had appointed Mr Rohan, and Monsarrat had no idea what their selection criteria were, but he presumed they'd want someone staid, above reproach. And someone pliable. So he knew he should assume that anything he said to Rohan might find its way to McAllister. That he should really state nothing of any importance; perhaps simply conduct an inconsequential polite conversation and then take his leave.

So it was with a degree of horror that he heard himself saying, 'Superintendent, if I may have a moment of your time, I'd like to discuss with you prisoner Grace O'Leary.'

'Ah. The riotous Irish woman. Very probably responsible for removing my predecessor from this world. What of her?'

'Well, as a man such as yourself will appreciate, it's a delicate issue, this whole business. Unfortunate, of course. Would that it hadn't happened . . . But as it has Mr Eveleigh's most anxious for it to be dealt with using the utmost discretion.'

'Yes, I suppose that's wise. Although it may be somewhat late for discretion. Have you seen the *Chronicle*?'

The *Sydney Chronicle* was a newspaper that delighted in pointing out what it saw as the failures of government. And one of the failures it particularly enjoyed reporting on was the government's inability to control the convict population. Monsarrat had seen several copies of the paper at Government House over the past few months. He had read about the riots at the Female Factory, which had occurred while he was still at Port Macquarie. He recalled that the paper rather enjoyed using language which could be described as florid, and had referred to the rioting women as 'Amazonian banditti', a phrase few in the colony would have heard before.

The *Chronicle* had little sympathy for those it had styled Amazonians, regarding the women in the Third Class as a lost cause. 'The awful fact is,' the paper opined, 'that the softer sex, to the disgrace of human nature, are a thousand times more obdurate in their minds, and determined in their vicious career, than the men.'

And now the superintendent was excavating a more recent issue among the scrambled documents, and sliding it across to Monsarrat.

'We have heard,' the paper said,

of the most heinous murder of the superintendent of the Parramatta Female Factory, Mr Robert Church.

Such a man is to be praised for taking on what must be described as an almost impossible task: the control of the colony's most refractory females.

Our readers will remember that the damsels inhabiting the Parramatta institution took umbrage to justly and lawfully imposed discipline, responding by rampaging through the streets. It was only the swift response of Church and several constables which prevented the citizenry of that fair town from coming to injury.

The Valkyrie thought to have concocted the idea for the insurrection, and to have urged other females in the commission of it, is called Grace O'Leary, and our correspondent informs us she has been confined to a cell in the Third Class penitentiary since being marched back through the Factory gates.

Now, as the constabulary investigates the foul slaying of the former superintendent, there are those who believe this woman may have had some part to play in it.

Yet although the superintendent was struck down on the grounds of the Factory itself, and although O'Leary and her cohorts might be presumed to have much to gain from his demise, no charges have been laid.

We understand that our legal system allows some benefit of the doubt to be given to those accused of crime, and that processes must be followed. But surely in the case of a woman fallen once from respectable society, and then again from the First Class to the Third Class at the Factory, some assumptions can be forgiven.

If the government fails to see what is so clear to others, fails to call this woman to account for the most wilful murder of her better, the honest citizens of Parramatta could be forgiven for questioning the strength of the very system of order on which they rely for daily protection.

Monsarrat looked up at the superintendent. His intention had been to acquaint the man with the issues Grace O'Leary had raised. He could see now that this course of action would be futile. Worse, the superintendent might decide he could not be relied on to extract the necessary information, and cut off his access to the Factory altogether.

'Ah, yes, the *Chronicle* is always rather entertaining,' he said.

'I find very little entertaining about that article, Mr Monsarrat. And I'm given to understand that part of the delay in charging the woman has been brought about by your enquiries. Is that correct?'

'I certainly hope not, sir, and I do apologise if that's the case, as my objective has always been to act with the greatest expediency.'

'Nevertheless, you have insisted on several interviews with her.'

'Indeed, sir, at the direction of Mr Eveleigh. In a matter of this gravity, he feels it is imperative to demonstrate that due process has been followed, and to present an unassailable case to the court in order to save time and money in securing a conviction. It is for that purpose that I have interviewed her, in order to prepare evidence to be passed to the police and the courts.'

'And what has she said to you in these interviews?'

'Only that she is innocent of the crime.'

'And you have seen her – wait – twice now? Yet all you have managed to attain has been a denial?'

'Superintendent – here we stray into matters which are somewhat . . . vivid. Perhaps . . .'

Rebecca, who had been tidying papers, looked up at this. 'You are kind, Mr Monsarrat, to be so scrupulous in ensuring nothing inappropriate falls on my ears. I shall make it easy for you, shall I? Leave you two gentlemen to discuss the issue? I shall go and check on Mrs Mulrooney, ensure the convicts haven't eaten her for lunch.'

After she left, Monsarrat turned back to the superintendent. 'Prisoner O'Leary did, of course, communicate more than a simple denial to me during the course of our interviews, sir. She gave me to understand that Mr Church had been using some of the younger prisoners to satisfy his carnal appetites, and, further, that he had been siphoning off the prisoners' rations to sell for his own profit.'

'Don't be so stupid, man, of course she'd say that! They would do anything, these ones, to cast blame on those who are tasked with controlling them. I fully expect to hear similar allegations in regard to myself, despite the fact that my behaviour is never less than upright. So I ask you again, Mr Monsarrat, why can you not simply conclude your interview so that charges may be laid?'

'No one wishes more than I to have this matter concluded, sir. Which is, in truth, part of the reason I have come today. I feel, sir, that I might be able to extract the confession you desire with one more interview. With your kind permission, of course.'

The superintendent exhaled sharply through his nostrils.

'Very well then. As you have been helpful enough to present a member of your household to assist Mrs Nelson, you may arrive at ten tomorrow morning to conduct one last interview with the O'Leary woman. But I must warn you that should you fail I will most certainly be taking the matter up with your employer, and several others who wield considerable influence in this place.'

Chapter 23

Hannah saw Monsarrat as he crossed the yard. He looked over and nodded, but he was walking with his hands clasped behind his back – a sure sign of some sort of consternation.

The women were trickling back to their work, into the rooms where even the dust smelled burned, under the eyes of men who didn't care how uncomfortable they were as long as they met their quota and didn't give any trouble.

Perhaps Monsarrat had been sent to see Rohan. She would be most interested to hear what he had to say this evening, as well as to find out why he was looking towards the Third Class penitentiary in an apparent state of agitation.

Tonight she would have some information of her own, of course. The discussion with Helen had been in equal parts horrifying and useful.

As the yard drained of all but Hannah, she glanced up to the second-storey window she knew to be Lizzie's. She looked around a few times for Rebecca, felt in the pocket of her skirt, closed her fingers around the metal in it. Rebecca sometimes entrusted her with the keys to various Factory buildings. Not the gaol, of course, or the stores, but some offices and workrooms and so on.

'I'm so absent-minded, Hannah. And I don't want to ruin the line of my dress with this big metal lump. Here, you take them. Then I'll know where they are,' she had said.

And really Mrs Nelson had not left her with any instructions as to what not to do with the keys. Any instructions at all, really. While she seemed to have changed her mind about Hannah visiting Lizzie, she had never actually forbidden it.

'The woman isn't here to instruct me one way or the other,' she muttered to herself, and made for the stairs.

As she hurried up the stairs to Lizzie's floor, Hannah felt nervous. 'You've faced worse than an old madwoman,' she said to herself. Had anyone been there to remind her that the old woman was around the same age as her, they'd have felt the corner of her cleaning cloth.

She knocked, gently. She suspected Lizzie wouldn't answer, but it seemed somehow worse to enter without knocking than it did to use the keys without permission in the first place.

She heard no sounds of movement from within the room so she turned the key and put her hand to the door, and scolded herself when she noticed it was trembling. She pushed. Those hinges were in a state, by the looks of them.

Lizzie lay on her small cot, facing the wall, not moving. A bowl of food lay untouched on the floor beside her. For a moment Hannah was concerned enough to watch to see whether Lizzie was breathing.

She was. It wasn't the slow, deep breathing of the sleeper, either. Hannah was sure that Lizzie was awake.

'Hello, Lizzie,' she said quietly.

Lizzie didn't move. But she spoke. 'Eddie scolded me for hitting you. But you shouldn't have done it. You shouldn't have done that to my Richard.'

'I did nothing to your Richard, nor to any one of yours,' Hannah said, keeping her voice soft, a soothing, singsong cadence she might have used to comfort Padraig when he was a boy. 'And you did nothing to my Colm, or to my father. Other people did all that. It was a long time ago, now, you know.'

'A month may be a long time for you, but not for me,' Lizzie said.

Hannah was walking very slowly closer to the bed. Half-bracing herself for the kind of attack only the insane seemed capable of.

'Lizzie, it was not a month ago. It was twenty-seven years. There are men who were not born then who are now officers in His Majesty's army.'

'My Richard might have been an officer in the army. He's dead now. The Irish killed him.'

'It was a terrible time, wasn't it?' said Hannah, reaching the cot. 'My son is grown now, and he had not yet been conceived when the trouble started, but I can still smell the smoke from the burning thatch, from the houses. I still hear the yells.'

'Yes, they never stop,' said Lizzie. 'Nor the screams, neither. But the burning – the burning of wood and thatch, I wish that was the worst of it. Those of us in our town, we smelled something different.'

'What did you smell, Lizzie?'

'When people burn, they smell like lamb,' Lizzie said, with a suddenly cheerful tone. 'Imagine that! You'd never have expected it, would you? Lamb roast. It's my favourite.'

She rolled over to look at Hannah. She was smiling, but tears were falling down her cheeks.

'Was it you? Did you?' she asked.

'No, Lizzie, it wasn't me. What happened to your dear ones also happened to mine. And I am no more pleased by the death of yours than I was by the death of mine.'

'Did yours die in Scullabogue too?'

Hannah almost fainted when she heard the name. Scullabogue. A place her father wouldn't discuss, nor Colm. The place that had made her realise brutality was not confined to the British. For after the rebels had lined up and shot some of the Scullabogue Protestants, they'd set alight a barn containing as many as two hundred other Protestants, including women and children. Twice the desperate occupants had managed to break down the barn door. But they were unable to get past the pikemen stationed there, who drove them back in. During one of the skirmishes a two-year-old child had managed to crawl through the feet of the rebels, moving as fast as he could towards the clear air. His last breath would have tasted of smoke. When he was noticed, he was piked through.

'No,' she said quietly. 'No, Lizzie, but they didn't die far from there. And any such death in any place is inexcusable. I can understand why hearing an Irish voice upset you so.'

'It's just thinking of Richard, you see. The last time I saw him, my head was full of Irish voices.'

'Was he a yeoman?'

'A yeoman! What a ridiculous idea!' Lizzie emitted a giggle, a surprisingly girlish one at that.

'But you said he might have been an officer.'

'He might have been, had he lived long enough. I left him with my sister, you see, told them to hide in the barn while I ran to try to get help. He was in the barn when they burned it. Yes, he might have been an officer. He certainly enjoyed waving a sword around. But when they burned him in the barn, you see, he was only three years old.'

Lizzie's face crumpled, almost fell in on itself, and she began to cry. Not dainty tears, nor the gasping of Helen. A keen, a wail, consistent, flat and hopeless.

Hannah sat down next to her and drew her into an embrace, wondering if she would be rebuffed. She wasn't, and for some minutes they sat there as Lizzie leaked and wailed onto Hannah's shoulder.

'Do you think you can stop them?' Lizzie asked finally. 'Maybe there's still time. Before anyone else dies.'

'Lizzie, my love. It's over. You can rest, now. It won't happen to anyone else.'

Hannah knew this was a ridiculous statement. It could happen again. But Lizzie was not in the kind of state to deal with nuances.

'Perhaps, Lizzie, we should try to be friends. People being friends – that's the best way to stop this sort of thing, isn't it?'

'Friends. Yes. Friends don't kill each other. Eddie said you just wanted to be nice. That's why she was so cross at me for hitting you. She couldn't understand why I would do that to someone who was just trying to be nice. And she told me it was rude to use that name in front of you.'

'Lizzie, can I ask you a question? Who is Eddie?'

'You know Eddie! You were here with her the other day!' Lizzie's face clouded then. 'Was it you? Or someone who looked like you? You're not a croppy in disguise, are you?'

'No, no. It was me. But the lady who brought me here the other day is called Rebecca.'

'She does like to pretend,' said Lizzie fondly, as though she was talking of an imaginative child. 'She always did. At night she would tell stories, you see. About dragons and castles, mostly, and handsome princes rescuing damsels. Not very popular with some, though. Not enough handsome princes to go around.'

'She told stories? To you? Does she come to you at night to do that?'

'No, of course not – she didn't need to come. She was already there. In the dormitory, with the rest of us. She spoke so beautifully. She sounded like a princess herself; it was hard to remember that she was no different.'

'No different from the rest of you? But she's a free lady.'

'Yes. She's a clever girl. But she'll always be Eddie to me.'

'Are you sure, Lizzie? It is a boy's name.'

'Well, I have known boys called Eddie, it is true,' Lizzie said. 'But my Eddie, her name is Edwina.'

'And you're certain it's the same woman, Lizzie?'

'I am not a liar,' Lizzie said, beginning to turn away. 'I've never seen hair like that on anyone else.'

'I know you're not, Lizzie. But the woman you call Eddie is the wife of a prosperous merchant, a Quaker at that. She's a free woman.'

'Yes, she's done well for herself.' Lizzie began to chuckle now. 'A kind man, too. Not like Robert Church.'

'Do you know what happened to him? Has Rebecca told you? Eddie, I mean? What did she say?'

A look of suspicion began to bleed into Lizzie's eyes. 'Eddie says I mustn't tell tales,' she said, like a child.

Of course, Lizzie could be imagining things, thought Hannah. There may indeed have been an Edwina living here, and she may indeed have looked like Rebecca yet borne no other similarity to her. But it didn't seem entirely likely.

Now, she left Lizzie's side and walked over to the window, suddenly anxious to get a sense of the vantage point Lizzie would have had if she'd seen the attack on Robert Church.

The yard was in almost full view. Church's body had been found in the middle of it. If he'd fallen where he was stabbed – and it was hard to see how he wouldn't have, for why would an assailant move the body from a secluded spot into plain view – anyone standing where Hannah was now would have had an unimpeded view of the whole business, although whether they could have recognised the murderer from this distance at night was a question Hannah couldn't answer.

But she could see Rebecca clearly enough now, walking across the empty space, seemingly looking for someone. She turned back from the window.

'Lizzie, does it get lonely here?'

'Sometimes, I suppose. I have my thoughts to keep me company, but sometimes they are thoughts I don't want.'

'Would you like me to come and sit with you one evening?'

Lizzie looked doubtful.

'I could bring shortbread.'

'I've always loved shortbread,' said Lizzie.

'So perhaps one evening soon I will visit you and help you count off the dark hours with the aid of my best shortbread.'

Lizzie said nothing, but smiled.

'One thing, though, Lizzie,' Hannah said. 'Rebecca – Eddie – said you mustn't tell tales, and she was right. My visits should be a secret. Not something to tell tales about. Do you understand?'

Lizzie nodded solemnly. 'When you come, bring some shortbread for Richard, too,' she said. 'He does love it. Sometimes the promise of it is the only way I can get him into bed of an evening.'

Chapter 24

Monsarrat did not possess a horse. The major's money wouldn't last forever, and in any case he didn't need one for the short distance between his cottage and Government House, both north of the river.

But now a trip to Windsor from Parramatta – the same journey that had seen him lose his first ticket of leave – became, in his mind, crucial.

After leaving a note on his kitchen table telling Hannah not to expect him home that night (there were certainly advantages to her new literacy), he was able to find a carter going to Windsor who was willing to take him for a small fee. Unfortunately the carter wasn't returning that night, so Monsarrat would either have to find lodgings, rely on Cruden's generosity, should he find the man at home, or walk through the night to be back at his desk tomorrow.

He told himself that it wasn't deceptive to keep Eveleigh ignorant of his conversation with Preston and his plans to visit Cruden. After all, one was a confidential communication with a friend, the other a social visit in his own hours.

Still, he felt uneasy about the journey, and was grateful for the elongated daylight hours which November brought with it – he would have hated to be on the road with a silent carter he had never met as night fell.

The man was kind enough to deposit him outside the Cruden residence – or at least what he hoped was still the Cruden residence. He did not know whether Cruden's pastoral activities had managed to make up for the shortfall in his magistrate's stipend.

It seemed he was in luck, for the door was opened by one of the Cruden boys, a young man now – Will. Tall and beginning to fill out around the shoulders, with the same grin and impatient shuffle Monsarrat remembered from the schoolhouse more than two years ago.

Will employed that grin when he saw who was at the door. 'I regret to inform you, Mr Monsarrat, that my education is now complete, so I have no further need of you.'

Monsarrat smiled back. He had wondered, recently, whether there was anyone in his world save Hannah who did not have a hidden agenda, and the uncomplicated and unapologetic larrikinism of Will was surprisingly comforting.

'Your education will never be complete, young Cruden, and you'd profit to remember that.'

Will stepped forward and surprised Monsarrat by enfolding him in a gangly, long-limbed embrace. 'And what is it that *does* bring you here, Mr Monsarrat?' he asked, standing aside to admit Monsarrat to the house, and leading him past the rooms where the pair of them, and Will's younger brother, had spent many hours wrestling with algebra and Latin conjugations of verbs. 'I take it you are no longer being fed and clothed by His Majesty?'

'After a fashion I suppose I still am. I am in the employ of the private secretary to the governor.'

'Must be a fairly easy job, with no governor in residence.'

'You'd be surprised to know, Master Will, that a tendency towards industry finds its own outlet.'

'I hope never to be able to confirm that statement, Mr Monsarrat. In any case, I imagine you want to see Father.'

'Yes, if it is convenient. And I do apologise for arriving without notice. I imagine he's busy.'

Will's smile faded for a moment. 'Less so than he was. He receives few visitors, now, and turns most of them away. Nevertheless, I'm certain he'll make an exception in your case – if only because you might still be able to curb some of my worst excesses. Would you mind taking a seat in the parlour? I'll tell him you're here.'

The Samuel Cruden who walked into the room a few minutes later was almost unrecognisable to Monsarrat. Still dressed austerely, still with his grey hair swept back from his temples. But thin and slow, eyes darting to the side as he approached Monsarrat, as if to ascertain whether an ambush was coming. His voice, though, was as clear and strong as it had been when it had echoed from the bench.

'Mr Monsarrat! What a delight – it hasn't been three years, has it?'

As briefly as he could, Monsarrat told Cruden of the events at Port Macquarie which had led him to an early ticket of leave.

'The governor's office! I always knew you would rise, given the chance – and if you maintained the presence of mind to get out of your own way every so often. It's very kind of you to call. I imagine that you've heard my circumstances are altered now.'

'I had, actually, sir. In fact, that's why I've come.'

Cruden frowned. 'If it's all the same to you, Monsarrat, I'd just as soon not go over the whole business again. Should you wish to satisfy yourself as to the particulars, there are many lurid accounts in the *Chronicle*.'

'Forgive me, sir. It's not prurience which brings me here. Rather, I am currently the subject of a certain amount of attention from the agent of your undoing – and I think it is possible, even plausible, that he more permanently dispatched another man who was inconvenient to him.'

Cruden sighed, sat down, his eyes still probing the corners of the room. 'Very well, then. I suppose you'd better tell me.'

'You've heard of the murder of Robert Church, the super-intendent of the Female Factory?'

'Yes. A barbarous end, but from what I understand he is unmourned.'

'Nevertheless, His Majesty's government wishes his killer brought to justice, naturally.'

'Naturally.'

'The current suspect is a convict at the Female Factory. But – and I must ask you never to repeat what I am about to say . . .'

Cruden nodded.

'It has come to my attention that Mr Church might have been in competition with Socrates McAllister in the business of sly grog.'

'Oh yes,' said Cruden, 'he most certainly was. But if you're thinking that is motive for killing the man, I doubt it.'

'Really? With respect, sir, the last person I would expect you to defend is McAllister.'

'Not defending him, Monsarrat. Simply stating a fact. McAllister could buy and sell Church. He'd simply need to lower the price of his merchandise – which I've heard was less diluted than Church's – and Church would lose his customers in a heartbeat. No, I can't see how he has anything to gain from the man's death. In fact, he has something to lose.'

'Really? I didn't think there was anyone who would profit from Church's continued existence.'

Cruden gave a brief chuckle. 'Think on it for a moment, Monsarrat. Church was a monster, but an efficient one. He made the books balance, you see. I'm not sure how accurate they were but the returns always showed profit. And as long as the Factory was running efficiently, there was no need for Sydney to give credence to the less savoury rumours emanating from the place. Now, though, I understand the talk has already started – the appalling privations of the women, the forced attention of the superintendent, even suggestions that the true financial situation of the Factory might not be as robust as Church implied in the official statements. And with him gone, who would be held responsible for that?'

'Of course. The management committee, on which McAllister sits.'

'Yes. It is not inconceivable that there might be an inquiry. And while an adverse finding probably wouldn't be fatal to McAllister, it would dent him. He does not like to be dented. No, I fear, Monsarrat, you will have to look elsewhere for your killer, even if your only wish is to congratulate them.'

'The problem, sir, is that elsewhere points to a woman who I'm reasonably certain is innocent – not of all crimes, but of this one.'

'Still, as much as I would love to see McAllister ruined, I don't think this murder will be the end of him,' said Cruden. 'You may have to cast your net a little more broadly, Monsarrat. Look sideways, is my advice. Putting an unaccustomed slant on the facts can often lead to the most remarkable epiphanies.'

Monsarrat was offered the guest bedroom at the Cruden residence, and driven back to Parramatta before first light at breakneck speed in a trap piloted by young Will.

It was galling but Monsarrat had to admit that Cruden's assessment was most likely correct. And of course there was no reason to suspect him of having a skewed view of the situation. But Monsarrat was equally certain Grace was innocent. Perhaps he was deluding himself – he had to admit that he wanted her to be so. Or perhaps he needed to take Cruden's advice and look sideways. It would have been helpful, though, if he had understood what the man meant.

'Why is it that I am the only one never to taste a square of your shortbread? I know you were prohibited from giving me any at Port Macquarie, but I'm no longer a convict. And might I point out that I am also your employer? I paid for the flour and sugar that went into that tray.'

Monsarrat sounded petulant, even to his own ears. A short sleep in an unfamiliar bed followed by a jarring ride home had made him cranky. He disliked the way he was acting. It was simply shortbread – why should a senior government official such as himself care about such a thing?

'When this is over, Mr Monsarrat, I'll make you all the shortbread you want. I'll make so much of it we'll be able to build a second oven out of it. Hopefully that will keep you from squalling.'

'Well, I think squalling is taking it a little bit far . . .'

'And I think it doesn't go far enough. Anyway, when you hear what it's for, I'm sure you'll not begrudge it.'

Indeed, when she told him, he didn't begrudge the shortbread. But he came as close as he ever could to giving her a command.

'Tonight? Is that your intention? Truly, you mustn't. It's far too dangerous. Walking about at that time at night by yourself is bad enough, but gaining entry to the Factory, creeping around – you could find yourself in there on a more permanent basis if you're not careful.'

'That's why I intend to be careful, Mr Monsarrat. I did not survive as long as I have without stepping cautiously. We must know what Lizzie might have seen from her window. I intend to drop a handkerchief around the spot where they found Mr Church so I can assess if it is visible from Lizzie's room.'

'How will you get in?'

'Ah, well, I have a plan for that, of course.'

'Of course. Is it something you would like to enlighten me on?'

'As you ask so prettily, Mr Monsarrat, and as I am denying you the solace of my shortbread, I feel it is the least I can do. Mrs Nelson, you see, enjoys her superior status. She pretends not to, but it leaks out in certain little ways. Including requiring me to carry her sewing bag for her.'

'Rather high-handed of her, I must say.'

'Ah, I don't mind. And the fact might prove useful, anyway. Because, you see, I intend to accidentally leave it this afternoon.'

'Why?'

'We usually walk out of the Factory together, part company outside. Rebecca's driver, Grogan, takes her home. She always offers to convey me here, but as it is out of their way I have always declined. Tonight I intend to accept.'

'I see. So we have a ride in a trap and a sewing bag languishing somewhere in the Factory.'

'Are you aware, Mr Monsarrat, that you're an impatient and somewhat irritating man?'

'So I've been told.'

'I'll answer you more quickly if you remain silent. When we are closer to Rebecca's home than to the Factory, I will exclaim over the forgotten sewing bag and mention that there are some items of value of my own in there which I would as soon not leave locked up with convicts overnight. She will, I'm sure, offer to take me back there. And I will accept, on the proviso that she be delivered home first.'

'So Grogan will take you back to the Factory gates, and you will go up to the guard . . .'

'And say I'm on an errand from Mrs Nelson, which the driver will no doubt confirm if asked.'

'And you will enter the Factory . . .'

'And take some time to find the item, of course. Naturally, I will have hidden this shortbread somewhere during the day. I'll deliver it to poor Lizzie, take a peek out the window and will be away again. Hopefully newly enlightened.'

'I am not at all sure that I should allow this,' Monsarrat said.

'Is it up to you to do the allowing, Mr Monsarrat? Would you truly forbid me from taking a course of action I have settled on?'

'I might, if I thought you'd listen.'

'Good man. Now, I have a task for you as well.'

'You are aware, of course, that I already have an employer.'

'Oddly enough, I was aware, yes. And in that employer's office there must be all kinds of records. I wonder whether you'd be good enough, at your leisure, of course, to trawl through them for any reference to any Female Factory convicts called Edwina.'

Monsarrat couldn't resist an occasional glance at the baking shortbread as Mrs Mulrooney told him of her conversation with Lizzie.

'Surely you can't think Rebecca used to be a convict,' he said when she finished.

'It's those wrinkles again, Mr Monsarrat. You always overlook them. This is one we cannot afford to overlook. It may come to nothing, but I'd rather know.'

'Very well. I'll do as you ask. As we are talking of wrinkles – I had a chat with Dr Preston yesterday.'

Hannah Mulrooney did not approve of Dr Preston. She had seen him come to the Female Factory to examine the women, and she felt that his efforts were somewhat perfunctory, and carried out in order to receive the stipend he was paid for the work rather than out of any genuine concern for the women themselves.

Her irritation was not lost on Monsarrat. 'I swear, Mrs Mulrooney, I've given considerable thought to the logic behind your likes and dislikes, and I can't discern anything resembling a pattern. You seem to take against people for no reason, and stay against them, what's more. What's the poor man done in your view?'

'More what he hasn't done. He may be forgiven, though, if he gave you some useful information.'

'He very well might have. In the period between Grace O'Leary's demotion to the Third Class and Church's death, Preston noticed more marks on the arms of the First Class women. Bruising. Always on the upper arms, possibly made by a hand.'

'By Church's hand, no doubt,' said Hannah. 'I spoke to the convict girl, Helen, yesterday. She suffered similar bruising, and worse, from Mr Church. What do we do with the information?'

'Nothing, for now.'

'You seem to be doing a fair deal of nothing. If you keep at it, that girl in the Third Class penitentiary will hang.'

Monsarrat was surprised to find his muscles clenching at the thought.

'I shall give some thought,' he said, 'to how to use my evening. Since there will be no one home to make my dinner anyway.'

Chapter 25

Grace O'Leary might not know it, Monsarrat thought, but this was probably the most crucial interview of her life. Superintendent Rohan would not, of course, have been the only one to see the *Chronicle* article. The management committee, the police and Eveleigh himself would very shortly be coming under intense pressure to take action. Monsarrat was reasonably sure that McAllister and Bulmer would happily instruct their selected jurors to convict the woman.

He was one of the only people in the colony with the slightest interest in helping her avoid a state-sanctioned death. And why should that be so? Surely it was none of his business? He was risking the disapproval of the colony's foremost men, those whom he had hoped to impress when he had stepped off the *Sally* with his new ticket of leave in his pocket.

He tried the notion on – submitting his reports to Eveleigh, leaving Grace to the magistrates, extricating himself from the whole business and settling back into his comfortable kitchen, spending his days ignoring those who didn't matter and trying to prove to those who did that a man could reform, could rise above his former penal status and become useful, perhaps even respectable.

He might, it was true, earn the respect in time of those who pulled the levers of the town. But he would lose his own. Indeed, the idea of walking away from the whole situation made him feel slightly ill.

His decision was made, then, and really it was no decision at all. Within the next hour he needed to find something in Grace's words that could be used in her favour.

Though she was strangely philosophical about her own survival, she seemed to exert more effort on behalf of her fellow inmates. The sisterhood of the Factory appeared to have relied on her heavily, and judging by Hannah's discovery that she was still directing activities from her cell, they continued to do so.

Perhaps those who relied on her included Lizzie.

By the time the guard had grudgingly opened Grace's door (which had had a new lock fitted, Monsarrat noticed), he had worked himself into a state of frustration.

'Tell me, Miss O'Leary, are you really content to die?'

'Tell me, Mr Monsarrat, what have I to live for?' The sentence ended in one of her rattling coughs. Even if she did want to live, the prospect was looking slim given her current state of health.

Monsarrat theatrically looked around the room. He went to the raw wool mattress, bent over and inhaled, gave a series of melodramatic coughs, clutched his chest and staggered, sitting down on the bench which had been there since their first interview.

'Yes, I do see your point,' he said, brushing imaginary dust off his sleeve. 'Understandable that you'd be happy to leave this place, even if it meant waiting in another cell for a rope necklace.'

Grace glared at him. 'Cruel of you to make light of my circumstances, Mr Monsarrat. I'd not have expected it of you.'

'But why shouldn't I make light of them? You are not expending any energy to extricate yourself from them.'

'And what would you have me do, grow wings?'

Monsarrat couldn't help smiling. The sentiment was startlingly familiar to one he had expressed while a convict at Port Macquarie.

Grace took the smile as more evidence of mockery. 'I'm glad to have entertained you, sir,' she said. 'Now, if you've had sufficient diversion, perhaps you'd care to leave.'

'In good time. It will be a shame, though.'

'I fear I can't agree with you.'

'I'm stung. But I wasn't talking about my departure from this cell. I was talking about your departure from this life.'

'Kind of you to say so. I think you are the only one who feels it.'

'I very much doubt that. You're missed already, you know. You remember young Helen? She has some fading bruises on her upper arm.'

The anguish that talk of her own death had not managed to call forth now appeared on Grace's features. She looked very young suddenly, her eyes shining, and Monsarrat noticed that her hair was growing back, covering her skull in downy chestnut.

'He wasted no time in getting back to her, then,' she whispered. 'The others are safe, do you think? Now that he's gone, surely they are unmolested?'

'Safe ... Well, I've had the pleasure of meeting the new superintendent, Mr Rohan. Who, by the way, wants you tried, convicted and hanged. He's not as ... carnal as Mr Church, I'll give you that. But his attitude towards those imprisoned here is less than sympathetic. I have no idea whether he poses any danger to anyone – on the basis of a five-minute interview with the man, I couldn't possibly say – but you can't rely on his good nature. And he may bring in a new storekeeper, for example. New guards. Who's to say they won't be worse?'

'Still,' Grace said. 'It's not certain that they, or the superintendent, will be worse, even half as bad. And if you say Rohan doesn't seem the type to ... help himself to the younger ones, perhaps they may be safe. What of the matron?'

'Mrs Church? She's gone, no one knows where to. A new woman is on the way, from Van Diemen's Land. Until she gets here, Mrs Nelson is doing her best.'

'Mrs Nelson . . . She continues to come to the Factory?'

'Indeed, every day. Why shouldn't she?'

'Oh . . . I thought a lady of her refinement might have been put off by the grisly event.'

'From what I know of her, she is not easily frightened. But it is a temporary arrangement until the new matron is settled in. And who can tell what level of protection, if any, she will provide?'

'Still, they may find a champion in her.'

'They may. They may not. It's to be hoped they do, as their current champion seems intent on dying.'

'And I ask you again, Mr Monsarrat, what am I to do about it?'

'Live.'

'Ah, yes, wonderful. I'll live then. Splendid. And how am I to do that? You've said yourself, it does not look likely that I will be spared.'

'Because you do nothing to defend yourself!' Monsarrat said, unable to stop himself pounding his fist onto the wood of the bench beside him. The sound, and the violence it implied, made Grace step forward. She turned from the window, walked towards him until she was a scant foot away and stood there staring.

He noticed now how tall she was, merely a few inches shorter than he. He wondered if the *Chronicle* journalist who had referred to the Amazonian banditti had seen her.

And then, without conscious direction, his hands reached out and took hers. 'Grace,' he said gently. 'The superintendent says this is the last interview I may have with you. And the governor's secretary says that you are to be charged if I cannot find the means to exonerate you. Your situation is as precarious as it could possibly be, and everything depends on what you tell me today. Please, for the sake of the women here and those yet to come, tell me the truth. Tell me what you know of Mr Church's murder.'

'Why do you care?' she said. Not bitterly, but in wonder that a hidebound clerk would take an interest one way or the other in the plight of the women of the Factory.

Interesting question, thought Monsarrat. Why do I? But as soon as he pressed the question, he knew the answer.

He thought of Sophia, found himself tensing with frustration and annoyance at her small pretensions, the rules she held herself to in order to gain approval from a society that would never fully give it. He thought of her treatment of Hannah, degrading a fellow former convict in order to rise herself up. Sophia did not care what rung of the ladder she was on, so long as there were more beneath her than above her.

Grace, with very little hope of a ticket of leave, saw her strength in the well-being of those around her. She seemed to view the Factory as an organism, and think that if there was a cancer in one part of the body, it would spread. Something in him, too, responded to her boldness. He realised that he would have quite liked to have seen the pirate queen leading the Amazons through the streets of Parramatta.

He looked down into her face and saw a frown on it, realised he was squeezing her fingers quite tightly. He relinquished them and stepped back, knocking over the bench as he did so.

'All well in there? She hasn't killed you yet, has she?' called the turnkey from outside.

'No, I am very much alive still, thank you for your concern,' Monsarrat called out. 'And I'll thank you not to interrupt an official interview.'

'Suit yourself,' the guard called back. 'When I hear you screaming, I'll ignore it.'

'As to why I should care what happens to you,' he said to Grace. 'Well . . . most of the women here will eventually leave this place. Marry, have children. Perhaps run businesses. It's them, really, who will decide the fate of this town, this colony. And I would rather grow old in a place whose citizens learned of benevolence rather than bitterness at their mother's knee.'

It wasn't the whole truth. Not even halfway there. But it would do for now.

Grace went back to the window. Monsarrat followed her.

Looking over her shoulder, he had an unimpeded view of the stores. Out of the corner of one eye, he could see the opening in the wall which led to the main yard where Church was killed. He could also see the beginnings of the stone wall which separated the women from the solace of the river.

'An ideal vantage point, really,' Monsarrat said, 'if you're overseeing certain nocturnal operations. Particularly if those operations involve the stores.'

Grace looked at him, but there was no sign of surprise or panic. He doubted he could have stopped his face, under the same circumstances, from betraying the sickening wrench of impending exposure she was probably feeling.

He leaned closer, unwilling to risk being overheard by the guard. 'Grace, I know what you've been doing, and I am not going to report you. But something went wrong that night, didn't it? What did you see?'

She sighed, turned away. 'I wasn't asleep as I told you I was. When the murder happened.'

'Was anyone else awake?'

'Not as far as I could tell. And I'm fairly good at telling.'

'And the turnkey? Was he there?'

'Yes. Asleep, judging by the snores from the other side of the door.'

'Hmm. Careful about saying that to anyone else. You could have sneaked out and done it yourself. Don't glare at me, I don't deserve it. I am simply telling you what they'll say at your trial. That your confinement was perhaps not as secure as it could have been.'

'All of this is true. And, yes, I probably could have got out many times, if I'd wanted to. But it would have done more harm than good.'

'Why is that?'

'Because the only reason for me to go is to check on the girls. And had I been caught, it would have been worse for them. Mr Church, you see, liked to find interesting ways to punish me. Among them was paying particular attention to those he thought I was protecting.'

'All right. You were at the window. That small one in your previous cell, with a view of the Third Class yard?'

'Yes. It was a hot night, and as well as keeping an eye on the stores I thought perhaps Providence might send me a little breeze off the river. These things, I've now learned, matter when you don't move all day, when you pace around the same four walls until you come to know every piece of oyster shell in the mortar, every splinter of the skirting board. It's the cruellest of measurements. It wears out the soul, but not the body. And the body can be the worst prison.'

'And you saw something, while you were keeping a lookout for your friends in the stores?'

'I heard someone. And I didn't want my girls to stumble into whoever it was, so I gave the signal – two owl calls – for them to hide in the stores. And I kept watching.'

'You must tell me what you saw in the greatest detail you remember. Omit nothing.'

'I will do as you ask if you make me a promise in return.'

'What is that?'

'We will come to it.'

'Very well,' said Monsarrat, reaching into his pocket for his pencil and paper.

'I saw a woman,' said Grace. 'Running from the main yard, along the river wall. Heavily cloaked, which struck me as odd given the heat.'

Monsarrat had been sure Grace was holding back some sort of information. But this he was not prepared for. The woman had seen the killer, and she was allowing the world to think that the killer walked in her skin.

'You're certain it was a woman?'

'I wasn't at first. But as she ran, the hood of her cloak fell back. She was wearing a sun bonnet.'

'A cloak in summer, and a sun bonnet at night,' said Monsarrat. 'You did not raise the alarm?'

226

'Why would I? Remember, I had two women hiding in the stores. They would have been found in any search. And of course I didn't know what she was running from.'

'Did you recognise her?'

'No.'

'The bonnet – some of the First Class women have them, do they not? They are provided with them for Sunday wear, if I am correct.'

'True. But this was no convict. She did not run towards the First or Second Class sleeping quarters.'

'Well, I spoke to the guard. He saw no one entering or leaving on the night in question.'

'He wouldn't have. She went through the gate to the wood yard. Do you know, they don't even keep it locked? No need.'

'No need? Wouldn't people try to escape?'

'Why? Where would they go? Even after the riot, most of us went back to the Factory without protest.'

'So have you seen this woman since then?'

'No. I'm sure I wouldn't know her if I did, though. I could not see her face. More's the pity – I should like to meet her.'

'Perhaps you shall. Your statement could lead to her apprehension.'

'I doubt that very much, Mr Monsarrat.'

'Why should you doubt it? It is the best information we have had so far!'

'You made me a promise in exchange for my testimony.'

'Yes, very well. What do you require of me?'

'My requirement is simple. The women in the stores – they were stealing, yes, but doing so for a good purpose. The authorities won't see the purpose – all they will see is the theft. There is too great a risk of their exposure if my statement becomes official. And they are still in the First Class, better placed than me to take things forward. So, you are not to use my statement, you are not to talk about it to anyone. It will stay in this room. And should you decide to write it up, I will deny it. Every last word.'

Chapter 26

Grace O'Leary, Monsarrat thought, could be the most head-strong, contrary woman he had ever met. And given that her competition for that honour included Hannah Mulrooney, he felt it was high praise indeed.

'What . . . why would you deny it?' he had asked. 'What possible reason could you have for doing so?'

'A few. For a start I don't think it will do any good. No one will believe me.'

'Let's test that theory, shall we?'

'No, we shan't. Because my usefulness is at an end, I fear. Superintendents come and go. The girls will still need a protector.'

'So, for the last time, why are you staying silent?'

'For the sake of a woman – a stranger – who has put herself at great personal risk, and in doing so has already helped more than I ever could.'

'But you have no idea who she is! And no guarantee she will continue to act in their interests. It is insanity!'

'A little more insanity, here, could hardly make a difference. Do you know, Church actually enjoyed snapping minds? There was one woman – unstable to start with – who lost her son, years ago, on the other side of the seas. Church reminded her of it again and again. Told her she could have, should have done more to save him. She wanted nothing to do with the actuality of life after that. And neither do I. I will deny the crime, of course, as I am not guilty. But that is all. I will not close off the way for someone who can do more than I.'

'Why tell me at all, then?'

'You are very persuasive, and I thought someone, at least, should know. But remember, you gave your word.'

He had no intention of honouring his promise. Of course he would write up a statement, of course he would present it to the authorities. He was not at all certain it would make any difference. And it might, as he'd feared, put his own position at risk. But he would try to save her life, whether she liked it or not.

By now it was mid-morning, and most of the convicts were still in the workrooms. Monsarrat decided to follow the invisible trail laid down by Robert Church's killer around the Third Class penitentiary to a grassed area where the convict women used to be able to walk down to the river and bathe, until concerns of escape had led to the erection of the stone wall.

He tried the gate. Locked. He considered finding Hannah to see if there was a key on the ring Rebecca Nelson made her carry which would work. But now, his muscles still stiff from sleeping in an unfamiliar bed and the rollicking cart ride which followed, he was expected back at the governor's office and did not wish to stretch Eveleigh's patience any further. Nonetheless, he had an errand to run on the way.

Twenty minutes later, after checking the address Henson had given him, Monsarrat was looking into the window of David Nelson's warehouse.

'Ah, I was hoping you might come today,' Henson said as he entered. 'Those beautiful – in my opinion – tea services have just arrived. All Meissen, as I said. The painting on one is particu-larly fine.'

He led Monsarrat into a room with a table. Crates were stacked around it, and Henson reached into one, plunging his hand into the sawdust, and pulling out a cup and saucer. He went through the process a few times, and laid out the pieces on the table for Monsarrat's inspection.

Monsarrat made complimentary noises about each one, holding them up to the light (he imagined that was what a connoisseur of fine china should do), exclaiming over the delicate blue flowers on one, the vines on another.

'Extraordinary to have so many treasures in one building,' he remarked. 'I'm surprised you don't have an army outside to guard them all.'

'I often wish we had, to be frank,' said Henson. 'Had a dreadful time of it recently. The last six months or so, stock has been draining away. Not in large amounts, of course, nor in any discernible pattern. A piece of cloth here, some silver plate there. But enough to cause consternation, particularly as the thefts were so frequent.'

'Were? You have the matter under control now?'

'Yes, thankfully. Mr Nelson hired a nightwatchman. For a few weeks it seemed to make no difference, almost as though the merchandise walked out of here under its own steam in the dead of night. But then, whoever the thief was, he must've noted the vigilance of the man. For it all tailed off, and we've had nothing go missing for the last week or two.'

'Good news indeed. I wonder, who is this fellow? We need additional guards from time to time at Government House. I don't want to rob you of your nightwatchman, but should you decide you have no further use for him we may be able to offer him employment.'

'Most certainly, and I'll hold you to your word as a gentleman that you will not offer alternative employment until he has left ours.'

'You most certainly have it.'

'Very well then. His name is Ernest Holford. He's been in Parramatta for only a short time, and I believe he is currently residing at a guesthouse – the Stag, I think it's called.'

Or more fully, the Prancing Stag, Monsarrat thought. Sophia's guesthouse.

'That's interesting, as I happen to know the proprietor,' he said. 'I wonder, would it concern you if I was to introduce myself to the man?'

'By all means, I see no harm in that.'

'Thank you. And now we come to one of the most difficult decisions I have made: which of these charming tea sets to acquire. I am rather leaning towards the green, you know. Those tiny clovers around the rim – they look like shamrocks, and I know someone to whom that would appeal very much indeed.'

~~~

Monsarrat's purse was discernibly lighter when he left the warehouse. He really must sit down and assess his financial situation – he feared it was becoming somewhat tenuous.

He returned to Government House to find Eveleigh waiting out front.

'You are far later back from the Female Factory than I would have anticipated, Mr Monsarrat. You have not been conducting your own investigations, I trust?'

'Sir, I do apologise. Superintendent Rohan gave me permission for one last interview with prisoner Grace O'Leary. New information has come to light which may have some bearing on the case. I am fully aware, sir, that you were kind enough to give me until Friday – tomorrow – to resolve this matter, and now we may be in a position to begin to do just that.'

'Where did this new information come from, may I ask?' said Eveleigh. He avoided looking at Monsarrat as he spoke – a bad sign from this man, who always took pains to engage with his eyes as well as with his words. He directed his gaze, instead, past the main house to the sloping, curved driveway, as if he was expecting the new governor to pull in at any moment.

'From the prisoner herself, sir. It seems that from her window in the penitentiary she witnessed the escape of the murderer. She confirms Dr Preston's suspicions: the killer is a woman.'

'And was she able to identify this woman?' He had turned, was walking back into the offices as he spoke, without checking to make sure Monsarrat was following.

'No, sir,' he said, taking care that his longer legs did not propel him ahead of Eveleigh. 'But after the attack, she saw the killer leave through the gate to the river. And I happen to be aware that the gate isn't always locked.'

'I see. So we have a gate which may or may not have been unlocked. We have the testimony of a woman who feels the noose drawing tighter, and suddenly claims to have witnessed another unidentifiable female flee.'

It did, Monsarrat had to admit, sound rather flimsy.

'Sir, there is another point to consider. Prisoner O'Leary is not aware of the suspicion that the murder was carried out by a woman. So if she were fabricating it, would it not make more sense for her to put a man in the role?'

'In a building full of women? No, were I the dissembling type, I would invent a woman too.'

'But there are other considerations, sir. She asked me to promise not to tell anyone of her confession.'

'I am quickly forming an impression of a woman who is skilled at manipulating good-natured souls such as yourself, Monsarrat.'

'Very well, sir. Thank you for your consideration. I will continue, with your permission, to attempt to find out what I can.'

'Is there any point, Monsarrat? I doubt there is anything further to discover. I have more than enough to keep you busy here, in any case. I suggest you write your interview up, for what it's worth, which is very little in my opinion. We will hand the whole matter back to the police.'

'Mr Eveleigh ... You did say I might have until tomorrow to work on this matter.'

'Oh, Lord have mercy, Monsarrat. All right then. In that case, I shall invite the superintendent of police to meet us here in the afternoon. By that time, I anticipate you will have all the depositions appropriately drafted so we can hand them over to him and end this business. Don't forget, Monsarrat, a new governor is on his way. We do not wish him to form an impression of us based on what the *Chronicle* says about the deplorable delay in laying charges.'

Monsarrat sincerely hoped Hannah would have more luck than he had when she visited the Factory tonight.

He wondered whether the woman Grace had mentioned – the one who had been distressed beyond bearing by Church's continual reference to her dead son – was Lizzie. It seemed likely, and he hoped to be in a position to pass the information on to Hannah before she left.

Monsarrat spent the afternoon transcribing Eveleigh's letters, orders and requisitions for supplies for Government House to ensure that the new man when he arrived would have sufficient provisions. Reports on the state of the grounds. A letter to the colonial secretary regarding what was to be done with the old governor's follies, the observatory and the bathhouse – the new governor might find them delightful or ridiculous, and Eveleigh would rather know which was more likely before the new man arrived.

Long past the hour when most men in Eveleigh's position would have left (but long before Eveleigh usually did), Monsarrat presented the results of the day's labour.

Eveleigh flicked through the pages, giving a small nod to indicate his satisfaction where, not long before, he would have praised the neatness of the writing, the lack of errors.

'I wonder, Mr Eveleigh, whether you would have any objection to me going through the archives?'

'That rather depends, Mr Monsarrat, on what it is you're looking for.'

'I simply wish to seek out some more background on prisoner O'Leary. To place in my final report to be handed to the police superintendent tomorrow.'

'I wish you the best of luck with it. As you know, the Factory archives are in quite a state. As a matter of fact, perhaps that can be your task come Monday morning, when you will certainly have a lot more time to devote to it.'

'I'll be delighted to assist in any way possible, of course. In fact, I had a notion I might make a start tonight, if you've no objection.'

'I intend to be here for the next hour. As I'm responsible for the security of this place – particularly in the absence of the governor and the extra staff who would be here if there were one in residence – I do not wish to leave anyone on the premises each night, without my supervision. You have until my departure.'

The disorganised state of the archives did not faze Monsarrat, given that he had managed to find what he wanted last time he was down there. Although this time he had no idea what he was looking for. No date, no ship, no crime. Just the name Edwina, and the second-hand ramblings of a madwoman to guide him.

Chapter 27

The evening was a warm one as the trap moved through the slow twilight, past cottages and slab huts which gave way to stands of gum trees, with underbrush choking the sides of the rutted road.

Hannah would have found the journey in the open trap rather pleasant had it not been for the task ahead, and the frown on Rebecca Nelson's face.

'Not like you, Hannah, to be so absent-minded. Imagine not realising you were no longer carrying the sewing basket!'

'Ah, but I fear it happens from time to time. As I get older, you know, things just drop out of my head.'

'Well, it can wait till tomorrow,' said Rebecca, sounding wearily annoyed.

'That's the problem, you see. Mr Monsarrat gave me some money to purchase some butter tomorrow morning, before I arrive at the Factory. So I'd as soon not leave the basket there overnight – there are some wonderful girls in that place, but there are others, as well.'

'True enough,' said Rebecca. 'Do you know where you left it?'

'I'm fairly certain it's in the corner of the drying grounds. I set it down there when I was helping at the meal hour.'

'Very unwise of you. We shall turn around and get it now then.'

'Oh, but aren't we close to your house? I would hate to detain you. Perhaps if you were to allow me the use of your trap just for a short while longer, after you are safely home I can return to get it.'

'Very well, then. Grogan will take you.'

Grogan had the hunched posture of someone who spent much time seated, but on hearing his name his shoulders squared slightly. She did not wish to know how he felt about having a forgetful former convict add an hour or more to his work day.

So with Rebecca safely deposited and farewelled – 'You must take care not to do this again, Hannah. I've come to rely on you' – Grogan turned the horse around.

As they approached the Factory again, Hannah was disappointed to see that she didn't know the night guard on duty. As she dismounted from the trap and approached him he made no move to stop her, but his eyes never left her.

'I'm assistant to Mrs Nelson, who is helping Superintendent Rohan with the running of the Factory until the permanent matron arrives,' Hannah said.

'Are you?' he said.

'Indeed. Mrs Nelson has sent me to recover something left on the premises. I shan't be long.'

'The superintendent says no one is to enter without his permission.'

'I simply need to find Mrs Nelson's sewing bag and I will be gone. Look, there's Mrs Nelson's driver to stand surety for me. Wouldn't it be a shame to interrupt the superintendent's dinner over such a trifle?'

The man looked over at Grogan. He seemed to recognise him, nodded briefly.

'Find what it is you're after, and then leave,' the man said.

'Of course, thank you,' Hannah said. Then, leaning in she dropped her voice to a whisper, 'I'm not entirely sure where I left it, but I didn't want Mrs Nelson to think me half-witted. It may take some time to find.'

'Fifteen minutes, and after that I'll come and find you.'

Hannah bobbed her thanks and raced across the yard, dropping a small red cloth on the ground as she ran towards the staircase that led to Lizzie's room. In an alcove underneath it was the sewing basket, which she would leave in place for now so she could pretend to be searching for it should the guard make good on his threat.

Underneath the basket was a tray of shortbread, wrapped tightly in oilcloth to deter the rats, who liked Hannah's baking every bit as much as Monsarrat did. This she did remove, together with her shoes, which joined the sewing basket under the stairs. The odd creak was unavoidable but she did not intend to announce her presence any more than necessary.

She had the key to Lizzie's room in her pocket, and on using it cursed the poorly fitted door, which scraped the timbers as it opened.

Lizzie was sitting on her bed in her nightdress, staring at the wall.

'Good evening, Lizzie. I came, as I promised. I'm very sorry I can't stay long tonight, but I can keep you company for a short while. And, look, I brought the shortbread for you.'

She placed the tray on Lizzie's lap and the woman grabbed a fistful, crushing it in her hands while she stuffed it into her mouth.

When the pace of her feeding slowed somewhat, Hannah patted her hand. 'Did you enjoy that?'

Lizzie nodded and smiled, showing crumb-littered teeth.

'Lizzie, my love, will you come to the window with me?'

So they walked together to the window, Hannah supporting Lizzie.

When Hannah peered out, the patch of red cloth was clearly visible. Lizzie was looking out too, through unfocused eyes.

'Now, Lizzie, have you seen anything from this window? Startling things, I mean.'

Lizzie frowned. 'Eddie won't get in trouble, will she?'

'Why would Eddie get in trouble?'

'I just wondered. Because I did see a startling thing. Eddie made a man lie down, you see. And she must have done a good job, because he never got back up.'

'Can you point to where it happened?'

Lizzie tapped the corner of her eye, smiled at Hannah, then turned and moved the tip of her finger forward.

When she did, she was pointing directly at the red cloth. She noticed it, with a jolt. 'Has someone else lain down now?' she said. 'Because there's red again.'

'No, Lizzie. No, there will be no more lying down, I promise. Would you like the rest of the shortbread?'

Lizzie nodded again, going back to the bed and sitting beside the tray as if to prevent anyone taking it.

Hannah knew that she must not spend one more moment in the Factory. She said a rushed goodbye, made sure she took the now-empty tray with her, and collected the sewing basket from under the stairs and the red cloth from the yard.

She already suspected she had overstayed. Especially when she saw the guard making his way towards her. She held up the basket to show him, and inwardly cursed. She had forgotten her shoes. She hoped he wouldn't notice.

'I'm sorry to put you to the trouble of coming to fetch me,' she said. 'It's my eyes, you see. They're much weaker in the dark than they once were, and it took them a little time to pick out my basket.'

The guard said nothing but nodded, gesturing her towards the gate and following close behind.

She will ask Grogan, Hannah thought. She will ask Grogan how long I took, and Grogan will tell her.

For the first time since she had been in gaol in Port Macquarie, she felt fear.

It was clear that no one else had been here since Monsarrat had last been down to look for Grace's letters to the governor – the place remained in a deplorable state. Some documents still bore the wax seals that announced them as unopened letters, others were torn or dog-eared, many faded to the point where Monsarrat wondered if his candle would be up to the task. And of course very few of them – save the ones he had already been through – bore any signs of having been organised in any way.

This would be done, Monsarrat thought, within days. And his likely reward would be more days down here, trying to impose some sort of organising principle onto these unloved pieces of paper. He imagined himself, in the days and weeks ahead, finding the one document which could have saved Grace. A pity it would be too late.

So, organised or not, he would have to find it tonight.

He picked up a stack of the less damaged papers, started laying them out on the table, looking for any link, and not holding out much hope that in fifteen years' worth of documentation he could find her.

After a short while, he found the work soothing, almost became lost in organising the disorganised, imposing his will on something, even if it was just paper.

He shook his head, glanced at his pocket watch. He had maybe a quarter of an hour before Eveleigh left for the night and would demand Monsarrat did the same. It would have to be enough.

As he looked down at a sheaf of papers he had already laid out, he noticed that there was, in fact, one link, a factor they all shared: the ship the convict had arrived on.

Monsarrat had come here in the hold of the *Morley*. There had been no women on his ship. Nor did he look for Hannah's ship, the *Minerva*, as the Factory hadn't been built when she arrived. As for the other ships, he hadn't the faintest clue where to start. So he simply started wherever his eye fell. And as he ran his eyes up and down the list of ship names, flicked through page after page to find where the reports of the human cargo of one ship ended and the next began, one vessel's name snagged at his eye.

Nemesis.

The name, if he recalled his conversations with Mrs Mulrooney correctly, of Rebecca Nelson's Irish wolfhound. And with his classical education, he knew Nemesis was also the name of the Greek goddess of divine retribution. Having nothing more to go on, then, he started flicking through these records. After three or four pages he met a woman called Edwina Drake. The manifest listed her as 21 years old. Her occupation was set down as 'governess'. She stood 5 feet tall – the same height as Hannah. Her skin was described as clear, her eyes blue. And her hair was listed as red.

She had been transported fifteen years ago for stealing cutlery, with a sentence of seven years.

The piece of paper had nothing further to say about Miss Drake, and nor did the others he had managed to peruse by the time he heard Eveleigh's footsteps at the top of the stairs leading down into the cellar. 'Mr Monsarrat, finish up, if you please. I intend to leave within the next five minutes, and you will be doing the same.'

'Very well, sir,' Monsarrat called up. 'I'll just set these files to rights, and I will be right up.'

He did exactly as he said he would do. But one piece of paper, now folded tightly, did not find its way back into the midst of its fellows, instead leaving the governor's domain in Monsarrat's pocket.

Chapter 28

Monsarrat kept no intoxicating liquor of any kind at his small house. No rum, no wine. He rarely drank – although in his younger life he had occasionally done so to excess – and Mrs Mulrooney had never touched the stuff, and never would.

Yet suddenly Monsarrat wished he had access to a cellar to store grog instead of documents.

He was not happy, when he got home, to find himself alone. He had been sure his housekeeper would be back by now. If there was anyone who could look after themselves, of course, it was she. But there were some circumstances no one could rise above, some dangers no one could deflect, and he tried hard to stop the corners of his imagination from suggesting possibilities.

He sat at the kitchen table, spread the page on Edwina Drake out before him, read it over and over. He wasn't sure why he was doing so – there was very little nuance in it, the sparse list of ship, crime, occupation and physical description. He didn't expect to find new information, and he didn't.

He had not realised how worried he was becoming about Mrs Mulrooney's whereabouts until he felt the loosening of relief as he heard her making her way up the hallway, through the back door and into the kitchen.

She sat down heavily opposite him. 'It's been a trying night, Mr Monsarrat,' she said. 'I find myself not quite up to making tea.'

'Of course! Would you like me to make some for you?'

'Would you? I'm sorry. But I could use the solace of it, and for once it's a solace I find I'm unable to provide for myself.'

Monsarrat got up, knelt so that he could use the bellows on the dwindling fire, careless of staining his trousers. Hannah Mulrooney's strength had become, for him, one of life's constants, and he would do anything to see it return, stained clothing or not. Once the fire had grudgingly started, he put the kettle on the hook above it.

As he worked, she told him about her conversation with Lizzie.

'I don't mind admitting, I'm a little frightened, Mr Monsarrat. Grogan – the driver – will have told her that I took longer than would be expected of someone dashing in to pick up a forgotten sewing basket. So if it was her, and she thinks I'm behaving suspiciously – well, I wouldn't have thought her capable of doing harm to me, but then before tonight I wouldn't have thought her capable of what I now believe she did to Mr Church.'

'You mustn't worry, really. You will be safe – I'll make sure of it.'

He set a cup of tea in front of her, moving the paper from the files out of the way.

'What's this?' she said.

'It's a page from the list of women sent to the Factory from the ship *Nemesis*. I suggest you examine the details for Edwina Drake.'

Mrs Mulrooney was a new enough reader to preen slightly at being asked to peruse a document for herself. She took it primly, held it out at arm's length to enable her eyes to focus on the cramped script in the low light. After a moment, she set it down again.

'Rebecca Nelson was a governess, you know,' she said.

'Yes, you told me.'

'And her hair – well, you know about that, too.'

'Yes. The age seems about right. The eye colour, the height. None of it is any guarantee, of course. But it does seem rather coincidental. You noted the name of the ship?'

'Yes, I did. The same as her wolfhound. I always thought it was an odd name for a house dog, to be honest. I intended to ask her the meaning of the word, actually.'

'Some use it as though it means enemy, which of course it doesn't,' said Monsarrat. 'It's more an invocation to revenge.'

'I can understand why she would want vengeance on Robert Church. But why now? If she was in the Factory for so long . . .'

'Yes, and I wish we had a means of finding out how long precisely she was there. I know that Church was there for a long time. It's conceivable he could have taken up the post while Edwina Drake was an inmate. And if Edwina Drake is Rebecca Nelson, then she may have received some unsolicited attention.'

'I'm sure he put her through all sorts of horrors, as he did with the rest of them. It was his chief enjoyment in life, from what I understand. But now, of course, we need to decide what to do.'

'At the moment, I believe we should do precisely nothing.'

'You can't mean that, Mr Monsarrat! Not with Grace O'Leary facing probable execution.'

'We have until tomorrow, don't forget. I am not Mr Eveleigh's most favoured employee at present, but he is a man of his word. And making an accusation like this, against a person like this – it has not the merest hope of standing, not without more to back it up. So for now, as I said, we do nothing. I will see what I can uncover in the morning, and then we can make a decision.'

'I may be able to find a little more out tomorrow at the Factory, as well.'

'Hannah, I think it is unwise for you to go to the Factory tomorrow. To go anywhere near Rebecca Nelson.'

'But if I don't arrive, as I have every day before this, won't she know, then, with certainty that something is wrong?'

'As soon as she talks to her driver, she will be suspicious of what you're up to.'

'Very well then. I'll stay here. Perhaps you could arrange for a message to be delivered to her. Pleading illness, or some such.'

'I'll do that. And you promise me that you will stay inside and not answer the door. I'll do my very best to discover what I can. Although how to accomplish it, I have no idea.'

The next morning Monsarrat set out half an hour earlier than usual. He had an errand to run before appearing, seemingly blameless, before Mr Eveleigh.

It had been a week now since he had last entered the Prancing Stag, and since then he'd avoided even walking past it. It was an inconvenient time, too, to call, as the respectable were still preparing for the day, and the less respectable dribbling home. But it was very possibly a good time to find a nightwatchman breakfasting before going to his rest.

His knock went unanswered long enough to make him wonder if after all he had chosen the wrong time, until he heard light footsteps approaching the door.

Sophia had clearly been up for some hours. Her hair was perfectly pinned up, her dress perfectly pressed, with an expression floating between mild annoyance and curiosity.

In an instant her face tensed. 'Mr Monsarrat. How may I help you? You don't mean to tell me you require lodging?'

'Nothing of the sort, although I do thank you for the offer. I'm here to enquire, as it happens, after a guest of yours.'

'You may need to make your inquiries at another time, then. All of my guests have either already departed for the morning or are still in bed. Save one.'

'Would I be correct in assuming that one is Ernest Holford?'

'And what business have you with Mr Holford?'

'I simply wish to interview him for a possible position should his current employer no longer require him. And as I've never interviewed a nightwatchman before, I wasn't sure which time would be most convenient. I chose this one.'

'I see. And would you welcome a prospective employer arriving unannounced at your house while you were at your breakfast?'

'I imagine that would depend on who the employer was. Now, you're very kind to be so jealous of your guest's privacy; however, I'd like you to announce me. Perhaps Mr Holford himself can decide whether he welcomes a visit.'

Sophia nodded briefly, left him standing on the doorstep as she went inside to confer with her guest. She reappeared a moment later, gesturing with her head towards the parlour.

'Thank you,' said Monsarrat. He received no reply, nor did he expect one.

Ernest Holford was a barrel-chested man, short and stocky, and the sleeves of his coat were tight enough around his upper arm to make Monsarrat suspect he was more than equal to anyone with designs on Mr Nelson's merchandise.

'I'm sorry to disturb your breakfast, sir,' said Monsarrat.

'Don't be, I can eat as well in company as alone. Sit. Miss Stark mentioned you might be looking for a watchman.'

'I understand you've been very successful at Mr Nelson's warehouse, and I don't wish to lure you away from your employment there. But on occasion we have need of someone with your abilities at Government House, and with Mr Henson's blessing I thought it might be wise for us to get to know each other.'

'Might as well. I've not been in Parramatta long, and I'm happy to meet as many people as possible, you included.'

Monsarrat inclined his head. 'So, tell me – where were you before this?'

'In Sydney. I was employed by a number of ship owners to guard their cargo as it came onto the docks. Have you ever been on the docks in Sydney, Mr Monsarrat?'

'Indeed, though not for some time.'

'Then you'll know what a mess it can be down there. People getting off ships, others trying to get on. Convicts wailing and crying, soldiers trying to control them. Merchandise being unloaded and back loaded, publicans buying rum by the barrel, merchants buying cloth by the bale. And thieves, of course. There are always thieves.'

'So presumably you were there to prevent them from attaining their objective.'

'Yes. And I was successful at it. No merchandise walked off a ship I was guarding, unless it was paid for.'

'And you've had similar success at the warehouse, I hear.'

'Yes, although not straight away. Bits and pieces still bled out, although not at the rate they had before.'

'A great concern, I'm sure. I know they had some rather fine porcelain there recently.'

'Yes, and it was the small items that seemed to go. Small and valuable. Silver plate. Cutlery. The porcelain you mentioned.'

'But then it stopped?'

'Yes, then it stopped. Not before time – I was beginning to worry, I have to tell you. No one went in or out, you see, yet things still vanished. Enough to make you believe in phantoms,' Holford said, reflexively crossing himself.

'And you say no one came in or out? No one at all?'

'No. Apart from Mr Nelson, of course, and occasionally his wife. Lovely lady – have you met her? She would bring me a pie sometimes. Or some bread. Said she was concerned for my health, working those hours. And I don't mind saying, those bits and pieces were very welcome, too.'

'I am sure they were. So apart from the times she delivered you the food, there really was no one near the warehouse?'

'Ah, sometimes she'd go in. Say her husband had allowed her to choose some fabric for a gown, or that she wished to select a new brush or some such thing. Then she let herself out by the side gate. I looked forward to her visits, to be honest. Lonely work, this.'

'I'm sure it is.'

'But Mrs Nelson's been busy at the Factory of late. She goes there to do good works, you know. So there's been no pies. Wonderful what she's doing with those women – she must have the patience of the Blessed Virgin herself. But, though I feel selfish saying it, I do miss the victuals.'

'Well, I shall leave you to those you have,' said Monsarrat. 'Thank you for your time.'

Holford nodded, unable to express himself verbally due to the large quantity of bread he had just put in his mouth. Bread that, Monsarrat noticed, had been taken from a rather fine platter. Silver, with a design of grapes and vines, one ornate handle at each end.

Sophia was waiting by the door, and doubtless had been listening to the entire conversation. She wore her pinched expression, which did nothing to accentuate her beauty. Come to that, now that he looked at her, Monsarrat found her features rather sharp. He wondered why he hadn't noticed it before.

'I must say, your establishment is looking far more genteel than I remember it,' he said.

'Thank you,' Sophia said. 'I do try – one will never be accepted here unless one acts like one already is accepted.'

'Well, the longer I am in Parramatta, the less inclined I am to act like some of those in the box pews each Sunday. But of course each of us must proceed according to our own instincts. And yours, when it comes to domestic decoration, have always been rather fine. Augmented now, I see, by the addition of a lovely silver platter.'

Sophia said nothing.

'Looks like something one might see at David Nelson's shop. Your business must be doing exceptionally well if you're able to afford such treasures. Wherever did you get it?'

'From a family who left. They found the Parramatta heat too oppressive and have moved back to Sydney town,' Sophia said.

'Interesting. You know that on occasion land deeds and the like pass at my desk. Which family, did you say?'

'I can't recall.'

'Ah. Well, you have always been an exceptionally hard worker, and fatigue can play tricks with the memory, of course.'

'I have, and there is further work ahead of me now. So if there is nothing else I can assist you with, Mr Monsarrat, I have a guest to clean up after.'

Monsarrat left her to set into order the mess in her house, while he made for the comfortable chaos of the road.

Chapter 29

Judging by the state of Eveleigh's desk – papers still stacked neatly from the night before, a fresh blotter with no ink spots on it – he had not been there for long. Monsarrat was relieved – he was sure he would have been able to explain any lateness, but he would prefer not to have to.

He rapped gently on Eveleigh's open door to make the man aware he was in, then took himself to his own desk and started transcribing a copy of Grace's statement. He left out Peggy and Bronagh – hiding in the store, they couldn't have seen anything, and he had no leisure to interview them now. Nor did he want to see them join Grace in her confinement, to see their sentences lengthened and their hair cropped.

The further he got into his transcription, the slower he went, his own reluctance to see the matter concluded dragging on his fingers. He was distracted by an impulse to bring Eveleigh into his confidence. But with a person as highly placed as Rebecca Nelson, and Eveleigh's current frustration, he did not think it was the time.

So when he presented a document to Eveleigh, it was a list of land grants made in the last days of Governor

Brisbane's administration, for perusal by his replacement. Eveleigh glanced at it, set it aside.

'And the statement of prisoner O'Leary?'

'It will be with you by this afternoon, sir.'

'Good. After that perhaps you may like to pass some time in the cellar, setting those documents to rights.'

'I'd like that very much indeed, sir. As we know, the worst of the heat never penetrates there, and I must confess I am soothed by the process of imposing order on the mess in which those files currently live.'

'Very well, you may soothe yourself then.'

'However, sir . . .'

Eveleigh, having returned his gaze to the list of land grants, looked up again, putting his pen down very deliberately.

'Yes, Monsarrat. There would be a "however".'

'My housekeeper was ill this morning, and I would as soon look in on her. I promise to confine myself to the cellar until long after nightfall to make up for it. Would you have any objection?'

'I suppose not. Those files in the cellar are not going to slide any further into disarray for the want of your company. But I do warn you, Mr Monsarrat, if word reaches me that you are continuing to look into the Church murder, you will be confined to this office in perpetuity. And I am glad to hear that you like it in the cellar, I'm beginning to toy with the idea of locking you in there.'

Surely, thought Monsarrat, there was no harm in strolling past the Female Factory. It was on his way from Government House. If there was no guard at the gate, he might be able to duck in to check that Mrs Nelson was there and Hannah Mulrooney wasn't.

The guard was there, however. He was deep in conversation with Stephen Lethbridge, while wiping some of the contents of one of Lethbridge's pies off his face with the back of his hand.

Lethbridge could afford the time to exchange pleasantries – there were no knots of men outside the Factory today looking for wives or servants.

Monsarrat decided that as he was here, there could be no harm in skirting the Factory to have a look at the other side of the yard gate. He had not examined the gate closely before. He had not had the leisure, nor could he afford the turnkeys or overseers wondering what a man wearing a silk cravat rather than a rough neckerchief was doing staring at the gate in the Third Class yard. On this side of the river, though, he was observed by a few white cockatoos, their sulfur combs stowed for now, and by those bats that happened to be awake among the hundreds which hung from the eucalypt branches above him.

Coming from the other side, he wondered for a moment if it was the same gate. The timbers he had seen in the Third Class yard were as smooth as could be expected for such a utilitarian structure. But clearly those who had built the Factory had felt the side of the gate mostly seen only by the tradesmen who occasionally passed through it did not deserve the same treatment. The wood was rough and splintered, as were the timbers of the frame that wedged the gate into the Factory wall.

'I've never seen such thoughtful contemplation of a gate, Mr Monsarrat.'

Lethbridge had clearly tired of his conversation with the guard – who, after all, was unlikely to be able to exchange views on Tacitus versus Seneca, or the merits of Herodotus. He still had his hot box around his neck, was still moving from foot to foot, making deep indentations in the river mud. If only I had thought to come here just after the murder, thought Monsarrat, I might have seen a footprint. Perhaps a small, feminine one.

'Mr Lethbridge. Had I the leisure, I would certainly relieve you of one of your pies.'

'Yet you're staring at the gate as though you have all the time in the world, Mr Monsarrat. One can't help but wonder why.'

'We have an agreement, you and I, about keeping our own secrets, do we not?'

'Quite right. Forgive my curiosity – if you are not offended by my asking, I shall not be offended by the lack of an answer.'

Monsarrat smiled, inclined his head to show he was perfectly happy with the agreement.

Lethbridge removed his hot box from around his neck and set it on a nearby rock.

'Keep half an eye on that for me, would you, Mr Monsarrat? The magpies love my wares nearly as much as the men.'

He picked up a stick and began to make indentations at small intervals. He seemed to be thoroughly enjoying himself, poking with his stick at the mud that was exposed when the hungry ocean drew the river waters to it. Monsarrat couldn't see the attraction himself. In the heat, the mud smelled nearly as bad as the bats.

'People walk by here and never notice it, you know. No one *observes*, now, Mr Monsarrat. Not as the philosophers did in Greece and Rome. But you can see the little kink here. The dogleg, where the river jinks to the side a bit before taking the path of least resistance and continue on towards Sydney.'

'Yes, I suppose . . . Rather subtle, though, isn't it?'

'Not to anything in the river. You can see, here . . .' – he waved the stick towards a crescent-shaped amalgamation of leaves and twigs on the riverbank – 'Things in the river tend to get snagged here. And then the river abandons them.'

His stick continued jabbing into the mud, withdrawing, plunging again. 'And sometimes it's not leaves and twigs, Mr Monsarrat. I know. I observe, and I keep my counsel. Sometimes things fall in the river – coins decide to leave pockets and go for a swim, to be found by one with the wit to look. Sometimes people throw things in the river. Thinking that the waters will do their part, carry the offending object out through the heads and to sea, where it won't be seen again until the waters boil and the Lord parts the skies to deliver the final judgement.

And it wouldn't surprise me if some of them were hoping to avoid judgement in *this* life.'

Soon his prodding, which seemed to be happening almost by will of the stick rather than the man who held it, slowed. He withdrew the stick from the latest of the dozens of holes it had made and frowned at it as though it had said something puzzling to him. Placed it carefully back in the same hole, and twisted it a few times. Withdrew it again, and inserted it at an angle, using it to remove as much mud as he could without getting his shirt dirty. Then he seemed to give up on the idea of a clean shirt. He knelt, pushed on the exposed end of the stick so that it opened a rift in the mud, and carefully inserted his hand, palpating whatever the stick had found for him.

When his hand drew back from the rift, it was holding an awl.

'Is this what you were looking for, Mr Monsarrat?'

Monsarrat was hesitant to touch the thing. It was possible that this implement had been forced into the eye of another human, as little as Church was worthy of the term.

'I'm not sure, to be honest,' he said. 'But do you mind if I take it?'

'Certainly not. I've no use for such a thing.'

Monsarrat turned the awl over in his hand as Lethbridge resumed poking at the mud, presumably looking for coins. He found none, retrieved his hot box and said a courteous goodbye to Monsarrat, who looked up and smiled distractedly before returning his attention to the metal spike.

There was no way of being certain this was the implement that had killed Robert Church. Any blood or other material would have been taken care of by the river. Or the thing might have only ever been used for the purpose for which it was made.

It was sturdy enough. And it was long enough too, at least six inches. A few rust spots on the shaft. If it was the agent of Church's death, it would have been here for a fortnight, so they were to be expected. A useful implement, still – not one ready to be cast away into the river. And who would have been in a position to throw such a thing away from the confines of the Factory? Certainly if they had pitched it into the river from the other side of the wall, they would need a reasonable throwing arm.

He turned, stalked back to the gate, stared at it for a little longer. He reached out a hand, ran it gently around the gate's frame, and found himself having to extract a splinter from his palm.

All was quiet on the other side of the wall, apart from the white noise of the cicadas. He braced both hands against the gate, and pushed. He tried not to use too much force. He didn't know if the gate was locked or jammed, and did not want to announce his presence by pushing it so hard it slammed flat against the wall.

The gate, as it happened, was closed, and firmly. But it wasn't locked. Bloated by years of exposure to the humidity of the riverbank, it barely shifted against its frame with the first push. The second had a little more success. The third did the job, without the explosive entry into the courtyard Monsarrat was dreading.

The yard, as he had thought, was empty. He didn't step into it though. Instead, keeping the gate open only a fraction, he examined the inside of the frame. This was rougher than the face of the gate. Rough enough to snag something.

He carefully ran his hand around the frame, watching its path until his eye came to a fine line of colour near one of the hinges. He cursed, for the first time, the fact that he kept his nails so closely trimmed. But after some effort, and a few more splinters, he was able to extract a single strand of red.

Monsarrat was disturbed by what he had found at the Factory, and equally by what he had not found – any sign of Rebecca Nelson. Her trap and driver were not waiting outside, and the guard, when Monsarrat asked him after his visit to the gate, claimed to have seen no sign of her.

It would add only another five minutes, ten at most, to go home quickly to alleviate the anxiety which had crouched in the corner of his mind since he'd left this morning.

He was happy to see the house closed up. The curtains drawn, no noise, no sign of activity from within. No smoke from the chimney – hardly surprising: if Mrs Mulrooney had shut herself away during a Parramatta summer with closed windows and drawn curtains, the last thing she would want was a fire.

There was, however, a slip of paper protruding from underneath the front door.

Dear Mr Monsarrat,

I do apologise that your tea service is not with you yet. Mrs Nelson very kindly agreed to convey it when she collected your housekeeper this morning. However, Grogan has returned with it still in the trap. I assure you it remains in pristine condition, and I look forward to delivering it to you at your earliest convenience. If you happen to be passing the warehouse, please do let me know when you anticipate your housekeeper will be home to receive it.

Yours sincerely,
James Henson

Monsarrat skimmed the note almost blithely, was even attempting to settle on an appropriate time to visit Henson at the shop, when the crux of the message struck him.

Rebecca Nelson had collected Mrs Mulrooney. This morning, when the doors were shut and the windows closed and the curtains drawn against that very eventuality.

So, assuming he and his housekeeper were right in believing that Rebecca Nelson was responsible for inserting a sharp object into the brain of the superintendent, Hannah Mulrooney was very possibly now in considerable danger.

Chapter 30

If only Hannah had been able to live with the sight of grey water. But she'd never liked it – water that had served its purpose, that had cleansed bodies or dishes or clothes, sitting there glowering at her, angry, she fancied, at being made to swallow the filth the household generated. And she thought, really, that she had waited more than long enough.

The hammering had started shortly after nine. She would have assumed it was Grogan, but she'd heard only one set of footsteps approach the door and those belonged to someone light.

'Hannah! Hannah, dear, are you well? I was worried not to see you today. Hannah, come out. Won't you answer the door, so I can satisfy myself as to your continued health?'

Rebecca sounded as sweet, as flawless, and as impeccably enunciated as always. But Hannah, of course, had no intention of answering the door.

Eventually the pounding stopped. She heard the footsteps recede, the sounds of hoof beats as the carriage pulled away. Still, she sat there in the parlour for some time. Not moving, barely breathing. Trying to ignore the dampness under her arms as the heat of the sun worked its way in through the bricks, amplifying itself in the process, and was given no chance to escape with the windows closed.

She guessed she waited an hour, possibly even more. While she could now read words, Mr Monsarrat had yet to get around to teaching her how to read clocks, so she couldn't be certain what the one on the mantle was trying to tell her.

But surely Rebecca must be long gone by now. In the meantime the grey water in the kitchen would still be sitting there, perhaps even stewing – who knew what would happen if you let such substances lie around long enough, particularly in extreme heat.

She moved to the front windows of the parlour, as close as she could to the curtains without disturbing them. She would not risk looking out, but she stood there. Heard nothing, not even the occasional rustling of a leaf.

So to the water, then. A relief the woman had gone. She could return to the kitchen and perhaps make a start on some bread. But as she opened the back door, she heard a sound which frightened her more than any had since the sounds of the distant Wexford battles.

'Hannah! I was so worried about you, and here you are, walking around and clearly healthier than one would ever expect. Why did you not answer me when I knocked?'

Hannah's only option, she thought, was to pretend delight at the sight of the lady.

'Do forgive me, Mrs Nelson. You must think me terribly rude,' she said, resisting the urge to approach the low fence between her and Rebecca. 'I should not come too close, though. I have been coughing for most of the night, have only just managed to take myself out into the sun. I would never forgive myself if I passed the malady on to you, with all of those women relying on you.'

'Not at all!' said Rebecca with exaggerated magnanimity. 'You clearly need someone to take care of you. I sent Grogan off to water the horse, but that's him back now. You will come to my house – no, I insist. I am very well stocked with medicines and I feel sure you will do better there.'

'A kind offer, but I couldn't possibly accept.'

'Nonsense. In any case it will give me an opportunity to return your shoes. You left them, don't you know, at the Factory last night. When you went in to get my sewing basket, although why that required you to take off your shoes is a story I would like to hear. I have them with me in the trap. Do come along, and you'll be as well shod as ever. We must get you better. We've been away from our post for too long – people will start to wonder about us.'

They could wonder all they liked. Hannah realised, with the first stabs of alarm, that no one except Rebecca and her coachman knew where she was. She tried to fathom, as she had every time the wheel hit a rut, and several times in between, why she was taking such a risk. But Rebecca was not, now, sounding like Rebecca. A new – or old – presence now inhabited her body, and with it had come a new frankness. Hannah desperately wanted to hear what this woman had to say, and would rely on her own wit to survive the experience.

Where it would normally continue on around the bend in the river towards the Female Factory, the trap turned and crossed the bridge, heading towards the part of town where the prosperous lived. Heading towards the Nelson house.

Rebecca turned and smiled occasionally, patted Hannah's knee solicitously, said she hoped Hannah's shoes hadn't been got at by rats in the night. It was amazing what happened when you left things unattended.

There was no gardener in the grounds, nor anyone else in evidence today. No doubt the domestic staff had found themselves with an unexpected day off.

'Grogan, kindly assist Mrs Mulrooney down from the trap, she's not well, you know,' Rebecca said, hopping down herself in a most unladylike way, and displaying more agility than Hannah had seen in her before.

Grogan seemed to believe this gave him licence to act like a royal coachman, fetching a box and putting it on the ground near Hannah's side, extending his hand with a flourish and helping her down.

'That will be all, thank you, Grogan. We are going to have a little time together now, just us. And of course my guest needs to recover – although the fresh air seems to be doing wonders for you, Hannah. I haven't heard you cough during our little journey.'

She took Hannah by the elbow with a painfully firm grip, while patting Hannah's forearm solicitously.

So Grogan drove the trap around to the rear of the house, where Hannah assumed the stables lay. It seemed the horses might be getting something of an unexpected respite as well.

Rebecca stood on the verandah for a moment, then suddenly laughed. 'Do you know, I was waiting here for the housekeeper to come and open the door for us. But she's not here today, of course. So it seems I shall have to do it myself.' She pulled open the door and gestured Hannah inside, closing it behind them and locking it.

They went into the dining room which Hannah had passed through last time she was here; the dark-green painted walls, the marble fireplace, the picture of David Nelson looking benevolently down on his wife and her guest.

Rebecca offered Hannah a seat at the table, by far the grandest Hannah had ever sat at. She adjusted the place settings, and sat down opposite her.

'Now, Hannah, I can't offer you any tea, I'm afraid. No one here to make it, you see. And I was never very good at it myself. That's not where my talents lie. Teaching – that's my forte. Don't you agree? Whereas looking, listening – they, my dear friend, are clearly yours.'

'And making tea, of course,' said Hannah. 'I could make some for you now, Mrs Nelson, should you feel the need of it.'

Rebecca Nelson smiled again. She had been all smiles during their ride to the house. But this was a smile Hannah had never seen from her before. It was satisfied, slightly arrogant, and showed enough teeth on one side of Rebecca's mouth to approach a snarl.

'Do you know,' said Rebecca, 'I would *so* like a cup of tea, but I fear I'll have to deny myself on this occasion. And as for the medicine, well, there is none, but we both know you don't need it. Now, shall I tell you, Hannah, what I've always liked about you?'

'Please do. It would be lovely to hear it.'

'Since we met, I've been impressed by your practicality. Your diligence, the primary importance you attach to getting a job done. So rare, especially when one spends one's days among convicts. Most of them would rather do as little as possible. It's not that they see any benefit from their labour, after all.'

'Well, I consider that a grand compliment,' said Hannah. 'I would consider it even grander were you to note that my practicality tends to come out at the same time as my compassion. One without the other is meaningless, in my view.'

'Ah, yes. Compassion. You think I'm not familiar with the concept? What have I been showing those poor wretches at the Factory all this time? I didn't want to go back there, you know. You can imagine, I'm sure. Last place I would put myself. But you know Mrs Bulmer . . . She's not of a strong enough constitution to withstand the presence of so many depraved females. David urged me to step in for her . . . He's always believed it's too small a place here for Quakers to be at odds with the likes of Bulmer, and bad for business besides. I suggested I could help out at the orphan school or the hospital, but you might have noticed he is somewhat fastidious – he would hate the thought of me walking in the door with the malodorous air of the sick still clinging to my clothes.'

Hannah was aware of a small pulse of sympathy, quickly smothered by her growing unease. To pass through those gates again, as a woman who had achieved a fragile freedom, to return to Church, who had taken so much and had the capacity, and no doubt the will, to take more. A certain amount of derangement was only to be expected.

'Well, you certainly seem to have made a great difference to the women,' she said.

'Yes, I have. So have you, in your small way. But you know, of course, what single act of mine made the most difference.'

Hannah felt suddenly desperate not to hear a confession from the woman, to stop her from saying the words that would likely signal Hannah's own death. 'Was it the reading classes? Or the sewing?' A slight but treacherous tremor had entered her voice, and she felt a compounding alarm to hear it. I must not, she thought, allow this to rise up and choke me.

'I've been so nice to you, and here you go insulting my intelligence,' said Rebecca. 'I suspect you have an accusation to make. One regarding a huge service I did for the Factory women.'

Hannah nodded. 'And yet you would do a great *dis*service to one of the women of the Factory, to Grace O'Leary. For she looks likely to hang for what you've done.'

Mrs Nelson stood, walked behind Hannah's chair, pushing her hands painfully down on Hannah's shoulders as though trying to stop her floating away.

'The pirate queen has done more than enough to provoke a hanging,' she said, as a soft rain of her spittle flecked Hannah's cheek. 'And what could she do, were she to survive? Organise the occasional meaningless rebellion which gets no one's attention? Have the women destroy their work, only to see it taken out of their pay, or their rations? Practicalities – why does no one ever see them? Which one of us is in a position to do the greatest good: the convict confined to the penitentiary, or the rich woman whose husband encourages philanthropy?'

There was no point, thought Hannah now, in keeping up the tea-party demeanour, in pretending she had been brought here for nothing other than a pleasant conversation. 'Your husband – does he know? That your name is Edwina Drake? That you were a convict?'

Rebecca cocked her head to the side, looking at Hannah as though the altered view might produce a revelation.

'However did you come by my surname?'

'Doesn't matter. You have your secrets, a great many of them, and you must allow me mine. As to my question . . . Your husband seems to prefer to do good works from afar. I doubt he'd have you if he knew.'

'No. I thought my hair might be an impediment – many detest red where they would prefer to see gold. He never seemed to mind, though. But you saw how concerned he was about thievery, how upset he was at the idea of convicts in the house.'

'Yet he has had one here for years.'

'Yes. And were he ever to be acquainted with that fact, you are right – I would never be allowed in this house again.'

Chapter 31

Red had been a curse on Edwina for as long as she could remember.

Her hair had always been viewed with suspicion. An unnatural colour and surely, to the superstitious, an indication of what went on in the head it sprouted from.

She detested the names. Witch. Devil child. From classmates, from playmates, and sometimes from their parents too.

So she was grateful that the family who employed her as a governess liked their servants to wear cloth caps at all times. And she became adept at scraping her hair back until her whole skull ached, so that no blood-strand could escape. She had spent more than she could afford on a fine-toothed ivory comb for the purpose.

Who knew where the comb was now. It certainly hadn't accompanied her to New South Wales or the Female Factory, where she had instead kept an eye out for large splinters of wood and used her fingernails to gouge grooves into them until the pads of her fingers bled. She used the finished article to tame her hair.

Nonetheless, she could never stuff every strand into her white cloth cap. She suspected she was the only one among the convicts who would have happily submitted to a punitive haircut.

The old superintendent, an ineffectual man named Donne, had never remarked on her hair, nor on any other part of her person. She was a name on a manifest, someone he intended to parade before the next man seeking a wife. It was the only way to stop her eating provisions and taking up space.

But the treacherous red that sprang out from her cap prevented her being selected. Then the colonial authorities decided that Donne was not getting sufficient return from these women whom they fed and clothed, and they brought in a new man, one rumoured to have a disciplinarian bent.

Of course, it turned out that Church's approach to discipline was somewhat unorthodox. And he noticed her hair. He told her it meant she was dirty, that it betrayed lust, which he was able to satisfy. He would ask her to let it down, and twist a section of it around his wrist before forcing her down onto the grass behind the Third Class penitentiary at the point of an awl.

But even Church couldn't argue with the passage of time, and when enough of it had passed, her ticket of leave arrived. Before she walked through the Factory gates, she stopped to make sure that all of her hair was contained within her cap.

She was now able to afford the best of bonnets, lined with gathered cloth which enabled her to conceal everything above her hairline. So perhaps it would not be such a risk to return to the Factory – not that she could have demurred after her husband beamingly informed her she had the opportunity to do God's work and advance the Nelson name in a single stroke. The staff must surely be different, and many of the women too. She certainly was, and if there were any still there who had shared cells or work-tables or stale bread with her, they would be unlikely to connect the well-groomed woman in the plain but costly dress with the half-starved convict – provided she could keep her hair hidden.

She had not expected Church to still be there – most functionaries here lasted a scant few years until the governor changed – hardly worth learning their names.

But his brutality was translating into sufficient efficiency to keep the authorities happy, and as long as the women weren't draining money from the colonial coffers and could be tucked away at the bend in the river and forgotten about, those in power were reluctant to make any changes.

There would have been so many women since her. The chances of Church recognising her seemed slim.

And he didn't. Not until the day she was late, thanks to Nemesis and an argument he'd had with one of the parlour drapes. She detested tardiness, and had jammed her bonnet onto her head in a rush. Her bun sat uncomfortably all morning, pressing against the back of her neck, and she could tell – there was no pain in her temples, as there generally was when her hair was tightly scraped back – it was in danger of unravelling.

She had been distributing religious tracts to the Third Class women, at the request of Charlotte Bulmer, who was resting at home that day. Her work done, she quickly backed into a shaded corner to remove her bonnet and put her hair to rights. And when she stepped back into the sunshine, she saw Church staring at her.

He crossed the yard, took her elbow in as gentlemanly a manner as he could manage, and whispered, 'How lovely to see you again! And how far you've risen. Perhaps I should meet your husband, speak to him. He may find what I have to say on the subject of our past acquaintance interesting.'

❧

Hannah faced Rebecca across a table weighted down by the silver and porcelain that had made her husband's fortune.

'Of course, theft was easier this time than when I was a governess. The chances of me being suspected was negligible – after all, I was in effect stealing from myself,' said Rebecca.

'And what did Church do with the items?'

'I haven't the faintest idea. I imagine a few of them adorn drawing rooms in Parramatta. I doubt he would have left the town with them – the constables at the toll roads would have posed too much of a risk.'

'And you really think he would have carried out his threat? Told your husband?'

'Oh yes. I think he would have enjoyed it. I had the sense he was waiting for me to get sick of our arrangement, to tell him I wouldn't steal anymore, wouldn't bring him silver and porcelain and silk. There was no chance of that, of course.'

'But then something changed.'

'Yes. He was getting bored of the arrangement. Not bored of the money it brought him, but I think he actually wanted to see me cast out by my husband, tried and convicted for theft, placed back under his control. So he changed our agreement. Shifted the terms to ones he knew would be unacceptable to me.'

'I'm assuming he wanted . . .'

'Me to submit to him again, yes. "To revisit our acquaintance" was the way he put it. He gave me a day to consider the proposition and informed me that any refusal would see him calling on my husband immediately.'

'What did you decide?'

Rebecca Nelson snorted. 'Really, Hannah, need you even ask? He gave me his ultimatum the day he died.'

'And you'll let someone else die too now.'

Rebecca inclined her head again, looking regretful, but politely so, as though she were declining an invitation.

'Yes, I'm afraid so. Grace tried her best, I know, to help the girls, but she hasn't done what I have been able to for the women at the Factory. She couldn't intercede with the superintendent on their behalf – do you know, he was going to cut rations? On his first week? I talked him out of it so they don't know it but they have me to thank for that.'

'Very kind of you. I promise to do everything I can for them once you . . . leave.'

'Where would I be leaving to?'

266

'Well, that's the biggest question of all, isn't it?' said Hannah. 'Theft and murder – once the sentence is carried out, who knows where you'll end up? It's a question that can't be answered in this life.'

'Wherever it is, I do hope you'll greet me when I arrive.'

Hannah Mulrooney felt the rising fear begin to fog her thoughts and clench her stomach.

'Now,' said Rebecca. 'I have a gift for you.'

'Very kind, but unnecessary.'

'It is, though. And I am the one who decides what's necessary and what isn't, not a former convict.'

Rebecca's denial of her own convict past, and her deliberate, almost ritualistic movements as she extracted a flat velvet box from the sideboard and placed it on the table, frightened Hannah more than anything she had yet experienced in this place.

'Well? Open it! I do hope you like it,' Rebecca said, as though this was indeed a gift given out of friendship, and she was excited to see Hannah's response, hear her fulsome thanks.

Hannah did as she was told. And she did very much like what she saw – or would have under different circumstances. It was a necklace of the deepest-blue sapphires, surrounded by little diamonds and converging on a larger, teardrop-shaped sapphire, which had its own moat of sparkling white stones.

'Well, I must say it's lovely. But I couldn't possibly accept it, kind as you are. It must have cost more than I've ever earned as a housekeeper, more than I could ever hope to earn.'

'Yes it did cost rather a lot as a matter of fact. A wedding gift from David, you know. I professed myself delighted with it, and of course I was. I only wear it on the very best of occasions, of course. Dinner at Government House, that sort of thing. Will the new man entertain much, do you think? I've heard he's not intending to reside in Parramatta like dear old Brisbane did.'

'I wouldn't have an inkling of the intentions of the new governor,' said Hannah.

'Well, no matter. I won't be able to wear this necklace anyway. For soon it will have been charred beyond repair. And I'll be dead, so there will be no invitations to dinner for me anyway.'

Despite everything, Hannah felt another surge of concern for the woman. 'Now don't be doing anything stupid like walking into the river or taking a knife to yourself. That's not the way, truly.'

'Oh, I've no intention of doing anything like that. I won't be dead, not really. Everybody will just think I am. They will mourn the beautiful lady who gave her life for the betterment of her less fortunate sisters. I would so love to hear the eulogies. Maybe the *Chronicle* will report on them, do you think? Then I can read about how much I am missed.'

'I find it hard to see how you can have a funeral if you're not there to be buried,' said Hannah.

'Oh, Hannah. They won't be burying my ashes. They'll be burying yours.'

Chapter 32

Alarmed by Hannah's absence and the note from Henson, Monsarrat was tempted to march up to the Nelson house, knock on the door and demand to see Hannah Mulrooney. He knew that was unlikely to succeed.

There was still a slim possibility that Rebecca was innocent and had simply collected Hannah for another day of good works at the Female Factory. Even as he tried to convince himself of the plausibility of that, Monsarrat discounted it. She must have been taken to the Nelson house, and he did not want to imagine what might be occurring there.

But storming the place as a one-man army would simply result in his removal from anything to do with the Factory and its inhabitants. It seemed that his only choice was to confirm Ezekiel Daly's worst suspicions about ex-convicts by appearing before the man in disarray.

There was no one at the front of the police building. No way of finding someone to help him but to run through to the offices. So that, he thought grimly, is what he would have to do. Breaching the sanctity of an office during the work day was something that did not come naturally to him, but letting Hannah Mulrooney suffer was the most unnatural thing of all.

A few moments later, without even consciously instructing his feet to move, the force of his shoulder had slammed the door of the police superintendent's office flat against the wall.

Ezekiel Daly jumped to his feet as Monsarrat entered the room, accidentally kicking his chair to the floor behind him as he did so.

'What the blazes is the meaning of this, Monsarrat?' he yelled, looking at Monsarrat while his hand felt on his desk for a pistol.

'I am sorry, sir. However, I have reason to believe that the life of my housekeeper is in imminent danger, and I was hoping for police assistance in changing that.'

'Your housekeeper? Danger from whom?'

'Rebecca Nelson, sir. I am certain she killed Robert Church. With this.'

He put the awl, wrapped in a cloth, on the desk. Daly showed no inclination to touch it.

'I also suspect she abducted my housekeeper this morning. I cannot guess what her intentions are, but I fear the worst.'

The superintendent made to sit down again, remembering just in time that his chair was no longer upright. He righted it with exaggerated care, and eased himself down into it.

'Monsarrat, if your housekeeper is with Mrs Nelson, I have no doubt that she is perfectly safe and probably having a whale of a time being plied with scones – that woman does have a fondness for former convicts.'

'Because *she* was one, sir. I have the proof of it. She is Edwina Drake. She came here per *Nemesis*.'

'This is a fantasy, Monsarrat. If you were the only one to be harmed by it, I would leave you to it. But you are seeking to besmirch the reputation of a fine woman, all to exculpate a convict who is a known troublemaker. I will not have it. Your housekeeper, if she is fortunate enough to be with Mrs Nelson, is perfectly safe. And now I will give you the opportunity to apologise and leave. I suggest you take it, for if you don't I will be reporting this behaviour to Mr Eveleigh. And I will ensure that you lose your ticket of leave.'

'My ticket of leave? On what possible charge?'

'I will think of something, I assure you. Maligning a free citizen, maybe. For the moment, I remind you that the only chance you have of keeping your situation – and your freedom – is to make your amends and leave.'

It stalled Monsarrat's thoughts for a moment – the prospect of losing his freedom. And even if the superintendent was unable to come up with an appropriate charge, if he lost his position with Eveleigh, he'd lose along with any hope of the respect he had so hoped to earn from the McAllisters, the Nelsons, the permanently free.

But he quashed the thought as it transited his mind. And for an instant he felt something close to elation. He did not, he realised, particularly care for the good opinion of those who viewed Parramatta as a pie to be shared between a few, with a bonded workforce that didn't require payment.

'Sir . . . I shall politely decline your request. I'm well aware of what this may cost me. However, I beg you to come with me to the Nelson household. A courtesy visit, if you will. You may satisfy yourself that my accusations are the ravings of a madman, and I will happily hand you my ticket of leave and present myself the following morning to the overseer of whichever work gang you nominate. You will be shot of me. Surely a brief visit to an elegant household is a small price to pay for that?'

Daly stood. 'Very well then, Monsarrat. If this is how you choose to end your freedom, I will accompany you. The road to Windsor is in a terrible state – I understand from Reverend Bulmer that you are well acquainted with it. As someone who has travelled it before, it would be a great benefit to have you on the work gang there.'

'Now, I can see a few problems with that,' said Hannah.

'Can you indeed?' said Rebecca, a benign smile on her face.

'Mr Monsarrat will miss me, for a start.'

'He will find another housekeeper soon enough. They have no more interest in differences between servants than they do in the difference between one leaf and another. And I intend to put it about that you were seen leaving Parramatta with a bundle of your employer's property under your arm.'

'Yes. Well. Then there's St John's cemetery. It's a resting place for Protestants, isn't it? Surely the earth would revolt if a Catholic was placed in it.'

'I suppose we'll have to see. Another factor that makes me sorry I'll miss it – it would be an entertaining spectacle, I'm sure.'

'Perhaps. But the other problem, you see, is that I'm not dead.'

'As to that . . . I don't want to spoil my surprise, but I would love, dear Hannah, to see how well you look in my necklace. Please put it on.'

Hannah did as she was told. The woman had gone quite mad, far worse than Lizzie. There was no point provoking her until Hannah knew her intentions and was able to formulate a plan.

The necklace was surprisingly heavy. Hannah had no idea if it was a property of this particular piece of jewellery, or if all precious stones had so much weight to them. She had no basis for comparison. Cold, too – the chill seeped from the stones into her skin, seemed to spread to her shoulders, doing its mistress's bidding, immobilising her.

Mrs Nelson regarded Hannah silently for several moments. 'I always wear it with a gown, of course. It does really need a fine dress to set it off. I doubt it's ever been near such coarse fabric before. Must be a shock for the poor thing. But it does bring out the blue of your eyes.'

'Thank you,' said Hannah. 'It's been a long time since my eyes were the object of attention.'

'My pleasure. Now, you've seen our study?'

'Yes. I didn't go in though. I had an idea Mr Nelson wouldn't welcome it.'

'I daresay you're right about that. He doesn't even allow me in there most of the time. Fortunate, then, that he is gone so much of the day. It has enabled me to become very well acquainted with his correspondence. What shipments are expected when, that sort of thing. I was able to plan my visits to the warehouse quite well. Preparedness is so important, don't you agree?'

'Of course, Mrs Nelson. You've always been impeccably prepared.'

'Indeed. And, as you know, my husband's not a very trusting man. If he had his way, he would not employ former convicts. Of course, it's all you can get when it comes to domestic staff so he's had to put up with the notion of having them in the house. But he has taken certain precautions.'

'Very wise. You can't trust anybody, it seems.'

'True, sadly. One of the precautions he took was investing in an exceptionally good lock for his study door. Had the windows painted shut, too. Madness, I feel. In this heat, you know. It would send me quite demented if I was unable to open a window. But he doesn't seem to mind. So, really, I doubt there are many more secure rooms in the entire colony.'

'A comforting thought.'

'David finds it so. Of course, he won't have to worry about one particular former convict. By this time tomorrow I shall be far away from here.'

'How on earth will you manage? What will you do for money?'

'Well, I didn't give Mr Church everything I took from the warehouse. I have quite a nice little store myself, or had – it's all been sold, of course. The money, would you believe, is under the seat of the trap – you were sitting on it! More money than you could ever dream of, Hannah, and it was under your posterior – is that not delightful?'

'I find it hard to think of few things more delightful.'

'I knew you'd appreciate the irony. So I should be quite adequately set up for a while. I can always get another governess position, I suppose, but I fully intend to find a rich man to marry before that becomes necessary.'

'And the fact that you are already married won't concern you?'

'Why should it? The clergy – the sensible ones, not the Bulmers – have always turned a blind eye to that sort of thing. And I will have a new story by then, of course. I'll probably become a widow. But allow me to assure you, if you don't already know, that there are a great many married men and women who have living, breathing husbands and wives in Dublin or Cork or Leicester or London.'

'Yes. I'm aware of that.'

'So if you were to ask David in a day or so, he would say he was unmarried – he'll be a widower by nightfall. Why should I not say the same thing? Really, I was quite happy here, but I think I'm going to enjoy this. The adventure of becoming someone else. I've had practice; it should go a little more smoothly. Now, do you know, Hannah, you're to be greatly honoured today.'

'I am?'

'Why yes! You're going to be the first woman to be invited into David Nelson's study!'

Hannah opened her mouth, closed it again. Any voice that came out now would be shredded by fear and not worth attempting.

Rebecca grasped Hannah's arm and eased her forward. The curtains in the study were drawn, the room was dark with a metallic smell from overheated dust. Everything looked neat. Hannah didn't know where the correspondence Rebecca had spoken of was stored, but David Nelson was clearly not the sort to leave documents on his desk. In that, he and Mr Monsarrat were alike.

'Now, why don't you sit in that lovely chair? You can pretend you're a rich woman writing orders to your servants. Sending requests to dressmakers, devising the menu for a ball. It'll be such fun! Until, of course … But a very pleasant way to live out your last moments.'

Mrs Nelson stopped, looking at the ceiling in thought. 'You know, I must be more precise with language. More than moments, actually.'

'I am glad to hear it,' Hannah said, her voice a dying rustle.

'Yes, probably minutes. For as long as it takes the house to catch.'

'The house to catch what?'

'To catch fire, of course. I am afraid, Mrs Mulrooney, that that skin of yours – so good for a woman your age – is going to have to go to waste. We're the same height, and when your blackened bones are found with my necklace resting on them, everyone will assume you're me.'

Chapter 33

Daly was moving infernally slowly, casting his eyes over anyone they encountered as though trying to ascertain at a glance whether they were up to no good. Monsarrat had to restrain himself several times from urging the man to greater speed. But he feared the police superintendent would abandon the exercise entirely if he brought any further pressure to bear.

'I don't know what you expect to find at the Nelson house, Monsarrat,' Daly said at one point. 'But I can assure you I expect a scene of domestic tranquility, which is likely to be the last such scene you are privileged to witness for quite some time.'

Monsarrat, in truth, didn't know what he expected to find either. And he was caught, now, between hoping that he had misinterpreted the situation, and praying he hadn't. The former situation might leave Mrs Mulrooney without an employer, but the latter might leave her without a life.

Perhaps it was the heat, but it did seem to Monsarrat that Daly's stride was shortening, his pace slowing, with each passing minute. Then the man stopped altogether, before breaking into a run.

And when Monsarrat followed the superintendent's gaze, he began to run too – towards the slight rise where the Nelson household commanded views of the town, and from where, now, a column of smoke rose into the air.

It didn't take long, not nearly as long as she had hoped.

The hot, dry air did nothing to contain the flames, and the wind stoked them until, within minutes, wisps of smoke began curling under the study door. Hannah had tried rattling and pulling at the door, of course. A sturdy little lock, just as Rebecca had promised.

She checked that the windows were indeed painted shut. When she drew aside the heavy green drapes, she saw Rebecca Nelson. The woman was several paces away from the house. She held a flaming branch, which she was using to set light to piles of kindling placed at intervals around the house.

She looked up, saw Hannah and smiled. An approving smile: good, you're wearing the gift I gave you.

I'm not going to die with this cursed thing on my throat, Hannah thought. So, making sure Rebecca could see her, she took the necklace off, held it up, and then very deliberately threw it on the floor.

Rebecca's face clouded, her brows drew together like a petulant child's and she glared at Hannah, clearly offended that such a present should be tossed aside so casually, probably angry that it would not be found close enough to the ashes to allow a definite link to be made between the necklace and the body.

But it won't be, will it, Hannah said to herself. You've no intention of dying today, surely? You've survived far worse. Fine words, of course. But what, she asked herself, do you expect me to do about it?

Rebecca had turned on her heel and walked off, setting light to the kindling as she went, and probably thinking that would be the last she would see of the Irishwoman.

Maybe, Hannah thought, the heat was making the lock slightly more malleable? When she reached her hand out to it, however, she snatched it back immediately. It was much too hot to touch and when she placed her palm against the timbers of the door, they too were radiating heat.

The floor. It would buy her a few more breaths, hopefully enough to think of something to do.

But the fire had no intention of waiting for Hannah to gather her wits. As she dropped to the ground to avoid the worst of the smoke and crawled towards the window, dragging herself up on the sill to look out, the flames had already closed ranks and consumed the careful topiary and minutely tended flowers. A shame, she thought. Some poor gardener had worked day after day on those, and in an instant they were ashes.

As you will be soon, if you don't think of something.

The noise was already beginning to build, a roar gathering in the throat of the fire; the door was beginning to blacken. Yet, thought Hannah, would you not think, with all of that lovely vegetation and newly laid kindling out there waiting to be consumed, the flames would have marched right up to the window by now?

She closed her eyes. Pictured herself walking from the kitchen, where she'd been sent to get the water for Helen. The cup, brought to the pump, to the dripstone. And the pump leaking dreadfully, causing a small rivulet of water to sneak around the side of the house towards the outer wall of the study ... And now, in her mind, she came back through the house, past the study. She recalled glancing in, seeing David Nelson, staring at that bronze dog ... The bronze dog that even now sat on the desk, waiting to be melted.

You won't melt today, she said to it. You might not look quite as pretty when I am finished with you, though. She picked it up, hefted it. It was even heavier than she had anticipated, but not too heavy – and almost but not quite too hot to touch – to propel it towards the window, whose frames were now blistering.

The house was fully alight by the time Monsarrat and Daly got near to it, breaching a bank of smoke which instantly turned the bright day into dusk.

The men pushed on through the unnatural nightfall, through the embers which studded the gloom and which, once or twice, settled on Monsarrat's cheek and would have burrowed in if he had not brushed them away.

He was blinking fiercely now, the heat burning his eyes as he got close enough to see the state of the place. One side of the building sagged: its weakened timbers had collapsed under their own weight. The rumble from the burning house was echoed suddenly by a low, vibrating boom from a nearby eucalyptus. Its sap had vaporised, expanding in the heat, pushing outwards until the tree could no longer hold it, sending large splinters of wood twirling through the air. One of these found a home in the upper arm of the superintendent, who had matched Monsarrat step for step through the smoke. Daly plucked it out as though brushing some dust off his jacket.

'Well, Monsarrat,' he called above the fire. 'I hold out little hope for anyone inside. I am sorry.'

His voice was odd now, an unnatural rasp, lacking any moisture to give it depth or resonance.

'Little hope, you said, sir,' Monsarrat yelled back. His own voice sounded no better, and the scalding air he breathed made his throat feel blistered and his lungs labour under its weight. 'Little hope. Not none.'

He ran to the side, skirting the perimeter of the worst of the blaze, looking for a way in, a way out, any weakness in the fire's armour which might help him.

What he found was Grogan.

The man was striding purposefully, seeming unaffected by the ember-strewn air, as though he was expecting Monsarrat. As though he was coming to meet him.

Odd to see Grogan here, walking towards him as though he was starting up the road to collect Hannah. And this was,

Monsarrat thought, the man who *had* collected Hannah, brought her here, where he very much feared she remained.

Grogan was saying something, but the scream of flames and the now-regular pop of the trees were drowning it out. Then he got close enough to hear.

'Stay away! Mrs Nelson's orders – no quarrel with you. Go back, or I am bound to stop you.'

'I couldn't care less about Mrs Nelson's orders!'

Monsarrat stepped to the side, gathering pace as quickly as he could, trying to run around the man. Grogan was bigger, though, and had anticipated resistance. He sped up too, and more quickly than Monsarrat. He propelled himself towards the clerk, drawing back his fist as he ran, and then shooting it forwards to connect with Monsarrat's jaw.

The blow threw back Monsarrat's head and knocked him down. For a moment he could see small fragments of blue above the smoke. His teeth jammed together, snipping off a small part of the side of his tongue, and his mouth filled with blood, which ran down his chin when he opened his mouth to speak.

It was a futile gesture – there was nothing to say. The words with which he customarily constructed his barricade against the world were useless against this man who was now bearing down on him, having availed himself of a smouldering branch which, Monsarrat suspected, was being aimed at his head.

It never got there.

From his prone position, Monsarrat couldn't see exactly how fast Daly was running, if such a thing were possible, requiring as it would great gulps of air, which would take more than they gave as they clogged the throat with ashes. But Daly must've built a reasonable amount of speed because he knocked this human bullock off his feet, when the bigger man was braced with one stout leg on either side of Monsarrat's torso, raising the glowing branch while sparks dripped down from it onto his shirt, which had once been white but never would be again.

He must have hit his head when he fell backwards. At any rate he felt no urgency to stand, to run, to do anything except realise in wonder that the man who had threatened to remove his freedom, who'd wanted him back on the work gangs, was rolling on top of Grogan and driving his knee down on Grogan's arm, making the driver's fingers reflexively release the branch in protest.

He's done that before, thought Monsarrat idly, weakly swabbing his slick forehead with the back of his hand and wondering if there was any part of him not covered in a film of moist grime. Not something I would have thought to do, or known how, he thought. He turned his head, peeling his cheek away from the dirt, to see if he could spot any more patches of blue through the smoke.

He fixed on one, and decided it was a nice sight to drift off to. If only that voice would stop barking at him.

'Get up, man! For God's sake, get up! I don't know how long I can hold this brute!'

Monsarrat had just enough energy to look for the source of the voice. Why on earth does he want me to get up? he wondered.

'Monsarrat, if you don't get up, I will hit you with this stick myself! If there is any hope for your housekeeper, it is quickly diminishing. Get to your feet!'

And then Monsarrat remembered where he was, and why.

After that, it was the work of a moment to make his legs bend, to get his brain to control the mechanics sufficiently to bring him to his feet. He did, however, feel somewhat concerned about leaving Daly to wrestle with a man almost twice his weight.

'Are you ...'

'Yes, I am well able to manage here! Now go!'

Monsarrat went.

The narrow avenue he had noticed around the side of the house was baking hot, embers littering the ground. This side of the house was still standing, but it could not long remain so,

Monsarrat thought. Beyond it, extending to the back of the house, the small gap in the fire persisted. It seemed to Monsarrat that there were two burning entities struggling to meet each other, one consuming the house and the other the garden, and each being prevented for some reason from joining hands. But they would achieve their objective soon, he had no doubt.

He stumbled down the narrow space between the two, holding his breath as much as he could. The heat of each wall made him dizzy, and the sweat in his eyes would have blinded him even had he been able to see through the smoke.

A moment later, he felt a minute reduction in temperature, a tiny easing of noise. He lifted his ruined shirtsleeve to his eyes, wiping the sweat and soot away, and blinked. He was in the yard behind the house, the one that led to the kitchen. The kitchen outbuilding itself was not yet aflame but the fire was hurling embers towards it, scouting parties before the major assault.

He could barely see the green of the kitchen's paint through the smoke. The fact that he could see at all, though, told him the worst of the fire was behind him. And as he stumbled on through the smoke, a scrap of white near the ground began to emerge. It was not any white Mrs Mulrooney would have approved of. Smudged and streaked and torn, rendered utterly useless as an apron.

The skirts were hitched up slightly, revealing a pair of shredded feet. The toes of one were facing their counterparts on the other, in a manner which was not supposed to be possible. Their owner was sitting on the ground resting her back against the blistering paint of the kitchen, her eyes closed, her lips slightly parted but slack.

No, he thought. You are not allowed to do this. I refuse my permission as your employer. You are not dismissed.

Monsarrat knelt, taking Mrs Mulrooney under the arms and hoisting her over his shoulder. As he stumbled away from the worst of the smoke, he prayed to a God to whom he rarely spoke (and usually had no wish to, if He was happy for the likes of Bulmer to represent Him). He prayed for the sting of a rolled cleaning cloth against his temple and a dressing-down for having the hide to lug a woman around as though she were a sack of grain.

Chapter 34

Under different circumstances, Monsarrat might have taken a small amount of guilty pleasure in seeing Grogan cry.

It had taken him some time to work his way back around to the front of what was once the house, carrying Mrs Mulrooney, not wanting to check whether she was still breathing.

The air lightened gradually, each breath less laboured than the last, until the patches of blue above him widened and he could see ten, twenty, thirty feet ahead.

By the time he gained the roadway leading to the house two constables had arrived, alerted by the none-too-subtle signal of one of the settlement's best houses being burned to the ground.

One of them had managed to get Grogan's wrists into a pair of irons. Grogan was not struggling. He was staring, instead, down the road which wound its way to the base of the hill before veering off towards Windsor. Monsarrat followed the man's gaze. In the distance he could see a trap pulled by a single horse, which was being driven at remarkable speed by a driver with red hair. Someone, or something, was seated beside her, a small grey figure that could well have been a wolfhound.

Grogan's mouth was open and tears were running freely down

his cheeks, cutting paths through the soot. Daly was standing nearby. He had removed his jacket, which he had somehow had the presence of mind to fold and place on the ground nearby, and he was dabbing gingerly at the wound in his arm where the shard of exploding eucalypt had impaled it.

He was berating one of the constables in a voice made hoarse by smoke.

'Delancey! Why on earth didn't you stop her?'

'There was no reason to stop her, sir. None that we were aware of, anyway. It *was* odd to see her without a bonnet. Or a driver. But we thought she was escaping the flames. We offered assistance but she ignored it, just drove on. We believed that as she was safe we should come up here and render any assistance necessary.'

Daly glowered at his subordinates. 'Assumptions. Never make them again.'

But he forgot his anger, and his wound, when he saw Monsarrat. He reached down, spread his coat across the soot-dusted grass and helped Monsarrat lower Mrs Mulrooney onto it. Then the superintendent snaked his hand into the pocket of the coat on which Mrs Mulrooney now lay and drew out a silver pocket watch, which looked even shinier than it would normally have against the backdrop of so much dirt. Without opening it he held its polished surface above Mrs Mulrooney's mouth and showed Monsarrat the thin film of moisture that had formed there.

'Still alive, miraculously. Has you to thank for it, no doubt. I would not have gone in after her, simply because I felt there was no chance of survival for anyone in that house, and I would have been adding another corpse to the pile. You are to be commended, Monsarrat.'

Monsarrat's relief at the sight of the mist on the silver overrode any surprise he might have felt at a commendation from this man. 'I thank God for it, sir,' he said, the last word truncated by the need to cough as his lungs revolted under the weight of so many flecks of burned house and immolated tree. 'But she needs help, that much is clear.'

Daly turned to the constable who wasn't actively engaged in detaining Grogan. 'Run as fast as your spindly little legs will allow, down to the hospital, fetch Dr Preston in a trap and come back here. Send a man in another trap after Mrs Nelson. The speed of your return will have a direct bearing on your future in my office.'

The constable turned and sprinted down the hill.

Daly turned to the other constable. 'Delancey, have you a water bag?'

The man nodded, motioning to a small leather bag on a strap which crossed his chest. Daly reached into the satchel, withdrew the water skin and poured a small amount into his hand, bathing Mrs Mulrooney's face with surprising gentleness and pouring a few drops between her lips. She didn't respond, not by the merest flicker of an eyelid, and the skin beneath the soot looked frighteningly pale. Daly handed the water bag to Monsarrat and turned to Grogan. 'Now, boyo. You're going to tell me why you are mewling like a baby.'

Monsarrat slowly emptied the bag, washing the worst of the filth off Mrs Mulrooney's face and dribbling small amounts of water onto her lips. He very much feared it was a useless effort. The water would rest on her lips for a moment before running off down the side of her face. He tried to ignore the ashen quality of her skin, instead observing her chest continuing to rise and fall, however shallowly.

When Dr Preston arrived in the trap driven by the constable, he looked stricken at the sight of the housekeeper. He made no attempt to treat her there, dashing the faint hope Monsarrat was holding that the doctor knew of strange arts that could save her on the spot. But he helped Monsarrat load her into the trap and ordered the constable to drive away as fast as he could towards the hospital, with Daly calling after them to send the trap back as soon as Mrs Mulrooney had been unloaded.

It could have been the juddering of the vehicle as it did battle with the worst of the ruts on the road down the hill. It could have been the change in the air, still heavy with the smell of wood smoke but clearer, and as sweet as any Monsarrat had ever breathed. But whatever the reason, as they approached the hospital, Monsarrat felt movement in his lap where Mrs Mulrooney's head rested. He looked down to see her eyes fluttering open. And now she was trying to speak, in a voice that would have been a whisper had it not been shredded by smoke.

'Rest, dear lady. I would give anything to hear you tell me what an idiot of a man I am, but it will have to wait until you are improved.'

Mrs Mulrooney ignored him, of course, and tried to speak again. He leaned his head closer to her so that he could hear her message.

'I hope,' she was saying, 'that you don't expect me to wash that shirt.'

'Well, Mr Monsarrat. I've stopped being surprised by you. No point. The only thing that will ever shock me is if you materialise in the place I expect you to be.'

'I'm sorry, Mr Eveleigh. As I believe you know, there was an urgent matter to which I needed to attend. If it's any consolation, Superintendent Daly provided me with the most unimpeachable supervision.'

Monsarrat's words were precise, their pronunciation less so. The small missing piece of his tongue was affecting his speech, the sibilants almost gurgling out of his mouth.

'Yes, I'm aware of your adventures. The superintendent sent a messenger. He has had constables knee-deep in the river looking for red hair on a drowned body. He has raided every shebeen in the district, and has ordered every ship searched. Nothing, I'm afraid. There is nothing, however, to prevent a woman so deranged from wandering into the trackless bush, where her trace may never be found. But for now I am more concerned with another woman. How, may I ask, is your housekeeper?'

Monsarrat could hardly tell Eveleigh the truth – his housekeeper was cranky. Homer Preston had insisted she stay at the hospital for another day. She had spent the previous night coughing up black emissions and one of her ankles was badly broken.

Preston confided in Monsarrat, 'You have to be so careful with these breaks. If it doesn't heal correctly, she'll hobble for the rest of her life.' It would be some time before Mrs Mulrooney could walk with her accustomed ease.

Monsarrat, who had prayed more in the past twenty-four hours than he had in the previous decade, had since entreated God to spare the world a lame Hannah Mulrooney. Mostly for her sake, but also for his. It would put her in a permanently bad temper.

'She is recovering, I thank you, sir,' he said to Eveleigh. 'It is yet to be seen how her ankle will heal, but she has escaped the situation with the rest of her intact.'

'Quite a miracle, I understand,' said Eveleigh.

'Yes indeed, sir. The fire was very fierce and I feared she would be trapped inside.'

'But the best miracles . . . Well, they tend to occur with earthly assistance. I understand it is you she has to thank for her survival, Monsarrat.'

When Monsarrat looked surprised, Eveleigh said, 'The superintendent presented himself here last night, after it all. I'm not a drinking man, as you know, but I felt if there was ever a time to decant one of the finer bottles in the cellars, this was it. You have impressed the man, you know. The first time I'm aware of a former convict doing so.'

Monsarrat said nothing. After the blessing of Hannah's survival, he barely dared hope for a second one – that he might actually have made an ally of the police superintendent.

'I, however, am less impressed,' said Eveleigh.

'Of course, sir. I do apologise.'

'Rightly so. I have a room full of documents that require sorting. It's the work of a month or more, yet I gave you the task a day or two ago and you've not yet accomplished it.'

Monsarrat looked up and saw that one side of Eveleigh's mouth was inching towards his cheek, the closest he'd ever seen the man come to a smile.

'And what's even more galling,' said Eveleigh, 'is that those documents will have to wait for some time before they are able to claim your full attention.'

Monsarrat inclined his head, with what he hoped was the appropriate amount of servility.

'For now, they will have to languish. You have another task.'

'Of course, sir,' said Monsarrat. Tickets of leave, perhaps? An inventory of the contents of Government House in preparation for the new governor's arrival?

'Since Mrs Nelson is no longer . . . available,' said Eveleigh, 'her driver — Grogan, I believe his name is — is best placed to provide us with some illumination regarding the death of Robert Church. I understand he's also been charged with assault on a certain clerk. The superintendent is interviewing him today.'

'Ah. I wish him every success.'

'You can wish him that in person, actually. And you may contribute to it as well. He requires a clerk to transcribe the proceedings. And he has requested, would you believe, one Hugh Llewelyn Monsarrat.'

For once Monsarrat walked into the gaol without a sense of foreboding, without feeling as though the building was measuring him, sizing him up, checking whether any of its cells contained a Monsarrat-shaped hole into which he could be slotted.

Daly was waiting for him just inside and nodded when he saw Monsarrat. He was wearing a new coat, a darker one. His tan jacket would surely be permanently out of action on account of the blood and soot stains, which had also led to the consignment of Monsarrat's shirt to his manageable parlour fire.

'Mr Monsarrat. You may be interested to know that a woman with red hair was seen boarding a sloop to Van Diemen's Land after Mrs Nelson escaped. We have sent a fast ship in pursuit.'

Monsarrat did not hold out much hope. The idea that a woman who had set a spectacular conflagration in Parramatta would so calmly take ship for another port somehow seemed unlikely. He could more easily imagine her raging into the bush and thus vanishing.

'I wish you the best of luck with it, sir.'

'Hmph. We'll get started, shall we?' Daly said.

'Of course, sir.'

'Eveleigh says you have a fine hand, and that's borne out by what I've seen in your report on the O'Leary woman.'

'Yes, sir.'

'Quick, are you?'

'As quick as you need me to be.'

'We'll see.'

Grogan didn't look up as the guard admitted them to his cell. He lay on a board that was suspended from the wall by two chains. He seemed fascinated with the ceiling.

Daly turned to the guard. 'Tell me, what's your name?'

'Barton, sir,' said the guard.

'Mr Barton, tell me, are you a halfwit?'

'Ah . . . no, sir. I don't think so.'

'You do not, eh? May I ask you what you think Mr Monsarrat here and I are intending to accomplish today?'

'You are to interview the prisoner, sir, is my understanding.'

'Very good. Perhaps you have three-quarters of your wits, rather than simply half. You certainly don't have them all. How do you expect this gentleman and me to complete our task – together with the transcription of the statement – while standing?'

The guard gaped. Perhaps he was wondering if there was any safe response. If he was, Monsarrat had no concern about his wits whatsoever – it was a sensible question to ask oneself in the circumstances.

'A table, man! A table and chairs! Procure them at once.'

The guard bobbed, almost like a maid, and scurried off.

'Lock the door behind you, for God's sake! He may be impersonating a log at the moment, but I assure you our friend is well capable of making a run at you.'

The guard hurried back, locked the door and hurried off again.

'Well, Grogan. It seems we are your cellmates for a short period.'

There was no response from the log. Grogan turned his head slightly, glared at Daly, and then resumed his examination of the ceiling.

'Not feeling loquacious today, my friend?' said Daly. 'To be expected, I suppose. Yours was not the primary crime, after all. But the person who did commit it has left you to pay her share as well as yours, it seems.'

Grogan was on his feet so quickly that Monsarrat had no time to react. He barrelled towards the superintendent, one arm outstretched, his fingers in a claw as though Grogan meant to close them around the superintendent's neck.

Daly seemed unconcerned. He simply snatched Grogan's wrist when the man was close enough and twisted it downwards, eliciting a yelp which seemed too high to have emanated from such a large mound of a person.

'Very unwise. Strangling me isn't going to change your situation. You can strangle Monsarrat, of course, but even that wouldn't help.'

Monsarrat was still glowing from Eveleigh's reports of the superintendent's approval. Nevertheless, he could not say with absolute certainty that Daly was joking.

'Best sit down,' said Daly. 'Your gaolers have enough intelligence to prevent you from escaping. Whether that intelligence extends to finding a table and chairs, and how quickly, I've no idea. It may be some time before we can begin the formal interview.'

Grogan declined the offer, pacing around the room. Finally he turned again to Daly and the meanness had returned.

'She wouldn't have left me, you know. She wouldn't have. Not unless she'd been given no choice. He forced her to go,' Grogan said, slashing an arm in Monsarrat's direction.

'Forced her?' said Daly. 'He did nothing of the kind. Nor did anyone else. If there was anyone doing any forcing, I suspect it was the lady herself.'

Finally Grogan sat down on the plank. 'She's done nothing wrong,' he said.

'Oh, I think she's done a lot wrong. Murder, attempted murder, arson. Theft, I presume.'

'Presume what you like. I'll not be talking to you of anything to do with it.'

'Such loyalty! A fine fellow you must be, to be willing to take punishment for your employer. Particularly when that punishment involves your neck being broken. A pity, though, that the loyalty isn't returned.'

'Mrs Nelson would do anything for me.'

'Yes, I can understand why you'd like to believe that. But surely you can't, not anymore. I saw your tears when you looked down the hill yesterday. When you saw her, whipping the horse into a lather, the seat next to her occupied by a dog rather than you. And you still wish to defend her?'

'I will not say anything else,' said Grogan.

'Very well. You rest your voice, for now. At least until the table arrives. Then, however, things will become ... official. Mr Monsarrat here will be transcribing your evidence. So by all means save it for then.'

The guard was back remarkably quickly with a table and two chairs. He managed to produce them in around a quarter of the time it had taken Tom Felton to grudgingly drag a splinter-infested bench into the room for Monsarrat. Clearly guards took requests from the police superintendent more seriously than they did those from a clerk whose role in the proceedings was murky at best.

'Now, you stay where you are. I don't want you to trouble yourself,' Daly said to Grogan. He moved the table over so that it was close to the bench where the prisoner was sitting, so the man looked as though he was about to dine. Then he dragged his and Monsarrat's chairs close as well, seating himself opposite the man, with Monsarrat in the unenviable position of being between the two.

'Table or no table, I will say nothing,' said Grogan.

'What can she have done, I wonder, to earn your silence?'

Nothing from Grogan.

'And do you truly believe, if you say nothing, that things will become easier for you?'

Still silence.

'Now, I wonder . . . There have been rumours for years that the magistrates can be bought. That justice is a commodity to be traded, and anyone with enough money can purchase a lighter sentence, perhaps even a transmutation of death into life – quite a power. I make no comment on the veracity of those rumours. I simply wonder whether you're hoping that the lady will use the funds from the items she stole from her husband to secure your freedom, even your life?'

Grogan must have grown sick of looking silently at Daly. He resumed his examination of the ceiling.

'But you must see that she would have to be here to do that.'

Monsarrat wondered why Daly persisted in pausing after each statement. He also wondered why Daly did not seem perturbed when he received no response.

'Perhaps you believe she fled simply in fear of the flames. That she is, even now, still in this area, seeking to make contact with an appropriately corrupt functionary on your behalf. Faith as well as loyalty – very laudable characteristics. Or they would be if they were combined with any intelligence.'

Grogan lowered his head again. 'I'm not stupid,' he said. 'People think I am but I'm not. Mrs Nelson could see it.'

'What Mrs Nelson could see was a strong pair of arms and an unquestioning character,' said Daly. 'She's no doubt looking for someone just like you right now, wherever she is. But I can assure you it's not here in Parramatta. Before I was able to get word to the toll gates of her crimes, she passed through them at a gallop. The constables there let her pass, and why wouldn't they? Respectable woman such as herself. But now they know the truth of it, they won't let her pass back in so easily, assuming she tries to return to Parramatta, which she won't. Lord knows where she has gone, but she will never return here, of that I can assure you. And there has been no attempt to bargain for your life, nor will there be.'

'Mrs Nelson said she would look after me,' Grogan said stubbornly, as though seeking to reassure himself of that truth.

'And did you think to ask yourself, lad, about the character of someone who would so lightly burn her own house to the ground? Someone who would engineer the death of a woman who had done nothing but assist her? Someone who would think nothing of consigning to the flames a necklace of such value that it could pay for another observatory for the governor, wherever he is now. She was willing to dispose of all these treasures. Are you a greater treasure to her, I wonder?'

Daly's voice turned soft, his tone became fatherly. It was more chilling to Monsarrat than his threats had been – the knowledge that this man of power was able to change his verbal coloration with such ease.

'I'm sure she made you promises, my boy,' said Daly. 'I'm sure she claimed that you and she would live like a king and queen

294

away from Parramatta's muck. Was it a farm she promised you? Or just a comfortable house without the need to drive a horse through this heat? Whatever it was, it will never come to pass. She has gone, and gone permanently. And I can guarantee you she has no thought of returning.'

Grogan stared at Daly, his eyes narrowing. 'You're wrong. She's a good woman. She saved me. Mr Nelson was going to let me go – felt I wasn't taking good enough care of the horses. He even accused me of selling their feed so I could drink. It wasn't true, but that didn't matter to him. She made him see he was wrong.'

Daly laughed, a harsh sound. 'Is that all? You bartered your life for your job? Wait . . . she came to you, didn't she? She did! I can see it in your face. She did more than promise you a comfortable future. She made . . . a down-payment.'

'I would never speak of such things.'

'Good lad, does you credit. And you need say nothing, for I already know. But it was all false. I doubt she's given you the merest flicker of thought since she left.'

This reality was beginning to settle over Grogan's mind. His face began to sag, as he gave up the effort of keeping it flint-hard and unreadable.

'I would have done anything for her,' he said in a whisper.

'The matter at hand is what precisely *did* you do for her?'

'I drove her around. She'd ask me to take certain items from her husband's warehouse to this person or that, exchange them for payment, bring the money back to her.'

'Tell me about the night of Robert Church's murder.'

Grogan inhaled and held his breath for what seemed like minutes. Perhaps, thought Monsarrat, he was savouring the sensation of full lungs while he could.

'The night the superintendent was killed, I drove her to the Female Factory. Waited until she came out – from around the side, not through the front gate – drove her home. That was all.'

'Did you know what she'd done?'

'No. She just told me she had removed an impediment to our future happiness. I didn't ask anything further – she didn't like it when I asked questions. But the next day, when I heard of the murder . . . I knew. And I was glad. That man pawed at her, she said, until she wished her flesh was not her own. He deserved it.'

'Well, there are many who'd agree with you, as it happens. But it was still a crime, you know. And one you assisted, wittingly or not.'

Grogan's eyes began to dart around the room. He can sense the net beginning to close, thought Monsarrat.

'And you made another night-time visit to the Factory, didn't you? With the Irishwoman, Hannah Mulrooney. A woman, by the way, who happens to be of significant interest to my friend Mr Monsarrat here, and a woman whom, it seems, you drove to her near-death.'

'I didn't know Mrs Nelson wanted to kill her.'

'Ah, but did you give her any information about Mrs Mulrooney's visit to the Factory that night?'

'I told her the woman had taken a long time to retrieve a simple item. And that she returned without shoes.'

'I see. And the next day you assisted her in abducting the woman, and driving her to the place where she was nearly killed. To say nothing of your attack on my scribe here.'

Grogan was silent.

'Well, Mr Grogan, I believe I have all I need.'

'All you need for what?'

'Why, all I need to hang you, of course. Dealing in stolen property; aiding in one murder and attempting another; abduction – more than enough to earn you a capital sentence. We may need some more information, of course, and when we do we shall be sure to return. In the meantime, I hope you have a pleasant afternoon. Good day.'

Chapter 35

Monsarrat was left discomfited by the exchange.

He seemed to have found in the superintendent if not a friend at least not an avowed enemy, and he was reluctant to change the situation, barely dared glance at the man in case he took it askance.

While Grogan was no doubt guilty of everything laid at his door, he appeared to Monsarrat simple rather than evil. Not someone who deserved to have their head thrust through a noose where Rebecca Nelson's neck should rest.

There was, probably, little he could do about the situation, and speaking out on Grogan's behalf would run counter to Mr Cruden's admonition to stay out of his own way. But the recklessness that prompted him to speak when it was better to stay silent was never far away, and as he and Daly made their way down George Street, Monsarrat was alarmed to hear the sound of his own voice. 'Sir, Grogan was a dupe. Is there no hope of mercy in exchange for the information he gave you? Is he not too stupid to hang?'

'He did what he did, and the gallows will have their fodder. I make no apologies for it. Without his collusion, Mrs Nelson – Miss Drake, whoever she is – would have found it much harder to commit her crimes. And I'd ask you to please not forget that your housekeeper very nearly died as a direct result of being abducted by him. No, spare your scruples, Monsarrat. They are a luxury we cannot always afford here.'

They were passing the Corner now, adorned as it frequently was by Stephen Lethbridge, who winked at Monsarrat and lifted his black cloth cap to the superintendent. Daly glared at him. Perhaps Lethbridge lacked some necessary permit for the distribution of pies on street corners.

'I will say this,' said Daly. 'You have earned my regard, and it is a regard I am not used to bestowing on people such as you – those who have contravened the law not once but twice. You would be well advised to do anything you can to stop me changing my mind about your character.'

Monsarrat knew he would do precisely that, and he felt like a coward. But he needed to hold onto his good standing with the man at least for as long as it took to accomplish one last task.

'Sir, about the prisoner Grace O'Leary.'

'What of her?'

'Clearly she has been exculpated. I wonder, in recognition of her innocence, whether it might be appropriate to recommend she be moved back into the First Class?'

'Absolutely not. The woman is a rioter. God knows what else she would urge the others to do if she had a chance. It's fortunate, and no accident, that we have removed her means of communicating with them by keeping her confined. She stays where she is, Monsarrat, and I wish to hear no more about it.'

Monsarrat bowed slightly. 'I shall make a fair copy of this afternoon's proceedings, sir, and deliver it to you as soon as it's complete.'

'See that you do. Oh, one more thing . . .'

'Yes, sir?'

'I'm told by many and various people that your housekeeper has a facility with shortbread. A weakness of mine. When you deliver the report, if some shortbread were to accompany it I might be better disposed towards any requests you have to make.'

'No, I'm not going to intercede with Superintendent Daly, Monsarrat. The man can be quite intractable, and I'm sure he will be in this matter especially. He's not above the occasional bout of wounded pride. In any case, she did foment a rebellion, you know.'

'I understand, Mr Eveleigh.'

'I have done one thing for you, though. Look at this.'

Eveleigh slid a piece of paper over his immaculate desk. It was the page from the Female Factory records which contained the information on Grace. Her name, date of birth, what she looked like (apparently her hair, when it grew back, would be brown) and her sentence. Seven years.

'So she will be free next March, Monsarrat. Well, as free as you can be on a conditional ticket of leave. And I thought you might like the opportunity to remind her of that fact.'

'I would, sir, very much. And to let her know what has transpired, that she no longer faces execution. But I'm sure Superintendent Rohan would not allow it.'

'Allow me to see what I can do. I'm not above interceding with officials when I believe it will do some good. As indeed it has done in another case. I've received word from Rohan that your application for an assigned convict has been approved.'

This was indeed good news. Mrs Mulrooney was recuperating at home, still unable to put any pressure on her shattered ankle, fretting that she couldn't kneel to say daily prayers of thanks to the Blessed Virgin, or stand to make Monsarrat a batch of shortbread he could have all to himself.

It had to be said, though, that she was in a horrendous mood from morning to night. The kitchen things were no doubt being allowed to run riot, she said, and she certainly couldn't trust

Monsarrat to keep up with the dusting. It wouldn't surprise her, she said, if when she was well enough to return to the kitchen she was greeted with a pile of rubble.

Dusting was not, in truth, one of Monsarrat's best-honed skills, and in any case Mrs Mulrooney needed a project. It might keep her from snapping at Monsarrat quite so much. So he had applied to the Female Factory for an assigned convict maidservant. Someone who would do the dusting under Mrs Mulrooney's vigilant eye. Someone young enough to be trained by her. Someone who would take her direction without complaint.

Monsarrat had requested Helen Down. She seemed to trust Mrs Mulrooney, and Monsarrat recalled his housekeeper's distress at Helen's loss of her daughter to the orphan school.

'I am grateful, sir,' Monsarrat told Eveleigh.

'She should be on her way to your home now. So you had best get there quickly and explain yourself to the woman before her new helper arrives unannounced.'

Monsarrat wasted no time in taking his leave, forcing himself to walk at a stately pace down the Government House driveway, but breaking into a run as soon as he was out of sight.

He needn't have worried, as it turned out. Helen had already arrived. She had assisted Hannah from her bed, and the housekeeper was commanding activities in the kitchen from the depths of the comfortable chair which, judging by the grooves in the dirt between the house and the kitchen, Helen had dragged in from the parlour. It was something Monsarrat had been offering to do since they had moved into the cottage, and the idea had always been rejected – Mrs Mulrooney said she couldn't be doing with sitting in comfortable chairs when there was work at hand.

And she was working now, for all that she was barely able to walk. She was showing Helen the proper way to handle each kitchen utensil; the amount of force to be applied to scouring the table; and, most importantly, the appropriate way to make a pot of tea.

But she was doing so with a smile and gentle coaxing words rather than the bald commands Monsarrat knew she was capable of. And Helen was smiling back, showing echoes, no doubt, of the innocent she had been before Robert Church had got to her.

Monsarrat stood on the threshold of the kitchen watching them both for some time, unnoticed.

Finally Mrs Mulrooney spotted him. 'You've organised some company for me,' she said. 'Thank you. It will surprise you to know I can become a little ill-tempered if left alone too long. So ill-tempered I almost forget to thank the people who preserved my very life.'

'Surely not *ill-tempered*,' said Monsarrat, gratified by what passed for Mrs Mulrooney as profuse thanks. 'How are you today?'

'The coughing has nearly stopped, thanks be to God. The ankle ... Well, I expect it'll get on with healing up at its own pace, but I fully intend to be on it by Christmas.'

Monsarrat had no doubt this would occur. He noticed, then, that Helen had backed into a corner of the kitchen and was standing very still, her eyes down. She looked, frankly, terrified.

'Good morning,' he said gently. 'Helen, is it?'

'Yes, sir,' she said, almost whispering.

'You are safe here, Helen. No harm will come to you, not from me.'

But he was chiding himself. He had given no thought to where the girl was to sleep.

He sat at the kitchen table next to Hannah, and Helen put a more than adequate cup of tea in front of him, and looked shocked when he smiled his thanks.

'Mrs Mulrooney,' he said quietly, out of the corner of his mouth. 'I know you love your kitchen room, but now that you're installed in the house, do you think ...'

'Of course, eejit of a man. She will have my room next to the kitchen, lucky girl. I shall stay in the house for now. When

301

I'm back to myself again ... we shall see. Perhaps you will have to buy a house with a kitchen that has two sleeping rooms next to it.'

That, he thought, would be a miracle. He didn't want to worry Mrs Mulrooney, but the fact that the major's gift was all but gone seemed of even greater concern now that more pressing matters had been resolved. The salary of a clerk did not stretch very far.

As he finished his tea, he heard a knock and a hail from the front of the house. On the other side of the front door stood James Henson, his hat off and his brilliant white hair on full display.

'Ah, Mr Monsarrat. I'm surprised to find you at home at this hour.'

'Yes, you're lucky to do so. My employer has given me leave to see to my housekeeper, who has suffered an injury.'

'I heard,' Henson said. 'And very sorry I am, too. In fact, it's partly about her that I've come. But first' – he gestured to a crate beside him – 'allow me to carry this in for you. I believe you know what it contains.'

Monsarrat invited Henson in, gestured to a place on the floor of the parlour where the crate could rest for now, and took Henson into the kitchen to see Mrs Mulrooney. She, more than anyone, had a right to hear what the man had to say.

Helen might have been perturbed by another male entering the kitchen, but this time she showed no sign of it. She simply busied herself preparing another cup of tea, displaying a quick agility that made Mrs Mulrooney nod to herself.

'How is Mr Nelson?' asked Monsarrat.

'Well, I doubt he'll ever quite recover. The loss and betrayal ... He is undone, has locked himself away in a back room at the warehouse, where he works and sleeps. He's not long for Parramatta though. He is making arrangements to move to Sydney, where he hopes to escape the stain of it.'

'Will you go with him?' asked Mrs Mulrooney.

'I might as well, missus. The only trade I know, and he's a

decent man. I should think we'll be heading east by month's end. He wishes to be in Sydney by Christmas, to pass that day in the busyness of setting up his operation there.'

'Poor man,' said Mrs Mulrooney. 'He mustn't think less of himself. She was an artful woman.'

'He does think less of himself, though. And he feels particularly culpable when it comes to you, missus. He says you nearly burned to death thanks to his gullibility.'

'I don't lay any of the blame on him.'

'Kind of you. I'm hoping, then, that you'll accede to a request he makes. There is a particular item he wishes never to see again. He very much hopes you are willing to accept it as a gift, but will understand if you are not.'

Henson reached into his jacket, pulled out a small velvet pouch, a vibrant blue though it had some dark smears on it. He passed it over the table to Mrs Mulrooney.

When she opened it and reached inside, the stones felt heavy and cold. But the necklace was in pieces, some of the links charred, some broken. The clasp was bent, and a few of the small diamonds around the largest sapphire had popped out of their settings.

'I don't want this, Mr Henson. It is too valuable a gift, with too many devilish memories attached.'

'Indeed. Mr Nelson said that under those circumstances I was to ask Mr Monsarrat to sell it and to give you the proceeds.'

'I shall certainly do so,' said Monsarrat. 'It is a most generous gift, and will be of far more use to Mrs Mulrooney as a tradable item than as a piece of jewellery.'

Mrs Mulrooney tipped the pieces of the necklace back into the bag, as though they were river pebbles. 'Take the cursed thing then, Mr Monsarrat. Do what you will with it on the condition I never have to look at it again.'

Helen, meanwhile, had placed fresh tea in front of each of them, together with a plate of freshly baked shortbread that Mrs Mulrooney had coached her to make. It was nearly gone by the time Henson stood, bowed to Mrs Mulrooney and wished her a speedy recovery and many happy years of use of her tea set.

As he left, Mrs Mulrooney smiled at Helen and turned to Monsarrat. 'What is this about a tea set?'

'Do you know, I nearly forgot the thing. I ordered it as a pretext for asking about the thefts at the warehouse. But I did have certain individual sensibilities in mind when I chose it.'

He fetched the crate, and as he drew each item from its sawdust packing Hannah's eyes widened. 'The finest china I've seen since Port Macquarie,' she said. 'And those clovers, they look almost like shamrocks. More than enough for me to forgive them for being green.'

'I thought they were clovers too,' said Monsarrat. 'Until I realised that in actuality they probably *are* shamrocks. Look.' He lifted the lid of the teapot, turning it over. Underneath someone had painted, with exquisite delicacy, the harp of Ireland.

'And what will a man like you do with a tea set so grand?' asked Hannah.

'It's your tea set, not mine. As to what's to be done with it, one presumes it will be used to make tea.'

Mrs Mulrooney's glare left Monsarrat in no doubt that he would be subjected to a flick of the cleaning cloth as soon as his housekeeper regained her mobility.

Then her face clouded. 'This sort isn't for the likes of me,' she said.

'I would have thought it was perfect. Someone of your wealth should have a tea set this fine.'

'My wealth? With the pittance you pay me?'

'Now don't forget, in addition to your pittance, you are soon to have the proceeds from the necklace.'

'I doubt a trinket like this will fetch all that much, damaged as it is.'

'I think you may be surprised. I think it's highly likely, Mrs Mulrooney, that you are now far wealthier than me.'

Chapter 36

Rebecca Nelson was still missing by Christmas, which was far from riotous, but still among the noisiest Monsarrat had experienced.

He had asked Eveleigh – again – to talk to those in power at the orphan school about the release of Helen's daughter Eliza into his household, at least for the Christmas season, and the child's watchful nervousness had slowly given way to smiles, and then laughs, as she sat at the kitchen table playing with jacks made from boiled-down pigs' knuckles while her mother worked, Mrs Mulrooney promising unlimited shortbread as soon as she was back on her feet. And on her feet she was by Christmas Day, moving a little cautiously but well equal to producing pan after pan of shortbread.

'You'll give her a stomach ache,' Monsarrat said as Mrs Mulrooney lifted the third square of shortbread to the child's lips that sultry morning.

'Nonsense,' Mrs Mulrooney said, not bothering to look at him. 'Do the poor thing some good, it will.'

'We must take care,' Monsarrat had said quietly, 'not to make things harder for her when she has to return to the orphan school.'

But he still acquired, from Henson, some marbles and a porcelain doll. And as the days after Christmas unfolded, no one came for Eliza, no one asked after her. Then February, with its grinding, slick humidity, arrived, and still the little room by the kitchen was occupied by mother and child.

With sleep elusive on the stickiest nights, Monsarrat was hoping for long, calm hours in the soothing cool of the Government House cellar, sorting the Female Factory records. But Eveleigh had other plans, for he had received word that the new governor, who had left Van Diemen's Land and had been stamping his authority on Sydney, was expected any day in Parramatta.

The man was known to have an eye for administrative detail, so Eveleigh insisted that an inventory be drawn up of the residence – every painting, chair and cushion; the number of logs in each fireplace, fire bellows and pokers; drapes, beds and hip baths. Monsarrat was required to stalk through the bedrooms upstairs and the fine, broad reception rooms beneath them, counting pillows and tassels.

Eveleigh had assumed the role of majordomo with the governor's pending arrival. Housekeepers and maids were being procured, with assistants for them sent from the Female Factory. They would turn the beds, wash the sheets, beat the curtains, clean the chimneys, and make everything ready for the house's new occupant. One morning Monsarrat was walking back into the administrative outbuilding, past Eveleigh's office, when he heard voices.

'Of course it's not impossible, man. Simply cut them all the same length. And get started. I've not yet been told when the governor will be arriving, but it won't be too long. We do not want him riding up the driveway to find that the grass on one side is a different length from the grass on the other.'

The convict groundskeeper had only just recovered from the post-Christmas tribal gathering, a tradition started by Governor Macquarie when local tribes were invited to sit and eat by the grace of His Majesty on land which, in the mind of any fair person, might have been considered as theirs alone in any case. He walked out of the office, glaring at Monsarrat on his way.

'Monsarrat. In here, if you please,' Eveleigh commanded.

'Mr Eveleigh,' Monsarrat said, entering his employer's office. He had become accustomed to sitting down without being invited to, but given the man's current mood he decided not to risk it.

'Oh, sit down, for God's sake. I hate it when you pace around. Have you done the inventory?'

'Yes. I've simply to make a fair copy.'

'It can wait. That matter you asked for my assistance with – I have word.'

Monsarrat had spent so many years without hope, he barely recognised it when it arrived nowadays.

'With regard to Grace O'Leary?' he asked tentatively.

'Of course with regard to her! Who else – the King?'

Whatever he was about to be told, Monsarrat thought, he'd best stay out of Eveleigh's way for the rest of the day. The heat and workload were clearly deranging the man.

'Rohan has approved your request – he doesn't know it's yours, of course. Miss O'Leary will be allowed in the yard during the day. The windows in the Third Class penitentiary will be fixed, and the women there will have proper mattresses. I told Rohan that the governor would be touring the place at some point – and who's to say he won't? – so he's motivated to get things in order.'

'Thank you, Mr Eveleigh. Truly. It is a good thing that you've done.'

'I know. Nice to have some good news. Had some disappointing intelligence from Daly. The woman he sent a ship after to Van Diemen's Land, the one with red hair, is not our miscreant. Still, it is hard to disappear. I believe the likelihood is that her bones lie in the bush, for they have not been sighted in incarnate form.'

'I am sorry, sir, for the disappointment.'

'Ah well. Best get on with that inventory.'

'Sir,' said Monsarrat, not entirely sure he was wise in doing so, 'I wonder if it's possible . . .'

Eveleigh sighed, met Monsarrat's eyes. 'Yes,' he snapped.

'But you don't know . . .'

'You're going to ask to see her.' Eveleigh snorted. 'Officially you're there to get her to sign a statement. Unofficially . . . I don't care to know.'

Monsarrat smiled. 'Thank you, sir, I can't begin to . . .'

'Don't begin then. I've had far too many people stampeding around here today as it is – just go; you're giving me a headache.'

Grace looked pale as she washed at the trough in the yard with the other women. She now had as much liberty, if that was the word, as any other Third Class woman. True, this meant she could break rocks with the rest of them, but it also meant she could bathe, eat, converse.

When the women had finished and the bell had gone, Monsarrat approached Tom Felton, who was herding them back into the workrooms.

'I'm to interview prisoner O'Leary,' he said to the guard.

'I've had no word of it,' said Felton. 'Can't allow it without the superintendent's approval.'

'Well, Felton, you can certainly go and check with the superintendent. However my orders come from the governor's secretary, and in the governor's absence they might as well come from the governor himself. Therefore you'd simply be delaying me, and Mr Eveleigh does not like it when I am late back. He is liable to take it out on those who caused the delay. So I suggest, man, that you allow me to speak to prisoner O'Leary.'

Felton muttered, shambled after a knot of women who were moving towards the weaving rooms and grabbed one by the shoulder, pulled her roughly backwards. She trod on his toe in a stumble which looked like it may not have been entirely accidental.

'O'Leary! This gentleman wants a word. See you back at the loom within half an hour, or your pay will be docked.'

Grace walked towards Monsarrat smiling. In the sunlight, he could see chips of green in her eyes, small but distinct flashes. Far more intriguing than Sophia's uniform blue.

'Mr Monsarrat,' she said. 'You wanted to see me? We had best get on with the interview. Felton rarely keeps his promises but I think he'll keep that one.'

'Well then,' said Monsarrat. 'Our former meeting room, I understand, is no longer our only option, and I am sure you feel you have spent quite enough time in there already. Unfortunately the only other possibility is the Room for Useful Purposes . . .'

'The dead are no concern to me, Mr Monsarrat. It's the living who are the monsters. I have no objection to that room.'

The windowless room smelled strongly of lye, and the thick walls were doing their best to keep the worst of the heat at bay. Nevertheless, even with the door open, the place was stifling and Monsarrat could feel a film of sweat forming over his face. The notion irritated him. Yet why should you, he asked himself, care whether a convict sees you sweating? His own response came straight back at him: not like you, Hugh, to ask questions you know the answer to.

'It's good to see you unconfined,' he said.

'Well,' she said. 'Less confined.'

'I urge caution on you, though, in pursuing those former activities that centre on the stores,' Monsarrat said. 'Superintendent Rohan is not the type to overlook transgressions.'

'It is my fervent hope I won't need to transgress as much. The new superintendent seems to be lacking in a certain amount of compassion, but, as you told me, at least he doesn't actively seek to harm the women. As long as that situation continues, I see no reason to disturb the peace.'

'On that point . . . I have spoken to the governor's secretary.'

'Well done. You do move in exalted circles.'

He looked at her, trying to determine whether the statement was a jibe, but she was smiling and after some years of Mrs Mulrooney's friendship he recognised an affectionate insult when he heard one.

'I do, as it happens, and you'll do well to remember it,' he said, grinning back at her.

'And what does the esteemed governor's secretary have to say?'

'Well, Mr Eveleigh has a great deal to say, on a range of matters. One of those concerns conditions at the Factory. I have convinced him that the matter requires urgent attention. An efficient factory needs an efficient workforce. One that is fed and clothed and not subject to continual abuse.'

'Ah, yes. We could do with some more . . . efficiency.'

'Quite so. And as it transpires, Mr Eveleigh believes he can spare me to interview you and a number of other convicts regarding the conditions you have been subject to until now. He will give the resulting report to the governor, together with recommendations. It is by no means a guarantee of change, but it is all I have to offer.'

'It is a great deal,' said Grace, and her eyes shone for a moment. Monsarrat knew that many convicts lost the capacity to shed tears, and he welcomed this small proof that Grace was not amongst them.

'First, though, I have another duty to perform,' he said.

Her posture immediately changed. She sat straight, her hands folded in front of her. The model of propriety.

'Grace, why are you guarded? What are you expecting from me?'

'I have learned to expect the worst from everyone, Mr Monsarrat. While I do not think I shall receive the worst from you, I must confess you have done me a cruelty.'

'In what way? Please tell me, so that I can set it to rights.'

'You've given me hope, Mr Monsarrat. And hope that cannot be realised is the worst torture.'

'Grace, I don't know what you hoped for, and it's true that if freedom is your hope, I cannot provide it now. But if you wish for a willing ear, and the promise of a friend once your sentence expires – which is less than a year away, I would like to remind you – that is something I am most definitely in a position to assist with.'

Her eyes shone again, and this time a small tear formed in the corner of one of them, quickly dismissed by her hand.

'Forgive me, Mr Monsarrat. I am being silly. What is the other matter you wish to discuss?'

Monsarrat knew it was costing Grace to keep her composure. Perhaps she would welcome it if he put matters on a more official footing.

'Only the legal niceties in relation to the murder of Robert Church,' he said. 'I am to take a statement from you. That statement you said you wouldn't swear to – I transcribed it anyway. Now, of course, someone else will hang, although not the person who should. Mrs Nelson, it seems, has disappeared into oblivion. I need your signature on that statement.'

She took the paper, holding it in front of her at arm's length as though afraid the lines of words would free themselves from the fibres and reach out to strangle her.

'Very well,' she sighed. He handed her a pen, and she inscribed a signature with almost as many loops and flourishes as Monsarrat's.

'I am relieved,' he said, 'that you are no longer insisting on going to your death.'

'No. I don't think I'll be doing that, Mr Monsarrat. It seems I might now have the shadow of a reason to continue breathing.'

The rhythms of the Factory were starting to return to normal. Production was steadying after a drop in the weeks following Church's death. Men who had been rebuffed in the weeks following the murder were being admitted again to select wives or servants from among the First Class women.

If there was one advantage in Grace remaining in the Third Class, Monsarrat thought, it was that no man would walk in seeking a wife and walk out with her. Unless, of course, one were able to make a special request . . . He had no idea what the Factory regulations said on that point, but resolved to ask.

There were a great many today who seemed in need of a spouse or servant. Stephen Lethbridge had appeared too, with his pie box, and was attempting to educate the crowd on Aristotelian principles. He was not having much luck, but as ever his pies were in demand.

Monsarrat wove through the men until he stood beside Lethbridge. 'I must thank you for your help. An innocent has escaped hanging because of it.'

'My pleasure, Mr Monsarrat. Here, beef and kidney. No, I insist, you can pay for the next one. I anticipate good business this week, for while a certain person has escaped, the gallows will have their fodder. Tell me, will you attend the hanging?'

As a convict Monsarrat had witnessed a number of executions. The most recent refused to leave his dreams.

'I think not. I've no stomach for hangings, and Grogan will be just as dead whether I am there or not.'

'That he will. But you'd be surprised how many people do have a stomach for that sort of thing. Seems to make them hungry. I do not take pride in this, but I am more than happy to assist them with killing their hunger, though I assure you I won't feel like eating. So you may indeed wish to stay north of the river, Mr Monsarrat, as the south side will be crammed with those who like nothing better than the edifying spectacle of a man choking to death.'

❦

Two days later, as the hanging was taking place, Monsarrat heard a flight of bats scrambling through the air above the office. A loud noise had sent them on their way: hundreds of people shouting as a man dropped through a trapdoor and into the beyond.

Monsarrat wrinkled his nose at the thought of the bats. He couldn't smell them, but he fancied a few of them had left a souvenir of their transit on the roof.

So Grogan no longer lived. The woman who had become Rebecca Nelson was highly likely still breathing, but who knew where she was now, living somewhere on the fringes of a world which she had thought to rob of Hannah Mulrooney.

The previous night Monsarrat had offered to make a journey into Sydney on behalf of Mrs Mulrooney. 'We'll get a better price for the gemstones there,' he said. 'And then I'll provide you any assistance you need in finding a house.'

'Why would I need to find a house? Am I not wanted here? Maybe I've done too good a job teaching Helen.'

It was true that under Hannah's tutelage Helen had become adept in the art of tea making and was an efficient but unobtrusive presence in the household. Mrs Mulrooney fretted, but tried to hide it, when Helen was absent on Sundays.

'Of course not, Mrs Mulrooney. No, I simply meant that now you are a woman of means, you may wish for your own household.'

'I've all the household I can stand here, thank you. You're not getting rid of me that easily.'

'As it happens, I don't wish to get rid of you at all.'

'It's settled, so. And don't think you can get out of paying me my wages. I am still the chief housekeeper in this establishment and I will be remunerated accordingly.'

'Of course.'

How on earth, Monsarrat wondered, was he to afford *two* housekeepers?

'You can stop looking so sour, Mr Monsarrat. I'm not expecting you to pay the both of us. I will handle Helen's upkeep. We need to be very clear on this point – she is employed by me, not you. So please don't go ordering her around.'

'I wouldn't dream of it, Mrs Mulrooney. She has someone to do that already.'

At this Mrs Mulrooney rose from the kitchen chair rather more slowly than usual, having to heave herself onto a cane. Half-upright, however, she abandoned her attempt to reach Monsarrat and instead plucked the cleaning cloth from its customary position in her waistband to throw it across the table at him.

'Mr Monsarrat,' she said, 'would you be kind enough to hit yourself.'

He threw back his head and roared with laughter the likes of which his throat was unaccustomed to producing. 'Forgive me,' he said, regaining his composure. 'What you heard from me was simply relief that all is right with the world.'

'All right, so,' she said, continuing to regard him with suspicion.

'What would you like me to do, then? With the proceeds from the sale of the necklace?'

'They have those banks in Sydney, do they not?'

'One of them, yes. The Bank of New South Wales. Very good with money, those bankers, but not too imaginative when it comes to nomenclature.'

'Whatever you get from those stones, I wish you to leave it in the bank. Half under my name, and the rest under Padraig Mulrooney's. That necklace will be transformed into a public house for him. An honest one, that doesn't water the rum or deal with the likes of Socrates McAllister.'

'Very well. I'm sure they will be good stewards of the money. Otherwise I know they'll have you to answer to, and if they have any sense they'll do anything to avoid that eventuality.'

Monsarrat wished he didn't have to keep replacing articles of clothing. He still had his pearl-coloured waistcoat with its red smear – it would never be worn again but he kept it as a reminder of the dangers of making assumptions. This morning he was wearing a new shirt as he walked into the office, looking into Eveleigh's rooms to nod, let the man know he was in attendance. He was looking forward to a soothing morning in the cellar.

Eveleigh was shuffling papers on his desk, and gestured distractedly to the seat as he got his thoughts in order.

'Is there anything I can do, today, sir, to assist in preparing for the governor's arrival?'

'Probably several hundred things. But they'll need to be done by someone else.'

Dear God, Monsarrat thought. If I'm to lose my job, I'll have to offer myself as a footman to Mrs Mulrooney. He must have visibly paled at the prospect because Eveleigh glanced up and said, 'Damn it, man, you look like you've seen a ghost.'

'Not recently, sir.'

'I didn't take you for the superstitious type. Nevertheless, there are all sorts of rumours of hauntings where you're going.'

'Where I'm going? The cellar?'

'Don't be ridiculous – the only thing that haunts that place is the occasional spider. No, Mr Monsarrat, I'm afraid you won't be here to greet His Excellency when he eventually gets round to showing us his illustrious face.'

'Sir, is there a problem with my work? If there's anything you wish me to change . . .'

'Ah, stop it now. I don't have time for this. Nothing wrong with your work, and of course your, shall we say, unofficial work has been noticed. I made a report, you see, on the death of Robert Church to the colonial secretary. Rather more detailed than the public version. And I wish I hadn't now. Because to be honest, Monsarrat, it's a pleasure to have someone with a bit of intellect around. Now I'll have to rely on those cellar spiders for conversation for the next while, and frankly they're not very good at it.'

'Why won't I be here, sir?'

'What are your opinions about Van Diemen's Land?'

Monsarrat shuddered. Port Macquarie was known as one of the least brutal penal settlements, and it had certainly had its share of brutality. But its reputation paled in comparison to the stories emerging from some of the more distant outposts. And as far as distance was concerned, Van Diemen's Land was as remote as it was possible to be, dangling off the edge of the world as it did.

'They've had a murder there. Not just the usual a-convict-splitting-somebody-else's-head, either. No, the head that got split on this occasion belonged to a free man. And no one has the faintest clue who did it.'

'Unfortunate. Nevertheless I'm sure a solution will present itself to them.'

'So am I, Monsarrat. And you will be the one to present it. You are to sail for Van Diemen's Land in two days. Which means, my friend, that you need to get to Sydney. I've arranged for you and your housekeeper to be on the first cutter leaving here. How does high tide tomorrow suit you?'

Authors' Note

The Parramatta Female Factory was the template for eleven similar factories which operated around Australia during the colonial period. Conceived as a means of keeping men and women separate in a society where one group greatly outnumbered the other, the Factory was also supposed to embellish the colony's coffers through the work of the women detained there. Far more than a factory, though, it was also a marriage and employment bureau. And for many women, particularly those in the Third Class, it was a place of punishment.

The Factory went through a few iterations, and during the period in which this book is set the second Female Factory was in operation. Its buildings still stand on land which is now part of Cumberland Hospital.

Around 5000 women went through the Parramatta Female Factory over the years, including Meg's great-great grandmother Mary Shields, who was transported from Limerick for stealing clothing. It is estimated that as many as one in five Australians are related to Factory women.

For all its influence, though, the Factory is not as well-known as it deserves to be. The Third Class penitentiary stands empty and is not open to the public. Neither is the Third Class dining hall, which still bears smoke stains from an internal fire some years ago. Several of the buildings, including the one housing the committee room where women stood to be selected for marriage or service, are now part of the New South Wales Institute of Psychiatry, who are sympathetic custodians of the site.

It is a tremendous shame, in the opinion of the authors, that those who have sprung from the outcast women, as one governor called them, cannot stand where their ancestors did. The authors support the contention of the Parramatta Female Factory Friends that the site should be preserved and parts of the precinct repurposed as a museum of Australian identity.

The Factory has a long and fascinating history, both as a convict site and later as an asylum. We have sought to represent that history as accurately as possible; however, for the sake of the narrative certain parts of the story depart from the facts.

Robert Church is, we believe, a worse character than any super-intendent who actually had charge of the Female Factory. However, some superintendents did indeed skim the women's rations for profit. The superintendents lived outside the Factory walls, but for the purposes of the story we have married Robert Church to the matron, and situated them both in her quarters.

While the fictional Church may be more monstrous than any actual administrators of the Factory, there is no doubt that conditions there were frequently inhumane. The story of the starvation of Emily Gray, for example, is based on an actual event, involving a convict called Mary Ann Hamilton. Head shaving was also a real punishment, together with the wearing of what were known as caps of shame, though there is no surviving record of what these looked like.

The first riot at the Factory did not occur until after this book is set, in 1827. The article in the fictional *Sydney Chronicle*, mentioning Amazonian banditti, is lifted from an actual article on the riot from the *Sydney Gazette*, published on 31 October 1827.

The Factory itself was twice a penal site, and we have conflated these for the purpose of the narrative. For example, the mattresses of untreated wool and the broken windows referred to here were features of the first Female Factory, not the second. The clock, described in this novel as above the entryway, was not installed in reality at the time this story is set.

As mentioned in the novel, the children of convict women were taken away from their mothers and placed in orphan schools from the age of four. However, only girls went to the Parramatta Orphan School. Boys went to a similar institution further away. We have also taken various liberties with the Factory's layout for the purposes of the plot, particularly in relation to the stores and the Dead House.

Ralph Eveleigh, private secretary to the governor, is a complete fabrication, as are his office and the cellar attached to it (but Government House, with its observatory and bathhouse, still stands today). We have been unable to find a record of anyone performing Eveleigh's function in Parramatta, although as in the novel Governor Thomas Brisbane did spend a significant amount of time at Parramatta Government House, and was criticised for doing so.

There was a gap between the departure of Brisbane and the arrival in Parramatta of his successor, Ralph Darling, and we have extended this for narrative purposes.

Two characters in the book bear some resemblance to key figures in Parramatta's history, although we'd like to stress the likeness is passing. Hannibal Macarthur, like Socrates McAllister, was the nephew of a great pastoralist, John Macarthur. Like Socrates, Hannibal struggled to win his uncle's approval, and there is some suggestion he dealt in sly grog. Hannibal was also a magistrate. However, Socrates' Machiavellian nature, and some of his more lurid adventures, are entirely fictional.

The Reverend Samuel Marsden sat with Hannibal on the bench and was on the Factory's management committee. While he was hardline in his views on morality and convicts, the fictional character of Reverend Horace Bulmer takes these attributes to extremes.

The smearing of Monsarrat's old employer Cruden was inspired by a similar event in which charges of immorality were brought against magistrate Henry Grattan Douglass, who was ultimately vindicated. Hannibal Macarthur and Samuel Marsden were removed from the bench as a result.

There was also a pieman in Parramatta: William Francis King plied his trade some decades after Stephen Lethbridge in this novel, styling himself the Ladies' Walking Flying Pieman, and dispensing his own brand of philosophy along with his pies. His feats of pedestrianism include beating the mail coach in a race between Sydney and Windsor, walking 309 kilometres around the Maitland racecourse in 46 hours and 30 minutes, and walking from Campbelltown to Sydney carrying a 30 kilogram dog between midnight and 9 am.

We have also made some small changes to the geography of the township of Parramatta. The intersection of George and Church Streets, known as the Corner, existed in 1825 as did a number of public houses, most notably the Freemason's Arms (now the Woolpack Hotel). Sophia's guesthouse, though, is fictional, as is Crotty's shebeen, although there were likely to have been a number of unlicensed drinking establishments operating at the time (that sly grog had to go somewhere). The bend in the river where Monsarrat finds the awl is also fictional.

In addition to more general works on Australian history (including Tom's *Australians Volume 1*, *The Great Shame* and *Commonwealth of Thieves*, as well as Grace Karskens' *The Colony*), we drew on a range of sources which specifically relate to the

Parramatta Female Factory, or to Parramatta's history more generally. These include:

- *These Outcast Women: The Parramatta Female Factory, 1821– 1848*, Annette Salt, Hale & Iremonger, 1984
- *Women Transported: Life in Australia's Convict Female Factories*, a project of the Parramatta Heritage Centre and University of Western Sydney, 2008
- *Colonial Ladies: Crime Reports from the Sydney Herald Relating to the Female Factory, Parramatta*, Judith Dunn F.P.D.H.S., 2008
- *Rules & regulations for the management of the female convicts in the new factory at Parramatta*, issued 31 January 1821, Government Printer
- *The Prisoners of Australia: a Narrative*, Charlotte Anley, Bodleian Library Oxford, 1841
- *Parramatta: A Past Revealed*, Terry Kass, Carol Liston and John McClymont, Parramatta City Council, 1996
- *The Cradle City of Australia: A History of Parramatta*, James Jervis F.R.A.H.S., Council of the City of Parramatta, 1961

Acknowledgements

One of the challenges of historical fiction is conjuring a sense of how a place would have looked, sounded and operated in the period you're writing about. For this reason we are hugely indebted to Gay Hendrickson of the Rowan Tree Heritage and Cultural Services, former president of the Parramatta Female Factory Friends and now vice president of Museums Australia. Gay organised access to the parts of the Female Factory which few people get to see, walked around with us, and answered innumerable questions over a period of months. She helped us to step out the murder of Robert Church and the escape of his killer, pinpointing the optimal spot for the event to occur. She was also kind enough to read the manuscript and provide feedback. Any errors are ours, not hers.

We're also grateful to Noela Vranich of the Parramatta Female Factory Friends for her advice, and in particular for sending us a tract by Charlotte Anley, a representative of prison reformer Elizabeth Fry, who visited the Female Factory in the 1830s. The scenes Monsarrat encounters in the Third Class yard are drawn from this work.

Karima-Gae Topp of Topp Tours was also generous in providing information.

We'd like to thank the numerous volunteers at Parramatta historical sites such as Government House, Elizabeth Farm, Experiment Farm and Hambledon Cottage (the kitchen of which was the model for Mrs Mulrooney's kitchen). These people live and breathe their local history and are a wonderful source of information. We are fortunate to have such custodians of our heritage.

As always, our thanks go to our family – our beloved and insightful first reader Judy; and Craig, Rory and Alex, all of whom have patiently accommodated the intrusion of Monsarrat and Mrs Mulrooney into their lives.